BRYANT LEE

Caught Up

*For the ones who made a list of what you wouldn't accept, then
quietly settled for less than what Heaven had in mind.*

1

Skylar

Awkward barely began to describe the drive back to my place. The silence between us felt like a thick, frigid winter night, stretching out like an icy gulf that neither of us dared to cross. I let out a quiet sigh, feeling the tension pool in my chest, and rested my head back against the leather seat, letting the warmth of the seat warmer become my only comfort. I turned my gaze toward the window, intentionally avoiding Titus's eyes, though I could feel them on me, studying my every move.

The city's lights flickered outside, blurring through the rain-splattered window. The familiar hum of New York life rolled past us, a stark contrast to the turbulence inside me. It felt like every stoplight conspired to drag out this silence, stretching each minute between us. Lenny Green's smooth voice filtered through the speakers, introducing a Luther Vandross classic that almost made me want to sway, but I held back, locked in this strange, stony silence. Titus tried to catch my eye a few times, but I kept looking straight ahead, hoping my indifference would mask the confusion churning within me.

Then, his soft and strong hand shifted over to my lap, covering mine with a warmth that made my chest tighten. I didn't pull away, and as his fingers gently stroked mine, the tension between us seemed to soften, little by little. By the time we were gliding across the Brooklyn Bridge, the frost in the air was beginning to thaw. I'd always loved this bridge—the way it connected the city and yet held its own strength, its timelessness. I glanced up at the night sky, finding a sense of calm as I placed my other hand over his, giving it a light squeeze. I wasn't even sure what I was trying to say, but Titus exhaled deeply, his tension fading, as if he understood.

The familiar scent of amber and sandalwood from his cologne drifted toward me, wrapping around my senses, making it hard not to lean in closer. His scent was always subtle yet grounding, and I found myself inching a bit toward him. But I stopped just short, feeling the console between us, reminding myself to keep a bit of distance.

"Sky," he started, his voice low and cautious, "can we talk about everything? I know it's a lot to take in, but I wanted to be open and honest with you."

His baritone voice wrapped around my name like a velvet ribbon—gentle but weighted with intention. As if on cue, Luther Vandross's voice crooned from the speakers, *"Never too much, never too much, never too much,"* giving the moment a strange sense of timing, like the universe itself was trying to soften the blow of what was to come.

Titus slowed the car to a stop in front of my building. The streetlights cast a warm, amber glow across his profile, illuminating the striking contrast of his polished look against the night. His complexion—a deep, smooth ebony—glowed with the kind of richness that reminded me of mahogany soaked in candlelight. His hair, always kept tight in fresh waves, gleamed beneath the faint specks of gray that framed his temples, a quiet crown that only made him more distinguished.

Before I could even unbuckle my seatbelt, he was already out of the car, the door closing with a soft thud before I saw him appear at mine. Titus had a way of moving—calm, deliberate, never rushed—that commanded attention without demanding it. The cold air kissed my face as the door opened, making me flinch, but he was ready with an umbrella in one hand and the other extended toward me. His hand—firm but soft, wide and sure—was like everything else about him: dependable, warm, intentional.

"We'll talk," I told him, though my voice wavered at the edges. The truth was, I wasn't ready—not tonight, maybe not ever. This moment felt like the slow drift before the final goodbye, the first page in a final chapter I wasn't ready to write.

Still, I took his hand, squeezing tighter than usual, holding on just a breath longer than necessary. Maybe it was a silent thank you. Maybe it was a silent goodbye.

As we walked toward my building, Titus instinctively stepped ahead, cutting off the doorman with a polite nod and reaching for the door himself. Always the gentleman. His presence next to me felt like a wall of quiet strength—broad shoulders, tailored coat draped over his 6'2" frame, his scent a mix of sandalwood, fresh linen, and something uniquely his. He looked like he stepped out of a GQ spread—dark wool coat, cufflinks peeking out just beneath the sleeves, shoes that shined even in the rain. Everything about him was curated yet effortless, like he'd grown up understanding the power of presentation and presence.

And still, despite all of it—despite the way his dark eyes looked at me with something close to hope, something knowing—I couldn't do it. When he leaned in, lips brushing close, I turned just slightly, letting him land on my cheek instead. The hesitation hung thick between us. He exhaled, a whisper of disappointment escaping, but said nothing.

Titus had been nothing short of intentional from day one. For one of our most thoughtful dates, he'd surprised me with two spots in a live Peloton class—something I'd been trying to make happen for over a year. He didn't stop there. Sushi from my favorite spot showed up at my office that afternoon, alongside a sleek black box of Peloton gear tied with a red ribbon. My coworkers had playfully teased me that he was a "keeper," and I'd laughed, my cheeks burning, not from embarrassment but from the rare warmth of being seen. Really seen.

And that date had been incredible. I could still picture him in his purple shorts and Kobe 6 Concords, looking like he'd stepped straight out of a Peloton ad, drawing curious looks as we strolled through Central Park. We'd spent hours laughing about his Lakers conspiracy theories, exchanging stories of Brooklyn, and debating how our neighborhood was changing. Titus made me laugh, think, and imagine—he even got me to picture us, together. I had felt something real forming, something solid and maybe even lasting.

It wasn't that I didn't care. It was that I cared so much it scared me.

But now, standing in the quiet after he had revealed he had two kids, everything felt... complicated. "Two Kids Titus," I muttered to myself, leaning into the soft glow of the lamp in my living room, trying to shake off the heaviness of it all.

As I settled onto my plush loveseat, I gazed out at the Brooklyn Bridge in the fading light of sunset, watching as the last rays caught the bridge's delicate latticework. I picked up my phone, my thumb hovering over Allie's number. She'd find a way to make this feel lighter, make me laugh, and probably tell me how ridiculous I was being. But a part of me was still wary, still trying to make sense of whether I could navigate this life of his—a life where an ex-wife and two kids would always be in the background.

The phone rang once, and then twice, before Allie picked up. "What's up, girl?"

I sighed, and without much preamble, launched into everything—Titus's confession, my hesitations, the sudden weight I felt. Allie listened patiently, only occasionally interjecting with her classic blend of sarcasm and realism.

"Truthfully, I am so tired of dating these men with poten-tial. I am over it," I told Allie, my best friend, with a groan that felt as heavy as the words I'd just spoken.

Dropping down onto my plush, cloud-like loveseat, I gazed out at the fiery orange and pink hues of the sunset framing the Brooklyn Bridge outside my oversized window. The view was one of the best things about this condo, and on nights like this, it was hard to stay annoyed—though my dating drama lately was definitely putting that to the test.

"Sky, estás loca," Allie replied, her voice buzzing through the phone's speaker. "We both know there are slim pickings out here. Vamos a tener que hacer unos compromisos, whether we like it or not."

I rolled my eyes, recalling the "compromises" I'd made

in the last few months. "Oh, I made compromises, Allie. Remember Rashard?"

"Of course! Rent-free Rashard!" Allie burst into laughter. "Chica, he was *fino, fino*. Muy chulo. A nice tall glass of milk chocolate."

"Uh-huh. Fine, yes. But living rent-free at his mama's house? A forty-something-year-old man still at home? Seriously, what kind of nonsense is that?"

"He had a good reason for being there!" Allie teased, clearly still amused.

I shook my head, practically glaring at my phone as if she could see the exasperation on my face. "Oh yeah? Because he loves home-cooked meals? Or maybe it was his decision to quit his high-profile, six-figure job after law school to write a memoir about his 'journey from the hood to the courtroom.' A grown man, chasing a dream while living with his mama."

"Potencial, Sky! A man who loves his mamá y tiene un sueño? That's potential, girl! He could write a New York Times bestseller, ¿quién sabe?"

"Allie, he is not Dr. King," I deadpanned, shaking my head. "I'm not dealing with a man who's got big dreams and no independence."

"What about Marc? Talk about caramel heaven with a body like Adonis and enough swag for both of you."

"Oh, mini Marc? My Latin Lover who was maybe 5'5" on a good day? You used to clown me for even entertaining his calls."

"Sí, pero what he lacked in height, he made up for in style, swag, and personality! Y el hombre era dueño de media cuadra en el Bronx! Why did you let him go?"

I rolled my eyes again, sinking further into my loveseat.

The fluffy blanket my mom had gifted me—clashing with every aesthetic detail in my apartment—was now wrapped around me. "I couldn't keep pretending to be okay with dating a man who made me feel like a giant. Allie, I love rocking a heel—a proper stiletto, not some kitten heel nonsense. And with my fabulous 5'9" self in Manolos, what did I look like on his arm?"

"Primero, you're 5'8," Miss Fabulous," she snickered, the sound of her laughter spilling through the phone. "Y segundo, don't pretend you didn't like his *other* assets. Ya tú sabes a lo que me refiero."

Biting my lip, I moved the phone to speaker, placing it on the glass table in front of me. I closed my eyes, memories of one particularly steamy night with Mini Marc flashing across my mind. "Okay, okay, you're not wrong. He wasn't 'mini' in all areas."

"¿Claro que si? And you let him go just because he was too short." Allie's tone shifted, playful but a bit more insistent. "If Mini Marc wasn't on your ex-list, I might have to hit him up myself."

"¡Ay, qué asco!" I scoffed, rolling my eyes even though a grin tugged at the corners of my mouth. "Gross, Allie."

"I'm kidding!" She laughed, but then her tone softened. "But seriously, what about this new guy you told me about—Titus?"

I could feel my heart flutter at the sound of his name. "Titus," I echoed, a little too softly.

"Ohhh," Allie sang out. "Sky, puedo escucharlo en tu voz. You're smitten."

"Shut up, Allie! You don't hear anything," I muttered, though I could feel myself blushing.

"Smitten, smitten! My girl is *enamorada!*" she teased, breaking into a little jingle.

With a sigh, I admitted, "He's... a nice guy."

"Oh, now we're using pet names? Just 'nice'? Girl, spill the details!"

Grinning, I shifted on the loveseat, my voice turning sing-songy as I shared his resume. "Well, he's a DC native, Morehouse grad, and has an MBA from Wharton."

"Morehouse and Wharton? ¡Ay, qué lindo!" she murmured approvingly.

"Plus, he's CEO of a multi-million-dollar company, owns a summer house in the Vineyard, and, yes, he's dark chocolate and fiiine."

"A Jesús-loving CEO with real estate and style? Chica, encontraste oro!" she laughed. "So, what's the problem, Sky?"

I took a deep breath, hesitating as I searched for the right words. "You really want to know what the problem is?"

"¡Claro que sí! Suéltalo ya, amiga! Spill the tea!" She sounded almost impatient, and I could picture her on the other end, eyes wide with anticipation.

"Well... in addition to his Vineyard house, his amazing resume, and all the charm and charisma..."

"Skylar, don't keep me waiting. Spill it!"

"Titus has... two kids. And a baby mama, well actually a step up, an ex-wife. A whole ex-wife."

A stunned silence fell over the line, and then Allie broke out into a dramatic, "*¡Dios mío! ¡No puede ser!*" followed by a "Damn, damn, damn!" in her best *Good Times* voice, which had me cracking up despite myself.

"Damn, Mr. T is now Two-Kid Titus? Damn."

As soon as she finished her sentence, my phone buzzed, and I looked down, the screen lighting up with a new message from Titus. Naturally, Allie noticed. "Let me guess—Mr. Terrific?"

I didn't respond, distracted by the message flashing on the screen: *"If it's too much for you, I understand. Just let me know where your head's at."*

I stared at the words, feeling a mix of emotions twisting inside me—excitement, nervousness, maybe even something more.

"He's got it all together, Sky. The job, the thoughtfulness, the sense of humor, the charm. And yeah, he's got two kids, but honestly? That's life. We're not dating 20-year-olds anymore, girl," she said, laughing.

I let out a soft laugh, too, realizing just how high I'd raised my walls over the years. And here was Titus, a man who had checked all the right boxes, but the moment something unexpected appeared, I was ready to close the door.

"It's just... I always pictured someone who was only mine, you know?" I admitted quietly.

Allie's tone softened. "I get that. But life doesn't hand out clean slates, Sky. The real question is, does he make you happy? Can you see yourself letting go a bit and seeing where it takes you?"

Could I?

I sank back into the cushions, still feeling the warmth of his touch, still hearing his voice and the way he'd made me laugh when I hadn't felt that light in ages. And as the city lights blinked on one by one outside my window, I found myself thinking of him again—not as "Two Kids Titus," but as the man who had been steadily, carefully working his way into my life, and maybe even into my heart.

2

Skylar

I am not sure how I made it into the office today, after hitting snooze on the alarm one too many times. If Allie did not call to complain about me missing a morning workout, I would have welcomed another rollover in my bed and squeeze of a soft pillow.

In between a marathon of meetings and an emergency, but not really an emergency, call from my mother. That woman drives me absolutely crazy. I could barely respond to the text messages from Titus.

Titus: Just saying hello, beautiful. Have a wonderful day.

In an attempt to pretend as if I was not moved by the kind gesture. I could just hear his deep vibrato saying hello and calling me beautiful, making my heart melt. Before my generic response.

Me: Good morning Titus. Have a great day.

What had become the routine phone banter between Titus and I before the start of a workday was sidelined. I figured he wasn't sure where my head was at after a rushed conversation yesterday. It has been less than 48 hours since "the confession". Yes, I listened to Usher Raymond all day yesterday to memorialize the occasion, don't judge me.

Between the bags of Chinese Food, my purse, my laptop bag and the mail I just collected from my mailbox, I could barely press my floor in the elevator and now the challenge was accepted to see if I could manage opening my apartment door without having to put anything down. I kicked off my heels relieved to free my feet from the 4 inch heels I was wearing all day and took in the cool hard wooden floors of my apartment. The bags in my hand slowly won the battle, as I made my way to the island in my kitchen, excited by the scent of the chicken wings I added to my Chinese Food order. I was going to eat my feelings tonight.

After a nice hot shower, I grabbed a plate from the cabinet and filled my wine glass with cranberry juice and started filling my plate with more Chinese Food than I could eat in one sitting. The buzz of my phone playing "Count on Me" by Whitney and Cece, made me smile with delight knowing it was Allie on the other end.

And in that moment, hearing her voice felt like home.

"What's up, Chica?" Allie's voice floated through the phone, warm like cinnamon tea on a cold morning. There was always something comforting about the way she spoke to me—half sass, half sanctuary. That familiar lilt, equal parts Bronx bite and big sister energy, instantly softened the edge I'd been carrying all day. "Crazy day at work?"

"Yes," I sighed, sinking deeper into my couch, my head leaning back against a velvet pillow I hadn't fluffed in days. "It was super busy."

"It better had been crazy," she shot back without missing a beat, "because you *stood me up* at the gym this morning."

I groaned. "I could barely get up, A. I'm so sorry."

I could hear her suck her teeth on the other end of the phone, a sound so specific to her I could practically see the raised brow that came with it. Her disappointment wasn't real—just enough to hold me accountable, just light enough to let me know she was still my safe place.

Her tone was playful, but I could hear the tiny undercurrent of concern beneath the teasing. That's the thing about Allie— she knew how to poke at you and check on you in the same breath. She didn't need to ask if I was okay to *know* I wasn't. There was a rhythm between us, an unspoken trust that came from years of showing up for each other in quiet ways. When I was low, she felt it before I said a word. When I went silent, she never pushed—she just waited with her arms wide, ready when I was.

As I stuffed my face with steaming House Special Fried Rice, the smell of soy and scallion fogging up my senses, Allie didn't even need a visual to read me.

"Let me guess," she said, her voice thick with amusement. "Chinese food. And you overordered?"

A soft chuckle escaped me, muffled by a mouthful of shrimp and pork. "Maybe."

"Mmhmm. Still avoiding Titus and eating your feelings?"

I paused, chopsticks in mid-air. She knew me too well.

"Sky," she said gently, her voice dipping into that sacred

space we reserved for heart talk, "I still remember you retelling every detail of that incredible date you had with Titus. It was amazing how a man could know exactly how to charm you after just a few months."

The memory she conjured bloomed in my mind like a slow-burn love song. That date. The rooftop dinner he orchestrated, string lights glowing like stars above us, jazz humming low in the background, the way he listened—*really* listened—as I talked about my father and Brooklyn and the reasons I rarely let anyone in. He didn't flinch. He leaned in.

My heart fluttered at the thought, a quiet betrayal to the storm of doubt I'd been wrestling with for weeks.

Allie could hear the silence stretch between us, could probably feel the blush creep up my neck through the line. That was the thing about our friendship—she knew when to push and when to let me sit in the truth I was trying to avoid. Our connection wasn't just built on time; it was built on soul-deep understanding, the kind that comes from showing up through breakups, late-night tears, career pivots, and every complicated twist in between.

She didn't say anything else right away. She didn't have to.

That date felt like it belonged to another lifetime—a pocket of joy untouched by doubt. I remember bouncing around my apartment like a teenager, screaming into the phone after he told me where we were going, thinking, *This might be it. This might really be something.*

But now? Now I was curled up on the couch in sweats, hair undone, scarf hanging half-off my head, chopsticks in one hand and a pint of fried rice in the other. The distance between that giddy girl and the one on the phone with Allie tonight felt... wide. Like something had shifted and I didn't even feel it happening until it was too far gone.

I sighed, still chewing. The warmth of that day, the ease of it, how seen and spoiled I felt—*he really had been trying.* And here I was, dodging his calls and hiding behind takeout.

The ringing voice of Allie in my ear brought me back to the present. "Sky, talk to me. What are you *really* afraid of?"

I swallowed hard. It wasn't just the rice. It was the truth.

I thought back to my first real date with Titus—the one that made me believe he might actually be different.

After convincing Ty that surprises weren't my thing— and yes, I relentlessly bugged him for 48 hours—he finally caved and told me we were going to a live Peloton class. I screamed so loudly that my neighbor actually called the doorman to check on me. When I opened the door, still bouncing with excitement, my favorite doorman, Jeremiah, burst out laughing. After I explained that I was going to a live Peloton class, he grinned and whispered, "He's a keeper," clearly relieved there wasn't a real emergency. I rushed back to my call with Titus, still buzzing with excitement.

"Make sure you tell Jeremiah he's officially MY favorite doorman," Titus teased.

He'd arrived at my place right on time that morning, his punctuality as dependable as ever. I convinced him to park in the garage, buying myself a few extra minutes, and suggested we take the subway across town. What he didn't know was that I was on my 100th attempt to tame my hair into a sleek bun—a workout in itself. All my natural sisters can relate. The last thing I wanted was to reveal my hair struggles to Titus this early on!

I glanced over my Peloton gear, grabbed my gym bag, and

spritzed a few drops of Gucci Guilty on my neck. Shouting for my smart device to turn down the Ledisi song blaring in the background, I headed out the door. As I rode the elevator down, I took a few deep breaths, catching my reflection in the glossy elevator doors, trying to calm my nerves. I felt like a schoolgirl with her first crush. Just before reaching the lobby, I popped a mint and quickly chewed it as the elevator doors slid open.

Titus and Jeremiah were deep in conversation, tossing around a few comments about the Lakers making a run this year and some NFL games coming up the next day. As I walked up, I couldn't help but chuckle at the idea of two men named after Bible characters chatting sports. Ty's eyes widened slightly when he saw me, his face struggling to hide a smile. Jeremiah gave me a nod and greeted me with, "Hello, Queen," before Titus had a chance to speak.

"Indeed, hello, Queen Skylar," Titus echoed, carefully pronouncing each syllable as he walked over to give me a warm embrace.

Titus looked like he had just stepped out of a Peloton ad, with his broad shoulders and athletic build, his black Peloton tee fitting every muscle just right. I'd even caught Alex giving him an approving nod at the class. His black Peloton shirt highlighted every muscle in his chest, paired perfectly with a jacket and those eye-catching purple shorts. Yes, purple shorts, matched with his Kobe 6 Concords. His sneaker game was seriously on point- my heart did a little flip.. I was grateful for the unusually warm October day, which gave him the perfect excuse to show off those legs—and, of course, those shorts.

"You look beautiful," Titus said, pulling me in for another

quick side hug.

"Thank you, handsome. And for the record, the closest the Lakers are getting to a win this season are those Kobe's on your feet," I teased, to which Jeremiah groaned in playful disapproval.

As we walked to the subway that day, conversation flowed easily, touching on everything from the Lakers' season to the gentrification of Brooklyn, earning us a few curious glances from other subway riders. I was intrigued by his dedication to supporting Urban development and using his impact in real estate investing to leave a legacy in inner cities. This man checked all my boxes, cultured, brilliant, distinguished and debonair. I was definitely smitten. By the time we'd reached Columbus Circle, we decided to ditch the train and walk through Central Park, laughing and sharing stories as we made our way through the park's winding paths.

As if that wasn't enough, a few days before our date—on what Ty knew would be a long day packed with meetings and proposals—he surprised me with dinner from my favorite sushi spot and a messenger delivery to my office. I could hardly contain my excitement as the messenger opened his neon satchel, revealing a black Peloton box wrapped in a red ribbon, along with a note addressed to "Skylar, the original around-the-way girl. From Ty."

That Peloton class had been one of the best dates I'd ever been on. And afterward, we'd ended up on the Brooklyn Bridge. I couldn't believe he'd never walked across it before, so I'd made it my mission to change that. We'd stood there, side by side, watching the lights of the city twinkle around us, feeling the warmth of his hand on my waist. I remember looking up at him and thinking I could get used to this, used to him.

When he'd kissed me that night, it was like he'd broken through every wall I'd built up. It started out soft, gentle, his forehead pressed against mine as our breaths mingled in the cool night air. But that kiss deepened, his hands steady yet tender, and I'd felt myself melting into him, feeling things I hadn't let myself feel in a long time.

"¡Oye!" Allie's voice crackled through the phone, snapping me back to reality with that familiar sweet-but-sassy Brooklyn accent that could slice through any mood. There was something grounding about it—like the warmth of a childhood home or the first sip of café con leche on a cold day. She had impeccable timing, always calling when I needed tethering.

But her voice couldn't drown out the lingering echo of *his* voice. Of *that* moment.

The other night had felt different. Not just the rain in the air or the slow jazz playing in the background, but the space between Titus and me—it shifted. It expanded. It carried weight. The kind of weight you feel when something is either about to fall apart... or finally fall into place.

I turned my head just before his lips could find mine, offering him my cheek instead. A silent detour. His exhale landed warm against my skin, soft and steady, but I could tell he wasn't too happy with the switch-up. His eyes flickered— not with anger, but with that aching mix of restraint and resignation. He didn't say much, but the look he gave me spoke volumes. He understood. Even if he didn't like it.

"Goodnight, Titus," I whispered, offering a small smile that felt more like a bandage than a goodbye.

"Goodnight, Sky," he replied, his voice low and gentle, the

edges tinged with something tender. And something tired.

As I walked away, I could feel his gaze on me like a second skin, trailing behind me, lingering. The lobby was quiet—only the soft hum of the night doorman's jazz radio filled the space. My heels tapped softly against the tile, but my heart pounded like a drumline. The doorman gave me a polite nod, but I barely registered it.

The door to my apartment closed behind me with a soft click. Final. Defining. I leaned against it, the cool wood pressing into my back as I closed my eyes, letting out a breath I hadn't even realized I'd been holding. That kind of breath—the kind that's been sitting at the bottom of your chest, wrapped around something you don't want to name.

My apartment was still. Soft lighting from the kitchen glowed against the dark, and the scent of the candle I lit earlier—eucalyptus and something sweet—lingered in the air like a question waiting to be answered.

I dropped my bag on the hallway bench and made my way to the couch, sinking into the cushions like they could absorb more than just my body—like they could carry my confusion, too. I pulled my fluffy blanket around me, the one Allie gifted me after a bad breakup years ago, and stared out at the city through the tall windows. The lights flickered like tiny fires across Brooklyn, each one holding a different story.

Mine? Mine felt unfinished.

"Earth to Skylar."

Allie's voice sliced through the quiet like a warm breeze cutting across a heavy fog. The memory of our first date—so full of light—and the shadow of what might've been our last, faded to black. Her voice, laced with concern and that familiar edge of playful annoyance, pulled me back from the spiral I hadn't even realized I was in.

I blinked, eyes still fixed on the window, the reflection of city lights dancing on the glass like restless spirits.

A small part of me—still clinging to hope like it was my last good dress, the one I only pulled out when I really wanted to believe—wanted this to work. Wanted *him* to work. I wanted to believe that love didn't have to come in a neat box with perfect timing and no complications. That maybe the mess— the mismatched schedules, the fears, the kids, the baggage— *was* the point. That maybe effort, when paired with patience and time, could soften the sharp edges of fear and write a different ending than the ones I'd known.

But another part of me—the part shaped by disappoint- ments, seasoned by the kind of heartbreak that teaches you to pack light—wondered if we were already drifting toward the end. Not with fireworks or betrayal, but with that quiet kind of unraveling, the one where *almost* and *not quite* take up all the space love needs to breathe.

"Skylar," Allie said again, this time softer, her voice almost a whisper. "Don't close the door just yet. He may not be perfect, but he might be *perfect for you.*"

Her words lingered in the air long after we ended the call, wrapping around me like a hush I didn't know I needed.

Outside, a light drizzle tapped against the window, delicate and steady, like fingertips tracing the outline of a goodbye. The city was still moving, still pulsing beneath me—horns in the distance, footsteps echoing in the alleyway, someone laughing faintly down the block. Brooklyn breathed on. But inside, it was just me—wrapped in memory, tangled in hesitation, unsure if I was holding on too long... or not long enough.

And somewhere across the city, I imagined Titus doing the same—sitting in the quiet, replaying our night, wondering if I'd call. Wondering if this silence between us was closure... or just another pause in our unfinished story.

Titus

Wanya's smooth tenor and the rest of *Boyz II Men* crooned softly through the speakers, their lyrics about love being "more than a crush" weaving through the air like a confession I wasn't ready to say out loud. Somehow, their words mirrored my own truth—the one I'd been trying to deny for months.

Skylar and I had become inseparable, though we hid it behind coffee runs and late-night phone calls. When our schedules refused to align for a proper night out, we stole fleeting moments over chai lattes at the corner café. She checked in on me when I was on the road, always thoughtful—sending snacks to my hotel room as if she knew exactly what I craved or teasing me with flirty texts that made her absence all the harder to bear. Yet it wasn't just the playful banter that kept me up at night. We dove deep into real conversations, ones that made me see the world differently: how I could make my next project more sustainable, the ripple effects of gentrification across Brooklyn and other neighborhoods that shaped us both.

What had started as a chance meeting one unforgettable evening—surrounded by vibrant art, soft neo-soul music, and the warm hum of a Brooklyn crowd—had quietly transformed into something profound. Skylar had become more than just someone I liked; she was a friend, a partner, and the person I'd been unknowingly waiting for. A dream deferred, now within reach.

The song playing now took me back to one of our late-night conversations, the kind that stretched well beyond reason and sleep.

"*Hey Lover* is definitely LL's best song for the ladies," I declared into the phone, my voice firm with conviction.

From the other end came Skylar's soft laugh, punctuated with that little shake of her head I could somehow hear. "You're wrong, *Around the Way Girl* is hands-down the best tribute to the ladies. Classic."

I scoffed, not ready to let this round go. "Listen, *Hey Lover* with Boyz II Men on the hook? That's smooth. But okay, okay... *Around the Way Girl* does hit different. I'll give you that."

Skylar's voice was smug, laced with laughter. "That's what I thought. I win this round, Titus."

"You win every round," I muttered with mock defeat.

She yawned then, soft and sleepy, and it made me smile. "Ugh, it's late," she murmured. "And I *promised* Allie I wouldn't miss another Tuesday morning workout. Plus, I have that big meeting tomorrow."

"Right, right," I teased, settling deeper into the comfort of her voice. "I better let you go before Allie blames me for corrupting your workout schedule again."

"That *was* your fault," she countered, teasing me back.

"You're the one who kept me up debating redlining and urban development until sunrise."

I chuckled at the memory but softened my tone. "Sweet dreams, Miss Skylar," I whispered, reluctant to hang up.

There was a pause, just long enough for me to hear her soft breath before she answered, her voice light and flirtatious. "Good night, Mr. Scott."

The silence that followed wasn't empty—it was full of things unsaid. As I lay there in the dark, Wanya's voice faded, but Skylar lingered, her laugh, her thoughts, her presence settling into the spaces I didn't know had been empty.

I leaned against the wooden doorframe, staring out into the quiet night, replaying everything that happened. Skylar's reaction kept echoing in my mind, catching me off guard each time I thought about it. She didn't just freeze—she practically turned to ice when I dropped the "I have two kids" bomb. Not exactly something you toss into casual conversation, I get that, but I thought she'd take it better. My brow furrowed, and I let out a sigh, turning back to the familiar comfort of my brownstone.

The place wasn't a bachelor pad; it was a dad's home, filled with memories, each corner echoing moments from raising Deuce and Kayla. Photos lined the walls, snapshots from family vacations and graduations, and my fridge still had traces of kid artwork, though mostly it was a mix of Deuce's Morehouse graduation pictures and Kayla's freshman send-off to Howard. Just a few steps from Fort Greene Park, my brownstone sat quietly between two working-class families. I'd grown proud of the life I'd built here, of the stability and love within these walls.

I grabbed a bottle of water from the fridge, taking a slow

sip as I drifted back into the memories. Deuce, my 23-year-old, had just started grad school at Wharton after Morehouse. My girl, Kayla, was just settling into college life at Howard. I thought back to the way I'd choked up when we dropped her off at her dorm, the familiar scent of her vanilla-scented lotion lingering even as she disappeared around the corner. My kids were adults, out in the world making moves of their own. But telling Skylar about them tonight? Man, that had thrown her completely off.

I took another sip, mumbling to myself, "I should've known better. Dropping that on her like, 'Hey, want fries with that?'—only, it's two kids and an ex-wife." The words sounded ridiculous even to me. I had practically laid it all out there on the table like some BET drama setup, but this wasn't some messy situation. Kelli and I had split amicably, stayed friends even. She had remarried, adding another little one to her family, and our co-parenting game was smooth. We handled birthdays, holidays, and the occasional call about Kayla's financial aid deadlines without a hitch. Sure, we'd had our moments, but we'd found a rhythm that worked, even with our kids well into adulthood.

I chuckled dryly, remembering the awkward silence in the car after I'd told Skylar. The air had been so thick you could've sliced it. I'd inched my hand over to hers—a silent plea, maybe? She didn't pull away, but the frost between us stayed. I liked her, really liked her. After six months of late-night calls, Spotify playlists, and a couple of incredible dates, I had thought she was feeling it too.

Sighing, I sat down on my couch, leaning back as I stared at the ceiling. Lenny Wilkins and Luther Vandross had been the only things filling the silence during that drive, and now my mind was just as quiet and cluttered as it had been then. What was so wrong with being a dad? Did she think my grown kids were going to pop up and interrupt date night, raiding the fridge and handing out unsolicited advice?

My phone buzzed, snapping me back to reality. Deuce's name popped up on the screen, and I smirked, already feeling my mood lighten.

Deuce: Hey Dad, just played a pick-up game here at the gym. These guys are serious, but I held my own. Dropped 15 points! 🤙⬛

I shook my head, grinning as I typed back.

Me: Nice! Bet you had them rethinking their defense. Any sore losers?

Deuce: Oh yeah. One dude kept talking trash until I hit a three right in his face. Shut him up quick. But hey, the real challenge is this paper I'm writing. It's kicking my butt.

Me: That's my boy! What's the paper on?

Deuce: Impact of social movements on economic policy. Comparing the Civil Rights Movement to now. Heavy, but I think I'm on to something.

I set my water bottle down, feeling that familiar surge of pride as I thought about my son taking on something so meaningful. I could still remember the nerves I felt when Kelli told me she was pregnant just before my own college graduation. My life had felt like a whirlwind, yet here we were, all these years later, and my kids were thriving.

Me: Sounds like you're on the right track. Just make sure you're connecting the dots between the past and the present. Remember, that hustle can't be taught in class.

Deuce: Thanks, Dad. Next time I'm home, I'll show you how much my game's improved—on and off the court.

I chuckled, shaking my head. The banter, the shared love for basketball—it was all part of the connection we'd built. I felt the swell of pride that always came when I thought about my kids. They were the best parts of my life, and no way was I going to hide that.

My phone felt heavy in my hand as I scrolled through messages, landing on Skylar's name. I hesitated, my thumb hovering over the keyboard, but finally, I started typing.

Me: Hey Sky, I know I dropped some heavy stuff on you tonight. Didn't mean to overwhelm you. We've got great chemistry, and I really like what we've got going on. If it's too much for you, I understand. Just let me know where your head's at.

I hit send and set the phone down, leaning back on the couch. I knew she might need time, but if she was as amazing as I thought, she'd come around. And if not? Well, that was her choice.

I wasn't about to apologize for being a dad. My kids were part of me—a big part, the best part. Anyone who wanted to be with me had to accept that. Smiling to myself, I stretched out, feeling a sense of calm settle over me.

"Two kids and a baby mama," I muttered with a laugh, pushing myself off the couch. "Guess it's never too much for Luther, but it might be for Sky."

I took one last glance at my phone before heading to bed. The screen stayed dark, and I felt a pang of uncertainty, but I let it slide. If she wasn't ready for the full *Titus experience*, I'd survive. And if she was? Well, we'd see.

With a shrug, I turned off the light and headed to bed, still smiling.

4

Skylar

I stood in front of my closet, the soft hum of music playing in the background as I prepared for the Board dinner. The evening carried weight—not just the usual formality, but the promise of something bigger. We were ironing out the details and funding for a new urban STEM program, one designed to expose inner-city kids to sustainable energy and open doors to future career paths they'd never imagined. It was work I believed in, work that mattered, and tonight was a chance to push it forward.

Still, I couldn't focus on the significance of the evening. My eyes lingered on *that* black dress—the one I'd dubbed my "safe" option. Timeless, understated, and perfectly reliable, it had been my default armor for dinners like this. I pulled it from the closet, the fabric soft and familiar against my fingertips. I would have worn it without a second thought had Allie not intervened with her usual bluntness.

"If you wear that black dress again, I'll kill you," she'd threatened, half-joking but dead serious, her face scrunched in exasperation. "You're not going to a funeral, Skylar. It's a

28

Board dinner—step it up!"

Her voice echoed in my mind, and I sighed, tossing the black dress onto the bed with reluctant defeat. I turned back to the closet, my gaze drifting over the array of dresses I rarely touched. There, tucked toward the back, was one I'd bought on a whim months ago—a deep teal green number with sleek lines and an open back that felt like equal parts confidence and risk.

I hesitated. It wasn't my usual style, far from the muted tones and reliable cuts I typically hid behind. But tonight, something tugged at me to take a chance—to move beyond the comfort I'd wrapped around myself like a shield.

When I finally slipped it on, I couldn't help but pause at my reflection. The green hugged me in all the right ways, catching the light and pulling warmth into my skin. It felt different—*I* felt different—like a version of myself I'd been waiting to meet.

"Allie better appreciate this," I muttered to no one in particular, a small smile playing at my lips.

As I grabbed my bag and stepped into the hallway, the black dress lay sprawled across the bed like a surrendered flag—elegant, safe, predictable. A relic from a version of myself I was finally learning to outgrow. Tonight, I didn't need to disappear behind the armor of classic black. I didn't want to feel safe.

For the first time in a long while, I felt *ready*.

The hallway light flickered slightly as I pulled the door closed behind me, casting a soft glow on the room I was leaving behind—on the woman I was leaving behind. I paused, just briefly, long enough to feel the electricity of this moment, the anticipation prickling at the edges of my nerves.

My mind drifted back to the last time I stood at this kind of edge, teetering between retreat and possibility.

Flashback – six months ago

"I *cannot* believe you're backing out on me at the last minute," I groaned, flopping onto Allie's couch like a wounded actress mid-meltdown. "Now I have to attend this entire event solo? This is betrayal. Like, Shakespeare-level betrayal."

Her living room was its usual riot of color and curated chaos—bold artwork leaned against the walls, candles trailing sweet and spicy aromas into the air like a whisper, and a towering bookshelf that looked like it might collapse under the weight of every art magazine ever published.

I sank into the kaleidoscope of pillows that covered her couch, each one more vibrant and dramatic than the last. It felt like they were mocking me, closing in with their cheerful hues while I wallowed in last-minute abandonment.

Allie didn't even flinch. She was perched near the mirror, applying her signature red lipstick like war paint. "First of all," she said, raising a finger without turning around, "I'm not backing out. I never said I was going. *You* assumed."

I groaned louder, tossing an arm over my eyes. "Same thing."

She laughed, the kind of laugh that always pulled me out of my drama—warm, familiar, just a little smug. "Sky, this could be good for you. You've been hiding out too long. Go. Smile. Make mysterious eye contact with a stranger. Maybe don't wear that sad black wrap dress, though. Let the girls out a little."

Then, as if reading my mind, she added, "And before you

guilt-trip me again, I already told you—I have to go to Philly for that gallery walkthrough. I *would* be your wingwoman, but someone has to make sure our next exhibit doesn't look like a Pinterest fail."

That night—against my better judgment—I listened. I wore something bold. I showed up. And then I met *him*.

Titus.

And everything after shifted.

"¡Ay, Dios! Ref, are you *blind*? That's a foul!" Allie shouted, practically lunging at the TV as if the ref could feel her fury through the screen.

It was game night, which meant the Knicks had claimed her full attention—and I was losing a battle I never stood a chance in. She was in full fan mode, hair pulled up in a pineapple puff, wearing her vintage Patrick Ewing jersey like it was sacred cloth. Her gold hoops danced every time she stomped or gestured wildly, and her socks—orange and blue, of course—peeked out from under her joggers like tiny team flags.

"Allie!" I called again, dragging out her name with the kind of exasperated flair only best friends deserve.

She didn't even flinch. Instead, a throw pillow smacked me in the face with impressive accuracy. "Focus, woman," she said without looking back, now pacing in front of the TV like a stressed-out coach. "This officiating is *criminal*. I'm about to call Adam Silver myself."

I rolled my eyes and flopped onto the couch, letting out a dramatic sigh that would make any Broadway understudy proud. "You are seriously choosing the Knicks over me right now?"

"Stop pouting, Sky," she said, shooting me a sideways

glance without missing a beat. "You've been to, what, 101 galas, panels, summits—solo and otherwise. What's the big deal with this one?"

As if on cue, the Knicks missed a free throw and Allie threw her arms up like she'd been personally betrayed. "*Mija*, what's the problem? You always kill it at these events—raising money for Urban Futures, repping Black girls in STEM like a queen. This is *your* thing. Why the sudden stage fright?"

I waited until the camera cut to commercial and leaned in with all the urgency I could muster. "Is it halftime yet? I need your *undivided* attention."

She smirked, already heading toward the kitchen. "You *have* my undivided attention. Except, of course, when Josh Hart's thighs are in motion."

Moments later, she reappeared with two paper plates, each holding a perfectly crisp slice of pizza—thin crust, just like we used to get after school. The scent of garlic, oregano, and melted mozzarella filled the room like a warm hug.

"And don't forget the crushed red pepper flakes," I called after her, knowing full well she wouldn't.

"Are you *seriously* telling me how you like your slice?" she said, scoffing with mock offense as she handed me the plate. "Like I wasn't there *every single day* after school at Luigi's, watching you shake half the jar on your slice like you were seasoning generational trauma?"

I burst out laughing. "Old habits die hard."

She grinned, finally settling beside me. "So what's *really* going on, Sky?"

"Oh, Luigi's," I sighed, taking a too-hasty bite and immediately regretting it as the hot cheese scorched my tongue. I fanned my mouth, trying not to laugh.

Allie shook her head, laughing hysterically. "Some things never change! I'll never understand why you always dive in like that." She waited, her smile fading as her voice softened. "Now, back to this Urban Futures event. Why the nerves? What's up?"

Setting my plate down on the side table, I glanced at the photo of Allie and me from high school, our arms around each other, smiling wide. The familiarity of her gaze in that photo made what I was about to say feel even heavier.

"A little birdie told me... that Rob's going to be at the event," I confessed, the words slipping out before I could stop them.

She froze mid-bite. "Our Rob? Like, Sterling Robert Jennings from middle school and high school?"

Her eyes widened, lips twitching as she fought back a laugh. "No way. *Rob Jennings?*"

I nodded, already cringing.

Rob Jennings. My very first crush—the one who made my stomach flip before I even knew why. Allie knew every beat of that story, front to back. She'd been there for all of it: the hallway glances, the sweaty palms, the note I rewrote five times before slipping it into his locker.

He was the boy who gave me my first kiss—right after a seventh-grade dance under the flicker of gymnasium lights and a chaperone's watchful eye. My first Valentine's Day gift too: a leather bracelet with a green stone at the center, meant to "match my eyes," he'd said. I wasn't sure if they really did, but I wore it like it was laced with magic.

Somewhere in the back of my closet, inside a chipped, heart-shaped box with faded gold trim, that bracelet still lived. Alongside it, folded notebook paper stained with time and the kind of innocent hope only a twelve-year-old heart could hold—dreams of a forever that we mapped out in the margins of schoolbooks and exchanged under playground monkey bars.

I remembered that Valentine's Day in eighth grade like it had just happened last week—every color, every flutter of nerves, still vivid. We'd exchanged gifts on an old wooden bench in Fort Greene Park, the one near the playground with the chipped blue slide and the giant oak tree that stretched wide like it was keeping our secrets. It was just a few blocks from where Allie lives now, though back then it felt like a world away from anything grown-up or complicated.

I'd doused myself in too many spritzes of my mom's Donna Karan perfume—*Cashmere Mist*, to be exact—trying to strike that impossible balance between effortless and unforgettable. When he arrived, I was already rehearsing how to sit so I didn't wrinkle my outfit. He smelled like Calvin Klein *CK One*—clean, sharp, a little mysterious. That scent hovered between us, mingling with the cold February air and the nervous energy of two barely-teenagers pretending we weren't terrified of the moment.

I held a little red gift bag with tissue paper I had fluffed just right. He had something wrapped in the Sunday comics. I remember thinking it was kind of perfect.

Allie's voice snapped me back.

"Wait—*not* Robert? Your first crush and official eighth-grade boo *Robert*?" Her eyes were wide now, her face lit with that mischievous curiosity she couldn't hide. "The Calvin Klein cologne-wearing, big-headed, Dwayne Wayne glasses-rockin' *Sterling Robert Jennings*?"

She dragged his full government name out like she was

reading it off a courtroom transcript and started cracking up.

Then, without missing a beat, she added, "Girl, the only thing that boy should've been giving you was space. And a refund for wasting your edges with all that stress."

I doubled over laughing.

Allie leaned in, still grinning. "Skylar. This is *big*. Like, full-circle romance novel *big*. Except, I'm still not convinced he doesn't have a secret lair where he stores all his bad decisions."

I let out a long sigh, torn between dread and nostalgia. My stomach twisted, and not just from the greasy slice of pepperoni in my hand. "Allie, come on. Give the man a break. You can't *still* hate him."

She shot me a glare over her wine glass, one perfectly arched brow raised. "Oh, I absolutely can."

"You're flaking out on me!" I groaned, slumping deeper into the couch. "I don't think I can do this. Seriously. I'm not going."

I took another bite of pizza—this time slower, deliberate— savoring it like it was my last bit of comfort before walking into emotional quicksand. The cheese stretched like the moment itself, heavy and melting at the edges.

Allie rolled her eyes with flair only she could deliver. "¡Dios mío! Skylar, get a grip."

The soft glow from the pendant light above us cast gold shadows across her curls as she leaned forward, her tone shifting from dramatic to sincere. "You know I'd be there if I could. But this gallery trip to Philly popped up last minute. I *have* to check out this artist—he's perfect for the next exhibit."

She reached for my hand and squeezed it with sisterly

conviction. "But listen—we're going to find you something bomb to wear, qué linda. You're gonna walk in there like a walking power ballad, and that fresh blowout?" She gave a satisfied nod, like she could already see it. "On. Point."

Then she sat back, smirking like she'd just delivered the closing argument in a courtroom drama. "And Sterling Robert Jennings—with his big head and weak apologies—is gonna wish he'd done something other than peak in middle school."

"Allie, te quiero mucho," I murmured, a relieved smile creeping onto my face. I knew she'd make sure I was ready, even if she couldn't be there. Sterling had been my everything once. I'd scribbled his initials across my high school notebooks, daydreamed about a future with him before I even knew what that meant. He was the first to break my heart, and somehow, a part of me had never let him go.

"Okay, halftime's over," Allie announced, grinning and settling back into her chair. "Back to my Knicks and mi hombre, Josh Hart." She turned up the volume on the TV, a playful gleam in her eye. "And Sky, just remember— absolutamente nada de lengua. No tongue."

Laughing, I tossed the pillow back at her, catching her smirk as the Knicks jogged back onto the court. And for a moment, I felt the warmth of friendship, pizza, and the memories of young love—all blending together into something that made me feel ready to face whatever might come.

5

Skylar

The Saturday morning air was crisp as sunlight spilled through my apartment windows, casting golden streaks across the hardwood floor. My phone was pressed to my ear as I curled up on the couch, mug of coffee in hand. It was our ritual, Dad and me. Every Saturday morning, without fail, we debriefed the week—the big stuff, the small stuff, and everything in between. It started back in college, me calling to vent about exams, roommate drama, or my nonexistent love life, and somehow, it never stopped. I loved these calls more than I cared to admit.

This morning was no different. I could hear the faint hum of birds and the rustling of leaves in the background, a sure sign Dad was either sitting on the porch or at the park, his favorite spots for these conversations. "I texted Miss Alejandra last night," he confessed casually, his voice carrying that familiar blend of mischief and sincerity.

I chuckled. "Miss Alejandra? Why?"

"She's our good luck charm," Dad declared. "I know she was yelling at the Knicks during that nail-biter last night, and somehow, they pulled out the win. Had me worried for a minute, though."

I laughed, shaking my head in disbelief. "Good luck charm, huh? You and Allie and your Knicks—dedicated to a team that hasn't won a championship since I was born."

"Don't you dare say it," Dad warned, his voice mock-stern, as though he could hear my grin through the phone. "Miss Skylar Madison, you get your Knicks jersey ready, because this is their year. I feel it."

Rolling my eyes, I sighed dramatically, glad he couldn't see me. "Sure, Daddy. I'll get right on that."

"Enough sucking your teeth and rolling your eyes, young lady," he teased, the humor in his tone shifting into something more pointed. "What's the deal with that young man you've been entertaining the past few months?"

"Entertaining?" I laughed, caught off guard. "Daddy, you make it sound so scandalous."

"What, you want me to use your generation's slang?" he fired back, the chuckle in his voice making me grin. "What is it now—'linking up'? Or are you 'boo'd up'?"

"Eww, Daddy, stop!" I protested, cringing at his attempt at modern lingo.

"Enough with the semantics, Skylar. How are things with the young man you're *dating*?" he asked, the shift in his voice subtle but unmistakable. He wasn't joking anymore. This was his serious tone, the one that let me know I couldn't dodge the question.

I hesitated, the words slow to form. Finally, I told him what had been weighing on me since Titus and I last talked. "He told me he's divorced," I said, pausing. "And he has two kids."

"Grown kids, right?" Dad clarified, his tone neutral.

"Yes. And he has a good relationship with his ex-wife," I added quickly, hoping to control the narrative before Dad could interject.

"Sounds like an upstanding young man," he said, his voice measured. "Not only did he tell you about his life and family, but he waited until he felt you were someone worth sharing it with. Do you know how hard that is for a man? To be a husband, not just a baby daddy, and a father? And a Black man, no less. This one *is* Black, right? Not one of your Latin lovers?"

I groaned, wanting to kick myself for ever giving him details about my past situationships. "Daddy..."

"Don't 'Daddy' me, Skylar," he cut in, his voice firm but not unkind. "You've been swooning over this man for months. Eager to talk to him, spend time with him, brag about his accomplishments. And now, after one evening of him being real and vulnerable with you, you're backpedaling? I'm disappointed."

The words stung, knocking the air out of me. Still, I wasn't going to let him steamroll me. "I'm not backpedaling, Daddy," I said, steadying my tone. "You raised me to have expectations and not to compromise. I wasn't expecting the man I'm dating to have an entire family and life outside of me."

"Skylar Madison," he said, his voice dropping into that no-nonsense tone that always made me sit up a little straighter, even over the phone. "I raised you to have expectations, yes. But I also raised you to be realistic. Did you ever stop to think about the fact that I was younger than you are now when I had a daughter and an ex-wife? I had a successful career, trying to navigate this thing called life. Imagine if I found a woman as remarkable as you are and wanted to see if I could share my life—and my family—with her."

His words landed like a sucker punch—subtle but bruising. I sat in silence, staring out across the city from my living room window. From this high up, the world felt quiet, distant. The skyline stretched in soft layers—concrete, glass, and morning haze, all bathed in golden light. A few clouds moved lazily above the rooftops, unbothered by the weight of anyone's emotions.

Inside, my condo was still—no footsteps, no morning playlist humming in the background, just the faint ticking of the clock and the echo of my father's voice in my ears.

He wasn't looking for a response. He never was. That was Daddy's way: say what needed to be said, sharp and true, then let you sit with it until it made its way to your bones.

Before the silence got too thick, he shifted course, his tone lighter. "By the way, did you see Allie's boy Josh Hart had a double-double last night? I swear, that girl is the Knicks' good luck charm. She's got playoff energy in her aura."

I couldn't help the soft laugh that escaped, even as emotion swirled beneath it—gratitude, affection, a touch of irritation. That was Daddy's gift: correct you, comfort you, and crack you up all in the same breath.

Just as our call ended, my phone lit up on the marble counter. One buzz. Then two. Then five.

Group chat.

Me, Allie, Quinn, and Eden. We'd started it in high school and never let it die. It had been through everything—late-night heartbreaks, new jobs, breakups, babies, engagements, betrayals, reconciliations, and endless debates about who was better: Usher or Chris Brown.

Quinn: I hear I need an update on your status with Titus. Hit me up—soccer mom duties 'til 3pm.

Eden: ◐◐◐◐ Spill.

Allie: I have *all* the tea. Don't tempt me.

I rolled my eyes and let out a small groan. Leave it to Allie to beat me to the story—again. And to announce it like a press release. I was still trying to unpack Daddy's sermon and now I had the Gossip Avengers assembling.

Eden: What's the tea, A? Don't play with us.

Quinn: Emergency conference call tonight at 11. Kids will be asleep and—God willing—I'll have Tatum satisfied by then too.

Eden: Eww, Q. Nobody asked for all that detail.

Allie: If you're scheduling your session *before* our sister call, we'll catch you mañana. Priorities, babe.

Quinn: Make it 11:30.

I stared at the screen, shaking my head as I smiled. This was our rhythm. The noise that somehow brought peace. These women had known me across decades and phases, highs and lows. They'd seen the before, the after, and the in-between— and still chose me, again and again.

I didn't know if I was ready to unpack everything. But with two out of three of them? I'd be just fine.

Though with Quinn and Tatum... it might just be me and Allie. Again.

6

Skylar

Six Months Ago

My bedroom looked like a fashion hurricane had torn through it. Heels, hangers, and handbags were strewn across every surface—scarves tangled with belts, clutches teetering on the edge of my dresser, and shoes that had somehow multiplied like rabbits overnight. In the middle of the chaos, three carefully curated outfits lay across my bed like contestants awaiting final judgment.

Each one had been vetted—read: handpicked and critiqued—by Allie, whose style compass was always set to "undeniably extra in the best way." She'd helped me prepare for the Brooklyn Renaissance: Art, Community, and Sustainability charity event, an annual who's-who of culture and change-makers. And this year, I'd be attending *without* her.

That was the part twisting my stomach into knots.

Even after her endless pep talks—"You're the main character, Sky. Act like it!"—I still wasn't sure I was ready to walk into a room like that solo.

Outfit number one was Allie's favorite. A bold lavender slim-fit pantsuit that hugged every curve like it had been sewn onto my body. The cut flattered my waist and hugged my hips just enough to make me feel like I had something to say—even if I didn't speak. The back view was, in Allie's words, "a sermon." She'd paired it with a sheer white blouse—clean, crisp, a little daring under the right lighting. The shoes? A pair of unapologetically loud, multi-colored heels that made my toes hurt just looking at them. A coral clutch and pearl drop earrings rounded it out, a bold departure from my usual palette of safe earth tones and neutrals. It was pure Allie—polished, fearless, and styled with love.

The second look was more my speed. A fitted, knee-length sheath dress with a mosaic of rich jewel tones—sapphire, emerald, deep burgundy—woven through the fabric like stained glass. It had short sleeves that subtly highlighted the arms I'd been toning in 6 a.m. barre classes and a rounded neckline that managed to be both modest and flattering. The midi hemline gave it just the right amount of sophistication. Allie had paired it with delicate black strappy heels and the sleek black clutch she'd brought me back from Paris last fall. It felt timeless, safe, *me*—but maybe a little too me.

Then, there was the third option.

My secret backup.

The one I hadn't even told Allie I'd pulled from the back of my closet. A classic black A-line dress—unassuming, unfussy, the sartorial equivalent of hiding in plain sight. No shimmer, no statement, just a dress that made me feel invisible enough to get through the night if the nerves got too loud.

If Allie knew I was even *considering* it, she'd revoke my fashion privileges and put me in timeout indefinitely.

But the truth was, as much as I wanted to channel Allie's confidence, part of me still craved the safety of fading into the background. The black dress wouldn't turn heads, but it wouldn't raise questions either. And on a night like this—without my right-hand woman—that felt like a comfort I might not be ready to give up.

Still, I stood there, staring down the lavender suit like it was a dare.

I was mid-routine, smoothing another layer of warm oil over my freshly showered skin. The scent of vanilla and almond wrapped around me like a soft memory, lingering in the air as Joe's voice floated from the speaker: *"I'll do all the things your man won't do..."* His smooth croon drifted through the room, a sultry soundtrack to my quiet Saturday prep.

Then the phone rang—cutting clean through Joe's promise—and I didn't even need to check the screen.

"Yes, Alejandra," I answered, already smiling.

Allie's voice came through, bright and familiar, like sunlight cutting through a cloudy morning. "What's up, Sky?"

Wrapped in a thick white towel, I padded into the bathroom, mentally bracing for the task ahead: makeup. Ugh. The part of getting ready I dreaded most. I could write a grant proposal in my sleep, but contouring? That was a whole other language.

"You all showered up and glowing, or do I need to send in a glam team?" Allie teased, her voice tinged with that playful rhythm she always carried.

She knew me too well.

I caught a glimpse of myself in the mirror—barefaced, hair wrapped in a satin scarf, skin still damp and gleaming under the soft bathroom lights. The vanity lights reflected the subtle shimmer of the oil on my collarbone, but my eyes zeroed in on the chaos behind me: makeup brushes, palettes, and the intimidating row of products Allie insisted I keep "just in case."

Makeup had never been my thing. It always felt like trying to color inside someone else's lines. But Allie? She'd been trained from birth, or at least it seemed that way. I could still see her sitting on the edge of the toilet lid while her older sister Luz painted her face like a canvas—electric blues, frosted purples, even lime green at one point, colors so bold they looked like they belonged in an MTV music video.

Mami Hermida would lose it every time. I could hear her now, stomping down the hallway in her slippers, wagging her finger like a conductor. "¡Tu hermana no es tu muñeca! No le arruines su carita bonita. Your sister is not your little doll—don't mess up her pretty face!"

But Luz never stopped, and Allie never flinched. Somewhere between rebellion and artistry, Allie learned to master her look. Now, her skill with a makeup brush rivaled her eye for gallery curation—flawless, expressive, and always with a little drama.

"Skylar," she said now, her voice shifting into coach mode, "just a bit of foundation, a smoky eye, and a natural lip. *Just like we practiced.* Eres preciosa, no necesitas mucho. You're gorgeous, you don't need a lot."

Her voice wrapped around me like a silk robe—firm, familiar, and comforting. Only Allie could tell you what to do and make it feel like a love letter.

I nodded, even though she couldn't see me, glancing at the lavender suit hanging near the window, glowing in the early light. That was her top pick—bold, tailored, unforgettable. Meanwhile, the black dress sat sulking across the armchair like a safety net I desperately needed to outgrow.

"I'll let you finish getting ready," she said, her voice softening again. "Just wanted to check on my girl. Make sure you're good. And keeping an eye on the time."

"Gracias, hermana," I murmured, heart full. "Te quiero mucho, Alejandra."

Her name tasted like home.

"Lavender, Sky. *Go with the lavender.* And please, ditch that boring black dress," she added with mock exasperation.

I gasped. "How do you *know* I even pulled it out?"

"Because I *know* you. And because you always flirt with the idea of hiding when you're about to shine."

Her voice lingered for a beat, then brightened.

"I love you too, Sky. And when you send me pictures tonight, you better be wearing that lavender suit. Don't make me FaceTime you from Philly in a rage."

I laughed, the nerves melting just a little.

Lavender it was.

7

Titus

Six Months Ago

Reluctantly, I pulled on the crisp grey suit, already longing for a different kind of night—one with buffalo wings on the coffee table, the NBA playoffs lighting up the big screen, and the familiar rhythm of trash talk echoing off my walls. I could practically hear the announcer calling out a clutch three, feel the tension of a fourth-quarter comeback, and the comfort of being in my own space, surrounded by my boys.

But tonight wasn't about comfort. It was about commitment.

The annual *Brooklyn Renaissance: Art, Community, and Sustainability* gala was more than just another charity event—it was a power hub. Last year, I made the kind of connections that helped move my Navy Yard development project from concept to conversation. And I wasn't about to let that momentum stall. This wasn't just business—it was legacy work. I wanted to build *with* the community, not over it. Affordable housing. Locally owned businesses. Opportunities that honored the families who'd called this neighborhood home for generations.

Kayla, my daughter and unofficial stylist, had insisted on the dark grey slim-fit suit with a soft pink dress shirt—no tie. Her instructions were precise, her tone pure young adult authority. She FaceTimed me as I dressed, making adjustments through the screen like a seasoned fashion director.

"Not that pocket square. This one," she said, holding up a vivid fuchsia handkerchief with subtle grey patterns.

We picked it together, and I couldn't resist pairing it with matching socks—a quiet act of rebellion against the sea of black tuxedos I knew I'd be walking into.

"That's the one, Pop," she'd said with a grin. "You're gonna look expensive but approachable."

That girl. She pushed me just far enough past my comfort zone without letting me lose myself in it.

The scent of lemon, bergamot, and a hint of star anise from my cologne clung to me as I adjusted my jacket one final time. The venue was already alive with soft jazz, curated conversations, and the muted shimmer of expensive fabric and ambition. I didn't come to be dazzled—I came to do business.

"You got this. Your crown has been bought and paid for. All you have to do is put it on."

I murmured Baldwin's words under my breath, steadying myself. My father's voice echoed in my mind—firm, steady, proud. Those words had carried me through boardrooms, city council meetings, and now, into rooms like this.

I straightened my back, gave the cufflinks one last check, and spotted a familiar investor across the room. I smiled at the memory of my father and moved with purpose, Baldwin's words still thumping like a heartbeat beneath my polished shoes.

After hours of schmoozing, nodding through elevator pitches, and dodging lukewarm wine refills, I finally found a small pocket of peace by the gallery's far wall. A plate of mini crab cakes in one hand, my phone in the other, I snuck glimpses of the game with Langston—my friend, colleague, and the only other person in the room who cared about offensive rebounds and missed foul calls as much as I did.

A trio of local musicians reimagined Erykah Badu and Lauryn Hill with soulful ease—layering jazzy riffs into "Didn't Cha Know" and "Ex-Factor" like love letters to the culture. It was the kind of vibe that made you slow down, exhale, maybe even believe in something.

And then *she* entered my atmosphere.

It started with a scent—soft and unexpected. Sweet vanilla and warm almond, delicate but commanding, drifting into our corner of the room like a quiet announcement. It wasn't familiar, but it was magnetic. I looked up, drawn out of the game and into something entirely different.

"Who's winning?" came a voice, honeyed and low, floating in just behind Langston's shoulder.

We turned in unison, and suddenly, nothing else in the room existed.

She stood there like the punctuation mark on a sentence I hadn't finished. A vision in lavender. Her suit fit like it was custom-made—sharp in cut, soft in tone, hugging her curves with understated confidence. The sheer blouse beneath it offered just a glimpse of collarbone, elegant and disarming. Her skin, rich and deep, held the light in a way that made everything around her seem dim by comparison. Shoulder-length curls framed her face effortlessly, partially veiling pearl earrings that winked with every subtle turn of her head.

I blinked, trying to remember what game I'd been watching.

Clearing my throat, I answered, "Knicks."

Her face lit up, and with a small fist pump she grinned, "Yes!"

I chuckled. "Don't tell me you're actually a Knicks fan."

"Let's just say I've got a soft spot for the orange and blue," she replied, her tone smooth and teasing.

"Not a real Knicks fan, then," Langston chimed in, smirking.

She shrugged, amused. "Not officially. But I've got friends who'd revoke my Brooklyn card if I didn't cheer when they win."

I glanced at Langston. "We go way back with the Washington Bullets."

Her brow lifted, playful. "You mean the Wizards?"

Langston and I exchanged a look.

"I mean, yeah," I admitted with a smile, "but old habits die hard. Still getting used to the rebrand."

"And when the Wizards disappoint us, we shift allegiances," Langston added. "Brown and the Celtics."

She tilted her head, mock judgment dancing in her eyes. "Boston? That's brave. A little scandalous, actually."

"Calculated," I said, eyes still locked on hers.

Whatever game was playing on my phone seconds earlier didn't matter anymore. In fact, the entire night had just shifted course.

She chuckled—a warm, infectious sound that rippled

through me before I had a chance to brace for it. Just then, a tall man appeared behind her, gently tapping her shoulder and extending a hand, wordlessly requesting her attention. She turned toward him with an easy grace, her gaze lingering on his face just long enough to acknowledge him before flicking back to me and Langston.

"Thanks for the score," she murmured, leaning in slightly, her voice soft and just for us. "And you might want to root for the Knicks... I don't think the Bullets—sorry, *Wizards*—even made the playoffs this year."

Her lips curled into a smile, sly and knowing, before she allowed herself to be guided away. The lavender suit caught the light as she moved, and the faint scent of vanilla and almond trailed behind her, wrapping around the air like an unfinished sentence.

Langston glanced at me, but I didn't return the look. My eyes were still locked on her retreating form as she disappeared into the swell of the crowd—graceful, magnetic, unforgettable.

I found myself smirking, the corner of my mouth twitching as I slowly slipped my phone into my jacket pocket, the game forgotten.

I could be a Knicks fan, I thought, *at least for tonight.*

Because if rooting for the orange and blue meant I might catch even one more moment in her orbit, then so be it.

8

Skylar

Six months ago

I'd just savored the final bite of a perfectly crisp crab puff from a nearby table, the buttery richness still lingering on my tongue, when my gaze wandered across the room—and landed on two striking men posted in the far corner. The *opposite* corner from where Sterling Robert Jennings had been shamelessly orbiting all evening.

So far, I'd managed to strike that delicate balance between looking effortlessly fabulous and avoiding my ex like a trained professional. But I knew better than to let my streak end early. I needed an exit—graceful, subtle, intentional.

And there it was.

The two men stood shoulder to shoulder, tall, sharp, and smooth-skinned, the rich shades of their brown complexions gleaming under the soft gallery lighting. From the way they glanced down at their phones, nodding occasionally, I could tell—basketball fans. A knowing smirk here, a side-eye there. They weren't just checking email.

Perfect. A convenient excuse to slip out of Sterling's line of sight—and maybe into something far more interesting.

Something about this lavender suit—the way it hugged my frame, the way the heels shifted my posture—made me feel like I could command any room, or at least reclaim this one.

I walked toward them with purpose, weaving between guests with practiced ease, and stopped just close enough to be heard over the gentle hum of conversation and the dreamy rhythm of Erykah Badu's *"Didn't Cha Know"* pouring from the speakers. The soulful melody floated through the gallery, slow and hypnotic, like it was soundtracking my next move.

"Who's winning?" I asked, letting the question carry the soft lilt of curiosity as I eased into their space.

Before he even looked up, a wave of warm, woody cologne greeted me—smooth and grounding, layered with something earthy and slightly sweet. It wrapped around me, mingling with the almond and vanilla of my own scent, as if we'd been made to stand this close.

Then he turned.

And smiled.

An easy, pearly white smile unfolded across his face, framed by a pepper-dusted goatee that sharpened the lines of his strong jaw. The contrast between his dark facial hair and bright teeth gave him that rare combination of polished charm and natural ease—refined, but not rehearsed.

But it was his eyes that stopped me cold.

A warm, honeyed brown, flecked with gold and something deeper—like bourbon kissed by candlelight. They caught the glow of the overhead pendant lights, shifting from amber to caramel as he tilted his head ever so slightly. His gaze met mine—not too fast, not too lingering—like he was quietly studying something rare.

And in that pause, I realized I'd let out a small breath, barely audible, but undeniably real. A quiet exhale of *damn*.

I had walked over to escape.

Now I wasn't so sure I wanted to leave.

I reveled in the rhythm of our banter, letting it carry me like a melody I didn't want to end. It wasn't just the conversation—it was the way I felt in it. Light. Bold. A little electric. There was something about basketball—the universal language of game nights and friendly rivalries—that had unlocked a rare ease in me. For once, I wasn't overthinking every glance or weighing every word. I was *flirting*, and it was working. I wanted more—names, stories, maybe a shared laugh that lingered longer than it should've.

I was just about to lean in, riding the momentum, when I felt a hand tap my shoulder.

Familiar.

And suddenly, I was back on solid ground.

I turned, pulse hitching, and there he was—*Sterling Robert Jennings*—standing as if summoned by some internal radar he'd never turned off.

His eyes, still that deep, penetrating brown, met mine without hesitation. They had once made me feel seen—truly seen—in a way that felt more dangerous than comforting. His gaze hadn't lost its intensity, but something in it had softened. Or maybe I had hardened.

The shadow beard that traced his jaw was as immaculate as ever, framing the warm, golden hue of his butterscotch skin, still sun-kissed and annoyingly flawless. A single diamond stud glinted in his ear—tiny, familiar, and triggering. I remembered the day he got it, grinning like a boy showing off a new toy, begging me to admit it made him look more "grown."

His low Caesar cut was tight, edged up to perfection, and the once quirky Dwayne Wayne flip glasses he used to rock had been upgraded to sleek tortoise-shell frames. Expensive. Polished. Like everything else about him—smoothed out, refined, curated to impress.

But not disarm.

"Thanks for the score," I said softly, turning just enough to glance back at the man I'd been speaking to. My voice dipped into something teasing, just for him. "And maybe you should consider rooting for the Knicks... I don't think the Bullets—sorry, *Wizards*—are even in the playoffs this year."

I caught the flicker of surprise in his eyes, a crack in his composure that made me bite back a smirk. I leaned in a breath closer—not too much, just enough to make it linger—and offered a parting smile that danced on the edge of flirtation and farewell.

Then I turned.

Sterling, the man who had tapped my shoulder, waited just a few steps away, and I let him guide me back into the current of the room, into the next part of the evening. But even as I walked away, I could feel it—the bourbon kissed man's gaze trailing behind me like a string unwilling to snap.

9

Skylar

Six Months Ago

"Allie, it's *2:00 a.m.* We can talk *tomorrow*," I mumbled, my voice thick with sleep and desperation as I cradled the phone against my cheek.

"It *is* tomorrow," she shot back, her tone light but commanding. "And I'm less than a block away. Quinn's up late working on briefs, and Eden said she'd jump on FaceTime once I get to your place."

I sat up, blinking at the ceiling. "A block away? I didn't even know you were back in the city."

"Philly's just down the street, Sky. No need to stay overnight. Besides, I want a recap *now*—before your memory turns everything into a polite summary instead of the juicy mess I know it was. Jeremiah'll buzz me up."

I barely had time to argue before I heard the familiar *ding* of the elevator down the hall.

Moments later, Allie breezed into my apartment like it was 2:00 in the afternoon instead of 2:00 in the morning. Her curls were piled into a loose pineapple, hoops still on, and she

was wearing her signature "I'm not staying long" sweats—
which always meant at least two hours.

She made a beeline for the kitchen, opened the fridge with
the confidence of a co-owner, and pulled out two ginger ales.
Then she flipped on the oven with a practiced flick of her
wrist.

"What are you doing?" I asked, watching from the couch,
half-amused and half-convinced she might start reorganiz-
ing my spice rack next.

She glanced over her shoulder. "Feeding us. I know you're
still hungry. Those artsy events never serve real food—just
tiny appetizers with names you can't pronounce."

She pulled two foil-wrapped sandwiches from her tote and
set them down with a flourish. "I grabbed us cheesesteaks
on the way back. From *that* spot on South Street. You can
thank me after you take the first bite. Now call Q and E while
I get our plates."

"Te quiero," I said, the gratitude spilling out in a sigh.

"*Mucho*," she grinned, cutting me off before I could finish.
We both burst into laughter, the kind that echoed through
the quiet apartment like home. I grabbed my phone, still
smiling, and opened our group chat to start a FaceTime.

Seconds later, Quinn's face popped up on screen, her eyes
narrowing as she spotted the sandwiches.

"Are those *cheesesteaks*?" she asked, adjusting her glasses,
voice equal parts horror and envy. "I'm really starting to
resent the fact that you two still live in the same city."

Eden joined next, hair wrapped in a silk scarf, yawning
as she clocked the food. "It's *after* 2:00 a.m. and y'all are
eating cheesesteaks? You're gonna need more than spin class
tomorrow to recover."

"Jealous often, E?" Allie said with her mouth full, taking a dramatic bite and sticking her tongue out at the camera.

I shook my head and laughed, sinking deeper into the couch as the late-night chaos settled into something familiar—girlfriends, food, and a story I was finally ready to spill.

I dove into the story between mouthfuls of cheesesteak, barely stopping to breathe as I recounted the night. My words tumbled out in bursts of excitement—new contacts, fresh leads, potential collaborators who could be *game-changers* for our next project on sustainable housing in Red Hook. These weren't just business cards and handshakes; they were real possibilities.

Allie and I polished off the first half of our sandwiches like it was a sport, our wrappers rustling in tandem. She stood and headed toward the fridge without saying a word.

"The jalapeños are on the second shelf," I called after her, grinning like we'd done this routine a hundred times before—and we had. From late-night study sessions to celebratory post-pitch snacks, she always knew where to find the heat.

Moments later, she returned, balancing extra napkins, a fresh ginger ale for herself, and a bottle of cold water for me. She handed it over without a word, already knowing I'd need it. She knew my habits better than I did.

"Enough with the business," Allie declared, flopping back down beside me with the kind of flair only she could manage. "Give me the tea, Skylar. Spill *everything*."

Quinn's face lit up on the screen. "Yes, Sky. I do *not* have until 2:00 a.m. *tomorrow* to get to the meat and potatoes of this story."

Allie leaned in, eyes gleaming, the wrapper of her sandwich crinkling beneath her hand like it, too, was waiting for the good part.

I exhaled dramatically, already laughing at myself. "I was doing everything in my power to avoid Sterling all night. I was ducking in and out of conversations, repositioning myself like a secret agent, even—at one point—hiding behind a decorative plant."

Eden choked on a laugh. "*A plant*, Sky? Not the shrubs!"

"But then," I continued, shaking my head, "he *pounced*. Caught me completely off guard."

"It was the lavender outfit," Allie giggled knowingly, biting into her second half. "You looked too good to ignore."

"You wore the lavender?" Quinn asked, surprised. "Wait—you *actually* wore it?"

"I had twenty bucks riding on you wearing the black dress," Eden chimed in, shaking her head. "Safe. Predictable. Classic Sky move."

"How did you *know* I went with lavender?" I asked, raising an eyebrow at Allie, suspicious but impressed.

Allie popped a jalapeño into her mouth and pointed a finger in the air like she was delivering gospel. "Because you value your life too much to ignore your fashion fairy godmother. And because I *never* steer you wrong. *Ever*."

Her laughter bubbled up, contagious and full of warmth, wrapping around the room like a soft blanket. I couldn't help but smile, the tension in my shoulders finally loosening. For all the chaos of the night, here—on this couch, with ginger ale, cheesesteaks, and my sisters on FaceTime—I felt grounded again.

Just as I was easing into light conversation with two strikingly handsome, cocoa-rich men—both in tailored designer suits and heads full of waves so crisp they looked airbrushed into place—I felt it.

A familiar tap on my shoulder.

Followed by the unmistakable warmth of a hand sliding over mine.

Sterling.

My breath hitched, just slightly. The kind of instinctive pause your body takes before memory crashes in. I didn't have to look to know it was him—the touch alone brought it all back. The firm yet gentle pressure of his hand, the way his palm always seemed to settle perfectly against mine, like it was made for that exact fit.

For a heartbeat, I stared at our joined hands—so familiar, so unexpected—and in that second, it felt like time folded in on itself. I remembered how his touch once anchored me, how it had once felt like home.

I slowly turned to face him, my expression guarded but composed. He looked... good. Familiar in all the worst and most wonderful ways. Still sun-kissed and sharply groomed, his scent was a smooth mix of sandalwood and something richer, something that whispered nostalgia.

We started with small talk—weather, work, surface-level chatter. Polite and careful, like two diplomats dancing around a peace treaty neither was quite ready to sign. But his eyes betrayed him. Beneath the practiced calm was something restless, unresolved, flickering just behind his gaze.

"Ten years, Sky," he murmured, shaking his head slightly, voice low and rough around the edges. "And yet... here we are."

His words landed between us like a stone tossed into still water, sending ripples through the carefully composed façade I'd worn all night.

I crossed my arms, grounding myself, and met his gaze evenly. "It's been a long time, Sterling."

"Too long," he said, his voice softer now, tinged with something like regret. The space between us seemed to tighten, thick with old emotion and things unsaid. He hesitated, his fingers brushing his jaw in that thoughtful way he always had when he was unsure of his next move.

"I thought..." he began, cautiously. "Maybe we could catch up sometime? Coffee, perhaps?"

Coffee?

My instinct was to laugh, but I didn't. Not out loud, anyway. Instead, I studied him. Searched his face for a tell—for context, for clarity, for an answer to the question he hadn't asked yet.

Because for all the weight hanging between us—for the love once shared, the pain never properly unpacked—coffee felt like... a placeholder. Too casual for the depth of our history. Too simple for the mess we never sorted through. Too safe.

Still, that old magnetism tugged at me like it always had. Quiet but undeniable.

I didn't say yes. But I didn't say no, either.

"I don't know if that's a good idea," I said, my voice calm but edged with hesitation. The words felt like they came from someone standing at the edge of a door—half-open, half afraid to walk through.

Sterling gave a small, almost imperceptible smile. His lips curved with a gentleness that wasn't quite smug, but something more... patient. Like he already knew the answer, even if I wasn't ready to say it out loud.

"Fair enough," he said softly, his voice a low, steady hum beneath the soft buzz of the crowd. "But I'll leave the invitation open. In case you change your mind."

He didn't press. Didn't plead. Just stood there with that quiet steadiness I remembered—one that once made me feel safe, and now made me feel... unsettled.

For a moment, we stood suspended in that silence, just looking at each other. His gaze didn't waver—warm, steady, but laced with something I couldn't quite name. Something older. Earned. Like he wasn't trying to be the man he once was, but was offering me a glimpse of the man he'd become.

And then, without another word, he let my hand go.

The physical contact may have been brief, but the sensation lingered—like the ghost of a melody I used to hum in the dark. I watched as he gave me a small nod, then turned and stepped back into the crowd, his silhouette swallowed by the movement and murmurs of the room.

I stood there, still.

Still unsure whether I should have said more.

Still unsure if I should've followed him.

Still unsure if the ache in my chest was nostalgia... or something deeper, something unfinished.

But one thing settled in, sharp and undeniable:

My heart hadn't forgotten him.

Not even close.

I was still caught in that haze when a napkin suddenly landed on my lap, snapping me back to the present.

"Okay. That's enough about *Sterling Robert Jennings*," Allie said from across the couch, her tone firm, teasing, and laced with the kind of best-friend authority you don't argue with. "We've been stuck on Chapter Ten of that book for a decade."

She pointed at my phone, her eyes dancing. "Now tell me—who's *this*?" she asked, grinning as she held up the screen with a picture I'd forgotten she'd taken.

Reality crashed back in—laughter, ginger ale fizzing in my glass, the scent of warm cheesesteaks still clinging to the air. And just like that, the moment passed.

But not the memory.

"There is a picture?" Eden asked with curiosity.

"Okay, your honor, we are entitled to the same evidence the prosecution has." Quinn laughed requesting the juice from Allie.

I picked up her phone, already familiar with her passcode. We'd swapped codes ages ago, right after watching a movie where a friend had died, leaving her loved ones locked out of her phone. Yes, we were *those* kind of best friends.

Scrolling through the photos, I saw a few shots from tonight. The two men in the picture? Titus and Langston. After Sterling's coffee invitation—which had left me con-flicted and flustered—Titus had swooped in, saving me from the lingering tension. We'd ended up talking for almost two hours, so engrossed that the time slipped by until the event finally wrapped up. Before parting, he walked me to my car outside the museum, where we exchanged not only names but numbers, along with a genuine promise to meet for tea sometime soon.

"That's Titus," I said, glancing down at the photo with a little smile tugging at my lips.

"Ugh, hello, you have friends that are not in the room. Send the picture over." Quinn demanded.

"Yes, NOW." Eden added.

I added the pictures to our group chat and pressed send

making sure Quinn and Eden had all the juice.

"I met him tonight at the event. He's a real estate investor working on a few projects in Brooklyn. His firm's all about urban development, but they're trying to push back against the gentrification that's been displacing people, you know? Trying to add real value for the community."

My voice softened, the memory of our long conversation lingering. "We talked for hours. And... well, we may have exchanged numbers."

"¡Ay, Dios! Skylar!" Allie laughed, clapping her hands in delight, her eyes lighting up with mischief.

10

Titus

Six Months Ago

"Please tell me you got the number of that fine, curvy lady in lavender we saw at the event last night," Langston said as we stepped into the glass-wrapped conference room on the 9th floor.

He dropped his everything bagel—extra schmear—on the edge of the sleek table and walked straight to the wall of windows that framed the Brooklyn Bridge like living art. The morning light caught the steel beams in gold, and even with all we knew about how this city had changed, it still felt like ours.

Our office in DUMBO had been a dream once—before it became a line item in a gentrifier's checklist. But here we were, holding space in a neighborhood where Black and brown stories were being rewritten in invisible ink. Every deal we inked, every block we reclaimed, was a small defiance.

I walked over to the table, setting down my coffee mug— a small, slightly lopsided piece of art handmade by Kayla in second grade. A deep maroon "M" for Morehouse was painted proudly on the front, the glaze slightly cracked, the handle just shy of level. She'd presented it to me on Father's Day with glue still drying. It never left my desk or my hand for long. A not-so-subtle reminder to lead with love. I set it down carefully on the polished walnut table and pulled out a chair.

Langston turned, grinning like a kid with gossip. "So, what's the story, Ty? Tell me you got her digits, man."

I tried to play it cool, clearing my throat like I had a speech prepared. His eyes narrowed with expectation. My smirk gave me away before I could say a word.

"My man!" He clapped me into a dap, loud and proud. "I knew you weren't gonna let that moment pass."

That's the thing about us—Langston and me. The bond ran deeper than business. We met as boys on the campus green during Morehouse's Parents' Parting Ceremony, scared and stubborn. Through late-night study sessions, broken hearts, family funerals, baby showers, and now real estate portfolios that stretched across three cities—we were still here. Still us.

After a stronghold in Memphis and Langston planting roots in D.C., we'd brought our vision to Brooklyn two years ago. It wasn't just about flipping buildings. It was about restoring legacies. His JD from Boston College and my Wharton MBA weren't trophies—they were tools.

Langston had run the Memphis office like a boss, but love brought him north. Zora—his law school crush turned wife and ride-or-die—was as brilliant as she was bold. They had three kids under six, and somehow still found time to name them after legends: Phyllis Giovanni, their precocious six-year-old who ruled the house; Baldwin Walker, the introspective middle child who probably journaled in crayon; and sweet little Audre Maya, all cheeks and dimples. That family was a walking syllabus of Black brilliance.

"So," I said with a smirk, "what's next? Toni for baby four?"

Langston groaned, holding up both hands in surrender. "Absolutely not. Zora says we're done. I'm tapped out. These kids are robbing me of sleep, peace, and Wi-Fi bandwidth."

"You said that after Baldwin," I reminded him, laughing.

He leaned back, eyes softening. "She's just... everything. Zora even saw me off with a smile. That woman's my whole heart."

"Sounds like she's plotting," I teased. "That smile had strategy behind it."

"Of course she's plotting," he said, rolling his eyes. "Her sister's bachelorette party is in Puerto Vallarta next month, then she's off to St. Thomas with her girls. Meanwhile, I'm gonna be home trying not to cry during 'Encanto.'"

"We don't talk about Brunco." I shook my head, still grinning.

"Anyway," he shifted, lowering his voice like he was getting serious, "speaking of weddings—"

"Stop right there," I warned. "You're about to take a hard left."

Langston held up his hands. "Wrong segue. We're staying in your lane. Back to Ms. Lavender."

I leaned back, the name still soft on my tongue. "Skylar," I said quietly. "Skylar Madison."

Langston raised both brows and whistled low. "Oh, we're using full government now?"

"She earned it," I replied, meaning every word.

"Alright, Mr. Sprung" he teased. "What's the verdict? You vanished for half the night and came back floating. Don't think I didn't notice."

"She's something else, man. Talking to her felt... easy. Honest. Like exhaling after holding your breath too long." I paused, smiling to myself. "Except her trash taste in NBA teams, she's incredible."

Langston howled. "Let me guess—Knicks fan?"

"Yup. All Orange and Blue."

He grimaced like he'd just bitten into a lemon. "Yeah, nah. That's grounds for annulment."

"She's worth the compromise," I said before I could stop myself.

Langston let that sit for a beat, then nodded slowly. "That's real."

A moment passed, filled only with the hum of the city rising behind the glass.

"She's also fine as hell," he added. "That lavender pants suit? I almost had to shield my eyes out of respect."

I threw a napkin at his chest. "Watch it."

He caught it, laughing. "Hey, I'm married, not blind."

"You keep talking and you're gonna end up in the kids' room while Zora and her girls are sipping piña coladas."

Langston held up both hands in mock defense. "I'm just saying, you better not fumble this one."

"I don't plan to."

He clapped his hands once. "Alright, back to business. We hitting the gym before this 1:00 call?"

"Absolutely," I said, standing. "Loser buys dinner."

"Oh, you mean you're buying? Great." He winked. "Junior's, please. With cheesecake. Or maybe that spot on

DeKalb…"

We were walking toward the elevator when he gave me a sly side-eye. "Skylar Madison…" he sang softly, drawing out every syllable like it was laced with meaning.

I didn't even bother denying it. My grin gave me away.

She was still in my head—lavender and laughter, confidence and calm. And I had a feeling she wasn't leaving anytime soon.

11

Allie

Six Months Ago

I paced the length of my apartment like it held the answers, my phone warm in one hand, a half-drunk malta sweating on the coffee table. Skylar had dropped a whole bomb on me the day before, and I was still trying to find the pieces.

Titus had kids.

Not "I helped raise my godson" kids. Not "my niece stays with me sometimes" kids. No. Two *actual*, living, breathing, birth-certificate-having children. And not toddlers either. These were grown-ish. College-age.

I flopped onto the couch, the cushions giving way with a soft whoosh, the kind of familiar comfort you crave when your best friend drops a truth you weren't ready for. I pulled the chunky throw over my legs and stared at the ceiling, still trying to absorb the headline: *Titus has two kids.*

Skylar's voice came through the phone, soft but laced with that anxious edge I knew too well. She was in her own head— probably curled up in her bed, wrapped in a robe that cost more than my rent in grad school, biting her lip like she always did when she was fighting logic with fear.

"Two kids," I repeated, letting the words settle like heavy snow. I could hear her breathing on the other end.

"Yeah... two," she murmured. "And an ex-wife. But there's no drama, he swears."

I let out a long sigh, blowing my bangs off my forehead and shooting a look toward the ceiling fan as if it could spin this situation into something simpler.

"Chica... that's a lot," I said, not sugarcoating it. "But are you seriously about to toss a whole Titus into the 'too complicated' bin over grown kids and an ex-wife who's clearly moved on?"

Sky didn't answer right away. Typical. She was probably halfway through imagining their family group chat and what her role would be in it—somewhere between "awkward interloper" and "forgettable phase."

"It's not just the kids," she said finally. "It's the *life*. He has this whole world that existed before me. A family, history, traditions. Sunday dinners and college graduations and whatever else. It just... feels like walking into a movie halfway through."

I got it. I really did. But that didn't mean I was going to let her self-sabotage.

"Okay. But let's slow this panic train down for a sec," I said, shifting deeper into the cushions. "He's a good father, right?"

"Yes," she said quickly, like that part was never in question.

"And he treats you well?"

"Yeah," she admitted, softening. I could hear the way her voice tilted at the memory. The way he talked about his son—Titus Jr., or Deuce—who'd just started his MBA at Wharton.

His daughter Kayla, a freshman at Howard, had his eyes and his wit. She'd told me how his face lit up when he talked about them. That kind of joy couldn't be faked.

"No drama with the ex?"

"She's remarried," Sky said. "They co-parent well. He said it's peaceful."

I sat up a little straighter, letting my voice ride the line between teasing and truth-telling. "So let me get this right. No baby mama drama. Kids are adults. He's thoughtful, fine, Morehouse-educated, got his stuff together. And you're about to let that go... why?"

"I just never pictured this," she said quietly.

"Well, yeah. None of us pictured this," I said, grabbing my malta. "If we had it our way, we'd be married to Idris Elba clones by now, living in brownstones with no baggage and infinite foreplay. But that's not real life."

Skylar chuckled faintly, and I knew I was chipping away.

"Real life is complicated. But this? This doesn't sound like chaos. It sounds like something real. Something *whole*. You're not walking into a mess, Sky. You're walking into a man who's already done the hard stuff—who chose to grow up. Do you know how rare that is?"

Silence. Then a sigh.

"I know," she whispered. "It's just scary. What if I fall for him and then I'm just... some footnote in his life? What if I don't fit into the picture?"

I softened, my voice gentler. "Sky... everyone has a past. The question is whether he's making room for you in his *present*. And from where I'm sitting? It sounds like he is."

She didn't answer. I knew she was spinning the scenarios in her mind like a Choose Your Own Adventure novel gone rogue.

"Sky," I added, "you've been raving about this man for *months*. He's not a project. He's not a fixer-upper. He shows up. You smile different when you talk about him."

Her voice cracked with a laugh. "I do?"

"Like someone just whispered a secret only your heart understands."

She let that land. I pictured her curled on her bed, staring at the ceiling just like I had been.

"Look, I'm not saying it'll be easy. But I am saying it's worth exploring. You've dated men who were all mystery and no intention. Titus? He's showing up with receipts, a blueprint, and emotional availability."

"That's rare," she admitted.

"Exactly. Don't let fear of the unknown keep you from something good. You're always overthinking, trying to calculate outcomes like this is a spreadsheet."

"I like spreadsheets," she muttered.

"I know you do, Excel Queen. But love doesn't work in formulas. Sometimes it's messy. Sometimes it's kids and ex-wives and unexpected blessings."

She sighed again—this one softer. Less resistance, more surrender.

"So you're saying I should give him a real chance?"

"I'm saying... yes. You might surprise yourself. Maybe the future you didn't picture ends up being better than the one you planned."

There was a pause.

Then a lighter, brighter, Skylar laughed. "I doubt it. But maybe."

"There she is," I smiled. "And worst-case scenario? You

meet the kids, they hate you, you run off to Paris and live your best aunty life with a poodle and a passport."

"Oh my God, Allie," she laughed, the real kind this time.

"I'm just saying, keep your options open. But don't close the door on something just because it didn't arrive wrapped in the box you expected."

"Alright, alright," she said. "You've talked me off the ledge... for now."

"Good," I said, satisfied. "Because if you dumped him over this, I'd seriously consider scooping him up myself."

"You hate kids."

"True. But girl, *he fine-fine*. I might make an exception."

We both laughed, slipping into the warm rhythm of our usual banter—work drama, petty celeb news, Netflix recs. But underneath the easy chatter, I held tight to one truth: Skylar was standing at the edge of something real.

And if I had anything to do with it, she wasn't going to let fear push her away.

She might not know it yet, but sometimes you've just got to leap, trusting that wherever you land, you'll be okay. And if anyone deserved that leap, it was Skylar. Now, I just had to get her to believe it, too.

12

Titus

Six Months Ago

I sat by the living room window, the morning light creeping across the hardwood floors in long amber streaks. The Brooklyn skyline stretched out before me in hushed shades of gray and orange, the buildings still yawning awake. My coffee sat untouched on the side table, cold and bitter now, its steam long since vanished—just like the warmth I used to feel when Skylar's name crossed my mind.

Her silence had weight. Not the kind that screamed or slammed doors, but the kind that lingered like fog—low, thick, and hard to see through. I tried to push it aside, to shake the ache off like a stubborn chill, but it clung to me.

Then my phone buzzed on the armrest, breaking the quiet. Langston. Right on time.

I answered, trying to smooth the roughness out of my voice. "Hey, man."

"T, what's going on? You sound... off," Langston said, his voice carrying that signature steadiness. He always sounded like a brother who'd climbed out of the same storm but remembered where the lifeboats were.

I exhaled slowly, the kind of breath that carried weeks of held-in tension. "It's Skylar. She's been MIA ever since I told her about the kids. I really thought we had something, L. Something different. But I guess I misread it."

Langston was quiet for a second, like he was weighing his response. "That's rough, man. But think about it—two kids, an ex-wife, a whole backstory? That's a lot for anybody to take in. Especially someone like Skylar, who's used to being in control of the picture. Doesn't mean she's gone, though. She might just be... recalibrating."

"Recalibrating," I repeated with a dry laugh, rubbing my temple. "Feels more like retreating. I've been texting, calling—nothing. It's like I scared her off. And I hate that feeling. I hate feeling like the thing that made me proud is the thing that pushed her away."

Langston's voice softened, like a balm. "Listen, don't let this eat you alive. You've got two incredible kids who love you, and this holiday? It's about family. Kayla's coming up early to see you, right?"

I nodded, eyes flicking to my suitcase in the corner— half-packed, half-forgotten. "Yeah. She's flying in before Thanksgiving. Said she wanted to check in on me. She knows I've been off. She could hear it in my voice."

"She's always been sharp like that," Langston said, his tone filled with quiet admiration. "Kayla sees you, T. Always has."

I could still picture her at seven years old, standing on her tiptoes, grabbing my face with those tiny, sticky fingers and saying, *"You're the best dad in the whole wide world."* Even now, just thinking about it brought heat to my chest.

"She's grown now, but she's still that same kid at heart," I said, my voice thick with something softer. "She's looking out for me, same as always."

"And Deuce'll be at your parents', right?" Langston added. "That boy's probably bringing all his Wharton energy to the table."

I chuckled at that. "Yeah. Can't wait to hear him try to analyze the Thanksgiving meal like it's a supply chain."

Langston laughed, and I could hear the warmth returning between us. "Point is, you've got your tribe, T. People who love you. Don't let Skylar's silence rob you of that."

I leaned back into the chair, letting his words find their way in. Outside, the skyline shimmered with the start of the day. Inside, I could feel the fog starting to lift.

"I know you're right," I said, quieter now. "It's just... I thought she might be part of that tribe one day. The way we connected, man—it felt different. Real."

Langston didn't jump in right away. When he did, his voice was calm, deliberate. "Sometimes real takes time. Sometimes it needs space to stretch into what it's supposed to be. If she's the one, she'll find her way back. And if not..." He paused. "You've still built a good life. One you should be proud of."

I swallowed that truth like a slow sip of bourbon. Bitter-sweet, but warming.

"How's your mom holding up?" I asked, pivoting gently. "First Thanksgiving without your pops."

Langston sighed. "She's got that Hughes steel in her. You know how she is—lipstick on, pearls clasped, acting like she's fine. But I know it's hitting her hard. That's why I'm making sure the whole family's under one roof. Kids, Zora, even my sister and her crew."

"It's going to help her. All that love in one house—it'll lift the weight."

"That's the hope," he said. "And she's already roped the kids into sweet potato duty. Told them if they mess up the dough, they're off dessert for life."

I laughed, the sound surprising me. "That sounds like her."

"Speaking of duty," Langston said with a grin I could hear, "you're still on cornbread biscuit detail. Don't think I forgot."

I groaned. "Man, can we rotate duties? I did that last year."

"And we *still* talk about how dry they were," he clapped back. "You've got a redemption arc this year."

I shook my head, smiling. "Alright, alright. I'll come correct."

"There we go," he said, the laughter easy between us now. "Just remember—family first. And hey, maybe Skylar just needs to sit with the truth a little longer. If she's worth it, she'll come back with clarity."

I looked out at the sky again—brighter now, the fog lifting. "Thanks, L. Really."

"Anytime, brother. Now go reheat that coffee and pack your bag. You've got a holiday to enjoy. And tell my goddaughter I'm ready to destroy her in Uno."

I laughed for real that time, the weight in my chest finally shifting. "Will do."

"And Titus," Langston added, voice full of mock warning, "don't mess up the cornbread."

I sucked my teeth. "One dry batch and I never live it down."

"That's the beauty of brotherhood," he said. "We remember everything."

As I hung up and turned toward the suitcase, I realized—

for the first time in weeks—I wasn't just getting ready for Thanksgiving. I was looking forward to it.

13

Skylar

The coffee shop had settled into that rare, golden lull between the chaos of the morning rush and the whisper of the midday crowd. The air thrummed with a low, peaceful energy, like a held breath between verses. Sunlight drifted lazily through the oversized windows, casting dappled shadows across the polished concrete floor and illuminating the lush cascade of hanging plants that trailed from the ceiling like green chandeliers.

The scent of cinnamon, honeyed syrup, and freshly ground beans hugged the room like a familiar song. Overhead, Musiq Soulchild's *"So Beautiful"* floated from the speakers, wrapping the air in a slow, aching sweetness. It was the kind of song that made everything feel intentional—like the universe was nudging you toward something... or someone.

I stood just inside the doorway, taking it all in. Books lined the walls, their colorful spines peeking between vines of ivy like secrets waiting to be told. It was all so soft, so intimate, that I felt the question rise in my chest again:

Why am I here?

Why had I agreed to this?

To sit across from the man who had broken my heart more times than I could count—not in some dramatic, final blow, but in subtle, slow fractures. Promises made and left hanging. Words that sounded sweet but never rooted into action. Hope that always managed to dissolve just before it could bloom.

Sterling had always looked perfect on paper—ambitious, articulate, polished. The checklist guy. But what lived beyond the bullet points? That was the question I'd stopped asking... until now.

Was he different?

Was *I*?

I adjusted my blazer, grateful I hadn't worn the sweater dress—it would've felt like armor, and today, I didn't want to feel armored. I wanted to feel honest, grounded. Present.

And then I saw him.

He was already seated, tucked into a sun-drenched corner beneath the windows. His gaze met mine instantly—those deep, dark eyes as unreadable as ever. My breath caught, not from longing, but from recognition. *That* look. The one that always made me forget the last disappointment... until the next one arrived.

He wore all black, his butter-pecan skin glowing against the crisp contrast. The white couch beneath him made him look like he'd been placed there intentionally, like art. When he lifted his hand in a quiet gesture—an invitation—I hesitated only a second before moving toward him.

He stood as I approached, tall and composed, and before I could speak, he stepped forward and pulled me into a hug.

It caught me off guard.

His arms wrapped around me like they remembered, like

they missed me. And even though every voice in my head told me to hold back, my body betrayed me and leaned in—just for a moment. His scent—warm, earthy, tinged with spice—wrapped around me like a memory I hadn't wanted to revisit.

The hug lingered longer than it should have. Not long enough to answer anything, but long enough to reopen everything.

When we finally stepped apart, there was a flicker of something in his eyes. Regret? Hope? I didn't know.

I sat beside him, my hand smoothing across the couch cushion like I needed to ground myself in something tangible. He sat close. Not presumptuous, but... present. A hand rested lightly on my knee. Familiar. Gentle. Too easy.

"Sky," he said, his voice low and careful, "thank you for meeting me. I wasn't sure you'd come. I know I haven't earned this—this space, this chance—but I'm grateful you gave it to me."

I nodded slightly, the weight of his gratitude settling into the quiet between us. But I couldn't let it carry the moment. I shifted slightly, creating a small, deliberate inch of distance—enough to breathe.

"Sterling," I said, my voice softer than I intended, "what did you want to talk about?"

The words hung in the air, suspended somewhere between past and present, braced for a future I hadn't decided I wanted yet.

Because beneath all the questions I had for *him*, the real one echoed in my chest:

Was I still the woman who waited on potential? Or had I finally become the one who knew her worth—and wouldn't settle for less than being truly chosen?

14

Allie

Sunlight spilled through the oversized windows of my kitchen, draping the space in a late-afternoon glow that softened everything it touched. The sleek marble countertops shimmered beneath it, catching the slow drift of dust motes suspended in the air like confetti in a snow globe. A lavender candle flickered quietly on the island, its scent curling through the room, mingling with the faint trace of that morning's coffee.

Skylar sat perched on a barstool, half in the present, half in her head. Her curls tumbled loosely over one shoulder, catching the light as they swayed with every restless bounce of her crossed leg. Her blazer was slung over the back of the chair, forgotten, and she absentmindedly traced the rim of her water glass like she was drawing a boundary she wasn't quite ready to cross.

I watched her in silence for a moment, trying to read the storm behind her otherwise calm exterior. Then, gently but pointedly, I broke the quiet.

"So..." I said, sipping from my mug. "What's the deal?

Have you talked to Titus?"

I kept my tone casual, but she knew better—my raised brow said everything I didn't.

Skylar exhaled slowly, tilting her head as if weighing how much of herself to hand over. "Our conversations have been... brief," she said, her voice floating somewhere between avoidance and understatement. "Just a few texts. A couple of calls. Nothing serious."

I narrowed my eyes, leaning forward with a grin that held just enough edge. "¿Lo estás evitando?" I asked, my voice teasing but not unkind. "You're dodging him. Admit it."

Skylar rolled her eyes, brushing imaginary lint off her jeans—her signature tell. "Not dodging. We've just both been busy. He's been traveling. I've had deadlines..."

"Right," I nodded slowly. "Deadlines and distractions. Sounds like my girl is ghosting with structure."

Just as I was about to push further, the doorbell rang, followed by the telltale creak of the front door opening.

"¡Luz!" Skylar nearly squealed, her voice rising like it belonged to someone getting a well-timed rescue. The relief on her face was so obvious it was comical.

Rolling my eyes, I turned toward the entrance. "Saved by the bell," I muttered under my breath.

Luz breezed in, a force of nature wrapped in a leather jacket and red lipstick, balancing three takeout bags from Cino's like it was her superpower. The scent of garlic, tomatoes, and shrimp parmigiana filled the room, and just like that, the kitchen became a memory of family dinners and full hearts.

"Tiempo perfecto, Luz," I said, kissing her on the cheek as I grabbed the bags.

"That eye roll better not be for me," she warned, tossing

her coat onto a hook. "Especially after I braved midtown traffic and double-parked for this shrimp parm. You're welcome."

"Yum!" Skylar chirped, already in motion—forks from the drawer, plates from the cabinet. "Shrimp parm—my love language."

"I hope you—" I started, ready to launch into a monologue about food boundaries.

"Allie," Luz cut me off with a pointed smirk, "I brought yours, relax. I've known you your whole life. Ms. I-don't-share. La reina mimada."

She winked and popped a piece of warm ciabatta into her mouth like punctuation.

"I'm starving," she said around a mouthful of bread.

"Same," I replied, pulling out my plate like it was the opening act.

But Luz wasn't about to let Skylar off the hook.

"Before we dive in, though—Sky's got boy drama to unload. Acting like she's in high school, avoiding a man with actual sense because he didn't show up with a blank résumé and zero history."

I raised a brow, instantly catching the rhythm. "Yes, Sky. No shrimp parm until we get the truth about you and Mr. Two-Grown-Kids."

Skylar groaned and reached for her plate.

I slid it just out of reach.

"Fine," she muttered, eyeing the pasta like she was negotiating a hostage release.

The sun had shifted by the time we finished—plates scraped clean, crumbs scattered, bellies full. The kitchen was bathed in that golden-hour hush, where everything felt slower and softer.

Skylar leaned back in her chair, tracing the rim of her glass again. But this time, her face wasn't guarded—it was raw.

"I'm scared," she whispered, the words barely audible. "Scared of what moving forward with Titus really means. His kids come first, and they always will. They're a part of him. And there's this tether—this invisible tie—to another woman who had a whole life with him before I even showed up. I don't know if I'm built for that. I don't know if I can be someone's bonus anything."

Her vulnerability quieted the room.

Then Luz leaned in, resting her elbow on the table, eyes locked on Skylar with that signature mix of blunt truth and big-sister love.

"Sky, I adore you," she said, her tone light but precise. "But let's be real. Titus hasn't proposed. He hasn't asked you to raise toddlers or share a bank account. You're out here overthinking a future that hasn't even happened yet. And girl... you're not twenty-five. You thought you'd meet a unicorn with no baggage at forty-something? The 40-Year-Old Virgin?"

Skylar huffed a laugh, shaking her head, but her eyes shimmered.

"She's not wrong," I added gently. "You spend so much time bracing for the worst, you forget to lean into what feels *good*."

Luz nodded, setting her glass down with intention. "Let me tell you something. If I'd let fear make my decisions, I wouldn't have Ari or Alec. And I wouldn't have known the love I had with Alejandro."

Her voice softened, memories stirring like sediment at the

bottom of a glass.

"You remember what it was like before we got married? His mother stopped speaking to him. Flat-out cut him off. And that wasn't the worst of it. After Ari, we lost two pregnancies. And just when we thought we couldn't handle any more... God gave us Alec."

She paused, eyes distant but steady. "And then, a week before Alec turned two, God took Alejandro."

The silence that followed was thick with reverence.

Even after all these years, the pain hadn't dulled. I felt my throat tighten, watching her relive it.

"But you know what?" Luz said, her voice stronger now. "I'd do it all over again. Every risk, every ache, every single tear. Because I got to love him. And be loved by him. And *that* was worth it."

Skylar looked down at her hands, eyes glassy but wide open.

Luz reached across the table and snatched the last piece of shrimp parm from my plate. Normally, I'd have launched into full protest mode, but not this time.

Some things weren't worth the fight.

Not when someone had just given you a piece of their soul.

15

Skylar

The autumn air nipped at our cheeks as we strolled through the tree-lined streets of Fort Greene, our boots crunching over a scattered patchwork of amber and rust-colored leaves. It was that perfect fall morning—where the cold woke you up but the sun kissed your skin just enough to make you forget the bite in the breeze.

Brooklyn buzzed in its own rhythm. The aroma of roasted chestnuts and fresh bagels drifted from a corner cart. Shop-keepers climbed ladders to string up holiday lights even though Thanksgiving hadn't arrived yet. That always annoyed me—this rush to the next thing. But Allie and I walked slowly, purposefully, like we had nowhere to be but exactly here.

We'd started our morning with her 8 a.m. yoga class over on Ashland and Lafayette. It felt like old times—pre-Thanksgiving rituals that had somehow survived college, breakups, new jobs, and everything in between. It was our way of pressing pause before the chaos of family and obligations swallowed us whole.

"Mija," Allie huffed beside me, dragging the sleeves of her hoodie across her forehead, "no matter what I do, I just can't get my brain to shut off during yoga. And today? *Muy caliente.* I thought I was gonna black out during downward dog."

I laughed, adjusting my scarf. "Isn't that your usual class?"

"Not with this new instructor. She cranked up the heat like she was cooking mofongo in there. And peri? She was no help. I swear I had a hot flash inside my hot flash."

"I'm just glad I pulled my hair back before class," I said, flipping the ends of my scarf over my shoulder. "Otherwise, I'd be walking around like Diana Ross after an encore."

Allie flung her arms out dramatically, her jacket unzipped and flapping in the breeze. Her neon yoga set—bold blocks of pink, orange, and lime green—caught the morning light and the attention of every passing pedestrian. Heads turned, but she didn't seem to notice—or care. That was Allie: full of color, confidence, and charisma, even with sweat on her brow and peri chasing her down.

"Sky, this woman Peri is not letting me live. I'm over-heating, and if I don't shower soon, I might melt into the pavement. You still have clothes in the guest room, if you want to clean up before we head to Sabór & Roots."

"You mean *my* room," I teased, nudging her shoulder with mine.

She rolled her eyes but grinned. "Don't say that too loud. Luz already thinks we're too close."

We both laughed, the kind of laugh that wraps around old memories like a scarf. But as we rounded the corner near Dekalb and started the familiar incline toward her brownstone, her mood shifted.

"So..." she said, her voice sliding into that signature tone she used when she wasn't playing. "Are we really going to pretend you don't owe me an update on Titus?"

I stiffened slightly, boots scuffing against the uneven sidewalk. I'd been sidestepping this conversation for weeks—dodging her calls, changing the subject, claiming work emergencies. But now, walking beside her in the cool morning light with the trees whispering overhead, there was nowhere left to hide.

"Ugh, there's not much to say," I muttered, stuffing my gloved hands deeper into my coat pockets. "He's been working, I've been working… there hasn't been time to really talk about what he said—or what it might mean for us."

The word slipped out—*us*—and I hated how soft it sounded.

Allie raised an eyebrow but didn't push—yet.

"There is something I forgot to mention though," I added quickly. "It's not a big deal, but I figured I should tell you. You know, since I tell you everything."

She stopped walking and turned to face me fully. "Do you need an invitation, Sky? Spit it out."

I hesitated. "Sterling and I… we ran into each other at the coffee shop. It was just coffee"

Her expression twisted into a cocktail of disgust and concern. "*Just* coffee?"

"That's what I thought it was going to be," I said. "But he asked if I'd be open to… trying again."

Allie blinked. "Trying again," she repeated flatly.

"I know how it sounds."

"You're smiling."

"I'm not—"

"You *are*," she said, narrowing her eyes. "Skylar. *Us?*" Her voice curled with sarcasm. "When you say it about Titus, it's warm and promising. But with Sterling? It sounds like bad credit. Something you should've paid off years ago."

I groaned. "You're reading too much into this."

"No, you're not reading *enough* into it," she fired back, starting to walk again, her pace just a notch quicker now. "You've been floating on air for months over this Titus guy—hell, you were ready to monogram towels. But then you find out he's a grown-ass man with a past and suddenly you're 'too busy.'"

She turned her head only slightly but didn't need to look at me. She could feel my expression. Somehow, she always could.

"And meanwhile, you're sipping espresso with the man who had you crying in the parking lot of Bed-Stuy Fish Fry. *That* guy gets access again? Make it make sense, Sky."

I kept pace beside her, swallowing my defense. Because honestly? I had none.

"What do you have to say for yourself? And don't even *try* giving me that look," she added.

We crossed the next street, dodging traffic like we had since we were teenagers. Her shoulder brushed mine, steadying me in more ways than one.

Walking with Allie felt like walking with a mirror—one that didn't distort or flatter. Just reflected who I really was.

And today, that reflection was hard to look at.

"¡Cuidado, estúpido!" she shouted, smacking the hood of a yellow cab that had tried to jump the light as we crossed. She pounded her fist on the car's hood a few times and flipped the driver off without missing a beat.

Once we made it safely to the sidewalk, she turned to me, grabbing my hand with a warm, reassuring squeeze. "You're calling him today," she insisted, swinging our hands as we continued down the street. "No more excuses, Sky. When we get settled in later, you're picking up that phone."

The warmth of her hand was a comforting reminder of how long we'd known each other, how many times she'd nudged me to do the hard things I was scared to face. She always had a way of guiding me, even when I resisted.

After hot showers and a mad dash through Allie's closet—where I ended up borrowing a cozy cream sweater and my favorite jeans I'd left in "my" guest room months ago—we finally made our way to *Sabór & Roots*. Fresh-faced, warm, and tucked into the rhythm of the late morning, we slipped into a booth nestled in the back corner of the restaurant.

The booth's plush terracotta cushions hugged my frame, a soft contrast to the earthy golds and deep olive-greens that bathed the space in a sun-drenched glow. The walls were lined with rustic wood panels and colorful Afro-Latin art, while the hum of easy conversation and soft jazz floated around us like incense. This place always felt like a warm embrace—a cultural heartbeat pulsing between comfort food and community.

Allie was still toweling off her curls with the ends of her scarf, cheeks glowing from the heat of her shower and the effort of getting ready in under 30 minutes. She looked like she belonged here—vibrant, grounded, full of energy. I, on the other hand, had been buzzing quietly ever since we'd stepped through the front door.

I didn't tell her, but I'd chosen *Sabór & Roots* on purpose.

I'd been here just a few months ago—with Titus. He'd discovered it one Sunday after a gallery visit and had raved about the food, the music, the soul of the space. We'd sat near the window, laughing over guava mimosas and sweet plantain hash. It had felt... hopeful. Light. Like something was beginning.

Now, as I settled into the booth beside Allie, my fingers traced the hem of my napkin while my eyes darted to the entrance more times than I cared to admit. I hadn't said a word to her about it, but part of me had picked this place hoping he might walk in—by chance or fate or divine inconvenience.

A passive-aggressive move, maybe. But not without purpose.

Was I looking for closure? Clarity? Proof that I'd moved on—or that he hadn't?

Probably all of it.

Allie, oblivious to my internal scramble, snapped her menu open like a woman on a mission. "If they don't have the peach empanadas again, I swear I'm writing a strongly worded Yelp review."

I laughed weakly, but my heart was stuck somewhere between the last time I sat here... and the possibility of who might walk through that door.

The scent of spices, grilled meats, and fresh herbs filled the air as Afro-Latin jazz played softly in the background. Allie grinned, tilting her head toward the speakers. "I bet you dessert that's Roy Hargrove," she quipped, raising an eyebrow knowingly.

I rolled my eyes, chuckling. Allie loved testing my jazz knowledge, which I barely had, but she knew how much I enjoyed our little challenges. The music flowed through the restaurant, its velvety notes echoing from walls adorned with colorful, mural-style artwork inspired by Afro-Latin heritage. Woven baskets, vibrant Afro-Latin art, and lush tropical plants filled the space, creating an atmosphere that felt both alive and intimate.

Our table was adorned with vivid plates: yuca waffles with tropical fruit, plantain French toast drizzled with guava syrup, and a vibrant açaí bowl topped with fresh mango and passionfruit. The steam from my café con leche rose from the mug, the warm, comforting aroma blending perfectly with the lively ambiance.

I took a sip, feeling myself relax into the moment. Allie had been nudging me about Titus since I sat down, but for a second, I let myself savor the peace. Outside, the autumn air was crisp and cool, and it seeped in slightly through the restaurant's door, mingling with the warmth from inside.

Just then, my gaze drifted to the door, and I froze. A strikingly beautiful woman, tall and regal, walked in, at least 5'8" with bronzed, radiant skin that seemed to glow under the soft lighting. And behind her was Titus. My stomach clenched, and I instinctively glanced at Allie. She was already watching me with a smirk that screamed "I told you so."

"Oh, la guinda del pastel," Allie muttered under her breath—the cherry on top. She said it like she was narrating a telenovela, eyes wide with mock drama, as if she could already see the plot twist coming. Then she turned to me, shooting a mischievous look over the rim of her mug, one perfectly arched eyebrow raised in full interrogation mode. Her grin tugged at the corners of her lips, barely restrained, like she was holding back a laugh—or a *told you so.*

I had half a mind to grab my fork and poke his eye out with it, thinking, *Really? Already with another woman?* But then, a small memory surfaced—the daughter he'd told me about. I realized that this beautiful woman next to him was his daughter, not a date. The relief that washed over me was so palpable I almost laughed out loud.

Allie, sensing my distraction, took the opportunity to sneak her fork onto my plate and nab another bite of my oxtail hash and eggs. "Earth to Sky," she teased, laughing as she claimed my plate as her own.

I caught her eye just in time to clear my throat and nod subtly toward the doorway. "Mija," I said in that familiar tone, letting her know something important was happening.

16

Allie

Skylar's gaze followed mine across the mellow buzz of *Sabór & Roots*, and we both froze at the sight near the entrance.

Titus.

And a young woman beside him.

They moved with quiet intention, threading their way through the softly lit café like they belonged here, even in a room full of regulars. The woman walked with a graceful confidence—elegant, unbothered, poised in a way that made people notice without knowing why. She was stunning: tall, slender, her mocha-toned skin glowing against the soft ivory of her blouse. Defined curls framed her face in perfect spirals, tumbling past her shoulders like a crown. She couldn't have been more than twenty-one, twenty-two, but she held herself like she knew exactly who she was.

And the resemblance to Titus? Unmistakable.

The shape of her eyes, the deep-set gaze, the stillness in her expression that carried weight without words. I didn't *know* she was his daughter—but something in me was certain. Who else would look at him with that blend of ease, familiarity, and unspoken trust?

Titus, meanwhile, was dressed like the kind of man who didn't have to try hard to make a statement. No suit today. Instead, he wore a crimson varsity-style cardigan with a bold ivory *M* stitched over the heart—Morehouse pride on full display. Underneath was a faded denim button-up and perfectly worn dark jeans that framed him just right. It was effortless—polished but relaxed. And somehow, it made him even more dangerous.

His milk chocolate complexion looked rich and smooth in the amber light, and the salt-and-pepper at his temples was just enough to remind you that this man had lived, loved, and probably broken a few hearts along the way. From the way Skylar's posture changed, I had a feeling hers might've been one of them.

Skylar's fork clinked against her plate as she swallowed her last bite too fast, suddenly flustered. Her hand shot to her napkin, dabbing her lips even though they were already clean. I caught the way she sat up straighter, checked her reflection in the window beside us, and gently pressed down a stray curl near her temple. She didn't bite her lip—barely—but I could tell she was fighting the urge.

Titus noticed us then.

His eyes scanned the room, landed on ours, and lingered just long enough for me to feel it. There was no drama in his gaze, no heat. Just acknowledgment. The flicker of recognition that passed between us felt like static—brief, but charged.

I kicked Sky lightly under the table.

My way of saying, *Girl, pull it together*.

She adjusted her sweater, straightened her shoulders, and

gave a subtle nod—like she could hear every word I wasn't saying.

Under my breath, I muttered one of my favorite D'Angelo lines, "Shit, damn, motherfucker," more prayer than profanity.

They were getting closer now. Titus with that calm, collected energy, and the young woman beside him—his daughter, I assumed—walking with quiet poise. Whatever this moment was about to become, he didn't look like a man ready to stir anything up. His expression was open. Gentle.

I turned toward Skylar, just enough for our knees to touch under the table, and whispered, "This is it, Sky. No more hiding. Time to find out what this really is."

She didn't respond right away, but I saw it in her face— that flicker of bravery that always showed up just before she jumped.

The smell of sweet plantains and coffee beans drifted through the air, mingling with the low hum of jazz spilling from the speakers. The entire café felt wrapped in gold and honey, a space too soft to hold anything sharp. Brooklyn was doing what it always did—making space for hard conversations in beautiful places.

And as Titus stepped up to our table, his maybe-daughter at his side, I had this strange, unshakable feeling that whatever came next... we'd been walking toward it for a while.

Ever observant, I caught Skylar mid-stare, her fork frozen in midair, oxtail hash forgotten on the plate before her. She didn't even try to pretend she wasn't looking. I arched a brow and nudged her ankle under the table.

"Looks like the oxtail hash lost its charm, huh?" I teased,

sliding my fork through the warm, syrup-soaked stack of plantain waffles we were sharing. I took a bite—soft, sweet, laced with guava—and nearly moaned. "Oh, *this* is good, Sky. Worth every minute in hot yoga this morning."

Skylar didn't answer right away. Just a quiet hum of agreement, her eyes still fixed across the room.

She'd been blissfully savoring her plate—oxtail hash, scrambled eggs, spicy sweet potatoes—the kind of brunch she lived for. The room was alive with warmth: sun filtered through the café windows, washing the terracotta and sage green walls in gold. The jazz playing overhead—something classic, Coltrane or maybe Etta—wrapped around us like a soft scarf. Plates clinked, laughter filled the air, and the rich scent of fried plantains, stewed meat, and brewed coffee made it feel like Sunday mornings were a love language.

Dining with Skylar was never just a meal—it was a shared feast. We always ordered like we had five stomachs between us, eager to try everything, to linger and talk and tease. But now, with Titus walking through the door, everything shifted.

My smile faltered for a moment, both concern and a flicker of secondhand embarrassment blooming in my chest. There he was. The man Sky had been giggling with like a teenager just weeks ago—late-night convos, FaceTime smiles under dim bedroom lights, deep talks about sermons and politics and dreams. The same man who sent "Hello, Gorgeous" texts like clockwork every morning at 7:00 a.m.

And now, here he was, strolling into the restaurant with the ease of a man returning to his regular spot—unbeknownst to me, this wasn't just any brunch place. It was *his*.

Skylar took a breath, shallow and careful, reaching for her

café con leche as if it could anchor her.

I leaned closer, my voice low and teasing. "Just breathe. Look fabulous. And remember—you are *unbothered.* As our girl Whitley would say…"

"*Relax, relate, release,*" Skylar whispered back, almost like a mantra, grounding herself in those words. She sat up straighter, pressed her lips together, and did a quick sweep over her bun, even though not a curl was out of place.

We clinked our mugs gently together—our own tiny toast to friendship, food, and impeccable taste in men, even if they came with complications. Our laughter hummed beneath the music, like it belonged there.

And then—there he was.

Titus stood at the edge of our table, his presence commanding even in something as simple as jeans and a crimson Morehouse cardigan with a bold ivory *M* stitched over his heart. The denim shirt underneath was worn soft, open at the collar just enough to be effortlessly cool. His smile was polite, measured, but warm—like he wasn't sure what version of this moment he'd just walked into.

"Excuse me," he said, that smooth, deep voice sliding into the air like butter on a warm biscuit. "Skylar. Alejandra. I didn't want to interrupt, but I had to come say hello."

"Titus!" I said brightly, keeping my tone easy and familiar. "Look at you, repping the alma mater and everything."

Skylar glanced up, her voice a touch softer. "Hey, Titus."

She didn't look too long—afraid her eyes might betray more than her mouth was willing to admit.

"I'm glad we ran into you," I added, following his gaze toward the young woman waiting near the front. She stood with the kind of patience and poise that caught the eye. "And is that your beautiful daughter?"

Titus's face lit with a kind of pride you can't fake. "Yes," he said, his voice softening. "That's Kayla. She's home for Thanksgiving break. First semester at Howard."

"That's wonderful," Skylar said, a little too quickly, her smile wide but tight, her fingers twitching near her napkin.

"Skylar, it's great to see you. You too, Allie," he said, sliding his hands into his pockets like he was trying not to stay too long. That signature baritone—smooth, grounded, with just a hint of knowing—settled into the air like an old record spinning on a Sunday afternoon. "I just wanted to say hello. Didn't mean to interrupt the oxtail hash."

"You're good," I said, waving him off with a smile. "Always good to see you."

He nodded, already stepping back. There was a faint awareness in the way he moved, like he sensed his presence had shifted the air around our table. Like he knew—without needing to ask—that there were things still unsaid.

But Skylar wasn't letting him walk away that easily.

Before he could fully turn, she reached out and touched his arm. Just once. Brief but steady. Enough to pause him.

"Thank you for recommending this place," she said with a small, knowing smile. "We might become regulars."

Titus chuckled—that low, husky sound that had once made her toes curl during late-night calls. "I can only hope," he replied, eyes holding hers for a second longer than polite. There was something in his gaze. Not longing exactly. Not regret. But... awareness. Recognition.

Then, just like that, he nodded again and turned to rejoin Kayla.

Skylar watched him go, her lips parted like she'd meant to

say more but thought better of it. Her breath caught slightly, eyes following him until he disappeared behind the hostess stand.

I took a sip of my coffee and murmured under my breath, "You and me both, *Titusito*." Then I shot Skylar a sharp side-eye, part amused, part deeply not impressed.

Skylar chuckled, shaking her head, but I could see the warmth blooming in her cheeks.

This story wasn't over.

Not by a long shot.

And we both knew it.

17

Titus

The kitchen was alive with the scent of memory and comfort—garlic blooming in olive oil, the bite of fresh rosemary mingling with the mellow sweetness of caramelized onions and chopped bell peppers. The low hiss of the stovetop played underneath the steady rhythm of Coltrane spinning in the background, his saxophone curling through the air like a conversation we hadn't had yet.

My cutting board was a mess of color: diced red and yellow peppers, chopped celery, ribbons of pale onion. The blade moved with practiced ease, though my mind wasn't fully on the food.

Across the counter, Kayla leaned with her arms folded, one hip hitched against the granite. She was wearing her favorite oversized Howard sweatshirt—faded, soft, clearly stolen from her dorm room—and black leggings. Her dark curls were piled in a loose bun, a few strands escaping to frame her thoughtful face. She didn't say much, but her eyes were fixed on me with that steady, quiet gaze that always reminded me of her mother.

"You okay over there, Chef Dad?" she asked, a teasing note in her voice—but underneath it, something more curious.

I glanced up, smirking. "Depends on who's asking."

She didn't smile, not fully. Instead, she tilted her head slightly, eyes narrowing just enough. "So," she said slowly, "that was *the* Skylar at the restaurant today?"

I paused mid-chop. The knife hovered over the celery. My stomach did that thing—it dipped, not with fear, but with the ache of something unspoken. I resumed slicing, trying to play it casual.

"Yeah. That was her."

Kayla's lips tugged into a smirk. She knew better.

"Mm-hmm. So *she's* the reason you've been moving around the house like a Jazmine Sullivan track—slow, dramatic, and kinda moody?"

I let out a soft laugh, even as I shook my head. "Really? That's how we're doing it?"

She shrugged, unapologetic. "I'm just saying... you've been humming sad girl energy, but in a grown man key."

I sighed, setting the knife down. She knew me too well. "Maybe."

Kayla pushed off the counter and stepped closer, her eyes sharpening. "Let me get this straight... she didn't know about me and Deuce until recently?"

"Not exactly," I said, leaning back against the opposite counter, folding my arms across my chest. "It's not like I was hiding you. I just—hadn't brought it up. Not yet."

She raised an eyebrow but stayed quiet, waiting for me to explain.

"It's been a minute since I tried this dating thing," I admitted. "Even longer since I wanted to get serious. At first, with Skylar, it was just... fun. Easy. But a few months ago, it stopped being just light. It got real. And I didn't want to complicate something good too early."

I glanced toward the window. The sun was starting to dip, casting long golden streaks across the floor. The last of the day slipping away.

"I wanted to be sure she mattered before I gave her the full picture. You and your brother? You're not footnotes. Y'all are my heart. And I didn't want to drop that over brunch like it was nothing. Every time I thought about telling her, it felt like the wrong moment."

Kayla nodded slowly, arms still crossed. Her brows pulled together slightly, not with judgment, but calculation. She was working through it like she did everything— thoughtfully, inward first.

"Did you just say you were getting serious with her?" she asked, her tone light but sharp. "Because that sounded a lot like the *L* word creeping up on you."

I chuckled, then stepped forward to press a kiss to her forehead. "Serious enough that I wanted her to know about the people who matter most to me."

"But when I finally told her," I continued, quieter now, "it shifted. She didn't say much. No big scene. Just... got quiet. Still. Like something in her pulled away."

Kayla looked down at the cutting board, then back up at me. "You think it scared her off?"

"I think it knocked over the version of me she had in her head," I said. "The version that was uncomplicated. Clean. No ex-wife, no grown kids, no full life already in motion."

She let out a slow breath, her expression unreadable for a moment. Then she stepped closer and gently placed a hand on my arm.

"You weren't wrong to wait until it mattered," she said. "But you're also not wrong to want someone who doesn't flinch at the full truth. We've been part of your life from day one, Dad. That's not changing."

Her hand steadied me more than I expected. I covered it with mine and gave it a small squeeze.

"I know," I said. "And I don't regret any of it. If anything, all of this has reminded me how much I already have. You, Deuce, your grandparents, your loud-ass aunties—Thanksgiving's gonna be a full house."

Kayla smiled then—slow, genuine, the kind of smile that made my chest swell with gratitude. "Good. Because you deserve someone who wants to be part of that. Someone who *gets* that."

"And maybe she still will," I added, my voice steady but measured. "But for now? I'm good with what I've got."

Kayla plucked a red pepper from the cutting board and popped it into her mouth, chewing thoughtfully. The saxophone swelled in the background, the garlic and rosemary deepening in the pan behind me.

For the first time in weeks, the ache I'd been carrying felt a little less sharp. The kitchen, the music, my daughter's steady presence—they anchored me.

And in that quiet, golden moment, I knew: I already had more than enough.

18

Skylar

The grocery store buzzed under the soft hum of fluorescent lights, their sterile glow casting a pale sheen over the produce section. The scent of just-misted cilantro and earthy root vegetables lingered in the air, mingling with the savory pull of roasted pork drifting from the deli counter nearby. I pushed the cart slowly down the aisle, the squeaky front wheel adding a soft rhythm to our path.

My cart was already loaded with everything we needed for a proper Puerto Rican Thanksgiving spread—green and yellow plantains, bunches of cilantro and recao, cans of *gandules* stacked like dominoes. Tucked beneath them were yucca, malanga, sofrito bases, and a few rogue items I always grabbed out of nostalgia. The air felt rich with memory—of my father's kitchen in North Carolina, of garlic sizzling in the pan, of laughter rising over old salsa records.

Beside me, Allie and her mother, Doña Herrera, moved like a unit. They chatted in a melodic blend of English and Spanish, flipping between recipe debates and gossip like only a mother and daughter could. You could tell Doña Herrera was in her element—pausing every few steps to examine labels, inspect produce, and toss things into the cart that weren't even on the list but were always in the meal.

"Allie," she called over her shoulder, her accent soft but firm, "we need coconut milk for the *arroz con dulce*, and don't forget the peppers for the sofrito. Ay, and grab another bunch of cilantro, por si acaso."

"Sí, Mami," Allie replied, catching the cans mid-spin like a pro and tossing them into the cart without missing a beat.

She looked over at me then, a wicked little grin forming as she held up a jar of green olives like it was evidence in court.

"Okay, Sky, I *have* to ask—what was that whole mute-in-the-corner act at *Sabór & Roots*? You barely said a word to Titus, like the cat caught your tongue. And don't think I missed the way you were watching him, either. Girl, you looked like you were about to fall face-first into your waffles."

I felt my cheeks flush hot and focused very intently on the handle of the cart, gripping it like it owed me something.

"It's... complicated," I muttered, barely above a whisper.

Allie raised an eyebrow. "That's what women say right before making terrible decisions."

I sighed. "I thought Titus and I—" I paused, trying to find the right words. "I thought we had something. Something good. But then he told me he has two grown kids, Allie. It caught me off guard. I felt like there was this whole other life he had that I didn't know about. Like I'd been handed a story with missing pages."

"So what?" Allie's voice was sharp but gentle, laced with that no-nonsense warmth only she could deliver. "You're not sixteen. Did you really think he was gonna be untouched by life? No ex, no baggage, no beautiful, intelligent, fully-formed children?" She folded her arms across her chest, daring me to hide behind more excuses. "Everybody's got something. The real question is—does what they come with scare you more than what they have to offer?"

Her voice caught slightly on the last word, just a tremor—but I heard it. Felt it. That wasn't just about *me* anymore. She was talking about her own missed chances, too. About love she maybe hadn't fought hard enough for. Her arms stayed crossed, but her heart was closer than she'd admit.

"Don't write off something good just because it didn't arrive in the package you pictured," she said, softer now. "Life never does."

I stared into the cart. Into the colors and textures of our meal-to-be. "I know," I said, slowly. "I just... I wanted something simple. Something fresh. No strings. No history."

Allie smirked. "Speaking of history," she said, voice rising theatrically, "Mami, did you know Skylar is entertaining your favorite—Sterling?"

She sang his name like a tattling little sister.

Out of the corner of my eye, I saw Doña Herrera freeze mid-reach by a display of garlic bulbs. She turned slowly, her expression unreadable at first, then unmistakably disapproving.

She walked over, holding a fragrant bunch of cilantro in one hand like a truth she was about to lay down.

"*¡Ay, Dios!*" she said, shaking her head. "I never liked that Sterling character. *Él es muy arrogante.* Always so full of himself. You were a shell of yourself around him, Skylar. You have to see that for yourself."

Her tone was soft, but her words were firm—cutting

through the noise like a seasoned cook slicing straight through fat.

"As for the two kids—*Titus*," she said, a glint of humor in her voice as she used Allie's nickname for him. "Sometimes the best things come in complicated packages. Good men, good relationships—they are not always neat. But they are worth it. *Vale la pena.* You just have to be willing to see past your picture-perfect version of love."

She dropped the cilantro into my cart, then reached over and gently patted my hand. "Don't throw away something precious just because it's a little tangled."

Her words landed in my chest like something warm and heavy. I looked at her—this woman who had shown me what consistency and unconditional care looked like since I was a child. She knew what it meant to love someone through flaws, to accept a life that was layered and real.

Allie nudged me, pulling me back to the moment. "Listen, Mami's right—especially about Sterling. That man might be familiar, but don't confuse comfort with compatibility. I saw how you looked at Titus. You *like* him, even if you're scared to admit it."

I let out a long breath, resting against the cart, the tension draining slowly from my shoulders.

"Maybe," I murmured. "Maybe I'm just afraid of getting hurt again. I thought I was ready for something real, but I guess I hoped it would be... uncomplicated. And Sterling? He's familiar. Predictable."

Allie rolled her eyes so hard I swear I heard it. "*Safe?* That's a funny way to describe a man who treats you like a prop when he wants to impress people and a ghost when he doesn't. Sterling isn't safe. He's *recycled drama.* You already know how that story ends."

The cart stood between us, brimming with flavors and traditions—and now, unspoken truths. As we turned the corner toward the checkout, I felt lighter, not because I had it all figured out, but because I didn't have to pretend anymore.

Love might be messy. But maybe—just maybe—it was still worth showing up for.

Doña Herrera's voice softened, like a lullaby seasoned with wisdom. "Skylar, sometimes life doesn't give us what we expect—it gives us what we need. You're lucky, *mija*, to find someone worth caring about. And maybe, just maybe, this *Titusito* is someone who deserves that care—messy life and all."

Her hand moved to her chest as her eyes grew misty, then sparkled with something warm and familiar—mischief laced with memory.

"*Mi amor*— Papi Herrera—he came into my life like a thunderstorm. Complications, chaos, pride, and all. But his love?" She smiled now, deeply. "His love held me through it. Because of that love, we've built a beautiful, loud, imperfect family over fifty-five years. Complications and all, *mi cielo*. That's what makes it real."

She winked at me, the fine creases at the corners of her eyes deepening like rivers carved by years of laughter and loss. Without saying another word, she looped her arm around Allie's shoulders and pulled her in close. The two of them walked ahead like they'd done this a thousand times before—mother and daughter, yes, but more than that. Co-conspirators. Keepers of family secrets. Lovers of sofrito and stories they'd only half told me.

Their heads leaned toward one another, their laughter

mingling with the faint hum of the overhead store music—
something Motown and warm—as the scents of ripe man-
goes and garlic from a nearby endcap wrapped the aisle in
something sweet and earthy.

I pushed the cart slowly behind them, my hands still curled
around the handle like it might answer the question I hadn't
asked yet.

"What complications, *Mami Herrera*?" I asked, tilting my
head with curiosity, leaning against the cart's edge. My voice
was playful, but there was a little thread of something else
running through it—an itch to know more.

Allie's lips twitched, amusement flickering across her face
like a flame she wouldn't let catch fire. She reached for the
cart, smoothly taking the handle from me like a baton, and
tossed me a look over her shoulder that felt... rehearsed. Like
they'd danced this dance before.

Their laughter echoed ahead of me as they glided down the
aisle—leaving my question suspended like steam in the air,
unanswered and increasingly intriguing.

I opened my mouth to push again, ready to call her out,
demand the truth Allie had clearly been dodging since yoga
class—but she beat me to it, her voice a picture of ease.

"Oh, by the way," she said, turning a can of pink beans in
her hand like it held sacred prophecy, "your mom mentioned
she's going down to North Carolina with you for Thanksgiving this year."

I froze mid-step.

The cart jolted to a stop, its metal handle digging into
my palms like the truth had teeth. The hum of the store's
lights suddenly felt brighter, harsher, almost accusatory.
Somewhere behind me, someone's toddler was whining.

Ahead, Allie hummed softly to herself like nothing had happened.

"What?" I choked, blinking like I'd misheard her, like maybe a can had rolled off the shelf and knocked something loose in my brain. "Since *when*?"

My voice cracked on the last word, the disbelief slicing through it like a splinter. I wasn't sure what stunned me more—the news itself, or the casual, almost smug way Allie delivered it.

There was something too relaxed in her posture, too practiced in her tone. Like she was handing me a coupon for arroz con dulce, not detonating a bomb wrapped in family dysfunction.

She didn't flinch. Didn't miss a beat.

"She told me yesterday," Allie replied, dropping a can of *gandules* into the cart with a definitive *thunk*. "Apparently your dad invited her. Said it just made sense. He's always looking out for her, isn't he?"

My heart gave a lurch, twisting around a familiar ache. My dad. The diplomat. The peacemaker. Always trying to smooth out the messes my mother made. And now— Thanksgiving? With both of them?

My stomach flipped.

Allie didn't look at me as she turned into the next aisle, but I saw the corner of her mouth lift in that knowing way.

She knew exactly what this meant.

And she was enjoying every second of watching me catch up.

That last part hit with the sharpness of a slap wrapped in velvet.

I knew Allie hadn't meant it to wound—*not fully*—but the

sting still bloomed under my skin like something I couldn't ignore. I could already hear my mother's voice, floating in from some imagined phone call, syrupy and sharp, wielding grace like a blade: *"Oh, your father insisted. He said it wouldn't feel right without me."*

Of course he did.

Because that's what he always did—bend. Twist. Reframe her presence as a peace offering instead of the power play it truly was. She'd show up with her too-bright lipstick and a tray of sweet potato pie no one asked for, gliding into the room like she owned it, while my father trailed behind her, polite smile in place, insisting it was "just easier this way."

I gripped the cart handle tighter, my knuckles whitening around the metal. A heat was rising in my chest, climbing up my throat like wildfire looking for air.

"Unbelievable," I muttered. "He can barely stand up to her, and now he's handing her a seat at *my* table like it's his to offer."

I turned sharply toward Allie, jaw clenched. "And you didn't think to mention this yesterday? When she *told* you?"

Allie's expression didn't waver—calm, a little amused, like she'd seen this movie before and knew all the lines.

"I figured it'd be better coming from me than hearing it from *her* the morning you were packing your car," she said, dropping a bag of rice into the cart. "Because let's be real—if she'd sprung it on you then, you would've canceled your trip, ghosted the whole family, and disappeared to some cabin in the Catskills with your phone on Do Not Disturb."

My chest ached—not just from anger, but from the deep exhaustion that came with trying to love someone who made it hard, and watching someone you love make excuses for her.

I didn't know who I was more upset with—my mother for slipping herself into plans uninvited, my father for letting her do it, or Allie for becoming the messenger in a game I never agreed to play.

I stared at the shelf of dried beans, seeing none of it. Just red, white, and black blur. My father's voice echoed in my mind—gentle, always giving her the benefit of the doubt.

"He's too nice to her," I said, the words raw as they left my mouth. "I don't get it. He knows exactly who she is. All the drama, the emotional sabotage, the guilt trips—she's put him through hell and still *does*. And yet..."

I trailed off, shaking my head. "Shouldn't she be enjoying Thanksgiving with her *husband*? Parker, right?"

Doña Herrera, who had been examining a pile of yuca with surgical precision just a few feet away, turned with a smile that held generations of lived truth.

"*Ah, Parker,*" she said, drawing the name out like the punchline of a story. "That's husband número *tres*, ¿verdad?"

Allie snorted, biting back a laugh.

Doña Herrera leaned closer, lowering her voice, but not enough to dull its impact. "Maybe your father understands what I've been saying, *mija*... Life is complicated. And sometimes, the people who hurt us are still the ones worth a little patience."

Her words landed like a slow exhale. Heavy. True. Uncomfortable.

I didn't answer right away.

Instead, I pushed the cart a few inches forward, the wheel wobbling slightly as if even it was unsure how to move through this moment.

I admired my father—his gentle strength, his faith in people, his ability to forgive. But that same softness baffled me, made me question whether I had any of that in me. Could I extend that kind of grace to someone who disappointed me? Someone who came with baggage, attachments, history?

Here I was, pushing Titus away because he came with a full, beautiful, complicated life... and my father? He was welcoming the woman who'd broken his heart more than once into a Thanksgiving dinner like it was nothing. Like she belonged.

He saw her clearly—flaws and all—and somehow still made room at the table.

Maybe I wasn't as ready for real love as I thought. Because if love was messy and layered and full of compromise... then I was still stuck on the fantasy version.

And maybe that was the most complicated truth of all.

As we rounded the corner into the baking aisle, the air grew sweeter—thick with the scent of cinnamon, nutmeg, and brown sugar, like it had been waiting just for us. The store's overhead speakers played a soft holiday tune—an old-school classic with a horn section that made the moment feel more like a scene from a movie than a simple trip to the market. Light filtered through the high windows, casting golden stripes across the linoleum floor, and everything felt... warmer.

I glanced down at our cart. It was brimming now—golden sticks of butter nestled against bags of flour and sugar, glass bottles of pure vanilla, bundles of ripe plantains, and small jars of fragrant spices labeled in both English and Spanish. Each ingredient was like a chapter in a story—Doña Herrera's story. One of flavor and memory, passed down through hands that had learned to stir and season with love and wisdom, not just precision.

Her cooking wasn't just tradition—it was testimony. Time woven into taste. A kind of love that required you to slow down and be present.

I let my eyes drift to Allie and her mother walking a few steps ahead. Their bodies moved in sync, like a pair of dancers effortlessly gliding to an old rhythm only they could hear. Their laughter—Allie's bright and teasing, Doña Herrera's low and knowing—curled through the air like music, the kind that stays with you long after it fades. Allie and her mother moved like a duet—shoulders brushing, laughter rising and falling like a well-rehearsed song. Allie's voice danced playfully between aisles, matched by her mother's steady, deep

Watching them, something tugged inside me.

A memory. A longing. A quiet ache.

I thought of my own mother—the opposite of light. A woman who could turn any conversation into a spotlight monologue. Emotionally manipulative in the most elegant, exhausting way. A master of quiet control cloaked in sugar and scripture. She didn't argue; she rewrote the narrative until I was questioning my own memory. She wasn't openly cruel—she just made everything about *her*. Her sacrifices. Her needs. Her image. And somehow, I was always the one expected to bend.

I'd spent so much of my life holding her at arm's length, waiting for her to be something closer to the image I carried in my head. But maybe that wasn't fair. Maybe connection wasn't always built on agreement. Maybe it was built on grace.

The realization sat in my chest, heavy but hopeful.

I reached for a small tin of cloves, my fingers brushing against Allie's as she turned to grab cinnamon sticks. She smiled at me, soft and unspoken, like she knew exactly where my thoughts had wandered. Maybe she did.

And then it came—a thought, light as breath, but sure.

Maybe it wasn't just my mother who deserved grace.

Maybe *I* did too.

Maybe Titus—his full, layered, complicated life—wasn't a detour from the future I wanted. Maybe he was part of it. And maybe the version of love I'd built in my head—neat, simple, perfectly timed—wasn't real love at all.

Maybe life wasn't meant to be solved like a puzzle, but cooked like a slow, careful meal—ingredient by ingredient, mistake by mistake—until something beautiful and deeply satisfying came together.

Like Doña Herrera's arroz con dulce.

Like the way Allie and her mother moved as one.

Like the quiet beginning of something that might actually last.

I stood there for a moment longer, my fingers grazing the edge of the cart, taking it all in—the sounds, the smells, the faces of two women who carried generations in their laughter—and felt something shift inside me.

It didn't fix everything.

But it softened me.

And that was a start.

19

Allie

After the last grocery run of the night, we pulled into Mami's driveway and helped her unload the final bags. The scent in the car lingered—ripe plantains, fresh cilantro, and warm pan de agua still piping through the paper bag from the Dominican bakery we found. Her house sat quietly on a tree-lined street in suburban New Jersey, the porch light casting a golden glow on the walkway like a gentle exhale after a long day.

As I slid back into the driver's seat, I glanced at Skylar through the rearview mirror, just as she was adjusting her scarf and sinking into the seat with a tired groan. I shook my head, smirking. "Every year. She *really* has to hit up five different stores to prep for Thanksgiving? Same routine, different year."

Skylar didn't even open her eyes, just gave a lazy shrug and a smirk that said, *You already know.* "Don't act new, Allie. This is sacred ground. Mami Herrera doesn't trust just *anybody* with her sazón or her yuca."

It was true. This chaotic grocery ritual had become our pre-holiday tradition: brunch in Brooklyn, then a full-court press across Jersey—Superfresh, the Caribbean market, Trader Joe's for the fancy stuff, and a last-minute detour to the big-box store with the best butter prices. Hours in the car, our patience tested and our stomachs grumbling again before we even made it back home.

But something in Skylar's voice felt a little too clipped. I looked at her again. "You've been quiet since we left Mami's. What's going on? Is it Sterling? Titus? Or is your mother back on her nonsense?"

Skylar sighed, her eyes still focused on the dim skyline in the distance. "I'm just mentally preparing for tomorrow's impromptu road trip-slash-therapy session with my mother. Nine hours in the car with Stitch. Can you imagine?"

I winced in sympathy.

"And the fact that she *called you* instead of just saying something to me directly? Classic emotional manipulation," Skylar continued, now sitting up straighter. "She knew you'd tell me, and she knew I'd fold. She plays the long game, that woman."

I kept my eyes on the road but softened my tone. "Maybe she just wants time with you for the holiday. A little one-on-one?"

"I wanted time with *my dad*," Skylar muttered, arms crossed like a kid denied her favorite toy. "Alone."

"Spoken like a true Daddy's girl," I teased.

She didn't deny it.

Changing the subject, I asked, "You're really not going to be here tomorrow to help us prep? The kitchen won't be the same without your playlist and your commentary."

Skylar smirked. "Please. Luz will be *thrilled*. You know

she's been plotting her kitchen takeover since last year. Watch your back. She's got passive-aggressive chopping down to a science."

I burst out laughing. "As long as she doesn't burn the rice again. I still remember the *great arroz debacle* of 2019."

Skylar clutched her chest. "Not the crispy-bottom tragedy!"

"She tried to pass it off as 'intentional tostones.' Mami nearly had a heart attack."

"Poor Ariana and Alejandro," Skylar said, her tone faux-serious as she shook her head. "Caught in the culinary crossfire."

"Please," I said proudly. "They've spent enough time with Mami and Papi to survive. Ari's basically Mami's shadow in the kitchen now. She'll probably be bossing all of us around tomorrow."

Skylar's expression softened. "That's sweet. She's becoming a little matriarch already."

There was a pause, warm and familiar.

"I'm just excited Elias is coming home," she said after a beat, her voice quieter, more sincere.

I smiled. "Me too."

Her eyes lit up like a kid on Christmas morning. "Is he doing the *pernil* again this year?"

"Of course," I nodded. "Papi officially passed the torch. But you know he'll still hover like it's a cooking show elimination challenge."

Skylar let out a dramatic groan. "That *pernil* is the highlight of my entire November. I'm not even kidding, Allie—if I don't get a plate, we're going to have real issues."

"Relax," I said, laughing as we crossed back over the bridge toward Brooklyn. "I'll save you a plate. Maybe even sneak an extra pastelillo if you're nice."

Skylar leaned back, eyes closed, smile playing at her lips. "Tell Luz to keep her hands off my to-go container. I don't need a repeat of last year's 'oops, it got tossed.' She knows what she did."

The laughter that followed filled the car like warmth, wrapping around us, lingering long after the scent of Mami's groceries had faded.

"You better talk to Mami about that," I teased, tossing Skylar a look as we cruised past rows of brownstone-style condos lit up with early holiday lights. "And don't even *think* about inviting him to Friendsgiving."

Her face lit up with a grin that could only be described as mischievous. "Why not? You scared someone might flirt with your precious big brother?"

I rolled my eyes so hard I gave myself a headache. "They're suddenly *your* friends when they're throwing themselves at Elias. And no—I'm not interested in watching a bunch of grown women lose all sense of dignity over him. Again."

Skylar smirked, completely unfazed. "Allie, please. They're just looking for a good man. And let's keep it real—if he wasn't your brother..."

"Don't you *dare* finish that sentence," I cut in, my tone sharp, but my smile betraying me. "He's practically *your* brother too, Sky."

Skylar leaned back in her seat, arms folded, her expression smug and unbothered. "Fine, fine. But you *know* I'm right— we're all just out here hoping for a man like Elias."

And I hated how right she was.

Elias wasn't just the golden child. He was *the standard*. At six feet, with that easy gait and island-born cool, he was the kind of man women noticed—and not just because of his thick curls, warm amber eyes, or that butter pecan skin that made everyone assume he spent his weekends on a yacht. He had this grounded energy, the kind that made people feel safe just being around him.

After finishing his law degree at Villanova, he planted roots in Philly and became a powerhouse sports agent. But despite the suits and high-rise meetings, he never stopped being our anchor.

I still remembered him walking Skylar and me to middle school, his long legs making us jog to keep up as he teased us about our oversized backpacks and colorful notebooks. He cheered us on at track meets, even though we were painfully mediocre. And when it was time for me to move into my freshman dorm at Brown, it was Elias who carried my mini-fridge up two flights of stairs and cracked jokes just to ease the lump in my throat.

He was the one who stepped in without hesitation when Luz's world collapsed. After her husband died in that awful car crash, Elias moved in for nearly a year. No questions asked. He helped with school pickups, midnight fevers, baseball practice and daddy daughter dances. He became the father figure Ariana and Alec Jr. desperately needed.

Yeah. He was that guy. The real deal. And I'd never say it to his face, but he was my favorite. Always had been.

Skylar's voice broke through the nostalgia. "Just make sure I get some *pernil*," she said, her eyes sparkling like holiday lights. "And don't worry—I'll keep the peace. No one's gonna throw hands over your brother this year."

I snorted. "You better. Or I'm putting you on clean-up

duty until spring."

She laughed. "Relax. Your brother will be safe from *my* so-called 'thirsty' friends. Besides, I'll be too busy shutting it down at the karaoke mic to play matchmaker."

I shot her a side-eye. "You better bring your A-game, señora. Elias might have the *pernil*, but I'm taking over the dessert table this year. I've got Mami's flan *and* my tres leches on deck."

Skylar arched an eyebrow, intrigued. "Oh, it's *on*. Don't get mad when my sweet potato pie gets a standing ovation."

"*Your* sweet potato pie? You wish," I said, turning the corner toward the bridge. "Just remember to bring your voice and your appetite. And maybe a little humility."

She grinned, stretching her arms behind her head. "Never that. But I'll bring the mic. And maybe... just maybe... an extra to-go container. You know, for leftovers."

We both laughed, the car filling with the easy rhythm of friendship and tradition—teasing, memories, and the promise of food, music, and just enough drama to make the holidays feel like home.

As we drove back toward the city, the last traces of twilight faded into a navy sky, pinpricked with early stars and the soft glow of streetlamps stretching across the highway. The car hummed beneath us, tires rhythmically gliding over the asphalt as familiar skylines slowly emerged in the distance— Manhattan's silhouette rising like a promise on the horizon.

The air inside the car felt lighter now, scented with leftovers from Mami's grocery bags and layered with the warmth of shared memories. I could already hear the clatter of pots and pans, the overlapping voices in Spanglish, the soundtrack of every Thanksgiving we'd ever known. It would be chaos, no doubt—someone burning the rolls, cousins arguing over who got the biggest slice of flan, and Mami micromanaging every dish like Gordon Ramsay in slippers—but it was *our* chaos. Loud, delicious, occasionally petty... and sacred.

Friendsgiving came right after, our self-declared encore to the family feast. It was less structured, more spirited—a night full of inside jokes, mismatched plates, and the kind of belly laughs that left you sore the next day. It was the one time of year when all our different worlds collided—lawyers, artists, educators, entrepreneurs—and no one cared about titles or timelines. Just the love that lived between us.

It was the dessert after the feast—the unofficial reunion of our crew. Loud music, mismatched wine glasses, overstuffed couches, and the kind of laughter that made your cheeks hurt. I could already feel the buzz in my chest at the thought of seeing Eden and Quinn again. The four of us, in the same room, no work, no distractions—just us, back together. The old rhythm we fell into so effortlessly, like no time had passed at all.

Skylar leaned over and nudged my arm, her voice playful. "So... about the karaoke playlist. Do we ease in with classics or just go full *crowd-pleaser* right out the gate?"

I grinned, already picturing her with the mic in one hand and a glass of wine in the other. "Why not both? It's Thanksgiving, Sky. Let's give them *everything* to be thankful for."

She threw her head back laughing, the sound rich and familiar, curling into the corners of the car like music. In that moment, with the city lights winking in the distance and Skylar beside me, everything felt... perfectly in place.

In that moment—with Skylar beside me, the city ahead, and the promise of stuffing, stories, and sisterhood just days away—it all felt perfectly in place.

Thanksgiving. Friendsgiving. Eden and Quinn. The beautiful, blessed mess of it all.

Ours.

And I couldn't wait to dive headfirst into every single, chaotic, heart-filling moment.

20

Skylar

The day had finally caught up with me. The digital clock on my living room console blinked *8:15 PM*, its blue glow casting a quiet pulse across the dim space. I yawned just thinking about it—yoga at sunrise, brunch with a surprise guest appearance from Titus that nearly gave me heart palpitations, hours of cart-pushing through aisle after aisle with Mami Herrera, and the great New Jersey traffic gauntlet we barely escaped.

I should've been excited to lay my head on a pillow. But instead, I stood in the middle of my apartment, rooted, staring down at the message that had been sitting unread for hours—like if I didn't respond, it might erase itself.

Mom: What time are you picking me up to head down to North Carolina?

My stomach dropped—again—as I reread it. My fingers tightened around the phone. For a brief, delicious second, I actually considered hurling it onto the hardwood floor, as if the shattered glass would save me from what I already knew: I was trapped. She was coming.

I took a deep breath, hit the call button, and dialed Allie. She had dropped me off less than an hour ago, after our pre-Thanksgiving chaos, and I wasn't sure if I wanted comfort, backup, or both.

She picked up on the second ring. I didn't waste time with pleasantries.

"Allie, there is *absolutely no way* I can ride with this woman for over nine hours. Alone. In one car. Just us. I won't survive it."

"Hello to you too, Sky. Did you miss me already?" Her voice oozed sarcasm, and I could practically hear the smirk. I pictured her barefoot in her kitchen, leaning against the counter, one brow arched.

"She just texted me!" I said, pacing the length of my living room. "*What time are you picking me up?* Like we discussed this. Like I agreed to this madness. The *nerve*."

I flopped onto the couch, one hand rubbing my temple while the other clenched the phone like a stress ball. "After the day I've had—Titus and his daughter showing up, running errands with Mami Herrera, fighting every New Yorker with a license in Jersey—and now this? I'm *done*."

There was silence on the line, the kind where I could feel Allie bracing herself.

"This is the first Thanksgiving since Daddy moved to North Carolina," I continued, my voice cracking. "I've been dreaming of this—me and him, his cooking, his old stories, just us. And now she's crashing it. I had a playlist, Allie. A *plan*."

Allie sighed gently on the other end. "I mean... it's not like your mom's *trying* to ruin your trip—"

"Oh, isn't she?" I snapped. "She always needs to be the

center of attention. I bet she overheard something from Aunt Mamie and decided she was part of the plan. Just slid herself in like a plus-one no one invited."

"I'd like to call a timeout," Allie interrupted.

"This is not the time for basketball banter, Allie. I'm spiraling."

"No, seriously. I think I need backup." She was already adding to the call. Before I could object, she merged the line and suddenly, Quinn and Eden were looped in.

I heard the chaos before I heard Quinn. Kids laughing, running, something crashing in the background. Tatum's voice calmly wrangling the circus.

"Hi Auntie Sky, Titi Allie, and Aunt E!" Quincy's sweet, sassy voice broke through like glitter—Quinn and Tatum's nine-year-old diva-in-training with hazel eyes and a freckled face you couldn't say no to.

"Say goodnight, Quincy," Quinn said with exaggerated patience. "Daddy's getting you settled. Go on now."

"I *am* settled!" Quincy insisted brightly, clearly planning her eavesdropping strategy.

"Goodnight," Tatum chimed in, his smooth tenor floating over the noise. "Good luck, ladies."

"Eden?" Allie called.

"*Present*," Eden replied, as if we were taking roll in our old homeroom. Her voice was dry, with a tinge of exhaustion. "Getting my wine. It's officially past Paris and Capri's bedtime, and I was on duty. Jayson's working late... again."

We all knew her four- and six-year-olds were named after her favorite travel destinations. We were just grateful she skipped over Tahiti—though, she had considered it.

I stood and wandered to the window, the city glowing below

me in that way it only does when the cold settles in and the holidays are close. My chest ached. My dad was already down there, in that tiny North Carolina town with no stoplights and too many memories. He had retired years ago and, with Aunt Mamie's gentle persistence, moved back to their roots— onto the land his grandparents once farmed. That land held history. That house held promise. And I had planned to have him all to myself.

"What's the deal?" Eden asked.

"Ms. Eva inserted herself into Sky's Thanksgiving road trip," Allie said.

"Yikes," Quinn murmured.

"She's riding down with you?" Eden asked, her tone teasing.

"And you have to share your beloved Daddy?" Quinn added with a smirk I could hear.

I groaned. "Yes. And no. I don't *want* to. I just... I wanted this one thing. One quiet drive. One peaceful Thanksgiving. Just my dad and me."

Allie's voice softened. "Sky... you've handled tougher things. This might not be ideal, but she's still your mom. And like it or not, she's part of your story."

I didn't answer right away.

"It's just..." I sighed. "I needed this. I needed him. No drama. No navigating her moods. No holding my breath, hoping she won't say something sideways. I just wanted peace."

"I get it," Quinn said gently. "But trust me... it's a blessing to have a mom around to drive you a little crazy. You know I'd give anything to have one more car ride with mine."

Her words pierced me in a way only Quinn's ever could.

Allie jumped in, always the mood-lifter. "You know Aunt Mamie's gonna take one look at your mom and have her baking pies, washing greens, and too busy to annoy anyone. You'll survive."

I laughed, despite myself. "You're probably right. I just hope she and Parker aren't going through anything. I do *not* need her getting nostalgic and trying to crawl back into my dad's good graces."

"Now *that's* a car ride I'd pay to see," Allie quipped.

And just like that, the pressure in my chest eased a bit.

Maybe I could handle it. Maybe I could survive one long drive with my mother, one unpredictable Thanksgiving, and the lingering aftershock of seeing Titus—with his daughter.

But just in case...

I was still making my playlist.

And adding noise-canceling headphones to my packing list.

21

Allie

My parents have been in this house for over 15 years, but on Thanksgiving mornings like this, I still find myself longing for the crowded Brooklyn brownstone where we used to wake up to the chaos of the holiday. Back then, the air was thick with the intoxicating smells of Mami and Papi cooking *pernil* and baking *pastelitos*, their laughter blending with the sounds of the city drifting through the windows. And then there was the *Tortilla Española*—Mami's specialty, reserved only for the most special occasions. The Jersey house is spacious and comfortable, but without the hum of taxis, street vendors, and bustling neighbors outside, it never feels quite the same.

Still, the rumble in my stomach had no complaints. The familiar aromas of garlic, roasted pork, and buttery pastry wafted through the air, waking something deep inside me, as if my body remembered before my heart did.

But if the smells of the kitchen weren't enough to wake me, Alec's boundless energy certainly was. At precisely 6 a.m., my unofficial alarm clock arrived in the form of an exuberant leap onto the too-small, full-sized bed my parents stubbornly insist belongs in "my room." I groaned as the mattress creaked under us. Don't they know a full-size bed is just a glorified twin? I'm far too grown for this.

"Titi Allie! Titi Allie!" Alec shouted, his little voice brimming with delight. I hadn't even had a chance to fully greet him last night after arriving well past his bedtime. All I managed was a kiss on his forehead as he slept soundly, curled up in his Spiderman blanket. My sister Luz warned me that he would come looking for me first thing in the morning—I just didn't expect it to be before my *café con leche.*

"Cariño!" I cried, wrapping my arms around him and pulling him close. His tiny body trembled with laughter as I tickled him mercilessly, his joy filling the room like sunshine.

Seconds later, Ari peeked her head around the door, her big brown eyes sparkling with mischief. "Tía chula!" she called out sweetly before bounding into the room and launching herself onto the bed. She tangled herself in Alec's arms and mine, the three of us collapsing into a pile of pillows that barely fit the bed's narrow frame. The mattress wobbled dangerously close to the edge, but none of us cared.

I kissed Ari on the cheek, brushing a strand of her curly hair out of her face. "Remind me to convince your abuela and abuelo to get me a bigger bed for this room," I whispered conspiratorially.

She giggled, her smile wide and knowing. "You're too old for this bed, Titi," she teased, mimicking what Mami might say.

I pulled both kids tighter against me, their warmth grounding me in the moment. The Jersey house might not have Brooklyn's crowded charm or its symphony of city sounds, but in this instant—with Alec's laughter ringing in my ears and Ari's arms wrapped tightly around me—it didn't matter. Thanksgiving wasn't just about where we were. It was about who we were with, and this, right here, was everything.

As soon as the day began, it seemed to race toward its chaotic, beautiful end. The house was alive, buzzing with the energy of family and the rhythm of Puerto Rican tradition. Titi Clara and Mami were deep in their annual coquito feud, their voices rising over whose recipe deserved the crown while Abuelita held court on the couch, regaling everyone with stories of Papi and Tito as mischievous little boys. Every now and then, her laughter would ring out like a bell, wrapping the room in warmth.

Meanwhile, the little ones were running amok, their sticky hands smudging everything in sight, much to Tía Carmen's exasperation. Javier, as usual, was on a mission to sneak pastelitos from the table, only to be caught mid-grab by Tía Linda. "¡Ay, gordito! Déjalo quieto," she teased for what must have been the tenth time, making Javier roll his eyes and mutter something about getting a new nickname.

And then there was Mami, who had officially stopped speaking to Tía Carmen after she dared to point out her gray hair. That small observation nearly sparked World War III, and if looks could kill, Tía Carmen wouldn't have made it past dessert.

I was mid-heist, sneaking scraps of pernil from the kitchen to stash away for Skylar, when Elias intercepted me with a smug grin. "Already took care of it," he said, holding up a container as if he were some sort of culinary savior.

Before I could thank him, Luz appeared like a thief in the night, swiping the container off the counter and popping the lid. My eyes widened as she jabbed a fork into the tender meat, taking a hefty bite with zero shame. "E, just make another one for Allie and Sky's Friendsgiving," she declared between chews. "You know this container is never leaving this house."

"Luz, ¡no seas glotón y deja algo para los demás!" I groaned, narrowing my eyes at her as she casually took another forkful. She grinned, though, breaking off a piece of crispy pork skin—my ultimate weakness—and held it out like a peace offering.

With a sigh of reluctant acceptance, I grabbed the skin, savoring every crunchy, flavorful bite. "Por favor, mi hermano favorito, ¡haz un pernil para Friendsgiving!" I begged, dramatically batting my lashes at Elias. "Por favor, por favor, por favor, te lo suplico!" My voice dripped with mock desperation as I gestured to Luz for another bite.

Elias chuckled, snatching the fork from Luz like a triumphant older brother. "You two are impossible," he said, taking a bite himself, much to our shared dismay.

Laughter erupted in the kitchen as we resigned ourselves to the fact that Elias, as the self-proclaimed King of Pernil, held all the power. With the container now a battleground, we turned our attention to the mountain of dirty dishes, pots, and pans, scrubbing and rinsing to the soundtrack of salsa pouring out from the living room.

Suddenly, the music shifted, and we all froze, drawn by the irresistible pull of the rhythm and the sight of our family dancing. Ari was spinning Alec around the living room, his giggles bubbling over as the crowd clapped in time. Mami and Papi swayed together, their movements as natural and familiar as the walls of the house itself. The dining room and living room had become one swirling dance floor, alive with laughter, smiles, and the kind of joy that smells as sweet as roasted pork and warm pasteles.

Luz stood at the edge of the room, her eyes locked on Ari and Alec. Her lips curved into a soft smile, but her gaze carried a depth of emotion that only a mother could understand. Watching her children laugh and move so freely filled her heart with something close to peace. Slowly but surely, they were mending from the loss of their father, finding moments of light amidst the shadows that had lingered. But as her smile lingered, a flicker of pain passed across her face, the kind of ache that comes from being here without him—without the man who should have been spinning her around the room, teasing her with his two left feet and making her laugh until her sides hurt.

Elias noticed her expression and, without a word, grabbed both Luz and me by the hands. "Come on," he said, his grin wide and full of mischief. Before Luz could protest, he whisked us into the crowd. We spun and twirled, tripping over each other's feet and laughing so hard our sides ached. Luz's laughter rang out, brighter now, as if for a moment she allowed herself to be carried by the joy around her.

The kitchen was forgotten, the mess irrelevant, as we let the music and the moment take over. Mami's voice soared above the clapping, calling out dance steps, while Tío Nino grabbed Ari for a spin. The room was a kaleidoscope of movement, warmth, and love. It wasn't just Thanksgiving in that house; it was something bigger, something deeper. It was family. It was home.

22

TItus

"That better not be cornbread burning!" Langston hollered as he strutted into the kitchen, pies stacked precariously in his arms. Baldwin, his identical twin, followed right behind him, as if tethered by some invisible string, while little Audre trailed behind, wobbling on her two-year-old toddler legs like a tiny, determined whirlwind.

Before Langston could get another word out, Zora breezed past him with the effortless elegance of a queen. Her salt-and-pepper hair caught the light, and her eyes zeroed in on the pies like a hawk. "You two play too much," she scolded, grabbing one of the pies from Langston. "Give me this before it ends up on the floor. You know neither of you have the balance for this."

Langston clutched his remaining pie dramatically, feigning offense. "You wound me, Zora! I've got balance for days."

"Yeah? Tell that to the cranberry sauce you dropped last Thanksgiving," Zora shot back without missing a beat.

The kitchen buzzed with the kind of organized chaos that only a family gathering can create. I wiped my hands on a towel and stepped forward, dapping Langston up before pulling him into a tight hug. Baldwin grinned as I scooped him off the ground, his little hands grabbing my face with pure, unfiltered joy. "What's up, big man?" I said, kissing his cheek. He giggled, his eyes sparkling with mischief.

Meanwhile, Kayla swooped Audre up like she was a feather, spinning her around in a mock airplane ride. Audre's giggles filled the kitchen, infectious and bright, wrapping everyone in its glow. Langston leaned over to kiss Kayla's cheek, winking at Audre mid-flight. "My girls," he said with a grin, his pride evident.

The clatter of heels announced the arrival of the matriarchs. My mother and Mrs. H. entered the kitchen like queens stepping onto their thrones. They tied their aprons with a practiced ease, silently commanding the room without uttering a single word. With a wave of their hands, they began shepherding us out of the kitchen like unruly sheep.

I turned toward Mrs. H., my "bonus mother," her presence grounding me instantly. "Mrs. H.," I greeted her with a wide smile, bracing myself for one of her legendary hugs. She didn't disappoint. Her arms engulfed me, her warmth pulling me in like the tide. Her embrace was all-consuming— part bosom, part sanctuary—and it had a way of making you feel both vulnerable and invincible at once.

As I inhaled the familiar scent of her Chanel perfume, memories of her unconditional support came flooding back. There she was, flying all the way from Memphis to campus one chaotic midterm season, armed with her homemade rolls and chicken noodle soup because Langston had broken out in hives and was running a fever for days. She didn't just nurse him back to health. She unknowingly found a frightened, nineteen-year-old me—torn apart by the news that my high school sweetheart and college love was pregnant.

I could still see her sitting beside me on the tattered sofa in our dorm, saying nothing at first, letting the silence fill the room like a balm. Her perfume, soft and familiar, hung in the air as she gently pulled me close, her shoulder steadying me. When she finally spoke, her voice carried an assurance I hadn't felt in weeks. "Whatever it is, we got you, Ty. God's got you, Titus. It will be okay. I promise you, it will be okay." I didn't know how she knew what I needed to hear, but at that moment, I believed her. She was the second person I'd told—after Langston—about the baby we were about to bring into the world.

Snapping back to the present, I squeezed her tightly and smiled. "Mama H, you have no idea how happy I am to see you."

"You just like getting close to these girls," Mrs. H. teased, patting her chest with a sly grin.

"Mama!" Langston protested, his face scrunching up in exaggerated disgust.

The kitchen erupted into laughter, the kind that bounces off the walls and settles into the cracks of your heart. Langston shot me a look that said *don't encourage her*, but it was too late. Mrs. H. and I were already sharing a conspiratorial grin.

As the real chefs took over the kitchen, we stepped aside to let them work their magic. The smell of Dad frying the turkey outside, the cinnamon-sweet aroma of sweet potatoes baking in the oven, and fragrant spices infusing the air mingled with the distant hum of laughter, chatter, and the soulful sounds of Marvin Gaye in the house.

Daddy started the prayer, his baritone voice filling the room like a cross between Teddy Pendergrass and a fiery Baptist preacher. His tone was rich, commanding, and deeply comforting all at once. "Heavenly Father, we thank you for another day, another opportunity to open our eyes and be known as your children," he began. Aunt Emma swayed at his words, her church hat bobbing with every syllable, before she belted out an impromptu "Amen!"

Her enthusiastic outburst triggered a ripple effect around the room. "Amen!" echoed the elders, their voices blending with the high-pitched attempts of the little ones, turning our prayer circle into an unintended chorus. Daddy took the encouragement as a sign to keep going, his voice deepening with renewed energy.

"Thank you for your goodness and mercy following us all the days of our lives," he continued, his words rolling out like a Sunday sermon. I couldn't help but peek at Cece and Leah on the other side of the table. My older sisters were doing their best to stifle their laughter, their shoulders shaking as they exchanged knowing glances. Momma, ever the disciplinarian, pursed her lips into a thin line, her eyes darting between them and Daddy like she was debating whether to intervene.

Deuce and Kayla cracked one eye open, both clearly wondering how long this was going to last, while their cousins covered their giggles behind cupped hands. Langston coughed into his napkin, a poor attempt to hide his snicker, but Zora, ever the enforcer, elbowed him sharply in the ribs, her glare daring him to try again. The room felt like a powder keg of suppressed laughter as we all braced ourselves for what we suspected would become a full-blown sermon.

"Dear Lord," Daddy's voice boomed again, but this time Momma stepped in, her soft, soothing southern accent cutting through the moment. With a gentle tug on his hand, she interjected seamlessly.

"Dear Lord," she repeated, her tone as steady as the breeze through magnolia trees, "thank you for the beauty and chaos of family—the ones we didn't choose and the ones we did." Her words carried a warmth that settled the room, her grip tightening on my hand and Daddy's as she brought us back to center. Her subtle glance in my direction told me it was my turn, her eyes urging me to be quick. Momma's Southern hospitality would not allow her carefully prepared feast to grow cold on account of a long-winded prayer.

Taking a deep breath, I offered a brief but heartfelt thanks, my words tumbling out just fast enough to avoid another wave of "amens" from Aunt Emma. Finally, after what felt like an entire church service, the collective "Amen" rang out, signaling the end of the prayer.

With that, we all broke formation, shuffling to our seats around the table, the tension from moments before melting into a hum of anticipation. The sight before us was enough to make anyone's mouth water: golden turkey, glistening honey baked ham, sweet potatoes topped with perfectly toasted marshmallows, and pies lined up like trophies. As plates began to clatter and voices rose in excitement, Daddy grinned, satisfied with his opening act, while Momma leaned into me with a quiet smile. "See," she whispered, her tone teasing but kind, "not so bad after all."

The chaos of family filled the air, and I couldn't help but think, for all its unpredictability, there was nowhere else I'd rather be.

The formal dinner hour had come and gone, but the evening was far from over. The living room buzzed with life as we all indulged in desserts and treasured second—or even third—helpings from the feast. The football game played on the oversized TV, a background melody to the laughter and chatter filling the space. Langston and I exchanged knowing glances, both of us shaking our heads at the outrageously fuzzy, brightly colored socks adorning our feet. My mother, ever the protector of her pristine living room, had insisted we remove our shoes before stepping onto her beloved carpet. Apparently, her solution to "cold feet" involved socks loud enough to be seen from outer space.

"I love the socks, Ty," Cece chimed in from her spot on the sectional, her grin wide with amusement.

"They really pull the whole outfit together," Leah added with a mischievous glint in her eye. She turned to Kayla, my baby girl, and asked, "Don't you think so, Lay?"

"Kayla!" I warned, tossing a throw pillow at her just as her laughter bubbled over. She ducked it easily, her giggles joining the chorus of teasing.

Langston groaned dramatically, lifting his own neon pink socks for the room to see. "Man, they left the frilliest pairs just for us. And I *know* my wife was in on this." He shot Zora a mock-accusatory glance as he settled on the floor in front of her.

Zora, unbothered, smirked and began running her fingers through his hair, her movements slow and deliberate. "And if I was?" she teased, her voice soft but playful.

"See? All that flirting is as good as an admission of guilt," I said, forcing my way onto the couch between Cece and Leah, much to their loud protests. The sectional, as massive as it was, seemed to shrink under the weight of our family, spilling over with limbs and pillows.

"She can be guilty any day," Langston said dreamily, leaning into Zora's touch as though the rest of us had vanished.

"Watch out now," I teased, leaning forward with a sly grin. "Are we going for Toni, Alice, or Claude?" I listed the names of iconic Black authors, hinting that all their antics might lead to an addition to their growing tribe.

"My vote's for Booker," Deuce chimed in from the corner, his smirk wide and deliberate. "That way, you can round it out with Baldwin."

Langston sucked his teeth and rolled his eyes with exaggerated annoyance. "Man, don't hate. Don't hate."

"Oh, we're not hating," Cece said, leaning into the banter. "We're just preparing to order the baby socks now. Might as well get ahead of it."

The room erupted in laughter, the kind that vibrates in your chest and lingers long after the sound fades. Langston shot us all a look that said he was done with our teasing, but Zora's knowing smile said otherwise. In the corner, the little ones squealed with joy, fully engrossed in their Christmas movie marathon in the den. Meanwhile, the sectional remained packed, the air warm and alive with the magic of family—the kind of messy, loud, and perfect chaos only we could create.

Leah, ever the instigator, leaned forward with a gleam in her eye. "So, Kayla, I heard you ran into your father's *special friend* the other day while visiting Brooklyn."

I shot her a warning glance, but it was too late. "Yes," Cece chimed in, tilting her head with mock curiosity. "Do tell us about this little outing where you ran into... what's her name?

Ms. Star? Is it Star?" She knew full well her name wasn't Star—it was Skylar—but she wasn't letting the opportunity slip by.

Before I could even open my mouth, I caught Langston's eye. He looked at me with complete innocence, blissfully unaware of the chaos about to unfold. My sisters, on the other hand, looked like lionesses closing in on their prey.

"It's Skylar," Deuce corrected, his tone dripping with sarcasm and wit. "And apparently, she doesn't know that my Dad is a *catch*."

"Her loss," Kayla chimed in with a dramatic flip of her hair, surprising me with the sheer attitude behind her words.

"Yes, it is her loss," Cece agreed, her voice firm and her protective big-sister energy radiating as she cut her eyes at me.

"Looks like it's Skylar's loss *and* the Cowboys' loss," Daddy interjected, his booming voice filled with an almost desperate attempt to change the subject. "They're about to take this L on Thanksgiving Day." He sauntered into the room, giving me a fist bump as if that would somehow shield me from the verbal firing squad. Momma and Mama H followed closely behind him, carrying plates of pie and wearing expressions that suggested they'd heard *everything*.

Langston's eyebrows shot up, his face a mixture of curiosity and panic. "How much did you hear?" he asked, half-joking but clearly bracing himself.

"We heard it all," Mama H confirmed, her voice steady as she shot Langston and me a knowing look.

"Yes, *every last word* about Ms. Star—oh, I'm sorry—S-K-Y-L-A-R," Momma added, dragging out each letter with exaggerated disapproval. Her lips twisted into a smirk as she glanced at Kayla and Deuce, who were now grinning like Cheshire cats. She lowered herself gracefully onto the couch next to Daddy, her body language oozing both authority and intrigue.

Langston, desperate to redirect the conversation, pointed to the television. "How about dem Cowboys?" he said, his voice unnaturally loud. The attempt landed with a thud, as not a single pair of eyes left me.

I exhaled dramatically, folding my arms and leaning back into the cushions, silently resigning myself to my fate. Kayla, sensing no mercy was coming, began recounting our run-in with Skylar and Allie, her storytelling animated and far too detailed for my liking.

Leah and Cece soaked up every word like it was the latest chapter in their favorite soap opera. Their reactions—"Umm hmm," "Ooh!" and "Ahh!"—peppered Kayla's story with an almost comical level of intensity.

Momma sat quietly, her sharp eyes fixed on me, while Mrs. H nodded along, her expression calm but clearly taking mental notes. I couldn't tell if I was being judged, pitied, or both.

By the time Kayla finished her dramatic retelling, complete with her reenactment of Skylar's polite but brief greeting, I felt like the walls of the room had closed in on me. "And then she just walked away," Kayla finished with a flourish, her voice dripping with mock indignation.

"Well," Mama H finally said, her tone neutral but somehow weighted. "Sounds like Ms. Skylar has *some* sense. Shame about that though." She patted my knee in a way that managed to feel both comforting and condescending.

Daddy clapped his hands together, clearly ready to put an

end to the interrogation. "Alright now, let's focus on this game! Cowboys need our support!"

Langston smirked, clearly amused at my plight, and returned his attention to the TV. But the look in Cece's and Leah's eyes told me this wasn't over. I sighed, sinking further into the couch, wishing for a distraction—or at least another piece of pie—to take the edge off.

I woke the next morning to the unmistakable aroma of waffles wafting through the air, a sweet invitation from the kitchen that tugged at my senses. The faint hum of activity downstairs told me that Momma and Mrs. H were already up and at it, their voices carrying softly through the stillness of the house. I glanced at the clock: 5:00 a.m. Only they could muster this kind of energy after a full Thanksgiving day. The scent of sizzling bacon joined the symphony, and I could almost hear the clatter of plates being set out for what had become a sacred tradition—the post-Thanksgiving breakfast.

This meal was the prelude to the chaos of Black Friday, a ritual my sisters relished with an enthusiasm that defied logic. For me, Langston, and the brother-in-laws, it felt more like a sentence we had to serve annually. This year, Deuce had joined the ranks of the "men on purse duty," a rite of passage that even he couldn't escape.

I could already picture the day ahead: a caravan of overstuffed cars snaking its way from store to store, the women diving into racks and aisles with laser focus while we loitered by the entrances, hands filled with purses, bags, and the occasional overzealous purchase. By the end of it, the vehicles would barely have room for all the electronics, gadgets, and designer bags they inevitably found, their triumphant smiles more satisfying than the deals themselves.

The creak of floorboards downstairs snapped me from my thoughts. I sighed, pulling myself out of bed and bracing for the long day ahead. At least I had waffles waiting for me. That was something.

"I just never imagined my life without him," Mama H said softly, her voice trembling as she looked down at her coffee. She sat across from my mother at the small wooden table tucked into the corner of the large galley kitchen. The early morning light filtered through the window, pale and cool, casting long shadows across the tiled floor. Outside, the world was just beginning to stir. Birds flitted around the feeders, their wings a blur against the backdrop of bare trees. Mama H's gaze followed them briefly before she shook her head, as if trying to shake off the heaviness in her heart.

She said it again, her voice quieter, as though repeating it might make the reality easier to accept. "I just never imagined. We had so many plans." A single tear slid down her cheek, catching the faint morning light before disappearing into her lap.

I stood just beyond the doorway, my presence unnoticed but keenly aware of the intimacy of the moment I was intruding upon. My mother sat still, her own hands wrapped around a warm mug of coffee. A tear silently escaped down her cheek as she looked into Mama H's eyes with a tenderness that spoke of years—no, decades—of friendship that had weathered life's storms and joys together. Two women who had become sisters through twenty-five years of shared triumphs and heartbreaks.

The quiet hum of the house waking up added to the stillness of the kitchen. The kettle on the stove still carried the faint scent of chamomile tea, and the aroma of freshly brewed coffee lingered in the air. It felt sacred, this moment between them, heavy with grief but also laced with love.

My heart ached for Mama H as I watched her. To lose someone who had been your partner in everything, who had shared your dreams and built a life beside you, seemed unbearable. But at the same time, I felt an overwhelming sense of awe at what she had experienced. To love someone so deeply that their absence left a void this profound—that was both a heartbreak and a blessing.

Mama H wiped at her cheek with the back of her hand, offering a small, rueful laugh that carried a mix of apology and acceptance. "He was my partner in everything," she said, her voice a little steadier, though still tinged with sorrow.

My mother reached out, her hand covering Mama H's gently. Her voice, when she spoke, was warm and steady, like the first rays of sunlight breaking through the chill of the morning. "It's okay to feel it all. To miss him like this. It means the love was real."

I stepped back quietly, leaving them to the comfort of their conversation. As I retreated, the scene stayed with me. The birds outside, the glow of the rising sun, and the quiet resilience of two women who had weathered so much. It was a moment etched in the kind of love and friendship that could hold space for both grief and hope, a poignant reminder of life's fragile, beautiful balance.

As I left the kitchen, the quiet weight of Mama H's words lingered in my mind. The house was waking up now, the soft sounds of footsteps and muffled voices filtering through the halls. I leaned against the wall in the hallway, letting the morning light spill over me, casting faint golden streaks across the wooden floor.

My phone buzzed faintly in my pocket—a gentle reminder of the unread message I had avoided since yesterday. I pulled it out, staring at the notification, hesitation and curiosity mingling in my chest. Finally, with a deep breath, I opened it.

Skylar: Just wishing you a wonderful Thanksgiving with the family. Grateful that our paths crossed.

Her words hit me in a way I didn't expect. Simple, kind, and somehow heavier than they should have been. For a moment, I stood there, caught between the tender scene I'd just witnessed in the kitchen and the subtle pull of Skylar's message.

I read it again, letting the words settle, wondering if she knew the weight they carried. In the quiet of the morning, surrounded by the echoes of love, loss, and gratitude, I couldn't help but wonder what paths lay ahead—hers, mine, and the ones that might still cross.

I started to type a simple "thank you," but stopped mid-sentence, realizing it wasn't enough. It was time to put my feelings on the line—time to let someone I couldn't imagine my life without know exactly how I felt.

Titus: Skylar, thank you for the kind message. I hope your Thanksgiving was as warm and meaningful as mine turned out to be. Sorry for the delayed reply—yesterday was a mix of family, reflection, and a lot of gratitude. I'm glad our paths crossed too.

23

Skylar

Elias carefully pulled the *pernil* from the oven, the kitchen lights catching the golden, crackling skin like it was something sacred. The rich, savory aroma filled every corner of the apartment—garlic, citrus, and slow-roasted pork so tender it practically whispered its way out of the roasting pan. He placed it gently on Skylar's marble kitchen island, pausing for a beat to admire the view behind him.

The New York City skyline glowed just beyond the floor-to-ceiling windows, the late afternoon sun surrendering to a deep indigo sky streaked with purple and amber. It looked like a painting. One of those rare, quiet moments when even the city seemed to exhale.

"It's *perfect*," Allie declared, practically bouncing as she clapped her hands together. Her cheeks were still flushed from setting the table, and her voice carried that same giddy disbelief she had when Elias first agreed to make his legendary *pernil* for Friendsgiving.

"Yes," I echoed, taking a step closer to admire it. "Absolutely perfect. This is going to shut the whole table down."

With more than twenty friends arriving soon—old friends, new flings, coworkers-turned-family—we knew this dish would be the crown jewel of the night. It wasn't just a meal, it was a legacy. And Elias? He took that seriously.

Tatum sauntered into the kitchen, rubbing his hands together with exaggerated anticipation like he was prepping for a heist. "Just one bite," he teased, eyeing the *pernil* like it might run off the counter if he didn't act fast.

"Don't even think about it." Quinn stepped into his path, one brow arched, already ready for his antics.

Tatum leaned in, grinning, and playfully tried to nibble at her neck. "Fine. If I can't get a piece of *pernil*, I'll just take a bite outta *you*, Mrs. Cross."

Quinn shoved him off with a laugh, swatting at him like a fly. "You try it, and I swear—Skylar's guest room will be off limits. *Off. Limits.*"

"Listen," Allie chimed in, not missing a beat, "if y'all sneak off to christen Sky's guest room, I'm calling both your parents. And your pastor."

"*Eww,*" Eden groaned from the edge of the kitchen island, a half-full glass of red already in hand. She took a dramatic sip, shaking her head. "It's not even 5 o'clock and you two are already giving 'Rated R' married energy."

"*Wine already,* Eden?" Quinn shot her a mock glare. "You don't want to pace yourself?"

Eden shrugged, raising the glass like a toast. "I've been wrangling toddlers all week. This *is* me pacing myself."

We all laughed, the kind of laughter that wraps around you, warm and familiar, the kind that only happens when your people are all in the same room, the kitchen smells like home, and the night hasn't even really started yet.

Outside, the city kept glowing.

Inside, we were just getting started.

"You're the best, E!" I exclaimed, my gratitude bubbling over like the pot of rice on the back burner. Elias had been running errands since sunrise—picking up fresh bread from our favorite bakery in Bed-Stuy, snagging mini beef patties from that tucked-away Caribbean spot in Fort Greene, and grabbing last-minute groceries that somehow none of us had remembered. Honestly, he was a godsend, the kind of older brother who showed up every time without needing to be asked.

"What do we owe you for all this?" I asked, trying to at least pretend like I was going to repay him, even if I knew he'd never take a dime.

"We?" Allie cut in, raising an arched brow in faux outrage as she popped a cherry tomato into her mouth.

I smirked without missing a beat. "Yes, *we,* as in all of us benefiting from his labor today. Don't get brand new."

Elias leaned casually against the counter, arms crossed, a mischievous glint in his eyes. That slow grin of his—half amusement, half strategy—made it clear he was already cooking up some kind of payback.

"You know he's gonna make us pay in karaoke duets later," Eden teased, lifting her wine glass and nodding toward Elias like he was the entertainment for the night.

"Looks like you survived the road trip with Stitch," she added with a wink, stealing an appetizer from the grazing board.

"We had the bail money ready," Quinn chimed in, reaching for a deviled egg.

"I don't do jail," Allie said, waving a hand in the air. "I

153

would've just sent a fruit basket and prayed for you."

I sucked my teeth, half-laughing, half-ignoring them. I wasn't ready to unpack the *thanksgiving misadventure* that was my nine-hour car ride with my mother. Not yet. Maybe not ever.

The warm pulse of '90s R&B flowed through the speakers, wrapping around the room like a soft hug. Outside, the sun was slipping beneath the skyline, casting a slow amber wash over the windows. Candlelight flickered from every surface—low votives on the coffee table, tall tapers on the counter—blending with the smells of cinnamon, orange peel, roasted garlic, and the buttery aroma of baked cornbread. The apartment felt full—of people, of stories, of the kind of joy that lingered longer than leftovers.

Quinn was tucked beneath Tatum's arm on the couch, her head on his shoulder, his fingers idly playing with the ends of her hair. What else was new? Their love was a cozy blanket that wrapped them in quiet, comfortable devotion.

Eden was already on her third glass of wine, her laughter louder now, looser. Across the room, Jayson sat staring at his phone, his thumbs moving quickly, his focus elsewhere. The space between them felt bigger than the few feet that physically separated them. It was the kind of distance you could feel, even in a crowded room.

From the kitchen, I caught a glimpse of Allie—who, despite hosting, had stolen at least three glances at Elias in the last ten minutes. He was sitting on the couch now, deep in conversation with Lupe, his laugh low and easy, a glass of Mami Herrera's homemade coquito resting casually in his hand. Their chemistry buzzed softly, like a current just under the surface. Smiles that lingered, eyes that said more than the words did. I made a mental note to ask Elias about it later—and possibly corner Allie in the kitchen.

The oven beeped, reminding me to check the turkey. I opened the door, the heat rising in a wave, and found the skin slowly crisping to a golden perfection. I leaned in to baste it one more time, the scent of rosemary and citrus wafting out like an invitation to gather and feast.

Then the doorbell rang—another wave of guests.

Allie floated across the room with the ease of a woman in her element. Her emerald green dress hugged her curves in all the right places, the color glowing against her butter-scotch skin. Her hair was pinned up in an elegant twist, with soft tendrils cascading around her face. Sparkling earrings caught the light as she moved, her steps graceful and sure, each one carrying her toward the front door like she was gliding through the opening scene of a holiday movie.

"Welcome!" she beamed, opening the door with arms wide and a warmth only she could summon. "Get in here, it's officially a party!"

And just like that, Friendsgiving unfolded into full bloom— love, laughter, music, and the sacred hum of chosen family.

Then—he walked in.

Sterling.

The name alone made my stomach clench, but seeing him in the flesh nearly made me burn my hand on the oven rack. He stepped through the doorway like he still owned every room he entered, and damn it, he did. That bald head caught the soft glow of candlelight, his neatly shaped beard now more of a shadow than a statement, but it only added to the rugged magnetism he'd always carried. The diamond stud in his left ear—same one from our high school days—glinted as he moved, a small reminder of the boy he once was... and the man he had clearly become.

His black T-shirt clung to his broad chest like it had been custom-made for him, tucked just right into dark-wash jeans that hinted at the kind of gym routine he never skipped. There was a precision to how he looked—unbothered, intentional. Every step he took exuded that smooth, almost arrogant confidence that used to drive me crazy—and maybe still did.

He approached the kitchen, slicing through the low hum of conversation and the soft swirl of Sade playing from the speakers. The warmth from the oven suddenly felt like nothing compared to the flush rising in my face as he came closer.

"Skylar," he said, his voice like warm honey wrapped in gravel. He leaned in, his lips brushing my cheek in a greeting far too intimate for a room this full. His cologne—woodsy, masculine, familiar—flooded my senses and almost buckled my knees.

"You look amazing."

I pretended to focus on the turkey, fumbling slightly with the roasting pan in my mitts. Thank God for distractions.

Against Allie's very vocal advice, I'd gone with the so-called "safe" little black dress. Only, tonight, it didn't feel very safe. The silky fabric clung in all the right places, the plunging neckline dipped just low enough to spark conversation, and the hem—well, it was shorter than anything I'd worn since college. Even Allie had done a double-take when I emerged from my bedroom earlier.

Sterling's eyes scanned me slowly, lingering just long enough to set every nerve alight. His lips curled into that slow, knowing smile I remembered far too well.

"I see you've been keeping up with those workouts," he said, a hint of playfulness threading through his tone.

I turned back toward the counter, cheeks burning hotter than the oven. "Just trying to keep up with Allie," I replied, forcing lightness into my voice. I could feel his eyes on me, like heat tracing the length of my spine.

From across the kitchen, I heard Allie laugh—low, amused, and entirely too knowing. She didn't say a word, but I could *feel* her eyes boring into the back of my head, waiting to pounce the moment we were alone.

But I wasn't ready for her commentary, not yet.

Not with Sterling's presence still clinging to me like a second skin.

The oven timer beeped, the smell of roasted garlic and herbs wafting through the air, grounding me again in the moment. But everything about this night had just shifted— because with one look, one word, one barely-there kiss...

Sterling had made it *very* clear:

The heat in this kitchen wasn't just coming from the food.

The long dining table stretched from the entryway into the center of the apartment like a runway of memory and intention. It was draped in a rust-colored linen that pooled at the edges like spilled warmth, flickering votives nestled between mismatched ceramic dishes and artfully layered serving platters. Everything was slightly imperfect—which, of course, made it perfect.

The air was thick with the kind of aromas that only show up after hours of love and labor: caramelized yams with cin-namon and brown sugar, rosemary-brushed roast chicken, truffle mac and cheese with that irresistible crispy edge. It was a scent that wrapped around you, clung to your clothes, and whispered, *You're home.*

From the speakers overhead, Solange's *"Cranes in the Sky"* floated through the space, all breathy melancholy and reflection, setting the tone like a velvet curtain drawing open. Moments later, Troop's *"Spread My Wings"* slid into the mix, and an audible hum of recognition rippled across the room. Heads began to nod. Smiles widened. The '80s babies claimed their moment, singing softly between sips of spiked cider.

The loft buzzed with a layered rhythm—laughter rising and falling like tidewater, the clink of glasses and forks tapping plates in sync, bursts of side conversations weaving together into a kind of joyful, lived-in symphony. It felt warm. It felt alive.

Friends from every corner of our lives leaned into one another—debating stuffing versus dressing like it was political philosophy, arguing over which version of "This Christmas" was superior, exchanging knowing glances when someone tried to claim the last spoonful of mac without earning it. There was no performance here. Just presence.

My heart swelled as I looked around. This beautiful, curated chaos wasn't just a dinner—it was the result of love, intention, and group chat coordination gone very right. Allie, Quinn, Eden, and I had birthed this gathering from scratch. What started as a cheeky rebellion against tense family holidays and polite small talk had become *our* tradition. Our third annual Friendsgiving. A night that blurred the lines between blood and bond.

Allie, radiant in an emerald green dress that hugged her curves like it was tailored for her soul, commanded the drink station with the flair of a mixologist and the joy of someone who *loved* the ritual. Her coquito was already the stuff of legend, and tonight was no exception. Her laugh—sharp, sparkling—floated above the music like punctuation.

Quinn stood near the dessert table, curls bouncing as she leaned into a conversation with one of my old coworkers. She had that signature Quinn energy—earthy, centered, magnetic. Her presence always felt like a grounding cord, her tone a mix of softness and sharp discernment. The kind of woman who could quote scripture and *Scandal* in the same breath.

And Eden, forever elegant, glided through the crowd in a sleek navy designer number, her hair pinned into a glossy chignon, her jewelry understated but exquisite. There was something timeless about her—like she'd stepped out of a jazz club in the '60s with secrets tucked behind her eyes. She didn't speak often, but when she did, the room leaned in.

Their presence filled me. Balanced me. Reminded me that sisterhood didn't always come from shared blood, but from showing up, year after year, with wine, wisdom, and whipped cream.

The joy in the room was undeniable. You could taste it. This was the kind of night that explained *why* we go to the trouble—why we stress over the playlist, over-season the food, light too many candles, and pull out the mismatched wine glasses. Why we choose, over and over, to gather.

Because this was sacred.

I glanced around once more as the Edison bulbs cast a soft, honeyed glow over the room. For a moment, I let go of what wasn't here—the old wounds, the unresolved conversations, the people who hadn't shown up. I let it all float away. And in its place, I leaned into what *was* here.

Laughter. Light. Love.

I let myself feel it fully—the gratitude, the nostalgia, the messy beauty of it all. And the quiet thrill of realizing that even in the chaos of life, even in the uncertainty of tomorrow...

I was exactly where I needed to be.

Every corner of the room whispered its own story, layered with laughter, music, and the scent of seasoning still hanging in the air like incense. My gaze moved across the space slowly, letting it all settle over me like a well-balanced melody— equal parts spice, soul, and something holy.

My cousin Keri—wild, unapologetic, and always three steps ahead of a good time—was holding court near the wine rack, one stiletto casually kicked off under the bar cart. Her Southern drawl had grown heavier with each generous pour of Hennessy, turning her words into velvet-coated thunder. She tossed her head back mid-story, her curls bouncing as she delivered one of her signature dirty jokes with a dramatic flick of the wrist. The crowd around her doubled over, snorting into their drinks, one poor soul nearly choking on a mini beef patty.

I shook my head, grinning. Only Keri could drop an R-rated punchline at a holiday gathering and somehow make it feel like a healing ritual. She was the kind of woman who could bring levity to a eulogy and somehow still have you crying *and* laughing through your plate of collard greens.

At the other end of the table, Brandon from the office perched stiffly at the edge of a cushioned bench like he was waiting for permission to exhale. His shirt was still perfectly pressed, his wire-framed glasses unbothered by the steam from the yams, and he held his glass of sangria like it might double as a shield. He blinked twice when Tiana yelled across the room, clearly not used to this brand of loud joy.

I caught Lala's eye from across the room. She arched one finely sculpted brow and smirked. Our bet was officially underway—she swore she could get Brandon to unbutton at least *one* button before the night was over. I had my doubts, but knowing Lala's charm and that devilish grin, I wasn't counting her out just yet.

Near the far corner, Quinn and Tatum stood like magnets locked in place—one arm wrapped around each other's waist, plates in the other hand, hips bumping as they laughed at something only they could hear. Married for over a decade, parents to three kids, yet they moved through rooms like they were still each other's prom date. Their kind of love wasn't performative; it was practiced. Worn in like denim and Sunday routines. The kind of love that didn't need an audience but always stole the scene anyway.

Then there was Tiana.

Our forever hype queen. Her presence was kinetic—braids swinging, voice lifted, and personality too big for any corner to contain. She rapped along with SWV like she had something to prove, threw in Biggie ad-libs with perfect cadence, and somehow managed to balance a second helping of *pernil* while simultaneously volleying flirtatious barbs across the table.

Her attention pinballed between Chad and Sterling, both of whom looked slightly stunned—equal parts entertained, intimidated, and low-key intrigued. Tiana flirted like it was an Olympic sport, and tonight she was breaking records.

The entire room buzzed with that perfect kind of chaos— messy, joyful, alive. There were stories in every glance, history in every laugh, soul in every second.

For a few sacred hours, the rest of the world faded out. No deadlines. No drama. No distractions.

Just the rhythm of the night, the glow of chosen family, and the rare magic of everyone being exactly where they were meant to be.

As dinner began to wind down, the warm hum of the evening shifted into something looser, more languid. Guests slowly peeled away from the long dining table, slipping into the comfort of the sectional couches or leaning lazily against the kitchen island. The clatter of plates gave way to the low murmur of conversation, punctuated by the sharp laughter of familiar company.

The Knicks were on, of course. Had I known they were playing tonight, I might have picked another date for Friendsgiving. But this was *Allie's* loft, and Allie was nothing if not loyal to her teams. The oversized TV flickered in the background, casting a soft blue light across the living room as a handful of guests—mostly the guys—watched the game with rapt attention, halfheartedly pretending they weren't "held hostage," as Allie had joked with a smirk and a fresh round of drinks.

Meanwhile, the dining table had transformed into a battleground of black joy—a rowdy, trash-talking game of spades now in full swing. Lupe, usually soft-spoken and reserved, had become a revelation. She smacked her cards down with the precision of a seasoned hustler, her calm delivery paired with spicy side-eye and unexpected swagger.

"Run it back," she said coolly, to the stunned faces around her.

The entire table roared with laughter, even as her partner—Keri—doubled over in her chair, fanning herself with a napkin like she'd just witnessed a spiritual revival. Who *was* this Lupe?

I moved quietly through the apartment, gathering stray glasses, wiping rings off the marble countertops, refolding napkins that had somehow found the floor. The smell of smoked turkey and vanilla-scented candles still hung in the air, mingling with the fading echoes of Solange and Mary J. from the playlist looping in the background. This was the moment I loved most—when the energy slowed, the vibe thickened, and the house felt wrapped in something warm and earned.

As I rounded the corner by the entryway, I noticed Allie gliding toward the door, her emerald dress catching the light like it had its own spotlight. I hadn't even heard the bell ring.

She opened the door with a wide, familiar smile—and then he walked in.

Titus.

His name escaped me before I could swallow it, my voice just loud enough to betray my surprise.

He stepped inside like a question I hadn't finished answering. That rich, warm scent—his signature cologne, layered with something darker, woodier—hit me first, curling around me like smoke. He looked as magnetic as ever: navy sport coat over a black sweater, crisp dark jeans, leather boots. Effortless, elegant, and unapologetically him.

We hadn't really spoken since Sabor & Roots. Not beyond a few distant text messages that carried more silence than substance. Things between us had unraveled quietly, like a thread being tugged beneath a door we both pretended wasn't opening.

I hadn't expected him to come tonight. The invitation had

been sent weeks ago, when everything still felt hopeful. I assumed he'd bow out, gracefully fade into the background like so many others had. But there he was—standing in the soft light of my entryway, looking at me like he wasn't ready to let the chapter close.

For a moment, the room fell away. The music blurred into white noise. The voices and laughter melted into a muffled hum. Even the clinking of glasses and the comforting scent of baked mac and cinnamon-laced coquito seemed to dissolve.

It was just him.

Titus.

Standing a few feet away, composed but unreadable, the corner of his mouth curving just slightly. His eyes met mine—steady, unflinching. And there it was again. That tether. That impossible pull.

There were no words between us, but the tension filled the space like steam from a boiling pot. Thick. Quiet. Electric.

Then, like a breeze blowing through to save me from drowning, Elias appeared—always with the perfect timing.

"Titus, right?" Elias said, his tone warm and effortless as he clapped a hand on Titus's shoulder and drew him away from the doorway. Just like that, the spell broke.

Titus gave a small nod, his gaze lingering on me for one heartbeat longer before letting himself be pulled back into the swirl of chatter and familiar distraction.

He disappeared into the living room with Elias, joining the others like nothing had ever happened. But the silence he left in his wake echoed through me, louder than any music, more disorienting than any flirtation.

It was the kind of silence that stayed with you.

And I wasn't ready to name what it meant yet.

He stood just a few feet away, sharp as ever in a navy sport coat that framed his broad shoulders like it had been tailored by fate. That smooth, baritone energy wrapped around him like cologne—low, magnetic, and unforgettable. His eyes—deep, dark, and quietly knowing—locked onto mine. And in that silence, something stirred. Something old. Something I hadn't let myself feel in weeks.

That familiar pull.

The ache that stretched like a live wire between us, taut and dangerous. Neither of us moved. Neither of us spoke. The room faded, blurred into static. For a heartbeat, it was just him and me in a moment we didn't know how to name.

Then, mercifully, Elias slid in like divine intervention.

"What's up, Titus? Good to see you," he said, clapping a firm hand on his back, his voice easy, grounding. He didn't ask questions. Didn't give me time to drown. Just gently steered Titus toward the living room, back into the current of noise and comfort and safe distractions.

But the silence he left behind?

It echoed through my ribs.

"So…" Allie's voice sliced through the moment like a warm blade, her hip already cocked as she placed a tray of flan and apple crostata onto the counter. Her tone was all casual charm, but her eyes—sharp, knowing—were locked on me. "Are we gonna talk about the six-foot-tall elephant in the room?"

I rolled my eyes and grabbed the cheesecake from the fridge, stalling. "What are you talking about?"

Allie let out a short laugh. "Please don't insult me with that fake innocence, Sky. The man walked in and you damn near dropped to your knees—or fainted. Not sure which."

Before I could form a comeback, Quinn appeared, wine glass in hand, catching the tail end of the conversation. "What's this about Sky dropping to her knees? I definitely came in at the right time."

"She's not denying it," Allie added, smug.

"I was caught off guard," I said, trying to hold on to what little composure I had left. "I didn't expect him to come tonight. It's been... weeks."

Quinn sipped her wine and gave me a long look. "Weeks and you still look at him like he's the last piece of flan."

"Oh, we're absolutely talking about this," Eden said, gliding into the kitchen, flawless as always, her heels clicking softly against the tile. She plucked a grape from a cheese board like she was too elegant for judgment, then tilted her head at me. "Because if Titus looked at *me* the way he just looked at you, I'd be trying on wedding dresses."

I groaned and leaned against the fridge. "Can't I just have one night where y'all don't psychoanalyze my love life?"

"No," Quinn, Eden, and Allie replied *in unison.*

Allie leaned closer, dropping her voice. "Sky, you pushed him away. You iced him out. And yet, he showed up. That's not nothing."

"Exactly," Quinn said. "It's not about what he said. It's the fact that he came. That man walked into a room full of your people, knowing there was tension. That takes courage."

Eden raised her glass. "It takes something else too, honey. That kind of confidence doesn't just show up—it lingers."

"I'm aware," I muttered, rubbing my temple.

"Sky," Allie said, her voice softening. "I know you've been hurt before. I know you're scared of making the wrong choice again. But pride is not a safety net. It's a cage."

I was quiet. The weight of their words settled heavy in the air.

Then, as if summoned by the tension, Elias reappeared with a grin—and the last slice of Aunt Mary's pie. Allie gasped in horror.

"Elias! That was *not* for you!"

He winked and took a bite. "This pie is delicious. And so is the truth. Which all of you clearly just served up to Sky."

Eden choked on her wine. Quinn gave him a slow clap.

Elias looked at me. "He's a good man, Sky. Maybe not perfect. But he showed up. That counts for something."

And then, just as my breath caught in my throat again, I turned—and there he was.

Titus.

Beside me.

"Sky. Skylar," he said, his voice warm, steady, and somehow still intimate despite the crowd. "Thanks again for the invite."

The way he said my name—low and deliberate—unraveled something in me. It wrapped around my ribs, made my shoulders drop and my pulse skip. I turned to face him fully, my eyes meeting his.

"Titus." His name was all I could manage.

The others had gone quiet around us, fading into the low hum of the Knicks game and clinking glasses.

"I know this isn't the time or place," he said gently, "but I didn't want to let another night pass without saying I'm sorry."

I stared at him, at the truth sitting in his posture, in the calm urgency of his gaze. "I... I want to talk," I said quietly. "Just us. Maybe not now. But soon."

His eyes softened. And this time, I swear I saw it—a flicker of hope. Something healing in the way he looked at me.

Before Titus could respond, the moment fractured.

"Ms. Skylar Madison!" boomed a familiar voice from behind me—just loud enough to turn heads and make my stomach knot.

Sterling. Of course.

He had the worst timing known to man. Like clockwork.

Without warning, his arm slid around my waist. I barely had time to brace before he spun me halfway toward him, the motion jarring and all too comfortable for the complicated, unstable thing we used to be. His grip was confident. Too confident. The kind that didn't match the distance I'd spent months building between us.

I stiffened, my smile slipping as I leaned away slightly, sidestepping his embrace with practiced grace. My shoulder brushed Titus's arm behind me—a small, fleeting contact, but enough to feel the quiet tension ripple through both of us.

"There are two minutes left in the game," Sterling said, flashing that signature grin—equal parts charm and ego. He pointed dramatically toward the living room, where the crowd had gathered in a knot of noise and anticipation. "And the Knicks need their good luck charm."

He winked, his hand still hovering near the small of my back like he was waiting for permission that hadn't been offered. The energy of the room pulsed with music, laughter, and game-night hype, but I felt none of it in that moment—only the sharp, uncomfortable shift as the warmth Titus brought was replaced by something colder. Something performative.

I glanced at Titus.

He hadn't moved.

He stood perfectly still, his jaw tight but composed, eyes unreadable. That cool, measured presence of his—the calm I used to crave—was back, wrapped around him like armor. But beneath it, something flickered. Disappointment? Resignation? Or maybe just... restraint.

"We'll definitely talk, *Ms. Skylar Madison*," he said at last, each word smooth and deliberate, laced with a softness that both steadied me and left me aching. His tone wrapped around me like velvet—warm, grounding—but there was an edge to it, too. Like a door slowly closing, waiting for someone to walk through it... or not.

His smile curved just slightly, enough to soften the blow. Enough to make it sting.

He glanced toward the living room with a small nod. "But right now, your Knicks need you."

I swallowed the lump in my throat, nodded with a breathless smile, and turned—feeling the weight of the moment slipping through my fingers like silk.

Sterling guided me toward the couch, his hand still resting lightly against my back, and the noise of the party rushed in like a wave I hadn't realized had gone quiet.

Allie, perched on the edge of the sectional in full Knicks fan mode, waved a hand toward the empty cushion beside her without even looking up. "*Sit! We need all the good juju we can get!*"

I dropped into the space between her and Sterling, my pulse still off-beat—not because of the game, but because of the man I'd just walked away from.

Across the room, Quinn stood near the drink station,

watching everything unfold with that sharp, lawyerly gaze of hers. She didn't say anything, but the look on her face said *plenty*. One brow arched, wine glass in hand, she gave me that "we're gonna talk about this later" face she'd perfected over the years. Beside her, Eden muttered something under her breath—something that made Quinn choke on her sip and nearly double over laughing.

I didn't need to ask what she'd said. I could guess.

Sterling slung his arm lazily across the back of the couch, his fingers grazing my shoulder like punctuation. I sat still, eyes fixed on the screen, pretending to care, pretending not to feel the empty space beside me more vividly than the one I was in.

The final minutes of the game were tense. The room was electric with hope and nerves.

Brunson stepped to the free-throw line. Silence fell, like someone had hit mute.

He sank it. *Tied game.*

The apartment *erupted*. Cheers, laughter, clapping. Sterling patted my back. Allie threw a couch pillow in the air like it was a confetti cannon. Someone from the spades table yelled, "It's destiny!"

"Come on, come on!" Allie shouted, halfway off the couch as the Knicks inbounded the ball.

The sequence was quick—give-and-go, perfect screen, and the shot went up just before the buzzer. The ball danced on the rim, every person in the room leaning forward like we could *will* it in with our breath.

Swish.

Pandemonium.

Allie screamed. Sterling stood up and high-fived someone

over the couch. People jumped, spilled drinks, someone dropped their phone. The room exploded in joy and disbelief.

And me?

I looked up.

Titus.

He stood near the kitchen, watching me. The chaos swirled around him, but he was still. Solid. Steady. His eyes found mine, and for the second time that night, the noise fell away.

He smiled—not flashy, not performative. Just *real*.

A knowing look passed between us—one that saw through the noise, through Sterling's theatrics, through the front I was still wearing like a shield.

And in that quiet exchange, I realized something:

The *real* play of the night had nothing to do with the Knicks.

It had everything to do with the man I'd almost let walk away.

24

Titus

A few hours earlier.

"Bro, what are you doing? Weren't you supposed to be at Skylar's *hours* ago?"

Langston's voice buzzed through the speaker, tinged with a blend of disbelief and brotherly irritation. I stood at the foot of my bed, staring down at the four outfits draped across the duvet—each one tried on, taken off, and now silently mocking me for the indecision I'd marinated in for the better part of an hour.

The clock on the dresser flashed 8:12 PM, a quiet accusation. Skylar's Friendsgiving had started more than two hours ago, and I was still standing here barefoot in sweats, completely stuck between wanting to show up and not knowing if I'd even be welcome.

"I think..." I said slowly, the words dragging out like they weighed more than they should, "I'm just going to pass. Grab something to eat, maybe stay in for the night."

There was a beat of silence—just long enough for the judgment to build.

Then Langston's reaction came fast and sharp. "You've got to be *kidding* me. After all the back-and-forth? All that closet chaos? The outfit changes, the internal monologue about what you'd say, how you'd walk in, what *tone* you'd use—now you're folding like a lawn chair?"

Before he could finish, I heard Zora's voice in the background, clear and unmistakably pointed. "Watch your mouth, Mr. Hughes!"

Her tone was sharp, but her affection was never far beneath it. Still, she wasn't done.

"And don't be so hard on him," she added with a hint of steel. "If I'm being honest, I'm not even sure *Ms. Skylar* is worth the gas money."

I winced at that, rubbing the back of my neck.

Zora hadn't forgiven Skylar for the way things had cooled off after I told her about Deuce and Kayla—my kids, my reality, and the part of my life that seemed to shift everything for Skylar. I never asked Zora to take sides. I didn't have to. She was loyal to the bone. Even when I didn't need defending.

But Langston wasn't letting up.

"You've got my wife pacing the living room like she's about to pull up on Skylar in heels and a wrap coat," he said, half-laughing, half-fed up. "Meanwhile, you're over there having a crisis about... what? Pride? Ego? Hurt feelings? Bro, what's *really* going on?"

I exhaled hard, dragging a hand down my face as I sank onto the edge of the bed. The floor creaked under me. The room was too quiet, except for the hum of the radiator and the occasional car passing outside the window. My jacket hung on the back of the door like it was waiting on my courage.

"It's complicated, Lang," I muttered, finally.

"Of course it is," he replied without hesitation. "It's *real*. Real stuff is always complicated."

I looked at the navy sport coat lying neatly beside a pair of dark jeans—the same one Skylar once complimented during our first real night out. The memory hit me like a whisper: her smile, the way her fingers brushed the lapel, the way she looked at me like I was already something solid in her life.

"I just..." I shook my head. "I don't want to walk into a room full of people and get greeted like I'm a question mark. Like she doesn't know what to do with me."

Langston's voice softened. "But you're not walking in for them. You're walking in for *you*. To finish what you started. You've been saying for weeks that you want clarity—well, clarity doesn't show up if you don't."

Zora chimed in again, her voice closer this time, less sharp, more sure. "Show up, Titus. And don't show up small."

I sat with that for a second. Let it land.

Then I stood, walked over to the coat hook, and reached for the sport coat.

"Don't listen to Zora," Langston said, dropping his voice into a mock whisper like we were sharing government secrets. "She's sitting here all cozied up with her Boaz, while your behind is out here still searching for Ruth."

He cackled, clearly proud of himself, the sound spilling through the phone like he'd just dropped a Bernie Mac-level mic. I didn't even have the energy to groan. He was ridiculous—and unfortunately, not wrong.

"Titus," he said, his voice softening now, "I better hear about how things went at Skylar's tomorrow morning. No excuses. Tonight, I'm handling Mrs. Hughes. We've got our own little Friendsgiving date night. And guess what?" He paused dramatically. "I didn't try on four outfits to get ready for it."

I let out a breath as the call ended, standing alone in the quiet of my bedroom, the city humming faintly outside the window. Frustration and envy warred in my chest—frustration at myself for hesitating... and envy over what Langston and Zora had. That kind of ease. That kind of steady.

Later that night, the brown paper bag holding my chicken parm from Cino's warmed my hands as I strolled the few blocks back toward my building. The cold air nipped at my face, but the smell of fresh pine from the corner Christmas tree stand softened it. A street vendor roasted chestnuts nearby, and the scent drifted through the air, weaving together with the buttery garlic from my dinner and the hint of woodsmoke curling from the brownstone chimneys.

Holiday lights sparkled from windows up and down the street—gold and red, blinking slowly. The city was wrapped in that magical November hush, just on the edge of December.

I chuckled, thinking about Langston and his corny scripture jokes. I wasn't surprised he and Zora were somewhere wrapped in a blanket, sipping wine and watching rom-coms. They lived for those little moments. But the thought of them together, laughing over a shared plate of something warm, made the chicken parm in my hand feel a lot colder.

By the time I reached my brownstone, the comfort of the Knicks game was the only noise waiting for me. I turned it on more out of habit than hope. The familiar voices of the announcers filled the space, echoing across the walls like company. Another reminder of Skylar.

I'd just sunk into the couch when my phone buzzed.

Deuce.

"What's up, son?" I answered, already smiling.

"Hey, Pops," he said, casual and upbeat. "What are you up to?"

I could already hear the judgment forming behind his tone.

"Don't tell me you're watching the Knicks again," he teased. "Weren't you a Wizards fan last time we checked?"

I laughed. "What can I say? When in New York..."

"Uh-huh. You dodging the real question, though," he said, not missing a beat. "Weren't you supposed to be at Skylar's Friendsgiving tonight?"

I paused, stretching out the silence like gum between my teeth.

"I decided to pass," I said finally.

"*Pass?*" he repeated, like I'd just told him I gave up on oxygen. "Dad. Are you running scared?"

"It's not that," I said, though it probably was. "The invite was from before... everything. Before I told her about Deuce and Kayla. Things changed. I wasn't sure she'd even want me there."

There was a pause on his end this time. Then his voice came back, firmer. Older.

"Dad. If she didn't want you there, she would've said so. Didn't she reach out on Thanksgiving? Sounds like she left the door open. The question is—are you too scared to walk through it?"

I leaned back into the couch cushion, one hand resting on my knee, the other gripping the remote. "This sounds suspiciously like Langston put you up to this."

Deuce laughed. "Nope. This is all me. Pops, you talked about Skylar for months. You told me how deep y'all's conversations were, how she challenged you. How she reminded you of yourself. You said she was smart, grounded, beautiful—and didn't just talk about purpose, she lived it."

His words landed with a quiet thud in my chest.

I stared at the TV, seeing nothing but that first dinner we had. The way Skylar argued about hip-hop rankings like it was a thesis defense. The way her eyes lit up when she talked about her friends, her work, her father. The way she said my name like it meant something.

"You finally found someone who fits," Deuce continued. "So don't waste your time looking at the door like it's locked if she's already cracked it open for you."

I sat there stunned. When did my son grow into the kind of man who could pull the truth out of me?

"And Pops?" he added, playful now. "Keep it simple. Blazer and jeans. *Not* dress shoes. Wear the Dunks. Trust me—Skylar seems like a woman who respects a good sneaker."

I laughed, shaking my head. "That's what you're going with? Fashion advice?"

"Better than advice from a man eating chicken parm alone in a hoodie," he said, and I couldn't even argue with that.

When the call ended, I looked toward the bedroom.

The clothes were still there—laid out like options and outcomes, waiting to be chosen.

Maybe it wasn't too late after all.

I was relieved when Allie opened the door.

We'd only met a few times during the stretch when Skylar and I were seeing each other, but I felt like I'd known her far longer. Honestly, I could've picked her out of a lineup based solely on the way Skylar talked about her—

their shared childhood in Fort Greene, their unshakable bond, their "sisterhood thicker than blood" kind of loyalty. Skylar didn't just mention Allie; she *invoked* her.

So when Allie swung the door open, vibrant as ever, that same familiarity washed over me like warm light through stained glass.

She was radiant—commanding the doorway in a sequined emerald green dress that clung in all the right places, shimmering with each movement like it had a rhythm of its own. Her curls were swept up into a soft, effortless updo, and her chandelier earrings danced with every word she spoke, punctuation to the joy written all over her face.

"Titus!" she gasped, eyes wide with delight before wrapping me in a bear hug that felt more like *welcome home* than *nice to see you.* Her embrace was real—bone-deep, no hesitation—and I felt something uncoil in my chest I hadn't even realized I'd been holding.

"You showed up," she said, pulling back to give me a once-over. "And look at you! The blazer? The Dunks? Dapper and intentional."

I laughed, shaking my head.

"Well, thank God you came," she said, grinning as she stepped aside. "Skylar's going to pretend she didn't care you walked in tonight—but I guarantee she did."

The shimmer of her dress caught the light again as she moved back into the apartment, the warmth of the party already spilling into the entryway behind her—music, laughter, the hum of a game on the TV, and the unmistakable scent of garlic, roasted meat, and something sweet and spiced baking in the air.

As I stepped inside, I realized something:

I wasn't just relieved Allie opened the door—I was grateful.

Because with one smile, one hug, and one perfectly timed joke, she made it clear:

I still had a place here. At least for tonight.

Before I could respond, my gaze drifted across the apartment—straight to Skylar, standing by the kitchen island, placing a strawberry cheesecake with careful grace. Her hair was straightened tonight, long and sleek, grazing her shoulders, with a silver streak at her temples that caught the light just enough to stop me in my tracks. She wore no makeup, and didn't need it—her cinnamon-toned skin glowed naturally, effortlessly. The black dress she wore was deceptively simple, hugging her curves and stopping short just above the knee, revealing more leg than I was prepared for.

Allie was definitely behind that, I thought. I made a mental note to thank her twice.

I set the bottle of wine I'd brought down on the kitchen counter and offered Skylar a quiet nod before speaking.

"Skylar."

She turned at the sound of her name, and when her eyes met mine, it was like a match to dry wood.

"Titus," she said, the word soft, familiar, and dangerously effective. Her voice stirred something in me I'd tried too long to quiet.

Before I could reply, Allie grabbed my hand like a lifeline and pulled me into the main room. "Come on. Save yourself. You've got the eyes of a man about to drown."

She led me to her brother, Elias, who stood by the bar cart, surveying the game with half interest and a glass of cider in hand.

"Please forgive her," he said with a slow shake of his head after Allie dashed off to yell at the Knicks. "The game brings out her inner maniac. *Allie, eres bien rude!*"

We both laughed, and it loosened something in my chest.

Elias extended a hand. "So, you're the infamous Titus."

"Infamous?" I repeated, raising an eyebrow. "Uh oh. That doesn't sound good."

Elias chuckled. "Don't worry—it's mostly love. Allie's team Titus. Honestly, most of us are."

"Most?" I asked, curiosity piqued.

He gave a subtle nod toward Skylar. "She's hard to crack. But she's worth it."

I glanced across the room and found her—Skylar—seated on the couch, laughing with her whole body, her hand resting lightly on her chest, head tilted back, eyes closed in that kind of full, unguarded joy I hadn't seen from her in far too long.

To her right was a woman with a cascade of soft curls and an easy elegance about her—Quinn, if I was guessing right. Skylar had mentioned her before: the no-nonsense attorney with a heart of gold, a mouth that didn't pull punches, and a husband she adored like he was her favorite playlist. She radiated a quiet fire, the kind you knew would defend her friends with a closing argument and a casserole.

On the other side sat another woman, posture perfect, wine glass cradled in one hand, her legs crossed with the kind of grace that didn't need to try. Eden, I guessed—the one who used to dance ballet and now managed motherhood, marriage, and curated chaos like it was art. She had that regal stillness about her, the kind of presence that didn't ask for attention but got it anyway.

I hadn't met either of them before tonight, but I'd heard

enough to feel like I had. The way Skylar spoke about them—like they were chapters in her autobiography—made it impossible not to connect the dots. *Her girls.* The ones who knew every version of her, who pulled up when it mattered, who didn't need to be asked twice.

And even from across the room, I could feel it—that rhythm between them. That unspoken code. They leaned into each other like they'd been orbiting together for decades, their laughter overlapping in perfect harmony. It was sacred. Earned.

For a split second, watching Skylar nestled between the two women I'd only known through stories, I wondered—*Is one of them Sterling?*

My chest tightened before logic caught up.

Of course not, I reminded myself. Skylar would've told me. She spoke about Quinn and Eden like family, not lovers. But even that tiny flicker of uncertainty was enough to remind me just how far I still had to go—how much of her life existed beyond the parts I'd seen.

And how badly I wanted to be let back in.

Elias followed my gaze. "I've known her since third grade. She's like a little sister. Loyal, brilliant, terrifying when she's mad. And *stubborn as hell.*"

I laughed under my breath. "Yeah. I've noticed."

He leaned against the edge of the bar. "She's got a soft heart, but a heavy guard. When someone gets too close, she finds a reason to push back. Sadly, you might've made that part easy for her."

I nodded slowly, the truth of it settling in my chest like a stone. "Yeah. I did."

Elias clapped a hand on my shoulder, firm and steady.

"Don't quit. She doesn't need perfect. She needs present."

Then, with a sly grin, he added, "Mind grabbing me some cider from the kitchen?"

I nodded, knowing exactly what he was doing.

Skylar stood at the island again, tidying up the dessert trays. The candlelight flickered gently behind her, catching the edge of her hair, framing her like a scene I'd been waiting to return to.

"Sky," I began, then corrected myself. "Skylar."

She turned, and for a heartbeat, it was just us again.

"Titus," she said, a small, hesitant smile tugging at her lips.

"I wanted to thank you," I said. "For still inviting me."

She looked up at me, eyes steady. "I know this isn't the time or the place," she said, her voice low but sure. "But before more time passes... I need to apologize."

I felt the sincerity before she even reached for my arm. Her fingers rested lightly on my sleeve, and it was all I could do to stay grounded.

"I can't say it all now," she added, her voice catching just slightly. "But I want to. Just us. If that's okay."

I opened my mouth to answer, but before I could speak, the spell broke.

"Ms. Skylar Madison!" a booming voice called from behind.

I am pretty sure that was the one and only, Sterling.

He appeared at her side like an interruption wearing cologne. He wrapped an arm around her waist and spun her toward him with theatrical flair.

I stepped back automatically, hands in my pockets, fury flickering behind my ribcage.

"There's two minutes left in the game, and the Knicks need their good luck charm," he said, nudging her toward the crowd.

Skylar glanced back at me, apology written all over her face.

I managed a small smile, tamping down every instinct to say more. "We'll definitely talk, *Ms. Skylar Madison*," I said deliberately. "But right now, your Knicks need you."

She nodded, her smile a little tight. She let him guide her back into the living room.

The room exploded minutes later as the Knicks hit a buzzer-beater. People jumped, screamed, hugged. Allie lost her mind, dancing in front of the TV like she'd made the shot herself.

I barely saw any of it.

Because I saw *him*. Sterling, leaning into Skylar, whispering something. His hand too familiar at the curve of her back.

Jealousy surged through me—sharp, fast, unwanted.

As the crowd settled, Allie reappeared beside me, her voice low.

"Titus," she said, resting a hand on my forearm. "You have no idea how happy I am that you came."

Her gaze flicked toward Sterling. Her smile faltered.

"You see it too," she said softly. "And so does she. Trust me."

My phone buzzed in my pocket. I pulled it out.

Group chat:

Deuce: *Shoot your shot, Pops.*

Langston: 🏀🚶‍♂️⬛♂

Deuce:

I stared at the screen for a second, then at Skylar across

the room.

Maybe it *wasn't* too late.

Not yet.

Hours later, the cold chicken parm sat untouched on my kitchen counter—a quiet reminder of the evening I almost missed. My stomach wasn't empty, though. Between the scraps of **Elias's famous pernil** he tucked away for me, the stolen slice of **Aunt Mary's legendary sweet potato pie**, and the warmth of shared laughter, unexpected closure, and undeniable *chemistry*, I was full in a way takeout couldn't touch.

But sleep? Not even close.

My mind wouldn't shut off. I kept replaying the night's moments—Skylar's voice saying my name, the look in her eyes, the way the room disappeared just before Sterling stormed in like a walking exclamation point.

I reached for my phone, thumb hovering over Langston's name before remembering it was *date night.* He and Zora were probably wrapped up on their couch, sipping bourbon and working on creating little Alice or Booker—future literary geniuses who'd quote Baldwin in preschool.

I smiled, set the phone down, then picked it up again, the urge to talk bubbling under my skin.

Dad? Nah. Even at nearly 1 a.m., he'd need it to be a true emergency. A "your son's in the hospital" kind of situation— not a "your son might still be in love" one.

Then it hit me.

Cece.

My big sister, Priscilla—Cece to everyone who knew better—was a night owl, wired to be wide awake when the rest of the world powered down. A call at this hour would barely register.

I tapped her name.

She answered on the first ring.

"Titus!" she sang, her voice chipper like it was 8 a.m. and she'd already finished yoga and a latte.

"Scilla," I said, grinning into the phone like I was fifteen again and about to get caught sneaking in late.

"Yes, Titus?" she replied, already suspicious, the edge of mischief sharpening her tone.

"I just wanted to hear my favorite sister's voice," I said, laying it on thick.

Cece sucked her teeth with the drama of a seasoned actress. "Please. You've never been a good liar, which is why you stayed grounded all of '99. This better be good—it's *almost 2 a.m.*"

I laughed, letting it all spill out.

I gave her the full saga—how I finally pulled up to Skylar's Friendsgiving like a man on a mission, dressed in my blazer and Dunks, goatee tight, confidence on ten. I told her about the buzz in the room, the soulful playlist, the candlelight flickering off Skylar's cheekbones like she was the main character in a romantic drama I hadn't realized I'd been cast in.

Cece listened from her couch, red wine in one hand, her head cocked to the side, smirk practically audible.

"Oh, *is that so?*" she said, one eyebrow raised from miles away.

"Mmm-hmm," she added, with that patented tone that meant *don't you dare leave out a single detail, boy.*

I kept going—describing Skylar in that black dress (*not*

cranberry, she corrected, laughing), the real conversation that started to crack through the surface between us, and how it all unraveled when Sterling waltzed in like he owned the joint.

"That Sterling dude sounds like an ass," she said flatly, not missing a beat. "Interrupting your moment? Too much bass in his voice and not enough sense."

I smirked. "He's got history. And presence. He knew it was a moment. He just couldn't let it happen."

Cece sipped slowly, her tone shifting slightly. "Okay, but what's *really* the story with Skylar and Sterling?"

Now she was serious.

When Cece asked questions like that, it wasn't idle curiosity. She was trying to measure the space between me and disappointment. And she didn't like open ends.

I rubbed my jaw, staring out the window at the flicker of holiday lights from the brownstone across the street. "I'm not sure," I admitted. "But he's not neutral. I can see that."

Cece hummed low and long. "Well, he's clearly too comfortable."

She let the words hang in the air, and I let them hang with her.

Then, with her signature switch-up, she fired off, "So how many hours did you waste talking yourself *out* of going? Let me guess—three hours, five outfit changes, and an identity crisis about whether to lead with charm or chill?"

I sucked my teeth. "Four outfits. And two full pep talks. Langston roasted me. Deuce guilted me."

Cece *cackled,* the kind of laugh that bounced off walls and healed old wounds. "I love them. Tell them they owe me for sparing them from your dramatics."

We fell into a comfortable silence, the kind that only comes with history and shared secrets.

After a moment, she said, "Titus, I know you. You don't show up like that unless it matters. Don't let fear let you fumble."

"I hear you," I said quietly. And I did.

Then, as if on cue, she glanced at the clock. "Do you *realize* it's almost 3 a.m.? My husband is about to wake up and ask why I've been on the phone with another man for an hour."

"I love you, Scilla," I said, voice softening as I stared at the photo of us on the bookshelf—me, her, and Leah, all grinning like fools at a family cookout years ago.

"I know you do. Hard not to," she teased. "Now go to bed. And tell Zora and Langston they owe me for sparing them from your late-night ramblings.."

I laughed, my heart lighter as we said goodnight.

Cece always knew how to check me, cheer me, and challenge me—all in one call.

And just like that, the night I almost missed became a story I wouldn't forget.

25

Allie

The apartment was quiet now, wrapped in that delicate stillness that only arrives after a long night of laughter and too much food. The soft hum of the refrigerator offered the only soundtrack—well, that and the occasional thunderous snore from Elias, sprawled like a retired gladiator across Skylar's oversized loveseat, one arm hanging dramatically over the edge, his sock barely clinging to his foot. The man had devoured two plates of pernil, three slices of pie, and at least four glasses of coquito before he'd passed out like a contented uncle at a family reunion.

A faint amber glow from the kitchen under-cabinet lights bathed the space in something cozy and cinematic. The clock on the stove read a little after 1 a.m. The last guest had left not long ago, their perfume and footsteps still lingering faintly in the air.

Gone were the sequins and stilettos, the curated curls and the carefully constructed confidence we wore like armor earlier in the night. I had traded my emerald green dress for fuzzy lime-green socks, a pair of blue cotton shorts, a purple tank, and a pink sports bra peeking through—my post-party *technicolor exhale.* My elaborate updo—Skylar's insistence— had long since given way to my go-to pigtails, keeping my curls off my face like a protective charm.

Skylar, now in gray sweatpants and a vintage T-shirt, had pinned her hair like it was sacred, determined to preserve the blowout she'd paid for—and rightfully so. She looked impossibly chill, perched on a barstool at the counter with a half-eaten slice of strawberry cheesecake in hand, fork in the other, her shirt slipping off one shoulder like she was starring in the final scene of a Netflix Christmas movie.

Meanwhile, I was loading the dishwasher with the subtle grace of a linebacker.

"Chica," I hissed, louder than I intended, as a stack of wine glasses clinked against each other like church bells, *"why the hell was Sterling here tonight?"*

Skylar didn't flinch.

"*Yes,* tell us, Skylar." Quinn appeared from the hallway in leggings and a sleep shirt that read '*I object... to your nonsense'.* Her expression was all lawyer, no fluff. "How *exactly* did Sterling make it onto the guest list?"

Skylar blinked, as if we'd just asked her to explain quantum physics without a calculator. She nonchalantly took another bite of cheesecake and kept her eyes on the fork, avoiding ours like she didn't just set the emotional grenade in the middle of her living room and walk away.

"Skylar *Madison,*" I said, using my mom-voice—low, sharp, and historically effective. "You better start talking before I throw this cheesecake out in protest."

Skylar sighed, finally placing the fork down with the kind of exaggerated calm that only made us more suspicious. "It wasn't that deep. He found out about it, and I didn't exactly un-invite him."

"*Not un-inviting* is not the same as *inviting*," Quinn snapped. "That man crashed your peace and flirted through the appetizer course like it was a sport."

"I didn't think he'd come," Skylar said with a shrug, like that somehow made it better.

Then Eden appeared, wine in one hand, dish towel in the other, still looking like a goddess even in sweats. "Jayson thinks Sterling should run for mayor," she muttered just as her husband wandered in from the den.

"Hey!" Jayson said, oblivious to the storm brewing. "I really like that Sterling guy. He's doing big things—expanding his wellness brand into the city. Real smart play."

Eden's eyes narrowed as she plastered on a tight, sarcastic smile. "*Jayson, honey,* can you help us clear the table?" Her voice was velvet-wrapped poison.

Jayson blinked. "Uh—sure?"

As he shuffled off, she turned to us. "Do you see what I'm dealing with? The *one time* he's fully present, he decides to co-sign the *villain.*"

Quinn huffed. "Read the room, Jayson. This is not a TED Talk about brand partnerships."

Skylar buried her face in her hands, groaning. "This is why I didn't say anything."

"This is why you *should've,*" I snapped. "Girl, you have Titus—*Titus*—show up looking like fine wine and emotional maturity, and then you let *Sterling* just slither in like we were doing a live taping of *The Bachelor: Harlem Edition.*"

Eden nodded in solemn agreement. "One man brought a bottle of wine and quiet clarity. The other brought ego and cologne."

"And chaos," Quinn added. "Don't forget chaos."

Skylar looked up, cheeks flushed, somewhere between guilt and disbelief. "I didn't think it would be a big deal."

"You invited your past and your possible future to the same party," I said. "That *is* the big deal."

The three of us stood in silence for a beat, letting it settle between us like the last note of a song we weren't sure how to follow up.

Finally, Quinn crossed her arms. "We're not mad. We just want to make sure you see what we see."

"Which is?" Skylar asked, her voice small.

Eden answered for us all. "That Titus came to *show up*. Sterling came to *show off*. And only one of those men left quietly, without needing to prove anything."

Skylar exhaled slowly, the truth of it written all over her face.

And in that late-night stillness, beneath the hum of the fridge and Elias's snoring crescendo, it felt like the emotional mess of the evening had finally begun to settle—one truth at a time.

"So...?" I said, eyes locked on Skylar, waiting—daring—her to finally give us the truth.

She froze mid-chew, guilt flickering across her face like a faulty streetlight. "Umm..." Her fork slowed as if maybe dragging out the bite would buy her a few more seconds of peace. "Remember when I told you I bumped into Sterling at the coffee shop before Thanksgiving?"

Eden raised an eyebrow, her tone sharp with suspicion. "*Coffee shop?*" she repeated, like she'd just caught a lie with a receipt in hand.

Quinn leaned forward, giving Skylar that slow, lawyerly once-over, her face already halfway into cross-examination mode.

I folded my arms and planted a hip against the kitchen counter, giving Skylar my signature *don't-play-with-me* stare. "Oh, I remember. You said *bumped into* like it was fate. What you didn't say was that it was a *scheduled bump.*"

Skylar winced.

Busted.

I sighed, lips pursed, disappointment sliding through my words like vinegar. "So what was the plan, Sky? Invite the ghost of boyfriends past to Friendsgiving and see if your new man could survive the heat? Or was this about not knowing which man you wanted at your table?"

"D-R-A-M-A," Eden murmured, sipping her wine and nodding solemnly like we were in a courtroom and I had just delivered a closing argument.

Skylar's jaw tensed, eyes flashing with that familiar mix of defensiveness and deflection—right before vulnerability softened her entire face. I knew that look. I'd seen it when she ghosted therapy after two sessions. When she lied about being over someone only to cry in the shower three nights later. She didn't need a roast. She needed the truth spoken with love.

Still, I wasn't backing down.

Skylar batted her lashes in that "don't be mad at me" way, but none of us were giving her the sympathy she was fishing for.

"What's going on, Sky?" Quinn asked, her voice steady but stern. "What are you really hiding?"

I grabbed four red Solo cups from the counter—refusing to

dirty one more dish—and walked them to the fridge. Skylar ducked behind me, suddenly very interested in beverage options.

"*Coquito or cider?*" she asked, the deflection practically screaming off her lips.

"Not coquito," I groaned. "Me and my mom's recipe already had our showdown earlier. My stomach's still in recovery."

We all cracked up—because that coquito was like dessert and danger in a glass—but the tension lingered underneath the laughter. We carried our drinks into the living room, slipping off our *chancletas* and curling up under throw blankets like teenage girls at a sleepover, though the wisdom and wounds between us made this gathering sacred.

The flicker of candlelight danced off the near-empty dessert trays and wine-stained napkins on the coffee table. The air still smelled faintly of cinnamon, vanilla, and something unfinished.

"*Chica*," I said, turning to Skylar, voice low, eyes locked, "la verdad y nada más que la verdad. The truth and nothing but the truth. No detours. Just say it."

She let out a deep sigh—the kind you only release when you're tired of running and realize the only way out is through. Quinn and Eden leaned in like seasoned detectives, ready to take notes.

Skylar finally set her fork down with a *clink*. Her eyes shifted to the window like freedom might be hiding in the fire escape.

Then she spoke.

The coffee shop "coincidence," she confessed, wasn't so coincidental. Sterling had slid into her DMs the night of the charity gala—*the same night she met Titus.* The charm was familiar, practiced, like the cologne he always wore too heavily. She brushed him off at first, caught up in the slow bloom of conversations with Titus. But after Titus opened up about his past—about Deuce and Kayla—she made space for uncertainty... and for Sterling.

"Just a few polite messages," she said, her voice low. "Surface-level. Platonic."

Then came a couple of lunches. A few *almost* dates. And before she knew it, she'd invited him to *Friendsgiving* without fully unpacking what that meant.

"And then," she added with an eye roll, "I casually invited him. It wasn't a grand gesture—I was just being nice."

I gave her a long, deadpan blink. "You *casually invited* your ex—the same one who ghosted emotional maturity and still thinks foreplay is optional—to the one night a year we pour wine, overshare, and toast to healing?"

She winced again. "It felt harmless at the time."

Eden let out a long, tired sigh, her diamond earrings catching the low light as she shook her head. "*Skylar Madison,*" she said, voice soft but laced with steel, "you gotta stop confusing *closure* with *curiosity.*"

"That part," Quinn added, her tone like Sunday morning *amen* energy. She even snapped her fingers.

Skylar went quiet, chewing on her bottom lip, the same way she did at the DMV when she realized she forgot her wallet. She was unraveling, and she knew it.

"It wasn't serious," she mumbled, more to herself than to us.

I blinked. "*Not serious?*" My voice climbed like it had somewhere to go. "Girl, that man was peacocking all over the party. He acted like Titus was stepping on his turf just by breathing the same air."

Skylar groaned and yanked the blanket over her head like it was a force field. "*I cannot with you right now,*" she muttered from beneath the throw, voice muffled but unmistakably irritated.

Before any of us could press her again, a sleepy voice cut through the moment like a record scratch.

"Facts." It was Elias—half-asleep in the armchair, head barely lifted.

"Sterling was definitely marking territory," he croaked. "It was giving possessive energy. Not platonic ex energy."

Skylar peeked out from under the blanket like a mole catching sunlight. "Who *asked* you?"

Elias shrugged, eyes barely open. "Y'all loud as hell. I figured I was already invited."

Quinn snorted. Eden rolled her eyes. And I just sat there, sipping my cider, watching Skylar wrestle with what we already knew:

Sometimes it's not about what you *didn't* mean to do.

It's about what you *chose* not to admit.

I rolled my eyes so hard I saw next week.

"Bitch move from an asshole," I muttered, grabbing my cider-filled wine glass and taking a long, judgment-flavored sip.

Skylar groaned and sank deeper into her blanket cave, as if cotton and fleece could shield her from the truth. But we weren't letting her off easy—not tonight. Not with me and Elias tagging every emotional foul like seasoned referees in the championship game of Skylar's love life.

"Alejandra Catalina Herrera!" Elias gasped, mock-offended, clutching his pearls like someone's dramatic auntie before we all cracked up.

"*Biiitch!*" Quinn added for punctuation, dragging the syllable out like it was her love language.

Now even Tatum and Jayson were fully locked in, their earlier side conversations forgotten.

"E," I said, turning to Elias, "you remember that clown when we were in college—the one who'd ghost Sky all week, then show up at her window like he was in a low-budget John Legend video?"

"More like a low-budget Boyz II Men video." Quinn teased.

Elias nodded, the memory hitting like a bad rerun. "I lost count of how many times I had to drive to that overpriced ice cream spot just to buy her that damn *vanilla with chocolate-covered Swiss almonds*. Every time he pulled a stunt, Skylar went into full emotional lockdown mode."

"Remember when he asked LaToya out at Skylar's *Sweet Sixteen*?" I added, glaring at Skylar, who tried to hide her laughter behind her cheesecake fork.

"That damn LaToya was a straight-up *thot*," Quinn muttered.

"*Not thot*, babe..." Tatum choked on his drink, turning to her with a half-laugh, half-warning.

Quinn gave him the look. You know the one.

"And *Skylar* was locked in my room for a whole weekend," I continued. "Curtains drawn, playing *Lady Sings the Blues* at full blast like it was her personal anthem of despair."

"I still have PTSD from *Lady Sings the Blues*," Elias groaned, tossing a pillow at Skylar, who had finally peeked out from under the blanket, laughing.

"We *all* have PTSD from *Lady Sings the Blues*," Eden chimed in, trying—and failing—to maintain her irritation at Jayson, who was now chuckling beside her.

"True," Jayson added. "E barely lets Billie Holiday play in the house anymore."

"Don't push it," Eden said sweetly, her diamond studs catching the light as she reclaimed her wine glass.

Skylar sat up straighter now, her curls now loose and tousled, cheesecake plate still balanced on her lap like a makeshift shield. "Okay—*enough* about Sterling," she sighed, her tone edged with exhaustion but not quite ready for surrender. "What about *Titus*?"

Nice pivot, I thought. Not slick. But I let her have it—for now.

"You looked *pleasantly surprised* to see him," I said, watching her closely over the rim of my glass.

"I was," she admitted, her voice quieter now. There was a softness around her edges I hadn't seen in a long time. Her eyes went a little dreamy, as if she was replaying his entrance like a movie scene. "I didn't think he'd actually show. I mentioned Friendsgiving over a month ago, back when..."

"Back before you found out he was a grown-ass man with responsibilities?" I grinned, nudging her.

"Back before the truth scared you," Quinn added, arching one perfectly shaped brow.

Skylar rolled her eyes but didn't argue. She dipped her fork into her cheesecake again, smiling—small and wistful.

"He looked happy to see me," she murmured, almost to herself.

"*And women say we're the ones playing games,*" Jayson muttered from the corner.

Eden gave him a pointed stare. "That is your final strike tonight. Maybe just... go back to scrolling."

Jayson raised his hands in mock surrender and sank deeper into the couch beside her.

I looked back at Skylar. That look in her eyes—it wasn't just nostalgia. It was *hope.* Quiet, tender, cautious hope. The kind that blooms when something real surprises you. The kind she hadn't let herself feel in a long, long time.

But before I could press her further, Skylar turned, ever the deflector, and locked eyes with Elias.

"Speaking of looking *happy*," she said with a sly grin. "*E*, were you flirting with Lupe tonight?"

"*Caught them exchanging numbers*," Jayson snitched from the sidelines.

Elias turned toward him like he'd just been betrayed on national television.

"*Really*, bro?" he said. "That's how you're gonna do me?"

Tatum shook his head, mock-disappointed. "You let him *in*, man. Rookie mistake."

Eden seized the moment and forked the last bite of Skylar's cheesecake before she could notice.

Elias ran a hand through his thick waves, trying to mask the slight grin tugging at the corners of his mouth. The string lights above the kitchen island bathed him in soft, amber glow, making him look like he'd walked out of a Hallmark movie and into our group chat.

"She was... interesting," he said finally, voice lower, more thoughtful than usual.

"Interesting?" I echoed, arching a brow. "Dime más, papí."

Skylar leaned in too, her curiosity matching mine.

Elias swirled the ice in his glass, his posture a little more relaxed now. "We talked. About family. About how neither of us ever really fit in the way people expected us to. About trying to figure out who you are when everyone else already has a version of you in their head."

He paused, his gaze distant for a beat.

"That hit," he said simply.

The room fell quiet—not heavy, just full. One of those moments where you realize maybe you're not the only one trying to figure it all out.

Skylar looked at me. I looked at Quinn. And for the first time in a long while, all of us were sitting in the truth of where we were, who we were, and what we still wanted.

We all leaned in, the teasing ebbing away as the room settled into something softer, something sacred. The shift was subtle but unmistakable—the laughter faded, and in its place, a stillness wrapped around us like a familiar quilt. This was our rhythm. The late-night quiet, wrapped in leftover warmth and layered truths. Vulnerability didn't knock here—it just walked in, uninvited but always welcome.

"E," Skylar said gently, her voice lower now, "you like her."

Elias didn't flinch. Didn't fumble. Just smiled—quiet and crooked—and let the silence hold.

For once, none of us filled the pause. We let it linger. Let it speak.

Then, Elias leaned forward, his forearms resting on his knees, eyes reflecting the flickering candlelight. "I spent a lot of years feeling... uncomfortable in my own skin," he began. "It got louder when you and Luz were born. The differences between me and Papi—they were obvious."

My heart pinched for him. He was the first of us. Mami was just sixteen when she had Elias in Caguas, and Papi—only seventeen—wasn't the one who made her a mother. That part of our family history was rarely spoken about in detail. Not because it was shameful, but because it carried weight. Still, Elias always bore it with quiet grace.

"Mami told us Eli was her first love," Elias said, his voice thick with memory. "He was from Loíza, visiting family in Caguas while his abuela was sick."

I gave a dry chuckle, nudging some levity into the moment. "Meanwhile, poor Papi was head over heels and getting *ignored* by Señorita Lucia like a side character in her novela."

That made Elias smile, but he kept going, his tone softer now, nostalgic.

"She said she and Eli used to walk the beach every afternoon—just talkin'. Dreamin'. She was falling for him, hard. But when his abuela passed, he went back to Loíza with his mom. Just like that."

The room grew still again, all of us listening not just to his words, but to the *weight* of them.

"She was devastated," Elias continued. "And a few weeks later, she found out she was pregnant. Her family and Eli's had been close, but he was gone. That's when she told Papi."

He looked up then, voice steady but heavy with reverence. "Papi didn't even blink. He told her he loved her, and that if she'd let him, he'd raise her child like his own. They were married a month before I was born."

"Papi sure was something," I said, my voice warm with pride.

"The *best*," Quinn chimed in, pressing her hand to her chest. "I always say, if every girl had a dad like Mateo Herrera, the world would be full of powerhouses and princesses."

"He *was*, and still is," Elias agreed, nodding slowly. "I may have looked different... but I never felt unloved. Not once."

His voice cracked just slightly as the emotion crept in, and then the tears came—quiet, steady. Not from sadness, but from *knowing*. From the weight of being loved fully, intentionally.

I leaned in, my eyes soft. "You know that Yankee tradition still lives. Just Papi and E, every year—one game, minimum. Sometimes they even fly out to away games just to keep the streak going."

Skylar perked up, her face warming with familiarity. "I remember that beat-up Yankee cap you used to wear all the time when we were kids."

Elias chuckled, wiping at his eyes. "Don't hate on the cap."

"That thing was more *gray* than Yankee blue," Eden laughed.

"Facts," Tatum added. "I swear you wore that dusty relic to the game with me and TJ last year."

Elias shrugged with a smirk. "It's called *character*, my friends."

"Sure," Eden teased. "It's also called *retirement.*"

The laughter swirled around us like a breeze, lifting the mood but leaving behind something grounding. Love. History. Home.

Elias sat back, staring into his now-melted ice. "Life has a way of twisting the story, but sometimes it ends up more beautiful than you planned."

I smiled, heart full, watching my brother—his resilience, his tenderness, the grace with which he carried our family's story.

"I just hope I find someone like Mateo Herrera—or his incredible son Elias Herrera—to help me write mine," I said, voice soft, eyes glinting with both longing and pride.

Elias shook his head, laughing gently. "Well, little sister... those are some *big-ass* shoes to fill. But you're a Herrera. You'll figure it out."

And in that moment, surrounded by the scent of coquito, the echo of Billie Holiday in our bones, and the steady glow of string lights above our heads, I knew one thing for sure:

Love—real love—wasn't just in our past.

It was sitting right here with us, worn Yankee cap and all.

26

Allie

It was a cold December afternoon, and the aroma of Mami's favorite holiday candles mingled with the brisk chill that swept in every time the front door opened. Allie's mother's house stood as a warm beacon, decorated with garlands, twinkling lights, and the faint hum of a salsa playlist emanating from the kitchen. The air inside smelled faintly of cinnamon and roasted coffee, a comforting contrast to the icy wind outside.

"Mami, why do you always have to empty the supermarket of every item when you go to the store?" I muttered, my voice heavy with mock exasperation. My arms strained under the weight of yet another grocery bag—one of what felt like a hundred—as I trudged in from the car. Setting it down on the kitchen counter with an exaggerated thud, I shot Mami a stern look, my frustration barely masking the amusement bubbling underneath.

Mami, standing at the counter sorting through her bounty, didn't miss a beat. She raised a perfectly arched eyebrow and responded with a dramatic flourish. "¡Ay Dios mío!

Alejandra, cuidado, cambia esa cara, fix your face" she said, her tone sharp but softened by the smile that crept into her eyes. She began organizing the bags with precision, separating produce, pantry staples, and holiday treats. The fluorescent kitchen lights glinted off her earrings as she moved, a force of nature in her element.

Luz, my older sister, followed close behind, balancing an overstuffed bag of her own. "Mami, she's right," she chimed in, her breath coming in short puffs from the effort. "You shop like it's the end of the world. It's just you and Papi here. What are you going to do with all this stuff?"

Mami ignored the chorus of complaints, her hands busy as she inspected a carton of eggs and rearranged cans of pigeon peas. Her concentration was unbroken, even as we grumbled. This was her ritual, after all—a monthly pilgrimage to every store she deemed worthy, stocking up on Papi's favorite cookies, her beloved spices, and a stash of treats for her grandchildren, Ari and Alec.

Despite our protests, we both knew we loved these moments—the chaos of shopping, the arguments over which brand of coffee was best, the shared laughter as Mami tossed yet another "essential" item into the cart. This wasn't just grocery shopping; it was a Herrera women's tradition that had been forged over a decade since Mami and Papi moved to New Jersey.

"Enough about my groceries," Mami said suddenly, snapping us out of our routine complaints. Her hands paused mid-motion, holding a pack of rice. "Tell me, what are you two up to?" She glanced at us expectantly, her sharp gaze softening with curiosity.

"Mami, there's nothing to tell," Luz replied, rolling her

eyes slightly. "Ari and Alec keep me busy when I'm not at the office dealing with doctors and patients."

"So busy that you missed Friendsgiving a few weeks ago?" I teased, raising an eyebrow. Luz shot me a glare.

"Allie! How many times do I have to apologize?" Luz's voice climbed an octave, and I couldn't help but laugh.

"Apology not accepted until I get a fresh batch of pasteles," I quipped, a sly grin spreading across my face.

"How was the Friendsgiving?" Mami asked, her hands resuming their work but her attention clearly on us.

Luz and I exchanged a knowing glance, mischief flickering in our eyes. Mami caught on instantly, her interest piqued. "¡Díganme todo!" she commanded, the familiar cadence of her voice prompting a laugh from both of us.

"Well," I began, dragging out the word for effect. "Tu hijo, your son, Elias..."

Before I could spill any further, Elias—my older brother— strolled into the kitchen, his presence announced by the exaggerated clearing of his throat. "Leave it to the Herrera shopping adventure to gossip about people's lives," he interrupted, a wide grin lighting up his face.

"Hola, Mami!" Elias exclaimed as he enveloped her in a bear hug, lifting her off the ground slightly. Mami laughed, swatting at him playfully as he placed a kiss on her cheek.

Without missing a beat, he began grabbing items from the bags and stacking them neatly on the shelves. His presence filled the room with a familiar warmth, adding another layer of comfort to the busy kitchen.

The kitchen buzzed with energy as we continued unpacking groceries, the warmth of Mami's holiday candles mixing with the savory scent of food yet to be prepared. Outside, the

December cold pressed against the windows, but inside, the atmosphere was as lively and warm as ever.

"Continúa. Mi hijo, Elias?" Mami asked with a sly grin, her eyes flickering with curiosity. She leaned slightly against the counter, her hands busy arranging bags of rice and cans of beans as she prompted us to tell the full story. Luz and I exchanged a quick glance, our gaze following Elias as he moved around the kitchen, within earshot but trying to appear aloof while putting items away.

"Well, Mami," I began, savoring the moment, "I think he may have met someone he's fond of at our Friendsgiving event. Between his thick eyelashes, wavy hair, and award-winning pernil, I think he might have impressed a certain young lady who was there."

"Alejandra, always laying it on thick," Elias quipped, his voice steady but laced with amusement. Luz and I erupted into giggles, making no effort to hide our enjoyment.

"I struck up a nice conversation with one of Allie's friends," Elias admitted casually, a small smile tugging at the corners of his mouth. "We exchanged numbers and have had a few conversations since then."

"Nice conversation?" Luz echoed, raising an eyebrow. She shot me a knowing look before adding, "Just how many conversations have you had?" Her tone was teasing but inquisitive.

"And were they all just conversations, or did I hear you met up for coffee once or twice?" I pressed further, leaning against the counter as if to corner him with my questions. I already knew most of the answers—Elias practically lived at my brownstone in Brooklyn whenever he came to New York for business. Having my older brother close was a joy

I didn't hide. My home became his home, which gave me ample opportunity to pry into his life and enjoy his cooking whenever he decided to take over my kitchen.

"I am not entertaining this inquisition," Elias declared, shaking his head as if to ward off our playful interrogation.

"If I'm correct," I added with a smirk, "they've had one coffee date, one dinner date in the last two weeks, and more than a handful of conversations." My words spilled out with deliberate mischief, earning me a dramatic eye roll from Elias.

"I'm staying at a hotel next time I'm in New York," he threatened, his voice full of mock indignation.

"No, no, no," I pleaded, hands raised in mock surrender. "I'll mind my business, I promise. But I absolutely love seeing you dating and having fun."

Elias tossed a bag of beans at me, his lips twitching in a suppressed smile. "Lo que sea," he muttered, "whatever, whatever," brushing past me to grab another bag of groceries.

"Mami, are you really going to let your favorite son hide behind you?" Luz teased as Elias darted behind Mami with a playful laugh.

"No te preocupes, mi amorcito," Mami said, shielding Elias with exaggerated protectiveness. Then, with a mischievous glint in her eye, she added, "Don't worry, my love. They're next on my list."

Elias peeked out from behind Mami and stuck his tongue out at Luz and me, his grin wide and triumphant.

"Did you ask your beautiful daughters when the last time was that they've been on a date?" he asked, shifting the spotlight to us with expert precision. His question landed like a well-placed dart, and Mami's eyes immediately sparkled with interest.

Luz and I exchanged a panicked glance, silently wishing we could disappear into the mountain of grocery bags surrounding us. The tables had turned, and Elias had won this round, leaving us to brace for Mami's inevitable interrogation.

The kitchen was alive with the usual blend of chatter and clinking dishes, but the energy shifted when Luz immediately threw up her hands. "Don't look at me," she said, her tone defensive yet playful. "I don't have any stories to tell you. I just told you, when I'm not dealing with..."

Elias cut her off with a dramatic flourish, his voice dripping with mockery. "Patients and doctors. You're busy with Ari and Alec. That story is getting old, Luz." He shook his head in feigned exasperation, earning a glare from Luz, who looked ready to defend herself further.

Mami, sensing Luz's silent plea for mercy, turned her attention to me, her brown eyes alight with curiosity. "Alejandra? You know all the juicy details of Elias' so-called love life. What's going on with you, mi amor?"

The jig was up. Mami's gaze fixed on me, a mix of desperation for a story and genuine concern. Luz and Elias, now united in their intrigue, looked at me expectantly.

I tried to avoid the inevitable by busying myself on the far side of the kitchen, grabbing a few stray items that needed to be put away. The ceramic jars clinked together as I worked, feigning focus.

"Allie?" Mami called, her voice cutting through the room with gentle authority. Her tone left no room for escape. I froze mid-motion, the air in the kitchen suddenly thick with anticipation. All eyes were on me now.

"There's nothing to tell, Mami," I said, turning back to face them with a practiced smile. "I've been busy working on a new exhibit at the gallery and an installation at a museum in Chicago. With everything going on at work, I don't really have time for a love life."

The look on Luz and Elias' faces told me they weren't buying a word of it. They exchanged a glance, eyebrows raised, as if to say, "Seriously?"

Mami, unimpressed with my deflection, stepped closer. "Alejandra," she said, her voice soft but firm, "you can tell that story to Skylar and the girls, and even your siblings, but please don't lie to tu madre." She reached out, her hand brushing down the long braids framing my face before cupping my cheeks. Her eyes searched mine, filled with tenderness and a touch of sadness.

"You've made everything and everyone else a priority for so long. What are you afraid of?" she asked, her voice barely above a whisper. Her words hung in the air, undeniable and heavy with truth.

I opened my mouth to answer, but the words caught in my throat. Mami's gaze softened even more, as if she could see the shadows of an unspoken story etched across my face. I felt a familiar knot tighten in my chest, the kind that came whenever I thought about the parts of my past I kept locked away.

Mami sighed, her hands dropping from my face but not before squeezing my shoulders gently. "You cannot keep your heart closed off forever," she said, her words a quiet decree that settled over all of us. The silence in the room deepened, but it wasn't uncomfortable. It was reflective, the kind that made you confront things you'd rather leave buried.

Elias shuffled his feet awkwardly, breaking the stillness. Luz busied herself with the groceries again, but I knew Mami's words had landed just as surely on them as they had on me. And for a brief moment, the kitchen, with its warm lights and lingering holiday scents, became a space not just for family chatter but for unspoken truths.

27

Skylar

The cold winter air clung to me as I approached Doña Herrera's house, the warm light spilling out of the windows like an invitation. I could almost taste the comfort of her home-cooked meal before stepping inside. Her pollo guisado — Puerto Rican stewed chicken with its rich, savory flavors — was calling my name, a culinary memory etched from countless evenings spent at Allie's house after school. And if that wasn't enough, the promise of arroz con dulce, her spiced coconut rice pudding with cinnamon, cloves, and raisins, sealed the deal. It was heaven in a bowl, and I was determined to snag an extra helping.

As I neared the door, the familiar aroma of cinnamon and spices wrapped around me like a hug, setting my heart at ease even before I stepped inside. Through the frosted glass, I caught glimpses of the Herrera family in their natural rhythm. Papi and little Ari twirled down the hallway, salsa music flowing from the speakers as they laughed and spun with carefree delight. In the kitchen, Doña Herrera moved with her usual purpose, a wooden spoon in hand as she bustled between pots and pans, tasting, stirring, and adding her magic touch. Luz darted back and forth, setting the dining room table with plates and utensils, while Elias crouched on the living room floor, racing Hot Wheels with Alec.

I knocked lightly before letting myself in, my arrival announced by a chorus of greetings.

"Hey, Sky," Elias called, looking up from his race car adventures with a grin. Alec, not to be outdone, piped up with an enthusiastic, "Titi Sky!" He pushed his tiny car with all his might, trying to beat his uncle to the finish line.

Papi paused his dance with Ari to embrace me in a warm hug. "Ahí está mi niña linda, there is my pretty girl, Skylar." His affection was unmissable as he kissed my cheek. Ari squealed with delight, her energy infectious as she wrapped her little arms around me.

"Titi Sky!" she exclaimed, prancing around me with a wide smile. "Dance with us!" She pulled me into the hallway, where Papi resumed his playful moves. Ari twirled, her eyes sparkling as she took in my lime-green, fuzzy oversized sweater draped off one shoulder.

"I love your sweater," she said with envy. Her tiny fingers brushed the soft fabric, and I laughed.

"Allie," I teased as I looked toward the kitchen, "I think Ari has her eyes on my clothes. I'm not sure I'll leave here with my sweater intact."

Luz's laughter rang out as she waved me over. "Skylar, come help me in the kitchen before Ari takes the sweater off your back."

Stepping into the warm, bustling kitchen, I was greeted by Doña Herrera's kind smile. "Skylar, how are you, my dear?" she asked, her voice rich with warmth as she stirred the pot of stewed chicken.

"Hola, Mami Herrera," I said, kissing her cheek. "I'm so much better now that I'm here with you, your pollo guisado, and your arroz con dulce."

"You'll have to fight Luz for the arroz con dulce," Doña Herrera chimed in. Luz gave me a playful but stern look as she reached for a stack of plates.

"No need to fight," Doña Herrera said with a knowing smile. "I made plenty for both of you to take some home."

"Whew, I was scared for you, Luz," I teased, winking at her.

Allie's chuckle came from behind me as she joined the conversation. "Skylar, you talk so much smack. You've been scared of Luz from day one."

"Who wouldn't be scared of Luz?" I replied with mock seriousness. "Look at her!"

"Yep, all five-foot-two inches of her," Allie teased back. "So intimidating."

"Don't let my height fool you," Luz said with a smirk as she handed me a stack of plates and gently nudged me toward the dining room. "I've got big sister energy, and you know it."

Laughing, I followed her lead, feeling the familiar joy of being wrapped up in the love and harmony of the Herrera family. It wasn't just a meal I had come for; it was a connection, a tradition, and a sense of belonging that I cherished deeply.

The warmth of Doña Herrera's dining room wrapped around us like a comforting embrace as we shared stories over plates piled high with stewed chicken, rice, and fried maduros. The table, long and worn from years of family gatherings, was a testament to countless meals filled with laughter, love, and the occasional interrogation. Just as I was about to savor my second helping of pollo guisado, Doña Herrera's voice pierced through the chatter.

"Skylar, what happened with 'Two Kids Titus'?" she asked with a raised eyebrow, her tone light but probing.

I froze mid-bite, my fork hovering in the air. Elias, caught off guard, nearly choked on a sweet fried maduro, while Allie pressed her lips together, fighting back laughter. Even Papi, ever composed, had a smirk playing at the corners of his mouth. I cleared my throat, stalling for time.

"Umm, Titus is fine," I offered cautiously, trying to keep my tone neutral.

Doña Herrera wasn't having it. "Just fine? You know I need more than just fine," she said, her piercing gaze making it clear she wouldn't let me off the hook so easily.

"Your turn," Allie chimed in, her knowing look adding fuel to the fire. "She came for me earlier today," she added with a playful grin.

"Alejandra, I am not done with you," Doña Herrera warned, her tone firm but affectionate. She quickly turned her attention back to me. "Skylar?"

I sighed, resigning myself to the inevitable. "Well, I'm sure you know we reconnected at the Friendsgiving event a few weeks ago," I admitted, shifting in my seat. "And we've had a few good conversations since then."

"Skylar, did you apologize to Titus?" Doña Herrera's playful demeanor softened, her question striking a deeper chord. Her words made me pause, the weight of her question settling over the table.

Caught off guard, I nearly choked on a mouthful of chicken

stew. "Yes, Mami Herrera," I finally admitted. "I apologized for giving him the cold shoulder."

Doña Herrera tilted her head, her expression a mix of warmth and sternness. "And for not being mature enough to see a good thing when it's right in front of your face," she added matter-of-factly.

I dropped my gaze, thoroughly chastised. "Yes, ma'am," I mumbled, my cheeks flushing.

"Mami, do you feed us your home-cooked food to disarm us before you swoop in and lecture us?" Allie quipped, sparing me from further scrutiny.

Doña Herrera's eyes twinkled as she replied, "No, mi amor. I'm trying to protect Skylar from herself." She turned to me, her voice softening as she continued, "If I hadn't been wise enough to see the man in front of me, I wouldn't be sitting here, surrounded by this blessing of a family."

Her gaze shifted to Papi, seated beside her. He reached for her hand, their fingers intertwining as he leaned over to kiss her cheek. The moment was so tender, so full of love, it left the room in a hush of admiration.

As I watched them, my thoughts drifted to Elias. After Friendsgiving, he had opened up about connecting with Lupe over shared feelings of being different in their families. Lupe, adopted, had shared how she sometimes felt like an outsider despite the love surrounding her. Their conversation had struck a chord with Elias. He had confided in me how he once wondered why he looked so different from Papi—his almond-shaped hazel eyes with green flecks a stark contrast to Papi's round, deep brown gaze.

It was then Elias revealed what he'd discovered: Papi wasn't his biological father. Yet in every way that mattered,

Papi had always been his dad—a man who chose to love him unconditionally, even before he was born. Papi's relentless love had erased any doubt, replacing it with a bond unshaken by blood.

"Skylar," Doña Herrera said, her voice pulling me back to the present. "I want you to experience the blessing of the unexpected." Her words carried the weight of lived wisdom, her eyes shining with the love and hope she held for me.

I swallowed hard, her words echoing in my heart as the room buzzed back to life. The smell of stewed chicken lingered in the air, mingling with the warmth of laughter and the promise of love that filled the Herrera home.

28

Titus

The crackling fire in the brick fireplace cast a warm glow over the living room of my brownstone, its amber light flickering against the exposed brick walls and hardwood floors. The chill of the evening was no match for the cozy ambiance that filled the space. I leaned back into the plush cushions of my sofa, savoring the rare sense of peace that only came from being surrounded by those who felt like home. The scent of wood smoke mingled with the lingering aroma of Southern comfort food, and the laughter of my long-time friend and Morehouse brother Langston and his wife Zora filled the room like a melody.

Langston sat at the end of the sofa, his arm draped protectively around Zora as she cozied up next to him, her laughter soft yet vibrant. The two of them had managed a rare escape from the chaos of parenting for the weekend, leaving the grandkids in the loving care of Mama Hughes. It was a treat to have them both here, especially after Zora had joined Langston in New York following a hectic week of meetings with investors and developers. My soul felt full from her home cooking and the hours we'd spent sharing stories, catching up, and simply enjoying each other's presence.

On the coffee table in front of us sat the remnants of a Sunday feast—a spread of fried fish, creamy potato salad, perfectly seasoned green beans, and cornbread so buttery it practically melted in your mouth. Langston's plate now only held a generous helping of peach cobbler, his favorite dessert, still steaming as he dug in with deliberate enjoyment. Zora, never one to miss an opportunity to tease him, reached over and grabbed the spoon from his hand, scooping up a large bite of cobbler before he could protest. The indignation in Langston's eyes was comically betrayed by the affection that softened his expression.

"You just can't let me have anything to myself, can you?" Langston grumbled, watching as Zora savored the bite with a smug smile.

"Sharing is caring," she replied cheekily, her eyes twinkling as she leaned back against him. Over the din of the football game playing on the TV, she turned her attention to me, her tone suddenly laced with curiosity and just a hint of mischief.

"So, when do I get to meet Ms. Skylar Madison?" she asked, her voice carrying the kind of playful sarcasm that told me she'd been eavesdropping on more than one of my conversations with Langston.

Langston's gaze flicked to me, his expression apologetic as if to say, *Good luck with this one.* I cleared my throat, stalling for time. "Umm," I began, but Zora cut me off with a raised brow and a grin.

"I'm assuming things are moving forward with Skylar," she prodded, scooping another bite of cobbler as Langston looked on in mild despair.

"Sky and I have been taking things slow," I said, carefully choosing my words. "We both realized we could have handled things differently. She apologized for shutting down after learning I have children. I made it clear that I would never apologize for having a life filled with two beautiful kids. But I also let her know I understand her initial hesitation and reluctance to move forward."

Zora's wide-eyed expression was a mixture of intrigue and skepticism. "Hmmm... you know it's going to take a lot for me to like her," she admitted, though her teasing tone couldn't completely mask the protective edge beneath her words.

"Zo, give the man a break," Langston interjected, shaking his head. "And fall back on my peach cobbler, will you?" He looked at her in mock despair as she defiantly took yet another bite, her smile growing wider.

"You're lucky I love you," she quipped, leaning up to kiss him on the cheek. Langston rolled his eyes, but his smirk betrayed his amusement.

I couldn't help but laugh, the warmth of their banter and the firelight cocooning us in a moment that felt both fleeting and timeless. In that space, surrounded by love and light, the uncertainties of life felt a little less daunting.

29

Skylar

Allie and I wound our way through the tight maze of tables inside Mike's Coffee Shop, the kind of old-school Brooklyn diner where the coffee's strong, the waitresses don't smile unless they mean it, and the booths still bear the initials of teenagers from three decades ago. The scent of sizzling bacon mixed with toasted bagels and burnt espresso hung in the air like a familiar blanket.

We had finally convinced the waitress to let us keep the back corner booth, even though the third seat at our party remained conspicuously empty. Eden was now twenty—no, twenty-two—minutes late, and we'd already given up two tables trying to hold out for her.

"This is so typical of Eden," I muttered under my breath, fidgeting with the chipped edge of the table.

"I'm starving," Allie said, her voice a little sharper than usual, as she pulled her hoodie sleeve up to glance at her watch.

Mike's was a neighborhood staple, tucked neatly on the corner of DeKalb and St. James, right next to the old pizzeria we used to haunt after school. The coffee shop hadn't changed since we were kids—still rocking the faded green booths, the dusty pie display, and a laminated menu so well-worn you could almost see through it. It was unpolished, no-frills, and familiar in a way that wrapped itself around you if you let it.

"Let's just order without her," I suggested, already halfway to committing to the blueberry pancakes and turkey sausage.

But Allie, loyal to a fault, shook her head. "She texted. Said she's close. Give her a few more."

The door chimed then, and speak of the devil—Eden swept in like a commercial break in the middle of a documentary. All movement and sound, as if the diner had been waiting for her arrival to kick up the drama.

She was a striking contrast to the setting, all high-shine and curated chaos. Her jet-black pixie cut looked freshly trimmed, her diamond studs caught the light like camera flashes, and her tailored leather jacket clung perfectly to the body-hugging black dress beneath it. The heels alone could've bought a week's worth of brunches. She looked like she was late for a rooftop cocktail hour, not joining two friends for pancakes in a booth etched with "K+M 4EVER."

"I thought we were grabbing breakfast, not auditioning for a music video," Allie said, tugging playfully at her oversized Knicks hoodie and black leggings.

I raised an eyebrow. "A heads-up that we were attending Fashion Week would've been nice."

Eden didn't even blink. She slid into the booth beside Allie with the grace of someone who hadn't just blown us off three weeks ago without so much as a text. "Parking was a nightmare," she huffed, draping her coat on the seat like we were in Tribeca instead of Clinton Hill.

And just like that, the air shifted.

It wasn't just that she was late. It was how she moved—like we were background noise to whatever story she was starring in. Like we hadn't planned that joint mother-daughter brunch that she ghosted without warning. No explanation. No apology. Just radio silence, leaving me to deal with awkward stares from church ladies and *both* our mothers, including Ms. Claudette, who made sure I knew I'd been left holding the bag.

And now? Eden strolled in, fresh-faced and glowing, like nothing had happened.

"Well, Eden, I'm *so* glad you could join us," Allie offered, handing her a menu with that gentle peacekeeper tone she'd perfected over decades of our nonsense.

I sipped my now-cold coffee, resisting the urge to let my sarcasm off the leash. Eden had been floating in and out for weeks, her texts spotty, her energy detached. She was here now—but only technically. Her phone sat face-up on the table like it had somewhere more important to be, and her gaze flitted between us with polite interest, but no real investment.

The food arrived—plates of golden pancakes, fluffy scrambled eggs, glistening bacon, and sausage crisped just right. It should've felt comforting. But the tension at the table lingered, heavy and unspoken, like a third cup of coffee you didn't ask for.

I forced myself to light up while telling them about the STEM program I was launching for middle school girls, hoping the enthusiasm in my voice could carve a wedge through the discomfort. Allie leaned in, genuinely engaged, her questions thoughtful as always. She started sharing updates on her upcoming gallery opening—a show she'd poured months of herself into, layers of grief and growth hidden in brushstrokes and light.

And Eden? She smiled, nodded, offered a well-timed "wow" here and there, but the warmth wasn't quite there.

She was present.

But she wasn't *with* us.

And I wasn't sure how many more brunches we were supposed to pretend that didn't matter.

Eden, as expected, commandeered the conversation the moment her coffee hit the table—diving headfirst into tales of color-coded calendars, chaotic carpool lines, and a nanny who apparently couldn't follow basic instructions.

"I barely sit down these days," she sighed dramatically, draping one arm along the back of the booth like she was waiting for applause. "Between coordinating Jayson's soccer schedule, managing the nanny's never-ending questions, and chairing the spring PTA gala, I'm just... *done.*"

Allie stirred her coffee slowly, gaze fixed on the swirling cream like it held an answer. I caught her eye, then shifted my attention back to Eden, a sharp edge forming in my voice.

"Sounds exhausting," I said, my fork poised mid-air. "All those drop-offs in between your gel manicure and edge-control appointments—must be rough."

Allie glanced up, her warning clear. Her eyes said *Not now, Sky.* But the words had already slipped out.

I shoved a forkful of syrup-drenched pancake into my mouth, hoping the sweetness would dull the rising bitterness. But Eden wasn't finished. She never was.

She turned to me with that polished, practiced smile that

glimmered but didn't glow. "Skylar, you're so lucky you can just... get up and go. No little humans depending on you. Must be nice to live so... *carefree*."

Her words stung more than I let on, but I held my expression flat. "Yeah," I said coolly, "I love my freedom. It's not for everyone."

Eden's smile tightened. "That sarcasm and attitude of yours—it's not cute. You're fortunate, Sky. No one relying on you. No one loving you enough to *need* you."

The air left my chest like a slow, cold exhale. The jab was surgical—precise, deliberate. I felt the heat rise behind my eyes, but I refused to blink.

I leaned in, my voice syrupy and lethal. "You're right, Eden. I've got freedom, and sleep, and a quiet apartment. Must be thrilling, making sure the nanny has Jayson's gluten-free chicken nuggets plated before your husband waltzes in to do bedtime prayers. So... *fulfilling*."

"Skylar!" Allie's voice cracked through the tension like a thunderclap. She looked between us, eyes wide. "Eden, stop. Sky, stop. This is supposed to be breakfast, not an audition for *Real Housewives of Clinton Hill*."

I exhaled sharply, but I wasn't done. The heat in my chest had simmered too long.

"Well, since we're already in the ring..." I leaned back against the booth, crossing my arms. "What is going on with you, Eden? You ghosted me. Left me to wrangle both *Stitch* and *Ursula* solo at that brunch—*your* brunch. You didn't even bother to send a text."

Eden rolled her eyes and sat up straighter. "Skylar, things happen. Life doesn't revolve around your calendar. Something came up."

My voice pitched up. "*Something came up?* Girl, this wasn't some casual happy hour. This was church folks and our mothers at *Emmanuel*, giving me the side-eye while I lied through my teeth. You left me stranded—*again.*"

"She's right, E," Allie cut in, her voice gentle but firm. "You stood up your mom. You stood up *your girl.* What's going on?"

I shook my head, the emotion threatening to spill. "And then you went dark. No replies. Just... silence."

That's when Eden snapped—voice low but sharp as glass.

"Not all of us have time to sip wine and debate whether the man behind door number one has emotional intelligence or the man behind door number two can build a bookshelf. Some of us have *real lives* to deal with, Skylar."

The insult landed with precision. I opened my mouth—but before the fire could leap from my tongue, Allie raised a hand.

"Excuse me!" she called out to the waitress walking past. "Can we get *three* hot chocolates? Extra whipped cream, please."

I raised an eyebrow, my jaw still tense. Eden blinked, confused. But the slight curve at the corner of Allie's mouth made it clear—she was calling a timeout.

When the waitress returned, she placed the steaming mugs in front of us, their peaks of whipped cream piled so high they practically defied gravity. The scent of chocolate and cinnamon cut through the stale hostility in the air.

Allie slid one toward me, another toward Eden, then wrapped both hands around her own like it was a peace offering.

"Remember when we used to come here on Sunday mornings after SAT prep?" she said softly, her tone a balm over the bruises we'd just left on the table. "And we'd fight over who got the mug with the most whipped cream?"

A reluctant laugh escaped my lips, small and surprised. Even Eden cracked a smile, the edges of her tension rounding off just enough to remember.

We sat in silence for a beat, the kind that hummed more than hovered. The diner buzzed around us—silverware clinking, dishes being cleared, the low hiss from the griddle filling in the gaps where conversation had grown too heavy.

The hot chocolate melted into us like memory. We weren't fully okay—but for a moment, we were seventeen again. Sitting in this same booth, waiting on buttered toast and dreaming out loud.

I didn't know what was going on with Eden—not really. But as the whipped cream softened into the rich cocoa, and the smell of syrup and bacon lingered like a song on repeat, I let myself breathe.

Even if we were bruised, we were still here. Still showing up. And sometimes, in friendships like ours, that was the first step toward fixing what had cracked.

The morning had begun to thaw—the tension, the silence, the tightness in my chest—just a little, thanks to Allie's nostalgia-fueled hot chocolate truce. The whipped cream had worked its magic, softening our edges. We were starting to settle back into a rhythm, even laugh. But peace never lasted long when Eden was around.

She tilted her head mid-sip, her tone light and oblivious. "Oh, Allie, I forgot to tell you—I was at this fundraiser last week with Jayson, and I ran into Bryan. *Your* Bryan!"

The name landed like a brick on the table.

Allie froze, fingers still hovering over her coffee cup, as if time had stuttered. Her face drained of color. I felt it too—the way the air seemed to crackle and still, the diner's background noise dimming around us like the world itself knew that name shouldn't have been spoken here.

Eden kept going, blissfully unaware of the grenade she'd just lobbed into our booth. "He said he's been thinking about you. Wanted to reconnect. Asked me for your number. I told him I'd ask you first, of course." She smiled, pleased with herself, like she'd brought us flowers and not a memory laced with trauma.

I froze mid-bite, my fork suspended over a plate of half-eaten pancakes that now felt like ash in my mouth.

"What the hell, Eden?" My voice cut across the booth, sharper than I intended—but I didn't care.

She blinked, startled by my tone. But I wasn't about to let her backpedal.

"Bryan is an asshole. Allie does *not* want to reconnect with him."

My mind reeled back to that brutal summer after sophomore year. Allie had shown up at my door with sunglasses on after sunset, her cheek visibly swollen, her voice so soft I had to lean in to hear her. I remembered rummaging through my makeup drawer, trying to find something—*anything*—to cover the bruises Bryan had left behind. Back then, she'd called it "just a bad argument." Back then, I'd believed her.

But over the years, the stories unraveled. Canceled plans. Sudden disappearances. Her light dimming with each phone call where her voice was hollow, robotic, afraid. The signs were there. I just didn't want to see them until it was too late.

He hadn't just hurt her physically—he had twisted her

from the inside out, piece by piece. Five years of subtle control and soul-crushing manipulation. And Eden thought this was *romantic*?

"Bryan? *That* Bryan? Are you serious?" My voice rose with each word. "The same man who isolated her, gaslit her, *broke* her down?"

Eden recoiled slightly, arms crossing, her glossy composure beginning to fray. "Well, people change, Skylar. It's been over a decade. He sounded sincere. He's doing really well for himself now—makes over six figures, he's involved in philanthropy, looks great—"

"That's the problem," I snapped, slamming my mug down on the table hard enough to rattle the silverware. "You're talking about resumes and charm. You didn't *think*, Eden. You never think."

Eden bristled, her face tightening into something defensive. "I was trying to help. We're not getting any younger. I just thought maybe Allie might want—"

"Eden," Allie said, her voice low but clear, the slight tremble cutting deeper than any shout. "Stop."

We both turned to her. Her eyes shimmered—not with tears, but restraint.

"I know you probably thought you were being thoughtful. But Bryan... that part of my life is over. There is *nothing* there to revisit. No curiosity. No unfinished story. There is no Bryan and I. And there never will be. I have absolutely no interest in reconnecting with him. Let's just leave it at that."

Eden shifted, her bravado folding into something smaller. She fumbled with her napkin. "I just thought... you know, everyone deserves a second chance."

I leaned in, locking eyes with her, my voice low and cold.

"Not everyone. And definitely *not* him."

A heavy silence settled over us. The clink of plates and chatter from other tables filled the void Eden's words had left behind. She lowered her gaze and quietly sipped her hot chocolate, her hands wrapped around the mug like she needed something to hold on to.

When we finally stepped outside, the late morning Brooklyn air was crisp and sharp, the kind that kissed your skin and reminded you you were still standing. The stoop of Mike's Coffee Shop creaked beneath our steps as we made our way to the corner of DeKalb and St. James.

Allie slipped her arm through mine, her grip light but steady. "Thank you," she whispered, her voice soft enough for only me to hear.

I squeezed her arm in response. "You know I got you," I said, then took a beat and broke the tension with an off-key, drawn-out: "Thaaaat's what friiiends are fooor..."

Allie laughed—really laughed—the sound bubbling up from her chest like it hadn't in a while. "You're the worst," she said, smiling through misty eyes.

"Yeah, but I'm your worst," I replied, nudging her as we walked past the pizzeria we used to hit after school. The scent of garlic knots and childhood memories lingered in the air.

We didn't look back at the diner. Bryan was behind us. And as for Eden—well, she had a lot of growing up to do. But for now, we had each other.

And that was more than enough.

30

Allie

The living room of my brownstone was dimly lit, the soft glow of the floor lamp casting long shadows against the exposed brick walls. Luz sat curled up in her usual spot—an oversized armchair in the corner, worn in all the right places. It had been her throne since the day I moved in years ago, a space she claimed as her own with an unspoken familiarity. Clutching a pillow tightly to her chest, she leaned forward, her eyes burning with frustration.

"Are we really going to pretend like Bryan isn't stalking you?" Luz's voice was sharp, laced with both anger and concern. She hugged the pillow tighter, her petite frame dwarfed by the chair.

Skylar, perched on the couch with one leg tucked beneath her like she was settling in for a storm, raised a perfectly arched eyebrow and shot me a sharp, questioning glance. "*Stalking?*" she repeated, her voice laced with suspicion and just the right amount of edge. The word hung in the air like an accusation dressed as a question.

"Allie," she said slowly, her tone shifting into the dangerously calm register she reserved for when she smelled bullshit. "Did you tell *Luz* about Bryan reaching out to Eden?"

Her lips curled slightly at the mention of Eden's name—subtle but unmistakable, like the word itself had left a sour taste in her mouth. It was a flicker of disdain she didn't bother to hide, and it made Luz chuckle, though not convincingly.

"Eden really pissed you off, huh?" Luz said with a half-smile. "Didn't see that one coming."

But there was a tightness around her eyes, a hesitation behind the tease, like she knew she was stepping into emotionally charged territory but didn't want to make it a thing—yet.

I sighed, not ready to meet either of their eyes, and reached down to pick at the frayed edge of the throw blanket in my lap, fingers working at the thread like it could unravel my anxiety along with it.

"I told her about Eden and... you-know-who asking for my number," I said quietly, the confession falling out of me like something I'd been trying to tuck away.

The room stilled. The weight of it all—Eden, Bryan, the mess left behind—settled around us like a fog, thick and suffocating, pressing into the silence that followed.

Luz rolled her eyes. "I still can't believe Eden's clueless enough to entertain that request." She shook her head, then added, "But that's old news. *El idiota* sent Allie flowers the other day."

Skylar's eyes widened, flicking toward mine in disbelief. I looked down, the weight of guilt heavy on my chest. I should have told her sooner. I thought back to that night, my hands trembling as I held the card that came with the flowers—

Bryan's neat, familiar handwriting scrawled across it. I had called Skylar, my voice shaking, my heart pounding. But she was tied up in meetings, preparing for a big project, and later meeting Titus. Instead of interrupting her, I dialed Luz.

"You were busy," I mumbled, avoiding Skylar's gaze. "I didn't want to bother you."

Luz cut in before Skylar could even open her mouth. "Allie called me frantic," she said, her voice tight and simmering with protective fury. "I could hear the fear in her voice—*real* fear. Don't downplay it."

The room fell quiet for a beat. The only sound was the soft whir of the heat kicking in, a low hum beneath the heavy silence.

Skylar sat across the room, still and watchful, her long legs tucked underneath her, a steaming mug cradled in her hands. Her eyes never left mine. I could see it all on her face—a blend of concern, frustration, and something deeper. Something unspoken. She didn't know the full story. Not yet. And the gap between what I'd told her and what I'd lived was starting to show.

"Allie," she said gently, her voice dropping to that tone she only used when we were standing on the edge of something fragile. She leaned forward slightly, mug forgotten. "Talk to us."

Wrapped in my fuzzy blanket like it could shield me from their eyes, I shifted on the floor, the hardwood cool beneath my legs. Oversized pillows surrounded me like soft barriers, but they couldn't muffle the weight of the moment.

"I wasn't scared," I said quickly, too quickly. The words came out sharp, defensive—my instinct kicking in before I had time to think. "I was just... caught off guard. I wasn't expecting him to find my office, let alone try to contact me."

But even as I said it, I felt the truth unraveling beneath my words. The trembling in my voice, the way my chest tightened at the memory—it said everything I wasn't ready to admit.

Luz glanced at Skylar, then back at me. She didn't speak, but her silence spoke volumes. And Skylar? Her eyes softened, but she didn't back down.

There was something they both felt—something I hadn't yet said out loud. Something they were now waiting for me to name.

Luz muttered under her breath, *"Él es un estúpido."* The anger in her voice vibrated through the room like an unspoken threat.

Skylar's eyes darkened. "What the hell, Allie? He's completely out of bounds."

Luz, always the overprotective sister, sat up straighter, her small frame suddenly towering with righteous anger. "Out of bounds? If I get my hands on him, he'll be in the hospital." Her eyes flashed with unrelenting fury, and for a moment, she looked larger than life.

A small smile tugged at the corner of my lips, but it didn't reach my eyes. The shame and anger that simmered beneath my skin began to melt away under Luz's fierce protection.

I exhaled slowly, the present blurring as my mind slipped back to her—the wide-eyed, unsure freshman I used to be. The one who still measured her worth by who noticed her, who believed that love came dressed in a perfect resume. That girl had no idea what was coming.

Bryan had been a campus golden boy. Wavy hair that never needed effort, eyes that sparkled with ambition, and a voice so smooth it made everything he said sound like a promise. People practically whispered his name in admiration—an engineering major from a prominent family, Student Government President, Dean's List every semester. The guy who could run a meeting and charm a professor in the same breath.

Everyone said he was a *catch*. And maybe he was—for someone else.

Me? I hadn't been impressed. Not at first. I clocked the type—Mr. Perfect with a polished smile and a plan for everything. I wanted no parts. But that only seemed to make him try harder.

He turned charm into a strategy: late-night "study breaks" at the library that felt suspiciously well-timed, casual pop-ups at the cafeteria, borrowing books from the same shelf I always used. Persistent didn't even begin to cover it—he asked for my number 101 times. I remember the number because he kept count. Thought it was cute. Romantic, even.

By spring semester, I gave in. Wore the "lucky girl" label like it fit.

It started small—so small, I almost didn't notice. Requests that sounded like concern, phrased sweetly enough to feel like love. The short skirts and bright colors I used to wear with pride? "Not really appropriate," he said, his tone light but laced with judgment. So I tucked them away, folded parts of myself into drawers I never meant to close. I swapped vibrant prints for muted tones, traded bold lipstick for chapstick, color for quiet.

My wild, unruly curls—those same curls he once ran his fingers through, calling them beautiful—suddenly needed taming. He liked my hair straight. Sleek. "Polished," he said.

I booked a flatiron appointment the next day.

Bit by bit, I began to shrink. I laughed softer, spoke less. I rounded off my edges and dimmed my shine to fit the version of me he preferred. The version he praised. The version that didn't challenge him.

Then came the control.

It started with "checking in" texts—harmless, even thoughtful at first. But soon they multiplied, timed like traps. If I didn't respond fast enough, the air shifted. The silent treatment would settle in like fog. Accusations followed. *Who were you with? Why didn't you answer? What are you hiding?*

Then came the name-calling. The guilt-tripping. The quiet manipulation dressed as devotion.

And still, I told myself he was just stressed. That he didn't mean it. That he had potential, he just needed patience—*my* patience.

I convinced myself I could fix it. Worse, I believed I could fix *him*.

Until one night, sophomore year, everything shattered.

I'd barely been back on campus a week. He was already on edge, complaining about how distant I'd been over the summer, how I didn't sound "as excited" on the phone. He picked at me all day—my tone, my laugh, my outfit for a party. "Trying to get attention?" he asked, his voice a knife wrapped in velvet. I brushed it off.

But words weren't enough this time.

I remember how fast it happened—how the argument escalated, how his face twisted into something I didn't recognize. And then, just like that, his hand cut across my face. A slap—hard, hot, and sudden—that stopped time.

I didn't cry. I didn't scream. I just... stood there. Frozen.

My skin stinging, my mind racing to catch up.

And then—I don't even know how—I apologized.

I *apologized*.

Like I had done something wrong. Like I had earned it.

That was the night I learned how quickly love can become a cage—and how quiet abuse can be until it isn't.

The cycle continued for five long years—an endless loop of his demands, my shrinking world, and the fear that crept into every corner of my life. His control didn't always come with bruises. Sometimes it came wrapped in silence, in the way I slowly stopped answering texts, declined invitations, pulled away from the people who loved me most.

I lied to them. But more than that—I lied to *myself*. Told myself it wasn't that bad. That I could handle it. That love just looked different for everyone. And before I knew it, my world had narrowed down to a single name: *his.*

I was drowning in a sea of self-preservation, surviving on scraps of affection he'd toss like breadcrumbs. And I'd convinced myself that was enough.

Skylar's voice sliced through the memory, pulling me back to the present like a lifeline. "Allie," she said, her tone fierce but trembling at the edges. "You *know* we're not going to let him near you again, right?"

I blinked, the weight in my chest easing just slightly as I met her eyes across the room. They weren't just filled with love—they were ablaze with something deeper. *Rage. Protection. Sisterhood.*

Beside me, Luz reached over without a word and wrapped her hand around mine. Her grip was tight, grounding, the kind that said *I've got you.* I could feel the quiet tremble of her strength beneath her stillness.

"Under no circumstances," she said, her voice low and steady, like an oath being made. "He will *never* hurt you again."

In that moment, I believed them. Not just because of what they said—but because of how they looked at me. Like I was still whole. Like I was still *mine.*

A lump rose in my throat, thick and uninvited, but I nodded, swallowing it down as best I could. The past might still linger in the corners of my mind, whispering its ghosts when I least expected it—but here, in this room, with my best friend and my chosen sister, I wasn't alone.

Skylar leaned over and bumped her shoulder into mine, her expression softening into something warm and familiar. "And next time? Tell me. Meetings or not, I'm *always* here. I don't care if I'm presenting to the Board—I'll pull up with hoop earrings and holy water."

There was a flicker of guilt in her voice, quickly masked with sass, and it made me smile through the sting in my chest.

"I know," I whispered, voice smaller than I meant it to be, but honest.

The tension in the room loosened like a zipper being slowly undone. Luz, ever the reset queen, reached for the remote with a dramatic flourish. "Okay, enough trauma for tonight. *Movie night?*"

Skylar perked up. "Yes. But we're vetoing anything sad. If someone dies, breaks up, or gets diagnosed with anything tragic, I'm throwing the remote."

I let out a soft laugh, the kind that starts low in your chest and catches you by surprise. I nodded and pulled the blanket tighter around me like armor. The ache in me hadn't vanished, not completely. Bryan's shadow still loomed.

Healing isn't linear—it loops and rewinds and stumbles.

But here, wrapped in warmth, in the safety of their presence and terrible movie opinions, I felt a little lighter.

And for tonight, that was more than enough.

31

Titus

The city pulsed with life around Madison Square Garden. Horns blared in frustration, the hum of rush hour swelling as bodies weaved through the streets, each person on a mission—some heading to Penn Station, others ducking into storefronts, and a sea of fans swarming toward the arena, decked out in Knicks blue and orange. The crisp New York air was thick with energy, the kind that made the city feel electric on game nights.

"Titus!"

I spotted Elias perched on the concrete steps outside the Garden, waving me over. His frame, relaxed yet commanding, cut through the chaos like he belonged there. I navigated through the throng of fans buzzing with anticipation for a Knicks win, sidestepping a group arguing about player stats before finally reaching him.

As I got closer, I couldn't help but feel grateful that we had connected after Friendsgiving. It wasn't often you met people who could challenge you, call you out, and still have your back. Elias was one of those people.

"Elias." I clasped his hand, dapping him up with a grin.

We made our way inside, the vibrations of the crowd palpable, the buzz intoxicating. The scent of overpriced stadium food—salty pretzels, buttered popcorn, and sizzling hot dogs—mingled with the metallic tang of the arena's chilled air.

"Don't worry, Allie is the Knicks fanatic. Not me. I just like a good game," Elias reassured me, catching the hesitation in my step as we neared the stands.

I chuckled, wiping an imaginary bead of sweat from my brow. "Allie is something serious."

Elias laughed, a glimmer of pride flickering in his eyes. "Tell me about it. My little sister is *something else*." He shook his head. "Allie and Skylar? Now *that's* a deadly combination."

I smirked. "Thanks for the warning, but it's a little too late."

The game was electric. The Knicks were on fire, the crowd surging with every three-pointer, every defensive block, every near-miss that had us holding our breath. We weren't die-hard fans, but it didn't matter. In that stadium, with that energy, we were honorary Knicks fans for the night. The final buzzer beater sealed the deal—a roar of victory erupted around us, hands flying up for high-fives, the city's love for its team pouring from the stands.

As we exited, still riding the high of the game, Elias nudged me. "Hungry?"

I eyed the concession stand, unimpressed by the trays of lukewarm chicken tenders and stale pretzels. My stomach growled in response.

"Starving."

"I know a great spot. Allie-approved." He glanced at me knowingly. "If you can convince your stomach to hold out until we get to Brooklyn."

Sabór & Roots was alive.

The line snaked outside, people lingering on the sidewalk, the air humming with conversation and the rich, sultry sounds of a neo-soul band inside. A velvet rhythm spilled into the street—smooth guitar riffs, the smoky croon of a vocalist weaving between the chatter. The scent of warm spices, slow-cooked meats, and caramelized plantains drifted into the night air, wrapping around us like a seductive embrace.

I walked straight to the hostess stand, catching the familiar face behind it. Her warm smile acknowledged me before she even asked how many.

"Two. Just us." I lifted two fingers, just in case my voice got lost in the frenzy.

She grabbed two menus and motioned for us to follow. We slid past the envious glances of those still waiting, their eyes tracing our steps as we were seated ahead of them.

"If the line outside is any indication of how good this place is, I can't wait to eat," Elias mused, rubbing his hands together in anticipation.

"You won't be disappointed," I assured him.

The appetizers arrived in a flurry of rich aromas and vibrant colors. The Ropa Vieja Empanadas—flaky, golden, bursting with slow-braised shredded beef, sofrito, and sweet plantains—melted in our mouths, the guava-lime aioli adding a citrusy punch. The Black-Eyed Pea Hummus & Avocado Dip was creamy, smoky, the perfect contrast to the crisp cassava and plantain chips we dipped into it.

Elias leaned back, chewing thoughtfully. "Yeah... I can

definitely see why this place is Allie-approved."

Between bites, he glanced at me. "So, Skylar."

I exhaled through my nose, already sensing where this was going.

"How are things since Friendsgiving?"

It had been months. It didn't feel that long, but also, it did.

I hesitated, rolling a piece of empanada between my fingers. "Better, I guess. But... still strained. It's like we never really got our rhythm back. We're... teetering. Almost just... friends."

The words felt foreign, like they weren't mine.

Elias studied me before shaking his head. "Man, just saying that out loud is depressing."

I let out a dry laugh. "Yeah."

He rested his elbow on the table, swirling his drink in thought. His voice was even, deliberate. "I love Skylar like a sister. But I also *know* Skylar like a sister. Don't let her use 'busyness' as an excuse to avoid hard conversations."

The words hit like a hard foul—unexpected, jarring, knocking the breath out of me.

I took a sip of my drink, letting the weight of his words settle. Then, after a moment, he changed the subject. "Speaking of Friendsgiving... has Skylar told you anything about Lupe?"

I raised an eyebrow. "Lupe?"

"Yeah. She was at Friendsgiving, right?"

I leaned back, rubbing my chin. "She was. Why?"

Elias shrugged, but it wasn't casual. "Just curious."

I smirked. "She got your attention, huh?"

Elias chuckled, shaking his head. "She was... intriguing. Seemed cool. I don't know much about her."

I nodded, taking another sip of my drink. "According to

Sky, Lupe's solid. Smart, got a good head on her shoulders. Works in community outreach or maybe she is a teacher. Something like that.."

Elias absorbed that, nodding. "She's got a vibe."

I grinned. "That she does. So what, you thinking about reaching out?"

Elias let the question hang between us before offering a small smirk. "Maybe."

I laughed. "Man, let me find out you're catching feelings over empanadas and Friendsgiving memories."

Elias chuckled, shaking his head. "Just gathering intel. This is just between you and me."

I lifted my glass. "Your secret is safe with me. Well, if you're serious, don't overthink it. Just reach out. Worst she can do is tell you she's not interested."

Elias nodded, rolling that thought around in his mind. "Yeah... we'll see."

I gave him a knowing look before he turned the conversation back to Skylar. "Alright, but back to what really matters—are you gonna actually fix things with Skylar, or just let it fade?"

The words hit like a hard foul—unexpected, jarring, knocking the breath out of me.

Had I been using busyness to avoid the same thing?

Before I could sit with the thought, Elias groaned in pleasure at his plate. "Yo, this Mofongo-Stuffed Smothered Chicken is *legit*."

I glanced down at my own plate—Guava-Glazed Short Ribs with garlic mashed yuca and braised cabbage—ready to dig in when—

"Elias!"

A voice, too familiar.

I looked up, my stomach twisting.

Walking toward us was *him*. The guy from the charity event. The same guy from Friendsgiving, the one who interrupted my conversation with Skylar in the kitchen.

Sterling.

Elias stood, greeting him with a pat on the back. "What's up, Sterling?"

Sterling's gaze flickered to me. His expression held recognition, then amusement.

"Friendsgiving, right?" He extended his hand in mock courtesy.

I gritted my teeth, shaking it briefly. "Titus."

"Nice to *officially* meet you," he said smoothly, that smirk still there.

Sterling glanced around the restaurant. "Great place, huh?"

"Yeah. Great place." My voice was even, but my grip on the fork tightened.

"I'm so glad *Skylar* introduced me to this spot," Sterling added, looking at me as if he knew exactly what he was doing.

The words landed like a gut punch.

Skylar introduced him here?

Why would she bring him to my spot after I brought her here?

Elias, sensing the tension, cleared his throat. "Great seeing you, Sterling. But I gotta get back to this mofongo before it gets cold."

Sterling nodded, smirking. "Enjoy your dinner, Elias. *Titus.*"

The moment he walked away, I exhaled sharply.

"What the hell was that?" I muttered.

Elias shook his head, stabbing at his plate. "He's an ass. Always has been." He nudged my plate forward. "Eat a rib. It'll make you feel better."

I grabbed a forkful, chewing through my frustration.

Elias' phone buzzed. He glanced at the screen and smirked. "It's Allie."

Allie: *Did you catch that game? My Knicks are on a roll.*

He rolled his eyes. "She's gonna kill me when she finds out I had tickets."

"Bragging about *her* Knicks?"

"Of course. Every day, all day."

Just then, my phone lit up, with a surprise text from Ms. Madison.

Skylar: Did I just spot you at the Knicks game on IG? You out here living your best life or what?

I turned my screen toward Elias.

He grinned. "Looks like *you're* in trouble now."

I sighed. "Maybe a plate of guava ribs will soften the blow with Allie."

Elias smirked, raising his glass. "And maybe a hard conversation will fix things with Skylar."

32

Skylar

I hugged my arms around myself, trying in vain to ward off the biting cold as my boots crunched against the ice-packed trail. The frigid air burned my lungs with every breath. "I still don't know how I let you convince me to come out here after a snowstorm. It's nothing but ice!" I huffed, rubbing my gloved hands together, desperate for warmth. My feet felt like blocks of frozen cement, barely able to navigate the treacherous terrain ahead.

Allie's laughter rang through the woods, bright and unbothered, as she leaped effortlessly from rock to rock. "How was I supposed to know the trail would be frozen over?" she called back, her olive-green coat barely visible as she disappeared behind a frost-covered tree. Her lime-green hat and gloves flashed like neon signals, making her look like some kind of winter Tarzan, swinging from branches and scaling icy ledges with impossible ease.

Behind me, Eden exhaled a dramatic sigh, stumbling in her impractical designer boots that had no business on a hiking trail. She looked like she had walked straight off a Fifth

Avenue winter display—fur earmuffs, a cropped fur jacket, sleek black tights, and buttery leather gloves. Fashionable? Always. Functional? Not in the slightest. Bent over, hands on her knees, she gasped, "Oh my God. Oh my God. I think I'm having a heart attack." Her wide eyes flickered between Allie's shrinking figure and the steep climb ahead, then down at the ice-covered path we had somehow already conquered. Neither direction looked promising.

"This is the last time I let you talk me into hiking." Quinn's voice carried from behind us, her tone as sharp as the wind slicing through the trees. "Tell my husband and kids I love them," she joked—just before yelping as her foot skidded on an unseen patch of ice. Our heads whipped around in horror, then, as she miraculously caught herself, we erupted into a fit of uncontrollable laughter.

"Quinn, are you okay?" Allie shouted from what felt like half a mile ahead, though her voice was distorted by laughter of her own.

"Girl, I'm done." Quinn plopped onto a fallen tree trunk, unbothered by the snow coating its surface. Eden immediately reached for her arm. "Stay right there—I need you to break my fall if I go down." She was only half-joking, her grip firm with the quiet desperation of someone who had already envisioned herself sprawled out on the ice.

"If Eden hits the ice in that fur coat, she's gonna slide right off this mountain," I muttered, barely containing my giggles.

"Skylar, lose the attitude!" Allie's voice carried through the crisp air, sharp and teasing. "And Eden, you're completely out of bounds for showing up in that fur." Then, as if the trail wasn't already humiliating enough, she turned her focus back to Quinn. "And Q, how is this your 'last' hike

247

when it's literally your first?"

Despite our collective groaning, we kept moving, our breaths puffing out in frosty clouds. When we finally reached the summit, I had to admit, begrudgingly, that the view was worth it. The entire town stretched below us, blanketed in pristine snow, rooftops shimmering like sugar-coated gingerbread houses under the pale winter sun. The sky, an icy blue, stretched endlessly above, making the world feel both vast and impossibly quiet.

Allie, our modern-day MacGyver, unfurled a small blanket and handed us tiny, steaming cups of hot chocolate that smelled like cinnamon and heaven. My lungs, my legs, my entire body thanked her. "Bless you, woman," Eden sighed in relief, sinking onto a nearby rock as she sipped.

Quinn greedily snatched a hand warmer from Allie's stash, stuffing it into her glove before accepting her own cup of cocoa. "Alejandra Catalina Herrera, we love you!" I declared dramatically, savoring every syllable of her full name.

Allie's eyebrows shot up in faux offense. "Oh, we're using government names now?" She held my cup hostage for a moment, a playful smirk tugging at her lips. I surrendered with a quick, "Sorry, sorry! Allie, we love you!"

We sat in companionable silence for a few moments, letting the warmth seep into our fingers as we took in the breathtaking view. But, of course, the peace didn't last long.

"So... what's the deal with Sterling and Titus?" Quinn asked casually, a little too casually. My hot chocolate nearly went down the wrong pipe.

Little did she know that Allie's been harassing me about ending things with Sterling for weeks. She continued, eyes locked on me. "And now I hear you and Sterling have been talking a lot? Two, three times a week, even? Sounds like something to me."

Allie's gaze snapped to mine, full of intrigue. I could practically hear the questions forming in her mind. I hesitated, then sighed. "It's nothing, really. We're just talking. Catching up."

"Uh-huh." Quinn's skepticism was thick enough to cut with a knife. "And what about Titus? He's definitely interested. I mean, you did reconnect at Friendsgiving. And didn't you apologize for icing him out when you found out he was, what was it—somebody's whole ex-husband and a father?"

The words settled between us, heavy as the snow that clung to the trees. I took a slow sip of my cocoa, my fingers tightening around the cup. "It's complicated," I admitted finally. "Sterling feels safe. Familiar. Titus... Titus is different. He scares me."

"Girl." Quinn rolled her eyes so hard I swore she could see her past lives. "This is not high school. You're not out here hoping to be someone's 'first' anymore."

Allie pursed her lips, her expression confirming that she had just been about to say the same thing. "Preach, chica. Preach," she muttered, nudging Quinn approvingly.

Eden, ever the pragmatist, smoothed her gloves, her eyes darting between us. "I get it," she said finally. "I would have never married Jayson if he had kids and an ex-wife. Too much baggage."

Quinn snorted. "Eden, please. We all know Jayson checked every single box on your 'perfect husband' checklist. You were on the housewife track before you even got to college."

"More like before she even finished high school," Allie added, exchanging a knowing glance with Quinn. They cackled, high-fiving like middle school mean girls.

"Ooo, wait a minute!" Quinn gasped, her grin wicked. "Didn't you have your eyes on Sterling way back when?"

Eden groaned. "Can we not dredge up ancient history?"

"Agreed." I exhaled. "Let's stick to my current crisis, apparently."

Quinn's laughter faded into something more serious. "Skylar, just be careful. These are grown men. With feelings. Expectations."

Allie nodded, gripping my arm gently as we prepared for the icy trek back down. "Sky, listen. There's no guarantee the person you want will still be waiting when you finally figure it out."

"Umm hmm. Preach, chica. Preach," Quinn echoed with a knowing smirk.

Just as we started descending, a loud thud rang through the air. We turned just in time to see Eden's legs and designer boots fly up as she slid down the trail like a human toboggan.

Laughter exploded from us as we scrambled to save her before she became a permanent part of the mountain.

33

Titus

We both had a rare lull in our schedules and decided to carve out the afternoon for tea at a cozy café in Brooklyn. Apparently, everyone else had the same idea—at 3 o'clock on a Thursday, the place was buzzing with conversation and clinking cups. I scanned the room for Skylar, and sure enough, she had beaten me there. Always punctual, always poised. She waved from the coveted corner table, her caramel complexion glowing against the soft hue of her off-white wool coat. Her twist-out, perfectly defined and cascading past her shoulders, looked as if she had just left a salon. As she shrugged off her coat and settled in, her presence pulled me in like gravity.

"Sky," I greeted her as her familiar perfume—warm, floral, and unmistakably hers—enveloped me. She stood, her embrace warm against the winter chill still clinging to my skin. As I took the seat next to her in the oversized chair, the café's mood lighting reflected off her cheekbones, accentuating the soft glow of her skin.

"Titus," she murmured, my name rolling off her tongue

like the lyrics of a jazz ballad.

"Thanks for meeting me, Skylar. I thought it'd be good for us to catch up in person." It had been over a month since I'd last seen her, though we still spoke a few times a week.

"Thanks for the invite," she replied, her voice carrying a note of curiosity.

After grabbing our drinks from the barista, I settled in, my mind racing with everything I wanted to say. Our conversations had felt too surface-level lately, too careful—like we were skirting around something we both knew was there.

"So, I'm just going to jump right in. Is that okay?" I asked, watching her reaction.

Skylar hesitated, her hands wrapped around her cup for warmth. "This isn't going to hurt, is it?" she joked.

"I can't make any promises I can't keep," I smirked.

I told her how I felt—no detours, no pretense. How I'd always been drawn to her brilliance, the way her mind moved in conversation, sharp and thoughtful and unapologetic. How I looked forward to our late-night calls, how I found myself waiting on her voice more than I cared to admit. And how, over time, I started hoping those talks were leading somewhere more than casual.

But I also told her the truth about what shifted between us—*after* I told her about my ex-wife... and Kayla and Deuce.

"I waited to tell you about them," I said, my voice low but steady, "because at first, I wasn't sure where we were heading. And I don't just hand my life out to people who aren't going to stay in it."

I paused, letting that land before continuing.

"But the way you looked at me that night—like I'd grown a second head—I'm not sure there ever would've been a *right* time to tell you."

Skylar exhaled, long and slow, as if she'd been holding her breath since the moment I walked in. Her fingers curled around the warm mug of tea in front of her, gaze dropping to the surface like it held answers she hadn't figured out yet.

"I get it, Ty," she finally said, her voice softer now, edges worn down by reflection. "If I'm being honest... your news surprised me. But not half as much as *my* reaction surprised me."

She looked up then, meeting my gaze with a mix of guilt and something lighter.

"I was a brat about it," she admitted, her lips curving into a faint, self-deprecating smile. "I panicked. And instead of asking questions or giving you space to explain, I just... shut down."

Her honesty disarmed me. It always did.

And for the first time in weeks, it felt like we were finally sitting in the same truth.

I chuckled, arching an eyebrow. "You're not the only one who thinks so."

Her mouth fell open in mock horror. "Excuse me?" she gasped, clutching at her imaginary pearls.

"I may have heard a thing or two from Zora and Cece," I teased.

Skylar rolled her eyes but smiled. "Okay, fair." There it was again—the self-awareness, the ability to reflect and own up to things, that made me fall for her even more.

"Listen, Sky, I enjoy talking to you. But I can't say I enjoy spending time with you, because we don't do that much."

"Low blow, Mr. Scott," she shot back, tilting her head.

"Just being honest," I shrugged. "That's why I wanted to

meet. You've been distant, and it feels like we're stuck in this 'buddy' zone. I need to know where your head's at."

Skylar smirked. "Straight shooter. Buddy zone?"

"I call it like I see it, Ms. Madison." I leaned in slightly. "I just need to know where we stand."

Skylar took another sip of tea, then shifted in her seat, inhaling as if she needed to steady herself. Before she could speak, I added, "Before my so-called 'confessions,' we talked about dating exclusively. About seeing where this could go."

"Titus—"

"I know things have changed," I said. "But are we working towards getting back there?"

She hesitated before finally admitting what I already suspected—she had been talking to Sterling again. Sterling, the same high school and college sweetheart I had mentally erased until he showed up at that charity event and Friendsgiving. My expression must have said everything because she rushed to add, "Titus, I don't want to promise you something I can't give."

Her words landed like a gut punch.

"I had my list of 'dealbreakers,'" she said quietly, her voice wrapped in equal parts honesty and hesitation. "And I never imagined myself with someone who'd been married. Someone who had..." She faltered, eyes lowering to the table between us. "Who had a built-in family."

The air between us thickened. Her words weren't cruel—they were honest. And that honesty deserved my full attention.

I sat up straighter, shoulders squared, not in defense, but in clarity. I met her gaze head-on. "I'm not here to convince you, Skylar."

My voice was calm, steady—but there was steel beneath it.

Her expression shifted. Caught off guard. Hurt, maybe. Or surprised I'd drawn a line.

"Titus," she said softly, her brows pulling together, "I don't need convincing." She reached across the table, her fingers brushing mine in a gesture that held more than apology—it held hope. An offering.

I let her touch linger. Let the warmth of her skin speak to what words hadn't yet. But after a quiet moment, I gently moved my hand back to my lap.

"I'm glad," I said, my tone even but resolute. "Because if a woman needs to be *convinced* to be with me... she's probably not the woman I need to be with."

I didn't say it to hurt her—I said it to honor me. To honor the version of me who had done the work, raised good kids, weathered heartbreak, and still had the capacity to love with his whole heart. Her eyes searched mine, wide and blinking back something—pride, regret, affection, maybe all three. And for once, we weren't talking in circles. We were speaking the truth.

Not as a performance.

And now the question hung in the air—not whether we liked each other, not whether we had chemistry, but whether she was *ready* for a life that came with roots. But as people trying to decide if love—*real* love—could still find them in the space between fear and forgiveness.

The café's playlist changed just then, the soft chords of Erykah Badu's *Next Lifetime* filling the space between us. The smooth, jazzy notes and mellow drumbeat wrapped around us like the moment itself, suspended between what was and what could've been.

Skylar sighed as she reached for her coat, the weight of our conversation settling in. I helped her slip her arms into the sleeves, my hands lingering just long enough for her to notice.

"Skylar," I said softly, my voice steady. "Let me walk you home."

34

Allie

The phone rang a few times before Skylar's voicemail picked up.

Automation: You have reached...

I hung up before the message could continue, muttering under my breath, "Damn it, Sky. Did you just send me to voicemail?" I frowned at the phone before tossing it onto the couch. Pacing the living room, I forced myself to take slow, deep breaths, but my mind wouldn't stop racing, replaying the events from earlier that day.

Just as I was wrapping up a meeting with a new client, energized by the prospects of an upcoming art installation featuring local talent, an unwelcome figure appeared in the reception area of my office. Bryan.

The loft space, usually expansive and full of life, suddenly felt too small, the exposed brick walls pressing in as I watched him stand near the entrance. As I bid my guests farewell, Javier—my assistant and self-appointed guardian—was already on high alert, stepping into Bryan's path. "Excuse me, sir. Can I help you?"

Bryan's voice cut through the space like a blade—deep, sharp, and impossible to ignore.

"You can't help me," he said, his tone loaded with something colder than frustration. "But I know *Ms. Herrera* can."

A chill ran down my spine.

"Ms. Herrera has another appointment," Javier interjected firmly, stepping between Bryan and the hallway with the practiced authority of someone who knew exactly what danger looked like. His stance was solid, arms folded, tone calm—but his eyes never left Bryan's.

I didn't wait to see how it played out. The moment Bryan's attention shifted, I slipped away, ducking into my office like my life depended on it—because part of me felt like it did. I shut the door quietly but quickly, locking it with trembling fingers. The second the latch clicked into place, I backed away like it might not hold.

I hid there for hours.

The rest of the afternoon passed in a surreal, foggy blur. I sat at my desk but didn't touch my computer. Answered no emails. My tea went cold. The sun dipped lower, casting long, tired shadows across the floor. What had once been a sanctuary—my space of color and calm—now felt like a holding cell. The vibrant paintings I'd carefully chosen for their warmth and inspiration looked dull under the weight of my fear. The air felt thick, like it was closing in, pressing against my chest.

Every footstep outside my door made my breath catch. Every muted voice in the hallway sent my pulse into overdrive.

Evening crept in unnoticed. And though he was long gone, his presence lingered—like smoke in the air, like a memory that refused to be buried. The air in my office felt thick, the once-vibrant paintings on the walls appearing muted.

"Javi, dinner's on me." I handed him a few crisp twenties, a silent thank-you for stepping in earlier.

"Mira eso. I can't believe it. dinner's on the boss! I guess hard work *does* pay. ¡Gracias, jefe!" He grinned, playfully snatching the money from my hand.

"Let's go. We're calling it a night," I sighed, grabbing my coat.

We exited the building together, ready to put the long day behind us, but the second we stepped outside, I knew peace wouldn't be ours just yet. Bryan was waiting.

Leaning casually against the entrance, he wore a navy wool coat, its open lapels revealing a fitted turtleneck and tailored pants that stopped above his ankles. In the dead of winter. No socks. Who does that?

His dark brown eyes locked onto mine, his thick lashes and perfectly shaped goatee only adding to the picture of a man who knew exactly how to command attention. "Alejandra," he called out, a polished smile stretching across his face.

I turned sharply, attempting to avoid him, but Javier wasn't having it. He stepped between us, his posture rigid, and I swore I heard him hiss.

"Dude, don't you get it? Take a hint."

Bryan's smirk didn't waver. "Allie, call your little friend off before he gets hurt." His voice softened, but his eyes carried the weight of history, making my stomach twist.

"Javi," I murmured, placing a hand on his arm, my only hope of preventing a scene. People moved past us, unfazed. This was New York, after all.

"Allie," Bryan's voice was almost gentle now. "I just want to talk."

I took a step back as he moved toward me. When he reached for my arm, my body reacted before my mind caught up. I jerked away, my voice steel. ""Ni se te ocurra. Don't you dare."

The phone ringing in my apartment yanked me back to the present. I shoved aside a pile of colorful pillows, fumbling for the device before it could go to voicemail. "Hello?" I answered, breathless.

"Allie!" Quinn's bubbly voice greeted me.

"Oh, hey, Q."

"Wow. Don't sound too excited to talk to your best friend," Quinn teased, her voice light—but I could already hear the shift in her tone, the subtle edge of concern starting to creep in.

I sighed—loudly, intentionally—knowing she'd catch the heaviness behind it. "What's up, A?"

Just those three words, spoken softer than usual, made my chest tighten. I could picture her on the other end of the line, eyes narrowing, posture shifting into that protective mode she always slid into when she knew something wasn't right.

And then I broke.

The words came tumbling out before I could catch them, the dam giving way under the pressure of a day I hadn't even fully processed. I told her everything—how Bryan had shown up at my office unannounced, how his hand brushed against my arm like he still had permission to touch me. How I locked myself in my office and cried for an hour after pretending I was fine. How I'd truly believed I was done with him— done with the fear, the anxiety, the memories that wrapped themselves around my ribs like vines.

"What the *hell* is wrong with him?" Quinn snapped, her

voice sharp now, no longer trying to cushion the blow. Her anger was immediate, fierce, and deeply loyal.

"I don't know," I said quietly. My voice felt small. Hollow. "But I don't need this. I've worked too hard to get here... to feel this way again."

There was silence for a beat—full, not empty. The kind that says *I'm still here. I'm listening. I've got you.*

And I let the weight of her presence, even over the phone, wrap around me like armor.

"I know, chica, I know." Quinn said softly.

Before she could say more, my phone flashed with Skylar's name and a picture of us on vacation. "Q, that's Sky. Hold on."

"Add her to the call. I'm not going anywhere, and *you* better not hang up."

I clicked over. "Sky! I was just calling you."

"Hey, Allie. Q's on the other line?"

"Yup, I'm merging us now."

"Hey, babes," Skylar greeted Quinn.

"You sound just as bad as Allie. What the hell is going on in Brooklyn?"

Skylar sighed. "What's up, Allie? I saw your call but was with Titus."

"Oh," Quinn said, the weight of Skylar's words settling between us.

I filled Skylar in on everything, the words tumbling out faster than I could control. By the time I finished, I was shaking.

"Oh, Allie," Skylar whispered. "I'm so sorry."

"I'm coming over," she added, her voice resolute.

"No, you don't have to," I protested weakly. "Besides, I

have to go to the gym in the morning."

"Allie, don't nobody care about your little gym," Quinn interjected. "Let us be there for you. You drop everything for *everyone* and never put yourself on the list. Skylar, take your ass over there."

A laugh bubbled up despite the tears burning my eyes, and they joined in.

"Between you and Allie, I swear I'm always being bossed around," Skylar teased.

Sniffling, I murmured, "That's because we make sense."

Less than two hours later, Skylar was at my door, holding up a bag. "Spicy noodles," she said with a small smile before sauntering inside like she owned the place.

From the speakerphone, Quinn scoffed. "You *could've* DoorDashed me some, so I wouldn't feel left out."

"Bye, Quinn," I laughed.

"Te quiero. I love you too, Alejandra," she replied softly. "We'll see you tomorrow night."

"Tomorrow night?" I glanced at Skylar, confused.

"Surprise girls' weekend at your place. Courtesy of a secret group text while we were on the phone." She smirked. "Eden's in too."

Before I could protest, she pulled me into a deep hug, and just like that, the dam broke. The secrets, the silence, the weight of it all—it poured out of me as I sobbed into her shoulder. And for the first time in a long time, I wasn't carrying it alone.

35

Allie

The chill of late winter clung stubbornly to the air, seeping through the aged walls of the Brooklyn brownstone despite the steady hiss and clang of the old radiator. Outside, the city lay beneath a heavy, wet sky—wrapped in a gray haze, with slushy remnants of last week's snow melting into grimy pools along the curbs. But inside, the brownstone pulsed with a different kind of weather—warmth, laughter, and the soul-deep comfort of good food. The rich, savory scent of curry chicken, oxtail, jerk chicken, and flaky beef patties drifted from the kitchen, curling into every corner of the house. It was the kind of warmth that came from takeout bags still steaming from one of our favorite Caribbean spots across town—food that felt like home even when the world outside felt cold and cracked.

"Make sure I get some of that curry chicken and an extra helping of plantains," Eden called from her spot on the couch, her voice carrying over the clatter of plates as I worked in the kitchen.

I smirked, popping a greasy, caramelized plantain into my

mouth as I heaped a generous serving of curry chicken onto her plate.

"Damn, Eden," Skylar teased, eyeing the towering portion I was preparing.

"Little Miss Demure is being greedy," Quinn chuckled, moving effortlessly through the kitchen, grabbing bottles of ginger beer and sorrel from the fridge. She popped the caps off with ease, passing the drinks around. "What happened to the salad?"

Eden scoffed, tugging the sleeves of her sweater down over her hands. "Girl, salad? Who needs salad when you have the best Caribbean food in Brooklyn?" Then, with mock impatience, she added, "Uh, Allie, am I eating today or nah?"

I shot her a look. "You might want to be nice to the person making your plate."

Quinn cackled, handing Eden her drink. "Right. You better talk nice to Allie before she adds a little Shug Avery pee in your curry."

Skylar and I burst into laughter while Eden recoiled, her face scrunched in pure disgust. "Ugh! Quinn, why are you like this?"

The tension I had been carrying all day—the anxious knots in my stomach over this impromptu girls' weekend—began to unravel. The familiar rhythm of their voices, the rich scents of comfort food, the easy banter... it was exactly what I needed.

I stretched out my legs, adjusting my thick, fuzzy socks, feeling the weight of my full belly settle into the moment. The lingering cold from outside couldn't reach us here, wrapped in the glow of food, warmth, and the kind of friendship that made the hardest days feel bearable.

Quinn took a sip of sorrel before launching into a story about her bonus daughter, Taylor.

"Taylor is a handful."

"Didn't she just turn 15?" Skylar asked, shifting on the sofa.

Quinn let out a weary sigh. "Yes. Fifteen going on twenty. And working my entire nerves."

Skylar shook her head. "I don't know how you do it."

Quinn arched a brow, biting into a now-cold beef patty. "Do what?"

Eden, never one to let a moment pass without stirring the pot, chimed in, her eyes glinting with mischief. "You know."

Quinn rolled her eyes. "If you're asking how I parent a teenager, the answer is: I have no clue. I'm just making it up as I go."

Eden scoffed. "Let's not pretend, Q. You weren't just co-parenting. You have to deal with baby mama drama from time to time."

Quinn pursed her lips, tucking a stray curl behind her ear. Her voice was calm, but there was steel beneath it. "E, don't make it sound like I am stuck in a bad situation. I have THREE beautiful children and the privilege of raising them with my amazing husband."

Skylar smirked. "You and Tatum have that 'Love Jones' kind of love. Like he's the mirror to your soul and all that poetic nonsense."

Quinn grabbed a throw pillow and launched it at Skylar. *"Shut up, Sky."*

I laughed, but I couldn't disagree. Quinn and Tatum had loved each other with a quiet intensity from the moment they met. They had an undeniable connection—one that weathered every storm. It was hard to believe they were celebrating ten years of marriage this year.

I could still remember when she first mentioned him back in college, back when he was just some guy she met on the quad. *"Easy on the eyes, but not my type,"* she had said. Tatum had been nothing more than an acquaintance—until years later, when life brought them both to Georgetown for law school, and the familiarity of an old friend became something deeper.

Eden sauntered into the kitchen, helping herself to what had to be her third plate of curry. "Please. Their love story is more like a Tyler Perry movie. Or Love & Hip Hop."

Quinn's expression darkened. "Eden, why are you always so damn miserable? The white picket fence and nanny life not all it's cracked up to be?"

Eden sucked her teeth, clearly annoyed. But Quinn wasn't finished. "And no, our situation isn't traditional. But neither Tatum nor I expected it to be."

Eden folded her arms. "Traditional? Girl, finding out your man has a whole toddler after dating for two years is beyond 'not traditional.'"

Skylar and I exchanged a glance, sensing the shift in the room.

Quinn's voice remained steady, but her eyes burned with something fierce. "Eden, if you're going to tell the story, tell it right. Don't make it sound salacious."

Eden scoffed. "How is it not salacious? It was a damn scandal. And you know it."

"Eden!" Skylar shot her a warning look, but Eden was already too far in.

"You expect us to believe Tatum had no idea he had a kid?

Come on, Q."

The words landed like a slap in the middle of the room—blunt, incredulous, and loud enough to still every other sound.

Quinn's head snapped up. "That's exactly what happened," she fired back, her voice shaking—not with uncertainty, but with fury barely contained. Her hands curled into tight fists in her lap, knuckles whitening, her jaw set so tight it looked like it hurt.

"Tatum was a stupid college kid who had a one-night stand. He didn't know. *Kelsey* didn't know. They were two reckless, immature kids, and it took *four years—four*—for him to even find out he had a daughter."

The room fell silent.

Not just quiet—*heavy*. The kind of silence that pressed in from all sides, thick with history. The kind that made everyone avoid eye contact because the memories it stirred were too complicated, too painful, too *real*.

We all remembered those years. Quinn, scared out of her mind, wondering if she could take on the mess that came with being the second woman in a story that had already begun. Tatum, terrified—not of fatherhood, but of losing *her*. The whispers behind their backs. The sudden text messages from Kelsey. The paternity questions. The court dates. The overnight transformation from carefree boyfriend to father of a four-year-old little girl with his eyes and someone else's last name.

We remembered Quinn smiling through it all, even as it cracked something deep in her.

But tonight, she wasn't hiding.

And no one had anything left to say.

"It wasn't like they exchanged numbers," Quinn continued, voice clipped. "It was one night. And that one night changed everything."

Eden scoffed. "It took her four years to find him? Please."

Quinn exhaled sharply. "Eden, your fascination with my life is a little much."

I placed a hand on Quinn's shoulder. "Q, I don't remember a single day when you wavered. Not once. You always knew you'd be with Tatum."

Quinn let out a soft laugh, shaking her head. "You have no idea how many times I questioned it, Allie. Imagine being in a serious relationship, thinking you're building a future together, and suddenly finding out your man has a four-year-old daughter. You think that didn't shake me?"

Skylar softened. "You handled it with so much grace."

"Yes, very demure," I added with a smirk, trying to lighten the mood.

The tension in the room finally cracked, giving way to laughter.

Quinn smirked, shaking her head. "I'm glad I stayed. I wouldn't change my family for anything."

Eden, still chewing on rice and peas, mumbled something under her breath.

"What was that?" Quinn challenged.

Eden smirked, swallowing. "Nothing, girl. Just thinking about getting another plate."

We all groaned.

Some things never change.

36

Skylar

The wind outside howled through the narrow alleyways between Brooklyn brownstones, rattling the bare branches of trees as they cast spindly shadows against the frosted windows. The street lights flickered faintly, their dull glow no match for the darkness of the early morning hour. Inside, the brownstone was warm, thick with the lingering scent of curry, oxtail, and spices from dinner, but the atmosphere was still heavy from the tension that had settled over the night.

It was past 1 a.m. on Saturday morning, and though we had all retreated to our rooms hours ago, sleep had eluded me. My mind replayed the look on Allie's face earlier that evening, the hollow way she carried herself after Bryan had shown up unannounced at her office. Even after Quinn insisted on gathering us all for a girls' weekend to lift her spirits, I could see the exhaustion in Allie's posture before she drifted off to sleep on the couch. My best friend—usually the strongest among us—looked like a mere shadow of herself, and it unsettled me.

Allie was always the fixer, the one who kept everyone else together. She had pulled me out of my lowest moments more times than I could count, but now, when it was her who needed saving, I wasn't sure if I knew how to be that person for her.

And then, there was Eden and Quinn.

The night had taken a sharp detour from its intended purpose when Eden arrived with more edge than usual, taking aim at Quinn like she had been waiting for the opportunity. The back-and-forth had been sharp, biting, almost cruel. Now, they had both surrendered to their respective corners—Eden retreating behind closed doors, Quinn curled up in the guest room, their battle unfinished but temporarily on pause.

I turned onto my side, staring at the dim glow from the hallway filtering under my bedroom door. My mind was restless, tangled between thoughts of Allie, the drama between Eden and Quinn, and my own lingering tensions with Sterling and Titus. Maybe it was the late-night curry still sitting heavy in my stomach, or maybe it was the anticipation of what the rest of this weekend would bring. Either way, sleep wasn't coming anytime soon.

Sighing, I pushed back the covers and slipped out of bed, wrapping my arms around myself as I stepped onto the cold wooden floor. The old brownstone had a way of announcing every movement—the creak of the floorboards beneath my feet felt impossibly loud as I padded toward the kitchen, careful not to wake the others.

The warmth of the kitchen enveloped me as I flipped on a low light, searching through Allie's cabinets for her stash of herbal teas. She always had the best blends. The kettle began to whistle softly as I settled on peach ginger, adding a touch of raw honey before perching on a stool at the island. The first sip sent warmth through my body, easing some of the tension in my chest.

I had just started to lose myself in thought when I heard the stairs creak.

I turned to see Eden descending, her silk pajama set draping effortlessly over her frame, the deep violet color complementing her skin under the soft kitchen light. Even at this hour, even in sleepwear, she was effortlessly put together— her matching silk bonnet in place, her nails pristine, her expression unreadable.

"Oh, hey Sky," she said casually, spotting me as she reached the bottom step.

"Hey E," I responded, my voice hushed. "Can't sleep?"

Eden ignored my question, moving through the kitchen with quiet efficiency—grabbing a bottle of water, scanning the counter for snacks, pretending as if I weren't even there.

"Eden, what gives? You're not your usual friendly self." My voice carried just enough sarcasm to catch her attention.

She exhaled sharply, not bothering to meet my gaze. "Skylar, I am not in the mood to argue with you."

"Who said anything about arguing?" I leaned forward, studying her. "But seriously, you went in on Quinn tonight. I thought you two were cool? The suburban moms club and all. You've been ghosting me. What gives?"

Eden's expression hardened. Her jaw tightened, and for a moment, I thought she was going to walk away.

"Okay, okay, all jokes aside. What's up with you?" I pressed. "I'm used to you being a bitch toward me, but now you're coming for everyone else. What was that earlier with Quinn?"

She hesitated, fingers gripping the water bottle just a little too tight. I could see the fight in her eyes, the resistance—but then something shifted. The tension in her shoulders gave way, and with a sigh, she sank onto the stool beside me.

"Sky, I am exhausted," Eden admitted, her voice barely above a whisper.

The vulnerability in her tone caught me off guard.

I stayed quiet, letting her find her words.

"I am absolutely exhausted. And before you make another joke about my nanny, don't."

I tilted my head, studying her. "Okay, no jokes. Talk to me."

She exhaled slowly, her fingers tracing patterns on the countertop. "I have this perfect life, right? The beautiful house, the successful husband, the two kids. On the outside, it looks like I have it all together. But do you know my girls—my own children—love the nanny more than they love me?" Her voice cracked slightly. "And Jayson... He's this amazing doctor, this brilliant researcher, saving lives, but he works insane hours. And when he does come home, it's designer bags and jewelry as some kind of apology for not being around."

I swallowed, unsure of what to say.

"And me?" she added bitterly. "I don't even know who I am anymore. I don't work. I don't have a purpose outside of making sure the house is in order, the kids are taken care of, and that I look good on Jayson's arm when we step out. I went from having all these dreams to being... a wife. A mother. That's it."

"And my mother? Ms. Claudette? The same woman who brags about my 'perfect life' to everyone who will listen? She holds me hostage with guilt. I pay her mortgage, her bills, her vacations—because she 'sacrificed so much' for me."

She paused, staring down at her perfectly manicured hands.

Eden let out a bitter laugh before slipping into her mother's thick Jamaican accent.

"Eden, yuh betta open yuh eyes, gyal! Di man have sense, eeh? Him have a good head pon him shouldahs, come from good stock—real quality! Him ah go mek sumting of imself, trus mi. Yuh nah go haffi want fi nutten! But gwaan, play di fool fool if yuh want to."

I tried to suppress my laugh, but I couldn't help it.

"Damn, you sound just like Ms. Claudette," I said between chuckles.

The sound of applause from the stairs startled us.

Allie and Quinn tiptoed into the kitchen, their laughter joining mine. The dark sky outside framed them as they settled into the stools beside us, the rustling trees beyond the window reminding us how late it was.

"Eden, yuh betta use yuh right mind, ah man like dat nuh come easy, yuh ear mi? Allie added, her Puerto Rican accent hilariously off but her effort commendable.

"Yuh betta grab im quick-quick before anothah gyal tek im! Anh gimme some granpickney before mi drop dead. Urrie up before yuh blessin gaan! Eden continued, her voice exaggerated before dissolving into laughter.

And then—just like that—she started to cry.

"I am absolutely exhausted," she whispered, her defenses crumbling in the presence of the only people who truly saw her.

And for the first time that night, we all saw it. There was

no such thing as picture perfect.

37

Titus

The crisp winter air nipped at my face as I carefully balanced the takeout bags, their warmth radiating through the thin plastic and seeping into my palms. The rich, tangy scent of fried wings drenched in extra mambo sauce teased my senses, making my stomach growl in anticipation. Stepping onto the wide, wraparound porch of my parents' home, I was met with the nostalgic creak of the wooden planks beneath my feet. The porch swing, slightly swaying in the evening breeze, greeted me like an old friend. The oak tree in the front yard stood strong as ever, its bare branches trembling under the weight of the cold, the familiar sight grounding me instantly.

From inside, the unmistakable sound of Sir Duke Ellington's fingers dancing across the keys floated through the open doorway, a prelude to the warmth waiting beyond. The house was more than a home—it was a living, breathing part of our family's history, its walls saturated with laughter, love, and the echoes of countless gatherings. The windows glowed with soft, golden light, and the scent of cinnamon and fresh-baked sweet potato cake mingled with the aroma of the food I carried

Before I could knock, my father appeared in the doorway, his tall, lean frame perfectly silhouetted against the golden glow of the entryway light. His dignified posture, one I had spent my entire life trying to emulate, was momentarily betrayed by the boyish excitement in his eyes. Rubbing his hands together like a mischievous child about to receive his favorite treat, he propped the door open with his foot, determined to prevent any potential catastrophe involving his beloved wings.

"Did you get extra sauce on the side?" he asked, his deep voice laced with both authority and delight as he reached for an overflowing bag. His expression was that of a man who knew exactly what he wanted and was pleased that it was finally within reach.

I couldn't help but smirk, taking in his impeccably polished appearance—maroon Morehouse joggers and a matching sweatshirt, the oversized "M" embossed across his chest. The look was completed with the fresh Nike Air Force 1 Low College Pack sneakers that Deuce had gifted him last Christmas. Even in leisurewear, my father exuded an effortless confidence that made it clear why my mother still looked at him the way she did after fifty years of marriage.

The sound of my mother's voice floated toward us before she even stepped into view. "Michael, let the boy get in the house," she chided, a mixture of affection and exasperation in her tone. When she appeared beside him, she was a vision of timeless elegance—her golden-brown complexion radiant, her skin glowing as if she had just stepped out of a high-end spa. She was dressed in her favorite white

Spelman sweatshirt, the blue lettering crisp against the soft cotton. The scent of her perfume—sweet citrus and fruit with undertones of coconut water and driftwood—enveloped me as she kissed my cheek and whispered, "Hello, baby."

With my father snagging his wings and my mother commandeering another bag, I followed them into the house, the familiar jazz riffs wrapping around me like a beloved childhood blanket. Family photos adorned the walls, spanning generations—my siblings and I frozen in various stages of youth, my children, our nieces and nephews grinning from frames, snapshots of our lives interwoven. The faint aroma of something sweet lingered in the air, a telltale sign that my mother had been baking. She always baked when we came home. It was her love language.

As I set the bags down, I glanced around. "Where's Leah and Cece?" I asked, knowing full well that Priscilla—Cece—was bound to be late. She always was.

"We all know Priscilla is running on her own time," Mom replied, unpacking the food with practiced efficiency. "And Lord knows where Leah and Lance are. They should have been here hours ago."

She eyed the sheer volume of food I had brought. "Ty, how many places did you stop by in D.C.? You have enough here to feed the neighborhood."

I laughed, shaking my head. "Blame Cece and Leah. They both had requests, and you know how they get."

I had made stops all over the city—Dad's wings, Cece's half-smokes loaded with chili and onions, lump crab cakes for Leah. And, of course, I had grabbed Mom's favorite sweet potato cake because some things just weren't up for debate.

As if on cue, Leah and Lance breezed into the kitchen, their entrance as rhythmic as the jazz filling the house. Leah immediately pulled me into one of her signature bear hugs, squeezing me tight. "How's my baby bro?" she asked, her voice warm and teasing.

Lance and I exchanged a look, silently acknowledging the unshakable hierarchy in which Leah still viewed me as her "baby brother."

"What's up, Titus?" Lance greeted, dapping me up. Before I could respond, Cece and Brandon strolled in, their playful banter preceding them.

"Is that mambo sauce I smell?" Cece cooed, sauntering toward the counter and shamelessly snagging a wing from the container.

Before she could take a bite, Brandon intercepted, plucking it from her hand with a grin. "You still know the way to my heart," he teased.

From the dining room, my father's voice rang out, his sixth sense kicking in. "Priscilla, stay away from my wings!"

Cece groaned, rolling her eyes. "Daddy!"

Hours passed in a blur of laughter, food, and storytelling. Plates were empty, glasses half-full, the fireplace casting a golden glow over the room as we settled in. Leah rubbed her cheeks, complaining that they hurt from laughing so much, while Cece, ever the instigator, giggled beside her.

Across the room, Mom and Dad had claimed the oversized chair they always shared, her legs draped over his lap as he whispered something in her ear. She blushed, giggling softly.

"Eww, Mom, Dad, get a room!" Cece chided, tossing a pillow at them.

Dad, never missing a beat, pulled Mom closer. "Every room in this house is ours, baby girl."

Mom chuckled, winking at him. "Don't be jealous, Priscilla. Your daddy was my boyfriend long before he was your father."

Brandon, ever the comedian, grabbed Cece by the waist and pulled her onto his lap with an exaggerated flourish. "Come on over here, Priscilla," he called out, winking across the room. "You can sit on my lap if you're feeling left out."

Laughter filled the space, warm and effortless, wrapping around the room like a well-worn quilt. The glow from the chandelier cast soft golden hues over familiar faces, the scent of food lingering in the air. The hum of conversation and clinking glasses set a comforting rhythm, a melody of family ties that remained steady no matter how much life shifted outside these walls.

I leaned back against the couch, watching the scene unfold, feeling both a part of it and apart from it. This was the pulse of family, the unbreakable thread that time and circumstance could not sever. And yet, as I sat there, a quiet ache settled in—a whisper of what once was, of a life I had envisioned but never fully realized.

There was a time I had pictured Kelli and me in this very space—surrounded by warmth, our laughter folded into the rhythm of my parents', the soft clatter of dishes, the low hum of familiar voices filling the room. I'd imagined us building a life together with the kind of ease you can only believe in when you're young and untouched by reality. Back then, we thought love was enough. Destiny, even.

But reality had a way of unraveling the fairytale.

The weight of an unexpected college pregnancy shifted everything before we were ready. Between law school applications, my long nights in business school, and the responsibilities that piled up faster than we could adjust, we barely had time to breathe—let alone build something sustainable. We didn't grow together. We endured together.

Our marriage wasn't built on freedom or joy. It was built on *duty*—on trying to do the right thing before we fully understood what we were sacrificing to do it.

Looking back now, it's a wonder we made it out with our friendship intact. That after all the unspoken resentments, the missed moments, and the quiet exhaustion of carrying each other's expectations, we still managed to be kind. Cordial, even. Grateful, in our own way.

It wasn't the life we imagined—but it wasn't a failure either. Just... a story that ended differently than we thought it would.

As two young parents, we lived in a constant state of negotiation—treading the tightrope between love and survival. Every decision felt like a trade-off: whose dreams could stretch, whose ambitions had to shrink, whose future would take the front seat while the other held it all together. We were only twenty—barely out of childhood ourselves— trying to raise a son while still figuring out how to raise *ourselves*.

Deuce deserved everything, and we did our best to give it to him. But behind every milestone, every birthday party, every late-night feeding, there was a quiet calculation. Could we afford this? Could we keep doing this? Could *we* last?

We were juggling college classes, part-time jobs, tuition bills, and a relationship that had started with sparks and late-night talks but quickly buckled under the weight of expectations. What began as love morphed into duty. Then duty became routine. And eventually, routine became the only thing holding us together.

Ours wasn't a story of failure—it was a story of two people doing the best they could with what they had. And though the love between us changed, it never disappeared entirely. It just matured—shifted into something more quiet, more respectful. A mutual understanding built on years of showing up, even when it was hard.

What began as a high school romance—full of promise, shared playlists, and whispered dreams—slowly transformed into something far heavier. Not a love story, but a life sentence we hadn't fully understood, let alone signed up for. We entered adulthood holding hands, determined to do the right thing, to build a family that mirrored the stable, loving homes we were both blessed to come from.

But good intentions buckle under pressure.

The dreams we once sketched out between classes and text messages—vivid and exhilarating—began to dim under the harsh light of reality. They became burdens, not because we didn't still want them, but because they demanded more than we had to give. Raising a toddler while juggling midterms and internships. Trying to show up for a marriage neither of us had the emotional maturity to maintain. Smiling through burnout. Compromising before we ever had a chance to grow.

We held on because it felt noble to do so. Because love, or what was left of it, was stitched to responsibility. And just when we began to find our rhythm—when Deuce turned four, when Kelli crossed the stage with her law degree in hand, when we both allowed ourselves to exhale for the first time in years—

Life blindsided us again.

Kayla was conceived during a time when intimacy had

become a rarity—something scarce and distant, like a language we used to speak fluently but had forgotten over time. By then, love had given way to routine, and even our moments of closeness felt more like flickers of memory than anything rooted in the present. Intimacy wasn't tender—it was exhausted. Desperate. A reminder of what we once had and no longer knew how to access.

Her arrival should have been a celebration—a fresh chapter, a second chance. But instead, it became the quiet breaking point. The final unraveling of whatever thread still tethered us together.

We smiled for photos. We said all the right things. But behind closed doors, we knew. We were no longer building something—we were surviving it. And Kayla, beautiful and innocent, entered a world where her very presence marked both a blessing and a quiet goodbye.

I still remember the night Kelli ended it—clear as a scar you stop noticing until someone touches it.

I had just gotten home to our cramped apartment in D.C., the air heavy with the scent of reheated leftovers and the faint whir of the dishwasher humming in the background. I was still in my buttoned shirt and blazer, wrinkled from the kind of day that starts before sunrise and ends long after it should've. I'd spent the last twelve hours grinding—early in my corporate real estate days, chasing approval, chasing paychecks, chasing everything but peace.

It was a little past seven. I had already missed Deuce's bedtime—again.

I stepped inside, the click of the door sounding louder than usual in the quiet. Before I could drop my bag or loosen my tie, I saw her.

Kelli was standing at the edge of the hallway, framed by the soft, amber light spilling from the kitchen. Her arms were folded tightly over her pregnant belly, her caramel complexion glowing even in the low light. Her posture was composed, but the weight in her shoulders said everything she hadn't said yet.

She wore her hair in a short bob now—practical, easy. A style that made sense with a toddler in the house and another baby on the way. I never said it out loud, but I hated that cut. I missed the way her long curls used to tumble down her back, wild and soft and free. This version of her—contained, clipped, tired—wasn't unfamiliar, but it reminded me how much life had shifted. How much we had both changed.

She didn't raise her voice. Didn't cry.

"Ty," she said, her voice quiet but unwavering, "I can't do this anymore."

Five words. Simple. Final.

She wasn't angry. She wasn't begging. She was done. And in that moment, I knew—this wasn't a conversation. This was a decision. A door quietly closing.

I moved instinctively, my body remembering the motions even if my heart was slow to catch up. I reached for her— ready to offer another worn-out apology for being late, for missing bedtime, for showing up in body but never quite in spirit. For the distance that had stretched between us, brick by brick, excuse by excuse.

But I stopped cold.

The way she looked at me—those wide, unblinking eyes— hit harder than any words could. They weren't just tired. They weren't pleading or angry.

They were hollow.

And suddenly, I understood. She wasn't talking about another late night. She wasn't talking about the meetings or the emails or the thousand ways I'd let time slip through my hands.

She was talking about *us*.

The slow erosion of something that used to be vibrant and alive. The love that had thinned into duty. The silence between our sentences. The way we had become two people living side by side, no longer reaching for each other.

This wasn't about tonight.

It was about *every* night.

"I'm suffocating," she whispered, and the words trembled as they left her lips—soft but devastating. "And I'm scared that if we keep going like this, I'll start to resent you. *Resent our life.*"

Her voice cracked just slightly at the end, and she gestured around us—not just to the cramped apartment walls, but to the weight that lived in them. The baby toys in the corner, the unopened mail on the counter, the tired remnants of dreams we once named out loud but hadn't dared speak of in years. Her hand floated in the air like she was reaching for something that had already slipped through her fingers.

"I don't want that," she said, eyes glistening. "Not for me, not for you... not for *them*."

The silence after her words was loud. A kind of grief neither of us had the language for.

"Kells," I said quietly, my voice stripped of defense, of ego. "We were just trying to do the right thing."

I looked at her—not the polished woman in front of me, not the tired mother or the worn-out partner—but the girl I once met in the high school cafeteria, full of fire and ambition and faith in the future.

"We wanted to give our kids a family," I continued, my tone rough around the edges. "The kind of family *we* had. The kind we thought could hold everything together."

Her expression softened, but she didn't speak. Because we both knew now: good intentions weren't always enough. Sometimes love wasn't either.

"Titus," she said, her voice low but steady, "it was never just about *structure*."

She shook her head slowly, eyes glistening—not with tears, but with clarity that had clearly cost her something. "It was love. Real love. The kind that holds space, that bends but doesn't break. Our parents didn't just stay—they *chose* each other, again and again. They made room for one another to grow. To fail. To dream."

Her gaze drifted toward the window, as if she were searching for something out in the D.C. night sky. "What we've been doing? This isn't that. This is survival. We're trading pieces of ourselves just to make it to the end of the week."

She paused, exhaling slow and heavy, like letting go of something she'd been holding far too long.

"If we hadn't had Deuce so young... if we hadn't been thrown into all this before we even knew who we were—" her voice caught slightly, then steadied, "—do you *really* think we'd still be here?"

The question hung between us, soft but loaded, echoing in the space where denial used to live.

I opened my mouth to respond. I wanted to argue. To defend what we'd built. To tell her that love wasn't always a feeling—it was a choice, a commitment, something deeper than butterflies or perfect timing.

But the truth settled in my chest like a stone.

Because deep down... I knew the answer too.

"Titus, I love you."

The words landed softly, but they didn't soothe. They felt like a memory—something that used to hold weight but now echoed hollow in the space between us. And even before she spoke again, I knew what was coming. I could see it in her eyes—the grief of someone who had rehearsed this in her head a hundred times.

"But I'm not *in* love with you," she continued, her voice trembling at the edges. "And I don't want a marriage built on guilt or routine. Our kids..." she paused, swallowing hard, "our kids deserve more than that."

Anger sparked in me like a reflex—a flare of heat rising from the cold fear I didn't want to name. A last-ditch effort to hold onto something that had already started to unravel months, maybe years ago.

"So what?" I snapped, my voice sharper than I intended. "You think they deserve a *broken home* instead?"

Her expression didn't change. She didn't flinch or fold. She met my frustration with something stronger—conviction.

"They deserve a home full of *love*," she said simply. "And that's not what we have anymore, Titus."

Her words pierced through my defenses, clean and brutal.

And the worst part?

She was right.

As much as I wanted to argue, as much as I wanted to fight to preserve the version of family we had been clinging to, I couldn't deny the truth staring me in the face.

We weren't in love.

We were *tired*.

And staying for the kids wasn't saving them—it was teaching them to settle.

In the end, we parted quietly—no dramatic exits, no screaming matches. Just the slow, painful unraveling of something we'd outgrown. What followed was its own kind of work: the delicate, often clumsy dance of co-parenting, learning how to speak to each other without the weight of resentment, and slowly unearthing the friendship that had been buried under years of sacrifice, silence, and misplaced expectations.

It didn't happen overnight. But over time, we figured it out.

Deuce and Kayla thrived. They were our reason and our rhythm—living proof that love, even when it changes shape, can still raise something beautiful. Kelli moved on, and truthfully, I was happy she did. She and Chris had been married nearly a decade now—a good man, stable, kind. The kind of partner who showed up for her in all the ways I couldn't back then.

And I meant it when I said I wished her happiness. I always had.

Because in the end, she found what she had been looking for.

And if I was honest, I was still figuring out what that meant for me.

But as I sat in that familiar living room, surrounded by love and laughter, an emptiness lingered beneath it all. My past was settled, my career established, my children growing into remarkable young people. And yet, something was missing.

Or maybe... someone.

Skylar.

The thought of her tightened in my chest. I had thought we were moving forward, but her hesitations about my "built-in family" had thrown me off balance.

From across the room, Mom's gaze softened as she watched me retreat into my thoughts. She had always been able to read me, even when I wished she couldn't.

"What's on your mind, baby?" she asked gently.

I swallowed, forcing a smile. "Just... thinking."

But the truth was, I wasn't just thinking. I was feeling. And for the first time in a long time, I wasn't sure what to do with it.

The room fell silent, all eyes turning toward me.

Leah, always the one to break silences, smirked from her spot on the couch. "Leave it to Mom to leave Ty speechless."

I exhaled heavily, rubbing a hand over my face as I leaned back. The weight of unspoken thoughts pressed against my chest. "I just pictured things being different," I admitted, my voice quieter than usual. "I have two beautiful kids, a successful career—"

"And amazing sisters," Cece interrupted with a teasing lilt.

"Priscilla, stop," Mom reprimanded her gently, though amusement flickered in her eyes. "Let Ty talk."

I shook my head, letting out a dry laugh as I offered Cece a half-smile—one that didn't quite reach my eyes. "I just... I want someone to share it all with," I said, voice low, honest. "The life I've built, the calm I fought for, the chaos that comes with it, too. I thought Skylar and I were on the same page, but..."

I trailed off, the words suddenly heavy in my mouth.

"She's hesitant," I finally admitted. "Told me she never pictured herself with someone who already has a family."

Cece let out a sharp scoff, not even trying to hide her disdain. She crossed her arms like she was bracing for a fight. "Then let her be uncomfortable."

Her tone was clipped, but not cold—it was the kind of tough love only Cece could deliver without flinching. Her eyes softened, just a little, but her stance didn't.

"She's not a villain for having doubts," she continued, "but you're not a villain for living your truth either. You're a whole-ass man with a life, not a half-empty glass waiting for someone to pour into you."

Leah, who'd been listening quietly, leaned forward now, her expression all conviction. "I'm with Cece on this one," she said. "If Skylar can't see the beauty in the life you've built—the kids, the growth, the peace you've created—then maybe she's not the right one. Because the *right one* won't need convincing."

Their words settled over me—not as judgment, but as a reminder. A challenge to stop shrinking just to fit someone else's comfort zone.

And as much as it stung, part of me knew they were right.

Dad leaned forward, his voice steady and firm. "Either she's not the one, or she's not ready. But you, son, have to decide if you're willing to wait or if you're wasting your time."

Mom, ever the peacemaker, shifted the mood. "Enough about Ms. Skylar Madison. Let's talk about something else— like how Leah and Lance had the audacity to wear Princeton and Bowie State sweatshirts in my house." She pointed at Leah and Lance repping their alma maters.

Dad shot up, grinning. "Spelhouse!" he declared, pointing to his Morehouse gear. His statement is an ode to my parents' alma maters. Although Dad was an emeritus professor at Howard now, the HBCU pride forever in his blood, he always repped Morehouse first and foremost. Mom and Dad stood up modeling their Morehouse and Spelman swag, causing the competition between everyone in the room to grow.

A full-fledged HBCU rivalry erupted, Cece and Brandon chanting "HU, you know!" while I stood, revealing my Morehouse sweater in solidarity with my father.

Laughter rang through the house, and for the first time in days, my heart felt light. Between the college pride and the coupledom my heart was full. No, I didn't have all the answers, but it did remind me of what I ultimately desire—a love that does not feel like a negotiation. Maybe, just maybe, it was time to stop waiting for Skylar to figure out if she wanted the same. And that realization makes me rethink just how much space I am willing to give Skylar before I start pulling myself back.

38

Allie

The city was still tucked beneath a blanket of quiet when I slipped out of the brownstone for my usual morning workout. The early dawn air was crisp, a faint promise of spring lingering beneath the bite of winter's last stretch. As I jogged past brownstones and bodegas beginning to stir, I thought about checking if Skylar wanted to join me—but when I peeked into her room before heading out, she was curled deep under her blankets, the colorful silk scarf barely visible against her pillow. She wasn't moving anytime soon.

On my way back, I stopped at the farmers market, picking up a little something for everyone—Skylar's favorite fresh berries, a bundle of crisp vegetables Quinn would appreciate, and a half dozen apple cider donuts for Eden, who had a love-hate relationship with carbs but could never resist these.

As I climbed my front steps, the scent of sizzling bacon and warm maple syrup hit me like a hug I didn't know I needed. It drifted through the air, thick and sweet, wrapping around me before I even reached the door. Only one person would take the liberty of turning my kitchen into a Saturday morning diner without warning: Quinn.

Sure enough, the scene inside was as chaotic as it was comforting.

A mountain of golden pancakes stood proudly on a platter like a centerpiece, steam rising off them like applause. Thick-cut bacon glistened under a foil tent, perfectly crisped, and a massive bowl of fresh fruit sat in the center of the island, spilling over with berries, kiwi, and mango like it had just come from a farmer's market run I definitely didn't make.

Quinn stood at the stove, flipping another batch with the ease of someone who'd claimed this territory a long time ago. Her curls were pulled into a high puff, and she wore one of my hoodies like it had always been hers.

Skylar, curled up on one of the barstools, was still in pajamas, her headscarf slightly askew like it had given up halfway through the night. She was mid-bite, clearly trying (and failing) to sneak a piece of bacon off the tray without Quinn noticing.

Eden, ever the picture of poise—even in sweats—was seated neatly across the island. And yet, with zero shame, she was absolutely *flooding* her pancakes with syrup, her silverware clinking against the plate as she piled on berries with surgical precision.

We all paused for a second, watching Eden—prim, polished Eden—go *to town* on her breakfast like she hadn't eaten in days. Lately, it seemed like she'd been eating—or drinking— her emotions, each bite a quiet rebellion wrapped in maple and denial.

"Damn, E. You good?" Skylar smirked, raising a brow.

"Don't judge me," she said without looking up, syrup dripping from the corner of her plate. "I've had a week."

That was all it took to break the silence. Laughter filled the kitchen—loud, unfiltered, real.

Quinn, cradling a steaming mug of coffee like it was sacred, brought it to her lips and inhaled deeply before giving me a pointed, knowing look over the rim. "So... how was your workout, Allie? And I *hope* you don't mind me completely taking over your kitchen."

The scent of cinnamon and bacon practically danced through the air, and honestly, I wasn't mad at it.

I reached over and snatched a strip of bacon from the platter just as Eden gracefully scooped another heap of berries onto her plate, still managing to look like a lifestyle blogger even while half-asleep.

"Absolutely not," I grinned, already chewing. "I might need to invite you over more often if this is what's waiting for me after cardio."

Without missing a beat, Quinn leaned over and plucked the bacon *right out of my hand,* biting into it with the smug satisfaction of someone who knew she was both petty *and* irreplaceable. "Don't get used to this," she mumbled between chews, eyes twinkling.

We all cracked up.

The kind of laughter that didn't feel forced. The kind that filled up the corners of the room and pushed out the heaviness that had clung to us the night before. The kind that felt like a reset.

Whatever tension lingered between us from the conversations, confessions, and late-night shadows—it softened in the warmth of buttery pancakes and sisterhood. The air felt lighter now, like we'd all silently agreed to put the weight down. At least for this morning.

A few hours later, we were fully sprawled out in oversized leather pedicure chairs, feet soaking in warm, eucalyptus-scented water. The smooth hum of jazz floated through the spa like a lullaby, while the gentle vibration of the massage chairs worked its magic on our tired backs. We flipped through tiny nail polish swatches with the seriousness of art curators, holding each shade to the light like it might reveal the secrets of the universe.

"I'm telling you, Elias and Lupe are *absolutely* a thing," I said, grinning as I pointed a deep burgundy swatch at Eden. "They can deny it all they want, but the man is basically humming love songs and baking banana bread."

Quinn snorted. "If Elias starts bringing herbal tea to work, we'll know it's official."

Eden, lounging with the grace of a woman who vacationed in silence, let out a long sigh as she examined a soft taupe. "I would love to care about someone else's romantic drama, but I've been too busy managing *mine.* Do you have *any* idea how exhausting it is to run a house that large? I haven't seen the west wing since January. And don't get me started on Jayson—he's been on three trips in the past six weeks. I'm basically raising these kids with the *housekeeper.*"

Quinn didn't miss a beat. "Oh no, not the *housekeeper!* The horror."

I leaned in dramatically. "I just... can't imagine the trauma of instructing the nanny on which organic snack to pack."

"Do you *have* to personally select the Evian bottle, or does the assistant narrow it down for you?" Quinn added, hand to her chest like she might swoon.

Eden narrowed her eyes, smirking despite herself. "Y'all are insufferable."

"You love us," I said, tossing a wink over my shoulder as I picked a bold coral for my toes.

She did. And we loved her right back.

Even when she was complaining about first-world problems from a literal mansion, we wouldn't trade her—or moments like this—for anything.

But the real tea? Ms. Claudette's latest *online dating saga.*

"Y'all," Eden groaned, dropping her sample palette onto the tray with theatrical flair. "She's dating a man *ten years younger* than her. Claims he's a retired firefighter turned amateur golfer. I swear to you—she is being catfished."

Skylar snorted, her headscarf slipping slightly as she leaned in with a mischievous grin. "Or maybe Ms. Claudette still got it! Don't be mad just 'cause your mama is pulling younger men."

"If by 'got it' you mean wiring money to a man she's never met, who keeps claiming his 'Visa is being reactivated,' then sure—she's got it," Eden deadpanned, flipping through nail colors like she was over all of humanity.

"Oh no," I said, eyes wide. "She's out here sponsoring a scammer with abs, isn't she?"

Quinn cackled. "Watch next week be: 'Ladies, meet my new stepdaddy, Tyrone from Turks and Caicos.'"

"Stop," Eden said, but she was laughing now, covering her face with her freshly polished hands. "Y'all are evil."

"Tell that to Ms. Claudette," Skylar quipped. "She's the one living her best 90-Day Fiancé life."

The laughter rolled through the spa like music, warm and familiar. The kind that made your stomach hurt and your heart feel lighter all at once.

Quinn, meanwhile, had her own updates—this time about

the latest workshop her nonprofit had hosted, focused on equipping social innovators with real tools to drive change in their communities. Her eyes lit up as she spoke, hands moving with that familiar rhythm that always surfaced when she was in her zone—passionate, purposeful, pouring from a deep well.

She talked about breakout sessions on sustainable development, funding equity, and grassroots organizing like she was describing a family reunion of change agents. You could see how much it fed her—how much *she* fed it. Quinn didn't just show up to work—she showed up for a movement.

And I loved hearing her talk about it. It reminded me why we'd always clicked—our shared love for community, for rolling up our sleeves and leaving things better than we found them. That was always our thing. Whether it was tutoring after school or protesting city council decisions in college, Quinn had always been one of the ones who *showed up.*

But of course, in true Quinn fashion, the work–life harmony was never without chaos.

"Between trying to save the world and managing TJ and Quincy's overlapping soccer schedules," she said, dramatically tossing her nail sample palette onto the tray, "I basically live in my SUV. At this point, I'm one missed game away from being reported to the *mom board.*"

"And don't even get me started on Taylor," she added with a sigh, referring to her teenage bonus daughter, who was currently testing every boundary like it was her job. "Last week she tried to tell me her 11 p.m. curfew was 'oppressive' and 'rooted in control.'"

"Not *oppressive,*" Eden gasped, nearly dropping her cuticle oil.

"She gave me a full monologue like she was defending her thesis," Quinn muttered, sipping her cucumber water like it was tequila. "Meanwhile, TJ's having a meltdown because Quincy got the blue Gatorade, and he didn't."

We howled.

Quinn was out here changing the world by day and refereeing tiny, emotionally complex humans by night. And somehow doing it all with edge control intact and a fresh gel manicure.

Skylar, ever the multitasker with a calendar fuller than a state senator's, had her own passion project in full motion. For months, she'd been pouring herself into a STEM incubator for local high school students—an ambitious, community-rooted initiative that was finally gaining traction. She wasn't just building a program—she was building possibility.

The hub, nestled between Bed-Stuy and Fort Greene, was more than science labs and 3D printers. It was a bold, creative space where Black and Brown kids could explore tech, entrepreneurship, design thinking, and their own brilliance without apology. Skylar had fought tooth and nail for the funding—endless grant proposals, community board meetings, late nights fueled by iced lattes and sheer grit. But now? It was happening.

She was mid-sentence, hands flying as she broke down the mentorship component and the startup pitch competition she was curating, when her phone buzzed softly against the tray beside her. The sound barely registered—but her reaction spoke volumes.

Skylar glanced down at the screen.

And in an instant, the energy around her shifted.

That sharp focus, always tuned to ten, softened. Her lips curled into a slow, involuntary smile. The kind of smile you don't even try to hide. The kind that catches you off guard.

Quinn, never missing a beat, took a long, smug sip of her coffee before tilting her head with a smirk. "A dollar says that smile is from Two Kids Titus."

Skylar rolled her eyes, but the smile lingered. "You mind your business."

"Oh, but your business is so entertaining," Eden chimed in, already leaning over for a look at the phone screen.

Eden, now intrigued, examined Skylar's expression before nodding. *"Nah, I think Quinn's right."*

I shook my head knowingly, already recognizing that look. *"Nope. Twenty bucks says it's Sterling."*

Skylar immediately tried to hide her grin, but it was too late. I knew that look anywhere. I had been reading her expressions since third grade, and this was the same one she always got when Sterling was in the picture.

"Shut up, Allie," she groaned, laughing despite herself. *"You swear you know me."*

"Because I do." I grinned.

Laughter bubbled up between us, our voices echoing through the salon as we settled deeper into our seats, the scent of lavender foot soak and fresh polish filling the air.

For all the chaos, for all the drama, this was why we kept coming back to each other.

This was home.

39

Skylar

The restaurant was alive with warmth and laughter, the scent of slow-cooked ribs and golden fried chicken hanging thick in the air. We were knee-deep in buttery biscuits, crispy fried chicken, smoky ribs, collard greens glistening with pot liquor, and candied yams that melted on the tongue like brown sugar dreams. Allie had, true to form, found us a Black-owned spot we'd all been meaning to try—her commitment to supporting our own never wavered.

Eden sat across from me, the picture of curated elegance—her silk blouse draped just so, diamond studs catching the soft overhead lighting like a gentle nod to her wealth. Everything about her was polished, composed, intentional. But I saw it before she even opened her mouth.

That barely perceptible flicker in her eyes. The too-perfect posture, the way she straightened her spine just a little too much, like someone preparing for impact. She was slipping back into her armor—that well-worn persona she wore when she needed to look untouchable. When she couldn't afford to be *seen*.

"Oh, the charity ball was absolutely exquisite," she began, her voice light, almost singsong—too bright to be real. "The floral arrangements alone were—"

"Eden, cut the bull."

Quinn's voice sliced clean through her sentence, sharp and unflinching. It wasn't harsh—it was honest. The kind of honesty that only comes from years of love and shared late-night truths.

All of us turned toward her.

Quinn leaned back in her chair, arms crossed over her chest, brow lifted in that no-nonsense way that made grown men rethink their decisions. "Less than 24 hours ago, we were holding your hand while you sobbed over how *exhausting* all of this is. How tired you are of pretending. And now here you are, feeding us fluff like we're the society column. Girl, *enough*. Tell us the real."

Eden froze, lips slightly parted, eyes darting—caught between fight and flight.

But I wasn't about to let her off the hook either.

"Yeah, E," I said gently, my voice softer but no less firm. I reached across the table, not for drama, but to ground her. "I could care less about the charity ball or the girls' dance recitals. *We* care about *you*. What's really going on?"

The mask cracked.

Just slightly. But it was enough.

Her shoulders dropped an inch. Her perfectly lined lips pressed together, trembling at the corners. And in that moment, under the softness of the restaurant lights, surrounded by the only women who could call her out and hold her up in the same breath—Eden exhaled.

And behind that exhale was the truth, waiting to be named.

We learned that Jayson—her husband, her partner, her person—had been drowning in work for over a year now. Twelve-hour shifts between his surgical practice and a high-stakes research initiative at the hospital had turned him into a shadow in their home. A ghost with keys. Someone who passed through rooms but no longer lived in them.

They barely shared a bed anymore, let alone intimacy. He missed the girls' recitals. Skipped the parent-teacher conferences. Arrived home long after bath time, sometimes after *midnight*, smelling like antiseptic and exhaustion. And Eden? She was left holding the weight of it all—homework, tantrums, teacher emails, sibling squabbles, and the quiet grief of doing it all alone.

Out of guilt, Jayson suggested hiring a nanny. He said it would help—take some of the pressure off. But instead of relief, the offer landed like an insult. As if she couldn't hold it down. As if she wasn't already *trying* to be everything, all the time.

The nanny came anyway.

And now the girls clung to her more than to Eden. They went to her for snacks, stories, even scraped knees. That quiet ache of irrelevance had burrowed somewhere deep, settling into Eden's bones like a second skin she didn't ask for.

She exhaled slowly, gripping the stem of her wine glass like it was the only thing tethering her in place. Her diamond-studded ring sparkled under the soft light, but her eyes looked tired. Dimmed.

"I live in a beautiful house," she said, her voice level, rehearsed. "I've got more designer bags and shoes than I could ever wear. A husband who's successful, handsome, respected. Two gorgeous daughters." She paused, her painted nails tapping lightly against the glass.

"What the hell do I have to complain about?"

She let out a brittle laugh, the kind meant to dismiss everything she'd just said.

But the bitterness in it? It was sharp. And unmistakable.

And for the first time in a long time, Eden wasn't perfect.

She was just a woman—exhausted, invisible, and wondering if having it *all* meant losing herself in the process.

Somewhere between Eden's confession and the second round of cornbread, I completely lost focus. My phone buzzed beside my plate, and one glance at the screen made the room fade into the background.

Sterling: What's up, gorgeous?

I swallowed hard.

Skylar: Hello, Mr. Jennings. How are you?

A beat later, another buzz.

Sterling: Dinner tomorrow?

My stomach flipped. My posture must have shifted because Allie's sharp gaze was already on me, curiosity flickering behind her knowing smirk.

"Do you want to fill us in on who's got you grinning like that, Ms. Madison?" she teased.

My throat went dry. "Uh... it's nothing. Nothing special."

The table went silent for half a second before Quinn, ever the dramatist, broke into an exaggerated, off-key melody:

"I can tell you're lying 'cause when you're replying you..."

Eden and Allie immediately joined in, laughing.

"Stutter, stutter," they sang in unison, their amusement loud and unapologetic.

I rolled my eyes, but the heat creeping up my neck betrayed

me. "It's just Sterling."

"We *know* who it is," Allie said pointedly. "He's been blowing up your phone all weekend."

I sighed, relenting. "He just asked if we could have dinner tomorrow." Even I heard the surprise in my voice, like I hadn't expected him to actually ask.

Allie's brows furrowed. "Dinner? You guys are doing *dinner* now?"

"I thought it was just innocent conversation and texting—nothing serious," Quinn added, her tone pure interrogation.

"We've been talking. Taking things slow. Getting reacquainted," I admitted. "Sterling's been pushing for more."

Eden smirked, tearing off a piece of fried chicken. "Sounds like classic Sterling. Moving in to make it *more*. He wants that old thing back."

"Just like Sterling, to want his cake and eat it too," Quinn quipped, shaking her head.

"You mean cake, cupcakes, cookies, and ice cream," Allie corrected, and Quinn high-fived her across the table.

The moment was broken when Eden choked on her sweet tea, coughing between laughs.

I exhaled slowly, eyes fixed on my plate as the quiet hum of conversation faded into the background. My mind, traitorous as ever, drifted back to the years I'd spent—middle school, high school, college—chasing after Sterling Jennings like some starry-eyed fool in a paperback romance. Back then, his smile could undo me. His attention, even when it came in fleeting, breadcrumb doses, felt like oxygen.

I thought I had outgrown it. Outgrown *him*.

But some small, foolish part of me—tucked away like an old journal I couldn't bring myself to throw out—still clung to the fantasy. The "what if." The version of Sterling I had created in my head: thoughtful, devoted, ready. A man who had never actually existed outside of my longing.

And maybe the truth was harder to face than the lie: that he hadn't changed... and I hadn't fully let go.

Not yet.

"Whoa, whoa, shots fired," I tried to joke, pushing the conversation away from the landmine it had become. "Come on, Sterling's a good guy. That was years ago."

Quinn snorted. "Years ago?"

"People change," Allie challenged, tilting her head.

I heard the skepticism in her voice, laced with the caution only someone who truly loved me would dare to say out loud. But the truth was, I'd already asked myself the same question—more times than I cared to admit.

Do people really change?

Could I trust the 40-year-old version of my first love—the man who once made promises with honeyed words and broke them with ease? The same man who had mastered the art of showing up just enough to keep hope alive, but never enough to stay?

Time had passed, sure. We weren't those reckless kids anymore. But when it came to matters of the heart, history had a way of wearing a familiar face.

And no matter how many times I told myself I was older, wiser, more guarded now... I still wasn't sure if I was strong enough to risk being wrong about him *again*.

But Allie wasn't finished. Her voice was calm, but laced with that sharp clarity she reserved for moments when the truth needed to cut. "Skylar, you seem to have *all* the grace in the world for Sterling's antics—but when it comes to Titus?

You've got none."

The shift in the room was immediate. My spine straightened, defenses rising before I could stop them.

"I've been honest with Titus," I said, sharper than I intended.

"Honest?" Eden's voice was soft, but firm—challenging me without blinking.

"Yes. Honest." I held their stares, refusing to shrink under the weight of their judgment. "Last time we talked, Titus asked me where this was going... if we were heading toward something real. Something serious."

The words hung in the air, and so did the memory—the café, the warmth of the lights casting a soft halo over Titus' face, the sincerity in his voice, that quiet vulnerability he didn't often show.

"I told him Sterling and I were talking," I said finally, the words tasting more bitter out loud than they had in my head.

Quinn muttered under her breath, barely loud enough for anyone to hear. "*Talking.*"

And just like that, I felt the weight of it.

The look in Titus' eyes that night. The pause before he nodded, the way his smile didn't quite reach his eyes. I had called it honesty. But sitting here, surrounded by the women who knew me best—who saw through my rationalizations like glass—I had to wonder if it had just been fear dressed up in truth.

"I never pictured myself with someone who had been married," I continued, my voice quieter now, barely above a whisper. "He has a built-in family. A *whole* life that existed before me."

There it was. The truth I'd been dodging, finally out in the open. Vulnerable. Uneasy.

Allie didn't miss a beat. She leaned in, her brows raised in disbelief. "*Wow*, Sky. You are being so shallow right now. Ay, *menso!*"

Quinn joined in without missing a beat, tossing a throw pillow at my legs with a scoff. "*Sí, muy loco*," she said, her voice laced with mock dramatics and just enough heat to make her point. "How is it that Titus gets benched because of your dealbreakers, and *Sterling*—of all people—*doesn't?*"

The room went quiet for a second, the weight of the question lingering longer than any of us expected.

I swallowed hard, staring down at my wine glass, the guilt creeping in like fog. I didn't have an answer. At least not one I was ready to say out loud.

Not yet.

Eden wiped her fingers on a napkin and looked straight at me. "Be careful, Sky. I get it—the fantasy of you and Sterling has been alive for years. But don't get so caught up in *what could be* that you miss out on *what actually is*." She picked up her sweet tea again, this time without choking. "I'm not saying Sterling *can't* change." She even made air quotes. "But let's hope *you've* changed too. Know your worth, Sky. Don't trade a real future for a recycled dream that may never be what you imagined."

Allie and Quinn exchanged glances, eyebrows raised.

"What?" Eden asked, catching our collective looks. "I make sense sometimes." She reached for the ribs. "Now, pass the damn food."

Laughter broke the tension, but my thoughts lingered on her words. Maybe, just maybe, she was right.

40

Allie

The soft glow of the city lights flickered against the towering windows of my Brooklyn brownstone, casting elongated shadows across the warm, earth-toned living room. The plush sectional embraced us, a cocoon of comfort as the faint scent of jasmine candles mingled with the remnants of our evening cocktails. Laughter rippled through the space, seamlessly blending with the velvety croon of '90s R&B, a nostalgic hum underscoring the years we had spent growing together.

Quinn, ever the instigator of deep conversation, set down her glass and looked at us expectantly. "Did you get the text about the 25th reunion?" she asked, her voice cutting through the comfortable stillness.

Skylar furrowed her perfectly arched brows, glancing up from where she had been tracing the rim of her glass with a manicured finger. "Twenty-fifth reunion? Whose 25th reunion?" Her expression betrayed genuine confusion, as if the notion of time applying to us was laughable.

I rolled my eyes, adjusting my posture against the pile of

velvet throw pillows. "Chica, it's *our* 25th reunion," I said, giving her a look. "Twenty-five years out of high school."

Eden let out a rich, melodic laugh, tossing her head slightly so the light caught the diamond studs at her ears. Her pixie cut, sleek and sculpted, framed her high cheekbones flawlessly. "I know, Sky, I can hardly believe it either. Twenty-five years feels... unreal." She smoothed the front of her silk blouse, its delicate sheen catching the warm light. There was no evidence in her face, her presence, her poise, that high school had been a quarter of a century ago.

Sky scoffed, waving a hand dismissively. "You may be celebrating 25 years out of high school, but—"

"Don't even say it." Quinn interjected, leveling her with a playful but stern gaze. "You *are* too."

Skylar, ever the skeptic, shook her head, still mentally calculating the math. "There's no way. I can't believe we've known each other for 25 years."

A quiet settled over us, thick with the weight of time, memories threading together like an intricate tapestry we hadn't quite stopped to admire before. The realization sat heavy, a mixture of nostalgia and disbelief. I watched as Sky took a slow sip of the mocktail Quinn had made, her fingers lightly tapping against the glass as if steadying herself against the passing years. Quinn curled her feet onto the couch, tucking her bare toes beneath a mound of pillows before draping a soft blanket over her lap.

Then, her voice, softer now, threaded through the quiet. "Twenty-five years... and do we really *know* each other?"

Her words were a match struck in the dark, igniting something unspoken between us. Quinn's gaze shifted to Eden, scrutinizing. "I mean, until this weekend, Eden, you had us all believing you lived this posh, privileged life, white picket fence, two kids, the whole thing."

Eden tilted her chin with a small smirk. "Minus the dog," she corrected.

Quinn pressed on. "And Sky, you walk through life like you own the damn place—smart, ambitious, conquering everything in your path. But somehow, you're still pining over a man who broke your heart one too many times."

I, ever the instigator of well-placed tension, grabbed a throw pillow and lobbed it at Skylar. "Correction—*the* jerk who broke your heart one too many times."

Sky caught it with a scoff, shaking her head. "We're not talking about me right now."

"No, we're talking about all of us." Quinn's voice was steady, intent. "How much do we actually let ourselves *be known* by each other? Are we even trying?"

Eden spoke first. "Quinn, we *know* you. We know you're an amazing mother and friend."

"You're the fearless, sassy glue that keeps us all together," I added, offering her a small smile.

She let out a dry, brittle chuckle—more survival than humor—and stared down into her glass as if searching for the right words in the swirl of red wine. Her fingers tightened around the stem, knuckles whitening.

"Yeah... on the surface, I'm all those things," she said, her voice steady, but barely. "Strong. Grateful. Resilient." She paused, her throat working around the weight of what came next. "But the truth?"

She exhaled, and when she looked up, her eyes shimmered with unshed tears, glassy with emotion she refused to let fall.

"The truth is—I'm *terrified.* Every single day. Praying I live long enough to watch Taylor, Quincy, and TJ graduate high school. Praying I get to see Tatum turn gray, grow slower. Grow old *with* me. Because my mom?" She shook her head slowly. "She was robbed of that. Breast cancer didn't just take her—it took *time*."

Her voice cracked slightly at the end, and she looked away, blinking fast.

The weight of her confession anchored the room. It cut through everything—the soft hum of the music in the background, the clink of ice in a glass, even the flickering candles on the table. The air shifted, like the walls themselves were holding their breath.

None of us spoke.

Because there are moments where silence isn't uncomfortable— it's sacred.

And in that stillness, we weren't just her friends.

We were witnesses. To her strength. To her fear. To her fight to still hope in spite of it all.

I took a deep breath, the weight of my own truth pressing against my ribs. "Twenty-five years together... and yet, we are not *fully* known to each other."

The words left my mouth before I could stop them, before I could convince myself to shove them back into the dark corners I had tucked them into for decades. And once I started, there was no stopping.

I spoke long into the night—my voice raw, cracking in places, my hands trembling in my lap as if my body remembered truths my mind had tried to forget. With each word, I peeled back layers I had buried so deep they barely felt like mine anymore. Layers stitched with silence, shame, and survival.

I told them the story I had never fully admitted to myself—the story of a confident, spunky Boricua from Brooklyn who had walked onto her college campus fearless, radiant, ready to take on the world... and fallen hard for a man who wore charm like armor and cruelty like second skin. A wolf in sheep's clothing.

I told them how I—*Alejandra*—the girl who always walked into rooms like she belonged, who cracked jokes louder than the boys and danced like the beat was made for her, had been told to shrink. To blend in. To make herself small enough to be manageable, digestible.

And when I didn't—when I dared to shine anyway—I was punished. Not with silence, but with bruises disguised as love.

I told them how I, the girl who had always been inseparable from her *familia*, had disappeared. How I stopped coming home. How I ignored my cousins' texts, my abuela's voicemails, my father's worried prayers. I avoided mirrors, avoided anything that might reflect the truth I couldn't bear to face: that I had been broken by someone who said he loved me.

And I told them how I, the girl who used to wear her hair wild, curly, *free*—a crown of defiance passed down through generations—had straightened it into silence. Week after week. Heat and shame pressed into every strand. Because he liked it better that way. Because control doesn't always come in screams—it comes in whispers that sound like compliments.

And yet, despite everything, I hadn't escaped even when the door was wide open.

"I almost forgot who I was," I whispered, the weight of it

sitting heavy in my chest.

And in that quiet, holy pause after confession, I felt something shift. Not just in the room—but in *me*.

The words poured from me, and as I spoke, I listened as if hearing someone else's story—detached, analytical. But it was mine. It had always been mine.

Finally, I exhaled, the confession settling around us, heavy yet liberating.

"Seeing Bryan again doesn't scare me because I think he could hurt me again," I admitted, my voice barely more than a whisper—fragile, but sure. "It scares me because it forces me to face the truth... that this isn't just something that *happened* to me."

I paused, feeling the words land like a confession I hadn't even realized I needed to say aloud.

"It's not a chapter I can skip over. Not a story I can tell in past tense, with neat edges and a safe distance. It's *my* story. And I have to own that. Every messy, painful, complicated part of it."

Saying it out loud didn't make it easier. But it made it *real*.

And maybe, finally, that was the beginning of taking it back.

The room, for once, was silent in a way that wasn't uncomfortable. It was a silence of understanding, of acceptance. Of finally, *finally* being seen.

And for the first time in twenty-five years, I let myself be known.

41

Skylar

I couldn't believe it had been almost a month since our girls' weekend. Somehow, time had slipped through my fingers like fine sand—familiar and fleeting—and we had all quietly eased back into the rhythm of our daily lives. For better or worse.

Quinn was back in her usual role: the master juggler of all things life, love, and liberation. On any given day, she was straddling the line between PTA duties and panel discussions, dashing from TJ and Quincy's soccer practices in muddy cleats to community board meetings in power heels. I still couldn't wrap my head around the fact that she was a bona fide *soccer mom* now—just with hoop earrings, a perfectly curated playlist, and a trunk full of snacks that were both organic *and* bribery-grade.

But beneath all the minivan chaos and color-coded calendars was Quinn, still tirelessly doing the work that lit her soul on fire. The political landscape had only grown more volatile, more hostile, and yet she stayed in the thick of it— fighting for the underdog, elevating social innovators who were constantly being asked to do more with less. She wasn't just showing up—she was building new lanes for people who had been locked out for too long.

And in between late-night legal brief review sessions with Tatum, trying to decode Taylor's latest mood swings (which were legendary at this point), and managing a home that never seemed to stop moving, Quinn still found time to check in on *us*.

That was her magic.

Even when her own world was teetering on the edge of chaos, she carried us. Quietly. Fiercely. Without asking for applause. She had this uncanny way of sensing when one of us was unraveling—and showing up before we even knew we needed her.

She was the glue. The grace. The grit.

And I don't think she even realized it.

Eden, on the other hand, had been drowning in designer labels and curated perfection. Her days were filled with cham-pagne luncheons and PTA meetings where the conversations had the depth of a puddle and the warmth of a showroom. It was all Range Rovers, renovations, spring break in Turks and Caicos, and whose husband just closed the biggest deal on Wall Street. The currency was clout, and Eden knew how to spend it—dressed to the nines, effortlessly composed, never letting the mask slip.

But I saw it.

Behind the subtle flick of her wrist as she sipped rosé. Behind the practiced smiles and casually dropped luxury names. She was tired. I saw the way her eyes searched for her husband across crowded galas, how her gaze lingered a second too long—like she was reaching for something just out of frame. Longing for the nights when they used to lie in bed laughing until their stomachs hurt, before their house became a showroom and their marriage a business arrangement.

We'd grown closer over the past few weeks—not in a performative, brunch-photo-op kind of way, but in the quiet, necessary truth-telling way that happens when women are just too tired to pretend anymore. Our bond had been soldered together by the wounds left by our mothers— emotional scar tissue that neither of us had fully healed.

We had nicknamed hers *Ursula*—the mother of manipulation. Calculating, polished, always two steps ahead with a compliment laced in control. Mine? *Stitch.* Because wherever she went, she left a trail of chaos, threading guilt and bitterness through every interaction, binding us in tension no therapist had fully unraveled.

It started as a joke—our code for surviving the women who raised us.

But underneath the laughter was an unspoken truth: we were still patching ourselves together from what they'd undone.

And then there was Allie.

Somehow, she had managed to avoid running into Bryan— not that it took much effort. The universe had given her a convenient out: a calendar packed to the brim with flights, meetings, and hotel check-ins that spanned coastlines. She'd been moving non-stop, bouncing between time zones like a woman running from ghosts she didn't want to name.

And maybe she was.

Meanwhile, I was left slightly off-kilter. Our daily check-ins—those quick, sarcastic texts, those late-night voice notes filled with half-whispered jokes and unsolicited life advice—had become sporadic, scattered like postcards from a version of her that always seemed just out of reach.

It was subtle at first. The lag in replies. The missed calls. The "let me call you back"s that didn't always come.

And though I'd never say it out loud—never admit how much her absence threw off my center—I *missed* her. I missed the rhythm of us. The banter that never needed warming up. The way her presence, even in silence, grounded me.

I wasn't counting the days until she came home.

But I was definitely counting *something*.

By Friday, I was more than ready to shed the weight of the week like an old coat. My brain still buzzed from back-to-back meetings, spreadsheets I never wanted to see again, and the final stages of planning our new STEM program launching in Bed-Stuy this summer. Excitement and anxiety danced in my chest, a familiar push-pull that came with birthing something that mattered. Something that might actually *change* something.

Nearly a year had passed since I first crossed paths with Titus—an unassuming introduction that had slowly unraveled into a quiet kind of magic. Somewhere between community board meetings and late-night texts about grant deadlines, we found common ground. And then, without realizing it, we built something real.

The Green Roof and Garden Project: Elevate Green.

It started with an idea—Allie, Quinn, Titus, Langston, and me tossing out dreams like puzzle pieces over brunch and brainstorming sessions that lasted longer than we intended. Now it had roots. We were partnering with local schools and community centers to transform empty rooftops and forgotten lots into vibrant green spaces—urban gardens where kids could get their hands dirty while learning about sustainability, architecture, food systems, and design thinking.

It wasn't just about plants or programming. It was about possibility.

We wanted to give Black and Brown students a chance to see the intersection of science and community not just as a class—but as *theirs.* Something tangible. Something they could shape.

And in the process, maybe we were reshaping ourselves too.

Allie had seamlessly woven her Urban Arts summer program into the project, curating a series of murals and community-led art installations that would breathe color and soul into every rooftop and garden wall. She had a gift for making concrete bloom—turning overlooked spaces into living canvases.

Titus and Langston, ever the dynamic duo, were spearheading workshops on real estate development and urban planning. With a mix of charisma and hard-won knowledge, they were showing students how to envision eco-friendly buildings using 3D modeling software, zoning maps, and the kind of language usually reserved for boardrooms. The kids? Ate. It. Up.

My team was knee-deep in the science. Solar panels. Energy-efficient construction. Rainwater collection systems. Sustainable gardening that fed both stomachs and minds. We were turning textbooks into touchpoints, theories into experiments. It wasn't just a project—it was a living, breathing classroom.

And somehow, against the odds, it was all coming together.

For once, things were moving forward without too many roadblocks. No derailed funding. No political delays. No internal combustion.

At least, not professionally.

Personally? That was a different story.

Langston—bless his ever-meddling heart—had become the unofficial glue holding it all together. Acting as liaison, buffer, and peacekeeper between Titus and me. Ever since things shifted between us—whatever we were now, unfinished or unspoken—avoidance had become the unspoken rule.

We worked in tandem. Just... never in the same room.

And while the project was thriving, some part of me wondered how long we could keep pretending that the tension between us wasn't still planted in the soil, growing wild beneath the surface.

I reached for my phone, thumb instinctively hovering over Allie's contact. The muscle memory of needing her—of wanting to hear her voice, her take, her *truth*—was second nature. But then I stopped, remembering she was probably somewhere over the Atlantic, midair and untouchable, on her way home from her latest international trip.

She had been working with a collective of Black and Brown artists abroad, curating exhibitions that told stories the world had tried to erase. It was so *Allie*—effortlessly moving between continents, translating culture into color, rubbing elbows with some of the most brilliant minds in the global art scene... and still texting us memes and checking in on Eden's latest meltdown like she never left the block.

That was her gift. Big stage, humble heart. She could be in

Paris or Lagos or Mexico City and still feel like home.

And even though I missed her—*deeply*—I couldn't help but smile. Watching her rise felt like all of us were rising too.

Leaving the office early felt like a small but necessary victory. A quiet rebellion against the grind that had consumed my week. The days were finally stretching longer, the remnants of winter loosening their grip, making room for spring to breathe again.

Outside, the scent of freshly planted tulips lingered in the air, framing the entrance of my building like a soft, floral welcome. Their vibrant colors nodded gently in the breeze, a reminder that even after the coldest seasons, something beautiful always manages to bloom.

Inside, the fading sunlight poured through my floor-to-ceiling windows, casting honey-gold shadows across the hardwood floors. The city outside was still humming, but in here—there was stillness.

I kicked off my heels with a sigh, the familiar ache in my arches giving way to instant relief. My bag slipped from my shoulder and landed with a soft thud against the wall. I didn't bother picking it up. I didn't have to.

Instead, I collapsed into my oversized sofa, its cushions swallowing me whole like an embrace I didn't realize I needed. My fingers swiped idly across my phone, scrolling without direction. Just noise to fill the quiet.

And then—finally—I let myself exhale.

Not just the shallow breath I'd been carrying all week, but a real one. Deep. Unrushed. The kind that empties your lungs and makes space again.

For the first time in days, I let myself *be*.

And in that stillness, I started to feel like myself again.

The golden hues of dusk bathed Brooklyn in a soft, amber glow, casting long shadows across brownstone rooftops and fire escapes. The city was easing into night with the slow elegance of a deep exhale. From my apartment window, the view stretched out toward the Brooklyn Bridge, its iconic arches lit in a soft shimmer. The lights danced along the East River like scattered diamonds tossed across dark silk, flickering with rhythm and restraint.

Inside, the low murmur of the jazz station filled the room, Coltrane's saxophone spilling through the speakers like a slow pour of honey—warm, deliberate, and just a little blue. It was the kind of song that held space for you to think, to feel, to unravel a little.

I stretched my legs across the sofa, toes curling into the throw blanket draped over the edge. The weight of the week still clung to me in invisible threads, but in this moment— this quiet cocoon of golden light and sound—I felt it start to loosen.

I picked up my phone and began scrolling, the screen glowing against the dim room. Messages had stacked up over the last hour, each one a tiny pull back into the noise. Work, family, people needing something—always something. But I moved slowly, not quite ready to rejoin the world.

For now, I just wanted to be here.

In the hush of twilight.

In the hum of Coltrane.

In the stillness I'd earned.

Sterling: Hello, gorgeous. Happy Friday. Dinner tonight?

I stared at the message, my thumb hovering, not quite ready to engage. Sterling always knew how to package his charm—warm, smooth, perfectly timed. He had that magnetic pull, the kind that could draw you in before you realized you were already tangled.

But tonight? I wasn't sure I had the energy for the performance dinner often required. The small talk dressed up like intimacy. The dance of flattery and ego. Sterling liked the idea of me—the curated, composed, captivating version. The real me? The tired, overthinking, quietly complicated me? I wasn't always sure he even noticed her.

I set my phone aside, letting the question hang like smoke in the air—unanswered, intentional.

Moments later, my screen lit up again.

Allie:

A cascade of images flooded in—photos of art pieces she'd clearly just discovered. Bold, arresting compositions. A riot of color and texture that leapt off the screen. Sculptures that twisted into emotion. Paintings that looked like movement frozen in time.

Absolutely amazing pieces, she wrote. I cannot wait to show you the treasures I found.

A slow grin tugged at my lips, unexpected but welcome. That was my girl. Allie didn't just collect beauty—she found stories in it. She *saw* things. And more than that, she brought pieces of the world back to the people she loved, like souvenirs of wonder.

I missed her fiercely.

And in that moment, I felt it clearly: the difference between someone who sought to impress me and someone who simply *knew* me.

Mom: Skylar, just saying hello. Call me when you have a moment.

My stomach clenched instantly.

I knew that tone—*too* polite, too measured. "Just saying hello" was her version of a loaded weapon dressed in pearls. Code for something unsaid, almost always a request draped in judgment, or worse, a reminder of some perceived failure I hadn't yet corrected. I'd been dodging her calls for weeks, not because I didn't care, but because I did. Too much. And caring came with a cost.

The guilt curled in my chest like smoke. The weight of obligation was a familiar ache—but I wasn't ready to carry it tonight. *Not yet.*

Allie: I get in early tomorrow. See you at the gym?

I groaned, half-laughing as I read it. The gym. Her not-so-subtle way of pulling me back to accountability. I had been ghosting HIIT classes since she left town—morning routines replaced by extended snoozes and a steady rotation of excuses. But the idea of seeing her again, sweaty and breathless on matching yoga mats, followed by overpriced coffee and an unfiltered catch-up?

Yeah. My heart lifted just thinking about it.

Dad: Hey, baby girl. I think I would rather drive up than fly. We'll talk.

A warmth bloomed in my chest at his message. My father, with his steady hands and quiet strength. No pretense. No layered meanings. Just presence. I could already hear the calm in his voice, feel the peace it always brought me. He was my lighthouse—never loud, never demanding. Just *there.*

I smiled, slow and genuine.

Three messages.

Three entirely different frequencies.

My mother's silence disguised as concern. Allie's light tug back into life. And my dad's quiet reminder that no matter how complicated everything else felt—*some* things remained simple, and good, and mine.

Quinn: I confirmed BK ROT will be able to help with the initiative! They're a Brooklyn-based composting program that supports youth employment and sustainability. The perfect partner for the Garden Project! I can't wait to give you the deets (♥).

I smiled, my fingers lingering over the screen for a moment. Leave it to Quinn to come through with a partner that not only made logistical sense but aligned perfectly with our mission. She didn't just check boxes—she built bridges. Her excitement crackled through the screen, and I felt it in my chest like a burst of sunlight.

I made a mental note to follow up and call her later—she deserved more than a "great news" text. She deserved a toast.

Sterling: ?

I rolled my eyes.

Of course. Patience had never been Sterling's virtue. A single question mark as if that would somehow compel a reply. No context. No grace. Just vibes and ego.

I ignored it and moved on.

Eden: Ursula is at it again. What's up with Stitch?

A laugh escaped my lips before I could stop it. Classic Eden. Our unofficial code names for our mothers had started as a joke and slowly evolved into a full-on coping mechanism. Ursula, with her velvet-tongued critiques and perfectly manicured manipulation. And my mother—Stitch—always weaving chaos into every conversation, threading guilt through even the smallest ask.

I tapped back quickly, firing off a string of laughing emojis and a reply:

Let's do lunch next weekend. I need the tea in person.

Because I already knew whatever Ursula was up to deserved a proper debrief—with wine, sarcasm, and maybe a little prayer.

The screen dimmed in my hand as I exhaled, the breath long and heavy—like I'd been holding it all week. My thoughts churned, circling the usual suspects: Sterling, my mother, the silent expectations tucked between the lines of her last message. The weight of it all—decisions waiting, feelings lingering, questions I wasn't ready to answer—pressed in, thick and unrelenting.

The evening stretched out before me, open and uncertain. I wasn't sure if I wanted solitude or distraction, silence or sound. Just not more thinking.

And then—buzz.

My phone vibrated in my palm, jolting me from the spiral. The screen lit up with a name that made my chest warm before I even answered.

I pressed the phone to my ear, already smiling.

A deep, familiar baritone wrapped around me like a well-worn blanket, comforting and sure. "Hello, beautiful."

My breath caught.

The one man who had never made me feel like I had to earn love. The only one who saw through the performance and adored every version of me anyway.

"Daddy."

The word tumbled out in a rush—soft, tender, unfiltered. The little girl in me stepping forward before the woman could think twice.

And just like that, the weight on my chest lifted.

Maybe not all the way. But enough.

Enough to breathe.

Enough to remember who I was before the world asked me to bend.

We sat on the phone for hours, effortlessly slipping into that familiar rhythm—the kind that doesn't need warm-ups or pleasantries. Just a breath, a pause, and we were there. Catching up on everything from work drama to family updates, to his long-suffering Knicks, who continued their decades-long tradition of breaking his heart right when he dared to believe again.

"Still think they're making the playoffs?" I teased, curled up on the couch with my legs tucked beneath me, a blanket around my shoulders and a half-empty glass of wine in my hand.

He chuckled, that rich, honeyed sound I loved more than any punchline. "Hope springs eternal, baby girl. You know we bleed orange and blue."

That was Daddy—faithful, even when things didn't make sense. Loyal to his core. And his voice carried that same deep, knowing timbre that always made me lean in, even through a phone line. It was a voice full of stories and strength, the kind of voice that could still talk me down from my worst days with nothing more than a sigh and a "You good?"

"I finally got the plans finalized," he said, his tone lifting with quiet pride.

There was a pause. The kind of pause that came when he was holding something sacred and couldn't wait to hand it to me.

I knew exactly what he was talking about before he even had to say it.

The house.

His dream.

The one he'd been sketching in his mind since I was a little girl. The one he'd described in vivid detail during long drives through red clay roads and overgrown fields on our summer visits down South. While other kids were listening to their walkmans or half-listening to their parents drone on, I was sitting shotgun, watching his eyes light up every time we passed *that* patch of land.

To anyone else, it was nothing—a sunbaked stretch of earth dotted with stubborn weeds and memories of what once stood there. But to him, it was sacred. A blank canvas. A promise in waiting.

"You see that over there?" he used to say, one hand gripping the steering wheel, the other pointing through the windshield, his voice swelling with conviction. *"That's where I'm gonna build you a castle fit for a queen."*

He said it with the same certainty he reserved for Scripture and Knicks predictions—unshakable, unwavering.

And I believed him.

Because when Daddy said something, he meant it. Always had.

I smiled at the memory, that old familiar warmth curling through me—Daddy's voice, his big dreams, the way he always made the impossible sound like Sunday gospel. But beneath that sweetness, my stomach tightened.

Now, it was really happening.

His long-awaited retirement was no longer some far-off idea he teased at family cookouts or talked about during halftime. It was around the corner. Concrete. Real. And he was preparing to leave New York for good.

He was heading South—to build the legacy he'd always

talked about. His own little sanctuary, nestled near Aunt Mamie's place in North Carolina. Five acres of promise, space to breathe, to plant, to *be*. He called it his "mini estate," and I knew he meant every word.

It sounded beautiful in theory—peaceful, intentional, exactly what he deserved.

But in practice?

It meant he wouldn't be a quick drive away. No more last-minute brunches in Harlem. No more popping by to fix a leaky faucet or surprise me with a box of cannolis from the old Italian bakery we both loved. No more of his steady presence just within reach.

The thought sat heavy on my chest—like grief in slow motion. A joyful goodbye I wasn't sure I knew how to give.

"Daddy, it sounds like you're down there giving everyone orders," I teased, as he explained his latest meeting with the lead architect and the scheduled groundbreaking.

"I wouldn't have to give orders if people just knew what they were doing," he shot back, the smirk in his voice evident.

I laughed, grateful for the levity.

We eventually shifted to lighter territory—his upcoming birthday visit.

"Why don't you just fly?" I offered, already bracing myself for the pushback. "It's faster, easier. No need to drive all those hours."

As expected, he scoffed, the way only a stubborn, prideful man raised on principle and practicality could. "No need to waste money on a flight," he said with a huff. "Skylar, I've driven from New York to North Carolina more times than I can count. I could do it in my sleep."

I rolled my eyes so hard I could practically hear them.

"That's *exactly* what I'm worried about—the 'in your sleep' part," I muttered under my breath.

He chuckled, that low, amused rumble that always made me smile even when he was being infuriating. "I'll be fine, baby girl. I like the drive. Gives me time to think, stretch my legs, listen to some Earth Wind and Fire. You worry too much."

"I learned from the best," I shot back, but there was no edge in it. Just love laced with anxiety, the kind that comes from knowing how much someone means to you—and how hard it is to imagine the world without them just a short drive away.

He caught that, of course. Nothing ever slipped past him—not my muttered worries, not the shift in my tone.

"Don't start treating me like an old man now," he warned, voice full of mock indignation. "I plan to stop in Virginia, catch up with some old friends, maybe spend the night in Maryland with your cousin before heading into the city. That okay with you, *Ms. Madison?*" His voice dripped with playful sarcasm, stretching out my name like he was reading it from a courtroom docket.

I rolled my eyes, unable to hide the smirk tugging at my lips. "If those are the definitive, approved-by-the-board plans, then I suppose they can be approved—pending final review."

He let out a low chuckle, relishing the back-and-forth. "Oh, baby girl, hold on a second," he said suddenly, feigning seriousness. "I need to check my birth certificate real quick. See if your name's listed under 'legal guardian.'"

And then came his signature laugh—deep, rumbling, and absolutely contagious. The kind that wrapped around me like a hug, even from miles away.

"*Daddy.*" I groaned, half-laughing. "You are *not* funny."

"You're right," he said with a grin I could hear through the phone. "I'm *hilarious.*"

"Tell Allie I'm looking forward to watching some *real* basketball with a *true* Knicks fan," he said, pivoting smoothly back to one of his favorite topics—basketball and bonding. Classic Dad.

I grinned, already picturing his face when I shared the surprise. "Actually... I was gonna wait to tell you in person, but I can't keep a secret from you. I got us tickets to a game while you're here."

There was a beat of silence before his voice lit up with boyish excitement. "Well, let me go ahead and pack my Knicks jersey while I'm at it," he said, full of drama, knowing full well he didn't own one—and had spent the last decade criticizing every front-office decision they'd made.

"You think you're a *comedian* today, don't you, Daddy?" I laughed, shaking my head.

He didn't miss a beat. "Nah, but I *am* your favorite act."

And he was.

No matter how grown I got, how far life pulled us in different directions, some things stayed the same—like the joy of making him laugh, and the way his love, even laced with jokes, always made me feel ten feet tall.

"Since we're keeping the laughs coming," he started, his voice dipping into something more knowing, "what's the latest on you and that knucklehead?"

My throat tightened. I knew exactly who he was referring to.

The silence stretched between us.

"Cat got your tongue? Or is it just that you can't find anything nice to say?" He chuckled, but I could hear the edge behind it.

I sighed, my voice softening as I slipped into that familiar, tender register I hadn't used in years—the one reserved just for him. "*Daddy*," I said, drawing out the word like a quiet plea, the way I used to when I wanted him to go easy on me after doing something reckless. "We're reconnecting... taking things slow."

He exhaled sharply, and even through the phone I could hear the restraint in it. The kind of breath that held back a thousand unspoken *I told you sos*. "Skylar," he said, his voice low and firm, "I'm not sure what needs to be reconnected."

The disappointment in his tone wasn't harsh—it was protective. Heavy with love and layered with memory. "He wasn't worth your time back then, and he damn sure isn't worth it now," he continued, not missing a beat. "And don't give me that '*people change*' speech. From what you've told me, he still only pops up when he thinks someone else is catching your eye."

I didn't respond, but I didn't need to—he wasn't finished.

"You are *not* a backup plan, Skylar. You're not a place-holder. You're not an option. You're the *only* option."

The conviction in his voice wrapped around me, grounding me. That was the thing about my father—he didn't just love me, he *saw* me. Even when I didn't want to be seen. Especially then.

And maybe, just maybe, he was right.

His words landed like a truth I didn't want to face—one I'd been sidestepping for weeks, wrapping in justifications and what-ifs. Because if I was being honest, these past few weeks with Sterling had been nothing new. Same script, different season. Missed calls that he never explained. Conversations so rushed they barely counted as connection. And the wandering eyes—*always* the wandering eyes—I tried not to notice when we met for coffee, pretending his gaze hadn't drifted to the hostess or the woman at the next table.

"*Dad, I know,*" I said quietly, more exhale than response.

A beat passed. Then: "Are you trying to convince *me*, or yourself?"

The question sliced through the air, not cruel, just devastating in its precision.

Before I could form a reply, my phone buzzed in my hand.

Text from Sterling: *Be ready at 8:00 p.m.*

No "hey." No "would you like to..." Just a directive. Casual command wrapped in entitlement.

I stared at the screen, the glow of it casting a cold, sterile light across my bedroom walls. The knot in my stomach twisted tighter, coiling into something I couldn't immediately name. Was it annoyance? Flattery? Guilt? Maybe a cocktail of all three.

Sterling was nothing if not persistent. Like a door-to-door salesman who didn't understand the word *no*, always showing up with empty promises and charm polished just enough to distract from the cracks underneath.

But I wasn't sure how much longer I could pretend that persistence and *presence* were the same thing.

Daddy's voice rumbled through the receiver, low and deliberate, tugging me out of my spiraling thoughts and back into the room. "*And what about that other young man?*" he asked, casually—*too* casually. As if he hadn't just lobbed a live grenade straight into my carefully compartmentalized mind.

Titus.

The name landed like a whisper wrapped in thunder. My heart gave a startled, almost betrayed little skip—like it had been caught holding onto something I wasn't supposed to feel anymore.

I turned away from the mirror, where my own reflection stared back at me, eyes wide and unsure. The expression I wore was complicated—part guilt, part longing, part *don't-go-there*—and I couldn't quite name the rest.

Before I could formulate a response, the soft wail of Coltrane's saxophone floated from the Bluetooth speaker on my nightstand. The melody was rich and mournful, unfurling into the room like incense—sweet, slow, and heavy with everything unsaid. Notes clung to the air, thick with memory and longing, each one a slow pull on a thread I had tried not to tug.

Titus had been the thread.

And my father, somehow, always knew where to find the loose ends.

My mind betrayed me, drifting before I could stop it.

I thought of the last time I saw him—the way his presence filled a room without trying, the quiet steadiness of him that always made me feel just a little less chaotic. And then, like muscle memory, the scent of him rose unbidden in my mind: warm, clean, laced with cedar and something darker, smoky—like night air after a summer storm. It clung to me like a ghost, intimate and inescapable.

I remembered how his arms had wrapped around me—not possessive, not performative, just *certain*. There was a tenderness there, unspoken but undeniable. A touch that said, *I see you. All of you. And I still want you.*

And for a fleeting, fragile moment... I had let myself believe it.

But then—*the truth.*

The moment I had let fear speak louder than love.

I'd weaponized Sterling's name like a blade, sharp and calculated. Told Titus that Sterling and I were "working things out"—a lie so bitter it scorched my tongue on the way out. It wasn't premeditated; it was instinct. A clumsy, panicked defense. Because I couldn't say what I was *really* feeling.

That I was terrified.

Terrified that Titus—good, grounded, intentional Titus— would eventually look at me and see every crack I'd worked so hard to conceal. That he would realize I was too complicated, too guarded, too *much.* Or worse—not enough.

I saw again the flicker in his eyes when I said it. The way his dark brows furrowed with confusion, then disappointment. The way his mouth pressed into a hard, unreadable line—like he was holding something back to protect us both.

I had hurt him. *Intentionally.*

And the worst part?

He hadn't deserved it. Not one bit.

How ironic, really—how bitterly ironic—considering how much Titus and I had shared.

The late-night conversations that stretched past midnight, where words flowed like jazz riffs—spontaneous, open, true. The easy laughter over ridiculous debates—*Usher vs. Chris Brown,* as if we didn't both already know the answer. Our shared outrage over politics, over broken systems and broken promises, sometimes finishing each other's sentences in frustration and hope.

How many mornings had begun with his *"Good morning, beautiful,"* steady and reliable as sunrise? How many of his random calls had turned into hours of comfortable silence and meandering dialogue that felt like soul work?

And yet, when he looked me dead in the eye—with that frustrating, beautiful bluntness—and asked where we stood, I folded.

I couldn't give him the truth.

So instead, I hid.

Behind Sterling. Behind the shadow of old wounds and the jagged ruins of dreams I never dared rebuild—dreams with white picket fences, 2.5 kids, and a man who'd never make me question my worth.

Sterling.

Sterling, who cheated on me in college like it was sport. Sterling, who tried to get with Eden back in high school, as if I wouldn't find out. Sterling, who had been the embodiment of every betrayal I swore I'd never live through again.

And still, I used *him* as a shield.

Titus had seen right through it. Through me.

He'd called it exactly as it was—accused me, fairly and gently, of retreating. Of dragging him into the "buddy zone" after months of him showing up with tenderness, consistency, and real intention. After we had both been stepping toward something that felt solid.

His voice, usually warm and laced with teasing, had grown quiet that night. Soft, but edged with hurt.

And I had nodded.

Pretended not to notice the way his shoulders tightened. Pretended not to hear the crack in his voice when he asked, one last time, if this was all there was going to be.

Things have changed, I had said.

The lie tasted like ash in my mouth.

But are we working toward getting back there? he had asked, voice low, almost pleading—like he was offering me one last door before walking away from it for good.

I hadn't answered.

Not because I didn't know.

But because I did.

The memory sank its teeth into my gut, sharp and unrelenting, gnawing at me with the kind of precision only guilt knows how to wield. It wasn't just what I didn't say—it was what I let hang in the silence. What I let die there.

"Skylar."

Daddy's voice boomed through the line, slicing through my thoughts like a lighthouse beam cutting through fog. "I've been rambling on, talking to myself for a good five minutes. Where are you, girl?"

I blinked, suddenly aware of where I was—perched on the edge of my bed, phone still pressed to my ear, my eyes locked on the dusky lavender wall across the room like it held the answers I was too afraid to speak.

"I absolutely love and hate how you can read me, even over the phone," I admitted with a sigh, flopping backward onto the bed. The mattress creaked beneath me, old springs groaning under the weight of more than just my body.

The soft scent of fresh laundry wrapped around me, mixed with the calming notes of rose and sandalwood from my room spray—familiar, grounding, and slightly melancholy. My sanctuary.

"I'm just..." I trailed off.

Lost. Torn. Afraid.

But I didn't say any of that.

I didn't have to.

Daddy chuckled, a sound as warm and familiar as a favorite sweater. "The mention of 'the other man' made you drift off, huh?"

I chewed my bottom lip. "You could say that."

"Baby girl, you can pretend all you want," he said, his voice softening, "but your heart wants what it wants."

I groaned dramatically, dragging a pillow over my face. "Ugh, Daddy."

The clock on my nightstand blinked 7:32 p.m. at me with quiet judgment. Sterling would be here in less than 30 minutes.

"I really have to go," I said, sitting up and swinging my legs over the edge of the bed. My bare feet sank into the plush cream carpet. "I actually have a date tonight. With your favorite person."

"Let's hope it's your *last* date with him," Daddy muttered.

"Dad!" I laughed, grabbing my robe from the foot of the bed and heading toward the bathroom.

"You and I both know you're just buying time," he said. "Sterling is exactly who you already know he is."

"Bye, Daddy. Love you," I said, feeling that familiar mix of gratitude and irritation only he could inspire.

"Love you to the moon and back, baby girl," he said tenderly.

As I hung up, I could still hear his parting words echo in my mind:

The heart wants what it wants.

I stood in front of the bathroom mirror, staring at my

reflection like it might offer answers.

My robe hung loosely off one shoulder, slipping slightly as if mirroring the unraveling inside me. My hair was pinned in a messy knot at the top of my head, tendrils escaping like little rebellions. My brown eyes—once bright and sharp—looked tired. A little sad. A little stubborn. Like they'd seen too much and weren't sure whether to cry or push through.

I leaned forward and splashed cold water on my face, the sting of it waking something up in me. The chill didn't just clear my head—it stripped away the haze of excuses and half-truths I'd been hiding behind.

Tonight wasn't about Titus.

It wasn't about Daddy's warnings or Sterling's persistence.

It wasn't even really about love.

It was about *me*.

About finally getting honest with the woman staring back at me. About owning the fact that I had been dodging myself—numbing, performing, clinging to patterns that looked like romance but were really just fear dressed up in expensive heels.

I reached for the towel and patted my face dry, then paused, fingers still at my chin, eyes locked on my own.

"You deserve more," I whispered to the woman in the glass.

More than mixed signals. More than pretty lies. More than being someone's maybe.

The words lingered in the air like a dare.

And yet, I still wrapped myself in the illusion—for one more night. One more dinner. One more moment of pretending I wasn't standing at the edge of a choice I had to make.

With a deep breath, I turned from the mirror and began to

get ready.

I danced barefoot across the cool hardwood floors, the smooth grain grounding me as Lalah Hathaway's velvet voice poured through the speakers. Her sultry tones wrapped around me like a favorite sweater—soft, familiar, full of soul. The kind of music that didn't just fill the space, it *inhabited* it.

Spinning in front of the mirror, I held up two outfits against my body—one in each hand, my brow furrowed with indecision. The apartment lights cast a soft glow over the room, but under the surface, my confidence flickered.

I found myself second-guessing everything. Tugging at the hem, tilting my head, wondering what Sterling would "approve of." The thought made me suck my teeth and roll my eyes at my reflection.

Since when did I start dressing for his gaze instead of my own?

Annoyed, I tossed the slinky black dress onto the bed. It pooled there like a dark question mark—suggestive, predictable. The obvious choice. Seductive. *Safe.*

But then, like a quiet whisper from the version of me I liked best, I heard *his* voice in my mind.

Titus.

"There's nothing like a sexy, clean white tee, some nice jeans, and heels on a woman who knows her beauty transcends the tight black dress."

I frowned at my reflection, the black fabric suddenly clinging to me like doubt. The kind that didn't come from the outside—it came from forgetting who I was.

With a sigh, I slipped the dress off, the satin whispering against my skin as I pulled it over my head. I tossed it aside, not delicately this time, but with purpose.

Then—*ding dong.*

The doorbell rang. Sharp. Unexpected. Like the universe deciding to move the night forward whether I was ready or not.

I stood still for a beat, breath caught between hesitation and instinct.

And then I moved.

I jumped, heart jolting in my chest.

This wasn't the polite chime of the doorman announcing a guest from downstairs. No, this was *at* my door. Someone already standing on the other side, uninvited but expected all the same.

"Just a second! Coming!" I called out, voice higher than I meant it to be as I scrambled across the room.

In a flurry, I yanked open a dresser drawer and snatched out a pair of tight blue jeans and a crisp white t-shirt—clean, classic, *me.* The outfit slid on in rushed motions, my fingers fumbling with the denim as I shimmied into the jeans and tugged the shirt down over my frame. The cotton clung softly to my curves, warm from my palms and still holding the scent of fresh laundry.

The doorbell buzzed again—sharper this time. Impatient. Familiar.

"*Coming!*" I shouted again, laughing breathlessly at the chaos. Of course Sterling couldn't just wait like a normal person. Of course he couldn't text *I'm outside* like everyone else in 2025.

As I neared the door, something else reached me first.

A scent.

Warm. Musky. Confident.

Amber and palo santo.

Sterling.

It seeped through the crack in the door like a warning—or a memory. Unmistakable. Expensive. The kind of scent that lingered too long, like his presence. Like his intentions.

I paused, hand resting on the doorknob.

And for a second—just one—I wondered if I was opening the door for a man or for a habit I still hadn't broken.

"*Damn,*" I muttered under my breath.

I tiptoed toward the door and peeked through the peephole, already knowing what I'd see.

Yep. *There he was.*

I quickly schooled my features into something presentable— a polite, almost-charmed smile—and unlocked the door with a slow breath tucked behind my ribcage.

Sterling.

All golden-toasted almond skin and effortless swagger, leaning against the doorframe like he owned the building. His low-cut hair was fresh, the lines sharp, and his shadow beard framed his chiseled jaw like an artist had drawn him that morning. He wore a charcoal suit tailored to perfection, the black shirt underneath unbuttoned just enough to whisper *I still got it.*

And he did. Physically, at least.

In his hands: a bouquet so vibrant it looked like a stolen piece of summer—sunflowers, lilies, wild daisies, and something orange and exotic I couldn't name. Bold. Loud. Beautiful. Just like him.

"*Sterling,*" I said, stepping back to let him in. "I wasn't expecting you to come *upstairs.*"

"Surprise," he said smoothly, holding out the bouquet. "Ms. Madison, I am *so* glad you're happy to see me," he added, flashing that crooked, mischievous grin that used to knock the wind out of me.

I laughed—a little too quickly, a little too bright—as I took the flowers and buried my face in them to buy a second. Their scent was wild and sweet, intoxicating in that way Sterling often was—beautiful, but overwhelming.

"I'm sorry," I murmured, still half-lost in the bouquet. "I thought I had a little more time to get ready. Time got away from me."

He shrugged, his eyes flicking down my outfit and then back up to my face with a slow, deliberate smile. "You're right on time to me."

Sterling's eyes drifted down my outfit—fitted jeans, crisp white tee—and lingered a beat too long. I saw it before he could catch himself: the faint flicker of disapproval, the silent recalibration.

"Going casual, huh?" he said with a forced lightness, the curve of his mouth trying to play it cool. "I was hoping you'd bless me with one of your little black dresses." He bit his bottom lip, his tone dipped in flirtation. "They always hug you in all the right places."

I tilted my head and raised an eyebrow, shifting my weight onto one hip, unbothered. Unmoved.

"A hot heel and a leather jacket," I replied, voice honeyed but edged with steel, "and you'll remember real quick that a little black dress isn't the only thing that hugs me in all the right places."

I gave him a slow, deliberate twirl, letting the denim do its job. His eyes followed, mouth parting into that slow, familiar grin—the kind he used when he realized I'd gotten the better of him.

Message received.

"Give me one minute," I said over my shoulder, already walking away. "Just need to tame this hair and add a little color."

He eased onto the arm of my sofa like it was his throne, gaze still fixed on me as if blinking might break the spell.

"The show starts at 9 p.m.," he warned with a smirk, elbows resting on his knees, hands clasped like he was praying I wouldn't make him wait too long.

I didn't turn around, just threw him a smirk of my own as I disappeared into the hallway.

He could wait.

After all, *I* was the main event.

I slipped into the bathroom, the soft glow of the vanity lights casting a halo over the steam-misted mirror. With practiced fingers, I gathered my wild curls into a loose, elegant bun—effortless but intentional—letting a few tendrils fall to frame my face just right. I dabbed a touch of shimmer onto my cheekbones, catching the light like a secret, then swept a rich berry hue across my lips. Bold. Striking. A color that didn't ask for permission—*it arrived*.

The effect hit instantly. A quiet rush of power. The kind that didn't scream—it whispered, *Watch me*.

Back in my bedroom, I crouched before my shoe rack like it was sacred ground. Classic nude pumps? Predictable. Sultry black stilettos? Too obvious. Then my eyes landed on them— fire-red heels with just the right attitude. A smirk tugged at the corner of my mouth as I slipped them on.

Add color. Always. Allie's voice echoed in my head like a style sermon, and I nodded to the air in her honor.

I plucked my short black leather jacket from the closet and

shrugged it over my shoulders, the soft leather molding to me like armor. Then, with a flick of my wrist, I snatched a sleek red clutch to match the heels—just enough heat to let Sterling know I hadn't dressed for his gaze. I had dressed for mine.

One last glance in the full-length mirror.

The jeans hugged my hips like they were custom-tailored by someone who loved me. The white tee—simple but surgical in its precision—fitted to perfection. The jacket brought just enough edge to slice through expectation. I didn't look done-up.

I looked *ready*.

Comfortable. Confident. Beautiful.

I smiled.

And this time, it wasn't for anyone else.

When I strutted back into the living room, the click of my red heels echoing softly against the hardwood, Sterling's grin stretched wide—satisfied, almost smug.

"No black dress," he said, eyes sweeping over me with slow appreciation, "but I must say, you clean up well, Skylar Madison."

His voice dripped with warmth and charm, practiced and polished—like he knew exactly how to say the right thing without saying too much.

I laughed, light and effortless, slipping my arm through his as we headed for the door. His cologne hit me again—amber, palo santo, and whatever spell he thought it cast. It clung to my senses like memory.

And for a fleeting moment, I let myself lean into the rhythm of the night. The quiet hum of city streets. The click of my heels against the hallway tile. The warmth of his body beside mine.

But just beneath that ease, in a small, stubborn corner of my heart, something stirred.

A whisper.

A truth I wasn't ready to say out loud.

It wasn't Sterling's approval I craved.

It never had been.

42

Allie

The past few weeks had been an exhilarating detour from the well-worn rhythm of my everyday life—a beautiful blur of passport stamps and unexpected magic. I'd wandered across two continents, crisscrossed a handful of countries, and lost myself in the intoxicating tastes, vibrant palettes, and soul-stirring sounds of cultures I had once only admired from a distance.

Every meal, every gallery wall, every bustling street market fed something in me—something deeper than wanderlust. My love for curating and storytelling through art had always been a passion, but experiencing history with my own hands, absorbing color and language with every step, reminded me why I fell in love with this work in the first place. It wasn't just about beauty. It was about connection. Legacy. The unspoken dialogue between past and present.

Still, as thrilling as it was to sip espresso on cobbled streets in Lisbon or haggle for textiles in a back alley in Marrakesh, the last leg of the journey came with an undeniable ache. Between Bryan's unexpected reappearance, the girls' weekend that turned into an emotional unearthing, and a cascade of spontaneous excursions that left me breathless—I was ready.

Ready for quiet mornings in my own bed.

Ready for routine.

Ready for home.

Bryan.

Just the thought of him sent a chill down my spine, unraveling the warmth I'd gathered from foreign cafés, sun-drenched rooftops, and stolen moments of peace. His unannounced visit had been a gut-punch—a violent jolt back to a version of myself I had fought hard to bury. Seeing him again was like being yanked through time, forced to relive every whispered apology, every twisted promise, every gaslighting loop that once left me staring at my reflection, wondering if I was too broken to be loved.

I had spent *years* stitching myself back together. Reclaiming my voice. Building boundaries. But the moment he stood in front of me, that familiar smirk curling at the corner of his mouth like a hook—*a weapon*—the panic returned. Uninvited. Unforgiving. A phantom fear I thought I'd outgrown.

But I wasn't that woman anymore.

I repeated it like a mantra every time my mind tried to rewind the scene. Every time the old fear crept in wearing new clothes. I clung to the memory of his face when he realized he no longer had access. The moment he saw it in my eyes— *she's gone.* The woman he used to unravel was no longer his to reach, let alone ruin.

My travels had given me more than new stamps in my passport. They gave me perspective. Space. A reminder of who I was without his shadow following me down every hallway.

The moment I stepped off the plane and into the hum of the arrivals terminal, a sudden burst of laughter bubbled out of me—unprompted, unfiltered, full of relief. The familiar buzz of tired travelers, rolling suitcases, and overhead announcements faded into the background as my eyes landed on one thing: *family.*

There he was—my big brother Elias—posted up by the baggage claim like he owned the place. Arms crossed, grin wide, eyes shining with the kind of sibling pride that said *about time you brought that beautiful self home.*

Before I could call out to him, I spotted Luz standing just behind him, her signature red lip already curling into a smirk like she'd been plotting a dramatic welcome. And just as I opened my mouth to say something, two blurs came charging out from behind a pillar.

"Tía *chula!*" Ari squealed, barreling toward me like a force of nature, all curly ponytail and excitement, her arms wrapping tightly around my neck as she leapt into my arms.

"*Tíita!*" Alec cried, not far behind, his little legs pumping with all the determination his small frame could muster. He crashed into my side, grabbing my waist with a grip that said, *don't you dare leave again.*

I wrapped both of them in my arms. The scent of Ari's vanilla body spray clung to her like a familiar lullaby, while Alec's bubblegum shampoo was still warm from his scalp. I pressed kisses to their cheeks, their hair, the space between them.

And just like that, in a pile of hugs and tiny sneakers and joyful chaos, I was *home.*

For the first time in weeks, maybe longer, I didn't feel

like a woman returning from far away—I felt like a woman returning to *herself*.

Just as I was about to open my mouth and float the idea of retreating to my Brooklyn brownstone for some much-needed rest, Elias—ever the timing assassin—gently burst my post-travel bubble.

"Mami and Papi are expecting *all* of us for breakfast," he announced with a smirk, slinging his arm around my shoulder like we were still teenagers sneaking in past curfew. "So consider yourself officially kidnapped. At least for the morning. Maybe the whole day."

I let out a dramatic groan, flopping my head against his chest for effect. "You're joking."

He only laughed harder. Luz gave me a knowing look as if to say *you knew this was coming*, and the kids were already bouncing with excitement like I'd just been summoned to a royal feast.

Truth was—I didn't mind.

As much as my body ached for a long shower, fresh sheets, and a few hours of uninterrupted silence, the pull of home—the real kind, filled with plantains frying in the kitchen, my father's booming voice over the radio, and my mother insisting I looked "too skinny"—was stronger.

And deep down, I knew... this was the kind of exhaustion my heart had missed.

As we loaded my bags into the trunk, I pulled out my phone and fired off a quick text to Skylar.

Text to Skylar:

You can thank Mami and Papi. You get to sleep in. No workout this morning. E's taking me to the house for breakfast.

Her response popped up almost instantly.

Skylar:

Ugh, I was really looking forward to working out.

I smirked.

Text to Skylar:

Lies.

Another bubble appeared right away.

Skylar:

Bring me some leftovers. And not just toast. I want plantains and the good cheese.

Text to Skylar:

I got you. If Mami doesn't try to wrap it in three layers of foil and bubble wrap first.

I slipped my phone back into my pocket, already picturing Skylar's eye-roll, and slid into the car. The familiar pull of home tugged at me again—this time, sweetened by the knowledge that my chosen family and blood family were never too far apart.

The car ride to my parents' house was alive with sound— mostly thanks to Ari, who held court from the backseat with the kind of energy only a teenager fueled by passion *and* gossip could conjure.

She animatedly recounted her latest culinary escapades, her hands flying as she described the dramatic rise and even more dramatic fall of a soufflé that refused to cooperate. "It deflated like my GPA after midterms," she said, dead serious, making all of us laugh. Then came the redemption arc—her proudest achievement to date: a seafood paella that even Abuelita had begrudgingly admitted was *"almost as good as mine."*

"She's taking cooking classes now," Luz said from the

passenger seat, glancing back at her daughter with a proud yet amused smile. "Outside of Abuelita's kitchen."

Ari leaned forward between the seats. "Fusion cuisine, Tía. We're talking Korean tacos, vegan arroz con gandules, goat cheese arepas..."

Luz rolled her eyes. "And a lot of cleaning up afterward."

"She never tells us about the drama at school," I whispered to Elias, as Ari effortlessly transitioned from food to which couples had broken up this week and who got caught making out behind the band room.

"She's warming up," he whispered back with a smirk.

Ari was a junior now—brilliant, expressive, bursting with ideas and opinions. The world was opening up for her, and I could feel the shift every time she spoke. She and Uncle E had planned a summer road trip to visit colleges and eat their way through every food truck between here and the Carolinas. They'd invited me to tag along for a few of the stops, and the thought of being part of that next chapter filled me with pride.

Our little Ari. Almost grown.

Still a whirlwind.

Still ours.

Just as Ari reached the dramatic peak of a scandalous tale involving a love triangle, a hallway confrontation, and a mysteriously deleted group chat, a small but determined voice cut through the chaos from the back seat.

"*¡Ya basta!* Okay, okay, *Ari!*" Alec huffed, throwing his hands up like a tiny old man fed up with *telenovela* reruns. "I want to tell *Tía Allie* about the video game I'm making!"

I blinked, caught off guard. "Did he just say he's *making* a video game?"

Luz turned slightly in her seat, catching my eye in the

rearview mirror with a grin that said *yep, your niece and nephew have officially entered the gifted-and-complicated era.*

"All thanks to Sky," she said, clearly impressed. "She found this coding course she thought he'd like. He started tinkering and now? He's obsessed. We've got sound effects, level design, character backstories... it's a whole thing."

Alec nodded solemnly, as if building an indie gaming empire was just another Tuesday activity.

Ari, never one to let anyone else hold the mic for too long, groaned and rolled her eyes. "Okay, coding king, but can we not act like that's more interesting than what *went down* at the Spring Formal?"

She reached over and affectionately messed up Alec's curls, earning a loud "*Hey!*" and a pout that was more adorable than effective.

Then Ari turned to me, eyes wide with curiosity. "*Tía*, tell us about your trip! I saw that post from Morocco. Were you really riding a camel, or was that, like, green screen or something?"

I laughed, leaning back in my seat as the city rolled past us. Just being with them—chaotic, bright, full of questions— was better than any souvenir I could've brought home.

"*Yeah!*" Alec chimed in, immediately shifting gears now that souvenirs were on the table. "And what did you bring us?"

"*¡Válgame Dios!*" I laughed, twisting in my seat to tickle his sides. "Is that *all* you care about? What did I bring you? Not 'Tía, how was your trip?' Not 'Tía, did you miss us?' Just—*gimme the goods?*"

He squealed and tried to wriggle away, but his giggles gave him away.

We pulled into the driveway just as I leaned back, breath catching slightly. There it was—my parents' home. The white stucco glowed in the soft morning light, its clay-tiled roof still holding the warmth of generations. The bougainvillea vines curling up the side of the porch, the wind chimes singing lazily by the front window—it was a scene etched into the very core of me.

Then it hit me—the smell.

The smell.

Café con leche, thick and sweet. Pan sobao, our beloved soft, slightly sweet Puerto Rican bread, warming in the oven. And something even more divine drifting from the open kitchen window.

My stomach twisted in anticipation, equal parts hunger and nostalgia.

Elias caught the look on my face and smirked like a man who knew *exactly* what buttons he'd just pressed. "Yes," he said, pulling the keys from the ignition. "Mami made your favorite *Mallorcas.* Fresh off the griddle. Extra powdered sugar."

I gasped, pressing a hand to my heart like I'd just heard gospel.

Luz laughed beside me. "Dramática," she murmured with affection, shaking her head as she stepped out of the car.

I didn't care.

Because standing in that driveway, surrounded by my chaos-loving, meal-stealing, sweet-talking family, I realized I didn't need to unpack my suitcase to feel at home.

I already was.

Hours had passed since the morning bustle in the kitchen,

when the scent of simmering sofrito and freshly baked *pan sobao* had first lured me in. The sun had made its full arc across the sky, and still, I was stuffed from morning to night, happily surrendering to the nonstop parade of homemade dishes Mami and Papi rolled out like culinary love letters. It wasn't just a meal—it was a marathon of flavor, a multi-course welcome home party in edible form. From breakfast through dinner, every plate was a tribute to my favorites, each bite steeped in memory.

Lunch was the crown jewel: a steaming, oversized bowl of *sopa de pollo con fideos*, courtesy of Papi. But this wasn't your average chicken noodle soup. This was *his* masterpiece—rich with golden broth, laced with homemade sofrito, sweet corn sliced straight from the cob, and just the right amount of fideos tangled at the bottom like treasure. It hugged every inch of me from the inside out, the kind of meal that made you slow down and *feel* loved.

And then there was Ari, sleeves rolled up, standing shoulder to shoulder with Mami at the stove. She'd boldly claimed the role of sous-chef, frying up the most mouthwatering *chuletas fritas* I'd had in years. The sizzle of pork chops hitting the oil, the fragrant blend of adobo and garlic dancing through the kitchen air—it was pure magic.

I smirked as I watched the two of them in their silent kitchen rhythm, passing ingredients, tasting sauces, arguing (lovingly) about whether the rice needed more salt.

Mami may have held the kitchen crown for decades, but I could see it in real time—Ari was rising. Fast. Confident. Proud of every perfectly seared chop she flipped.

Mami better watch her back.

The next generation of culinary royalty was coming for her

title—and she was doing it with flair.

The afternoon melted into a blur of laughter, lounging, and a thousand telenovela plot twists—each one met with dramatic gasps, perfectly timed side-eyes, and Mami muttering "*¡Qué descarada!*" under her breath like it was her job. The drama unfolded on-screen, but somehow, we were just as entertaining, cracking jokes between scenes and arguing over which character deserved to be slapped next.

Alec, meanwhile, was in a universe of his own. Tucked into a corner of the living room, he toggled between coding his latest video game and constructing a Lego fortress with all the focus of a pint-sized engineer. He barely looked up, except to offer a fact about pixel design or ask if anyone had seen his red ninja brick.

Between episodes, there were hugs on repeat—one hundred and one kisses from Mami, who seemed to think I could still be spoiled back into staying forever. She caught me up on the neighborhood gossip she somehow found herself at the center of, sipping from her cafecito and delivering every juicy detail like a seasoned reporter. And Papi, of course, launched into his usual Yankees sermon, passionately dissecting stats and strategy like he was calling the shots from the dugout instead of his favorite armchair.

It was chaotic. It was comforting. It was everything.

Before we knew it, the sun had dipped low, casting that golden glow through the kitchen window as Mami and Papi retreated to their bedroom, Mami muttering something about her novena and Papi already pulling on his house slippers. The house settled into a soft, familiar silence—the kind that hugged the walls with decades of love.

Ari tried to keep up, insisting she wasn't tired, but her

heavy eyelids betrayed her. Alec had already crashed, slumped on the couch mid-sentence, his Lego masterpiece halfway finished. Elias scooped him up with that quiet dad strength, murmuring something into his curls as he carried him upstairs. Ari gave in shortly after, yawning as she shuffled to her room with her bonnet and phone in hand.

I lingered for a moment, standing in the hallway, watching the quiet envelope the house.

This home—this exact one—had been built with all of us in mind. And now, seeing that Mami and Papi had carved out rooms, routines, and rituals for their grandchildren too... it hit me differently.

They didn't just open their doors.

They made sure we *belonged*.

All of us.

Always.

Elias returned, arms full of blankets like a quiet offering, a silent announcement that the night was far from over. It was our unspoken tradition—these late-night living room huddles, long after the house had settled. He tossed the blankets onto the couch, and Luz and I instinctively curled up like muscle memory, sinking into the comfort of soft cushions and each other's presence.

As the glow from the muted TV flickered across the walls, Luz's voice drifted into the quiet, light at first, carried by pride. "I'm really excited for Ari's senior year," she said, pulling a throw across her lap. "She's growing up so beautifully."

But then her voice faltered, just a touch. "Alec doesn't want her to go," she confessed softly. "He spends the day complaining about her—rolling his eyes, telling her to stay out of his room—but tonight, he crawled into my bed and told me he didn't want her to leave."

I saw it then—that glimmer in her eyes. Love. Worry. A little grief tucked into the corners.

I reached over and nudged her gently. "Sounds familiar."

She looked at me, confused for half a beat—then the memory hit, and I saw it flicker in her eyes.

"Remember when you used to complain about Elias non-stop?" I teased. "And then his first year away at school, you snuck into his bed like a lost puppy?"

Elias turned toward her, one eyebrow cocked in exaggerated amusement. "*Snuck in?* Is that what we're calling it now?"

Luz rolled her eyes, but there was softness behind it. "I was tired of sharing a room with *you*, Loquita. You always talked in your sleep and stole the covers."

"No need to lie, Luz," Elias added, grinning. "You missed your favorite brother."

"My *only* brother," she said, before launching onto his lap and smothering him in loud, obnoxious kisses.

He laughed and squirmed, but didn't pull away.

Because underneath the antics, there was history. When her world shattered—when her husband died and everything went quiet—Elias was the one who showed up. Moved in. Picked up Alec from school. Paid bills. Held her while she sobbed in the middle of the night. He filled in the silence with steady love and never once asked her to be okay before she was ready.

They didn't talk about it much. But it lived in the way she leaned on him now, like her bones remembered who held her up when everything else fell apart.

I leaned back, heart full, watching them. Their laughter filled the house like music from our childhood—familiar, healing, loud in all the right ways.

This was the kind of love you couldn't name.

"Ay, yuck!" I laughed, nudging Luz off like we were teenagers again, both fighting for space on the old living room couch. She flopped to the side dramatically, and I slid right into her spot, perching on Elias's lap like it was my rightful throne. I rested my head on his shoulder, breathing in the scent of laundry detergent and faint aftershave—comfort wrapped in cologne and familiarity.

"He *is* my favorite brother," I declared, my voice all mock-formal with just a hint of sincerity underneath.

Elias chuckled, giving my waist a gentle squeeze. "That's 'cause I'm your *only* brother."

But his tone shifted a moment later, softening like it always did when he turned his full attention toward Luz. "Alec's gonna be okay when Ari leaves," he said, his voice threaded with that calm certainty only he seemed to possess. "He's tougher than he lets on. But the real question is..." He paused, watching her closely. "*Will you* be okay?"

Luz straightened slightly, her lips parting in a practiced smile. "Of course I will be," she said quickly—too quickly.

I lifted my head and gave her the look. The one that said *I know better.*

"*Luz?* Really?"

Her shoulders dropped a fraction, the façade cracking just enough for us to see the truth beneath.

Because we all knew her. Knew the strength she wore like armor. Knew how often she used that strength to avoid admitting when she was hurting.

This wasn't just about Ari leaving for college. It was about the quiet that would echo through the house once she did. About the empty seat at the table, the space in the car, the quiet hallway. It was about change—the kind that shifts the floor beneath you in ways no one else sees.

We sat in silence for a moment, wrapped in the weight of what she couldn't say.

But she didn't have to.

Because she had us.

Always had.

Always would.

She exhaled, sitting a little straighter, forcing the strength into her spine even if her voice faltered. "I have to be okay." Then, softer, more fragile: "Ari's growing up and..."

Elias reached over, no fanfare, no grand performance— just steady, quiet truth. "And Alejandro would be so proud of the amazing job you're doing with the kids."

Luz froze.

Her breath hitched, her fingers instinctively reaching for the fraying edge of her sleeve, twisting it between her fingers like a lifeline. That was Elias. Always knowing exactly what needed to be said, and exactly when to say it.

Six years.

Six years since Alejandro's accident stole him from their story. Six years of Luz carrying more than any one person should—without complaint, without pause. She had never really talked about it, not in the way grief demands. Instead, she had armored up, raised two brilliant, beautiful children, and pushed forward because there wasn't time or space to collapse.

But now... now Ari was stepping into a new chapter, and

Alejandro wasn't here to turn the page with them.

"It's just…" Luz began, her voice barely above a whisper, "…it's incredible to watch her grow, you know?" Her lips trembled. "She is so much like Alejandro."

She didn't finish the sentence.

She didn't have to.

We felt the weight of the words she left hanging in the air.

If only.

If only Alejandro were here to see the fierce, funny, intelligent woman their daughter was becoming. If only he could hear Alec's laughter, see the glimmer of his own expressions in his son's face. If only he could hold Luz's hand again and remind her—*you don't have to carry this alone.*

The silence between us wasn't empty—it was sacred.

I reached for her hand, and Elias shifted closer. We didn't offer platitudes. We didn't change the subject.

We just held space.

For her.

For Alejandro.

For the *if onlys* that lived inside all of us.

"Luz, it's okay," I said gently, scooting closer and wrapping my hand around hers. "No tienes que cargar con esto sola. Aquí estoy contigo." You don't have to carry this alone.

Her lips trembled, and she nodded slowly, her throat tightening as she fought to maintain control. Her eyes glistened, but she held my gaze, her voice steady despite the emotion rising behind it.

"Alejandro and I used to talk about this," she said after a long pause. "How we'd follow Ari wherever she went for college. Even if it meant moving to another country—he swore we'd just get a tiny apartment down the street." She gave a soft, teary laugh. "She was always his *princesa*."

The smile that bloomed across her face was painted in memory and love, even as tears tracked silently down her cheeks. She shook her head, her eyes shining as she leaned back into the couch cushions. "She chews like him, you know? Loud and dramatic like it's the best thing she's ever tasted. And she's been playing all his old Spanish records like they're buried treasure."

She glanced up at us, her grin widening. "And Alec? Just the other day, he was banging on the bathroom door yelling, '*¿Pero qué haces con tanto tiempo en el baño? ¿Estás escribiendo una novela?*'"

I nearly choked on my tea, laughing so hard I doubled over. The cadence, the attitude—it was *so* Alejandro.

Stop!" I gasped. "*He* used to say that to me *all the time!*"

Luz doubled over with laughter. "Right? He'd stand outside the door huffing and puffing, then walk away muttering, '*Eso no es normal...*'"

"Because *you* take forever in the bathroom," I teased, giving her shoulder a playful shove.

Luz wiped her eyes, still smiling, and Elias chuckled beside us, shaking his head. The laughter faded, but it left something behind—a softness, a stillness. Not sadness, exactly. Something deeper.

A knowing.

"It's like... every day, they do something that brings him back," Luz said quietly, her voice barely above a whisper. "A phrase. A look. The way Alec leaves his shoes in the middle of the floor, just like Ale used to. It's like I'm constantly reminded that he's still here. Just... not the way I want him to be."

She paused, her eyes glistening as she looked at the two of us. "I know you're here. For me. For the kids. I *know* that. And I'm grateful."

Her voice cracked, just a little.

"It's just... some things are hard to say out loud. Some losses are too big to fold into words. I never imagined life without Alejandro. And having to say it... having to *feel* it every day?" She exhaled slowly. "It's been a journey."

We didn't rush to fill the silence this time.

We just held her.

Because love—real love—doesn't always need language. Sometimes it's just a hand, a memory, and the courage to sit inside the ache without looking away.

Elias squeezed my hand and kissed my forehead, his touch quiet and steady. "As long as you know we're here for the ride," he said, his voice a soft anchor.

I hesitated, feeling the full weight of the moment—the warmth in the room, the safety wrapped around me like a quilt. It wasn't planned. It wasn't rehearsed. But something cracked open inside me, and I knew. *This* was the moment.

"Since we're saying hard things..." I exhaled, voice barely above a whisper. "Maybe now's the time to tell you guys."

I hadn't expected to say it—not tonight, not like this—but once the door cracked, everything came pouring out.

I told them about Bryan. Not the version I'd sanitized. Not the vague mentions I'd let slip over wine and silence. The *truth*. The *whole*, raw truth.

How he had shown up at my office without warning. Uninvited. Unannounced. How the sight of him—just his *presence*—had rattled me in ways I hadn't felt in years. How it triggered something I thought I'd buried long ago.

And then I told them the things I had never, *ever* said out loud.

The nights I stayed on campus or slept in friends' dorms just to avoid coming home with bruises I couldn't explain. The phone calls I ignored, terrified he'd accuse me of something—of everything—if I didn't pick up on the first ring. The way I learned to shrink, to silence myself, to second-guess every word, every outfit, every breath. How I kept telling myself *he's stressed, he's just insecure, if I just loved him better, this would stop.*

I confessed to the shame—the thick, suffocating kind. The shame of knowing better and still staying. The shame of *loving* someone who made me feel so small. The shame of judging women in similar situations until I became one of them. How I skipped alumni events for years because I couldn't bear the idea of seeing him across a room. How the fear lingered like perfume I couldn't wash off.

My voice cracked. My throat burned. But I kept going.

Because once I started, I couldn't go back.

And when the last of it fell into the quiet space between us, I looked up, half-expecting discomfort or pity in their eyes.

But I didn't see either.

I saw Luz, her hand now wrapped tightly around mine, her eyes glassy and fierce, holding back tears.

I saw Elias, jaw clenched, his gaze locked on mine like he was mentally rewriting time—like if he could, he'd go back and rip Bryan out of every memory with his bare hands.

No one spoke for a long moment.

But I didn't need them to.

Because in that silence, I felt it:

The muted thrum of love, ever-present and warm.

The weight of truth met with unwavering grace.

And—for the first time in a long time—the lightness that comes when you finally stop carrying something alone.

The room was silent.

But in that silence, there was understanding.

A history we shared, the laughter, the pain, the way we carried each other through.

I exhaled, looking at the faces of the people who knew me better than anyone.

I was safe. I was seen. And I was so, so grateful for my family.

43

Skylar

"My stomach is in knots. I don't know what I ate," Daddy groaned, rubbing slow, deliberate circles against his belly, his signature swagger briefly humbled by the reality of overeating.

I narrowed my eyes, lips curling into a smirk as I watched him shift in his seat like an old man who knew he'd done too much. "Maybe it was all of Aunt Dinah's pig feet you kept sneaking like you thought nobody saw you," I teased, crossing my arms with dramatic satisfaction.

His eyes widened with mock innocence. "Pig feet? Who, me?"

"Uh huh," I shot back. "Don't play. You had a whole stash behind the deviled eggs like it was a covert operation."

He chuckled and groaned at the same time, his laughter cut short by another cramp. "That woman still knows how to season the mess out of some swine."

Donny Hathaway and Roberta Flack's *Where Is the Love* drifted through Uncle Zo's brownstone, each note dipping through the air like silk. The melody wrapped around us in a warm, familiar cocoon—equal parts nostalgia and comfort. This house had always been more than brick and wood; it was a memory bank, thick with the sounds and smells of Black joy passed down through generations.

The scent of fried fish popped and crackled from the back kitchen, golden and sizzling in well-worn cast-iron skillets. The tang of fresh lemon juice mingled with the syrupy sweetness of bourbon and sun-steeped tea, creating that unmistakable perfume of a family gathering: love, laughter, and just enough mischief to keep things interesting.

Uncle Zo, seated at the spades table with all the regality of a seasoned champion, leaned back and let out a low whistle. He wasn't even looking at his cards—his eyes were on Ms. Barbara Jean. His newest flame.

She sat beside him in a crisp linen set and gold hoops the size of bangles, her salt-and-pepper curls styled high and tight. Ms. Barbara Jean wasn't just *fine for her age*—she was fine, period. According to family lore, they had met at a neighborhood association meeting where Uncle Zo was arguing about potholes, and she corrected his math *and* his attitude. He'd been smitten ever since.

Trips to Atlantic City, brunches at the parkway diner, long drives with classic Luther playing low… and, if you asked any of the cousins, a whole lot of slow dancing in the living room after the grandkids were tucked away upstairs.

"They're like teenagers," my cousin Tasha whispered to me once. "Only with orthopedic shoes and matching life insurance policies."

From across the room, Uncle Zo caught my eye and winked, then turned to Barbara Jean, who giggled behind her glass of sweet tea like she was sixteen again.

I shook my head and laughed softly. Love, food, music, family—sometimes it really was that simple. And sometimes, a pig foot too many was just the price of joy.

"Barbara Jean, come on over here, girl," Uncle Zo called out, patting his cheek with theatrical flair. "I know a fine girl named Barbara Jean who owes me a little sugar for good luck."

She rolled her eyes, but the soft flush in her caramel cheeks gave her away. "Boy, don't make me act up in front of your people," she said, fanning herself with the score sheet like she had half a mind to oblige him.

"If this hand don't hit, it's gon' be all your fault," he warned, grinning. "You robbed me of my good luck kiss!"

A ripple of laughter circled the table. Asia nearly choked on her sweet tea. Buddy hooted, slapping the table with a cackle. Someone shouted, "Don't blame the lady when your hand is trash, Zo!"

"Zo, play your hand and stop delaying the inevitable," Daddy called out, his voice laced with amusement as he leaned back in his chair, folding his arms like a king waiting for the crown to be passed.

Before Zo could respond, the unmistakable pulse of *Earth, Wind & Fire* kicked in through the speakers. Maurice White's voice rode in on that classic bassline like a funky sermon, and the entire brownstone seemed to shift with the groove.

Daddy's eyes lit up the moment the horns blared, his grin stretching wide with recognition. "*Now* we talkin'!" he said, already on his feet before the first verse dropped.

With a dramatic flourish, he tossed his cards down like a royal flush in a movie scene. "*That's game!*" he declared, his voice booming, arms wide like he'd just dropped the mic in a stadium.

"Cheating!" someone yelled from the peanut gallery. "Ain't nobody call game mid-song!"

But Daddy was already shimmying away from the table, two-step in full effect, hips loose, shoulders rolling to the rhythm like it was 1978 and he had something to prove.

Barbara Jean clapped along, clearly amused, while Uncle Zo waved off the protests. "He been waiting all night to dance," he muttered, trying to hide his own smile. "Let the man have his moment."

And just like that, the cards, the teasing, the sore losers— all of it faded behind the joy of the music, the laughter, and the undeniable magic of a house full of love, soul food, and a well-timed Earth, Wind & Fire track.

Laughter burst through the room as he stepped away from the table, shoulders bouncing to the beat. The music seemed to breathe life into everyone, pulling us all into motion. We clapped, swayed, and glided across the living room floor in perfect, unspoken rhythm. No choreography, no need for instructions—just bodies moved by memory and melody, a dance passed down like heirlooms through bloodlines.

Barbara Jean was the first to join him, laughing as she matched his steps, hands in the air, curls bouncing with every sway. Then Aunt Dinah, then Zo himself, dragging his sore knees into a rhythm that somehow still had flair. Even the kids peeked in from the hallway, drawn by the beat, pulled in by the joy.

It was one of those rare, golden moments when generations folded into one heartbeat. Where pain took a backseat. Where the music reminded us who we were and where we came from.

And in that brownstone, full of fried fish, good bourbon, old stories, and second chances—we all danced like it mattered. Because it did.

And then, as if no time had passed, Allie shimmied her way into the makeshift Soul Train line, right on cue. The room erupted with cheers. She moved with the effortless grace of someone who had long mastered the art of joy—shoulders relaxed, hips rolling in time with the beat, her hands slicing the air like the rhythm lived in her bones. She twirled halfway down the living room floor, letting out a signature "¡Oyeee!" that sent a ripple of laughter through the crowd.

I caught her mid-spin, wrapping my arms around her and pulling her in tight. The scent of her familiar perfume— something soft and citrusy—wrapped around me like a hug from home. "I've missed you," I whispered into her shoulder, feeling the weight of the weeks we'd spent apart dissolve in the warmth of this moment.

She leaned back to meet my eyes, her smile bright and teasing. "Who knew Earth, Wind & Fire could make you so sentimental?"

"I'm always sentimental," I replied, only half lying.

Her laugh was easy, like sunlight.

But before I could say more, a voice cut through the music— low, rich, and unmistakable.

"Alejandra Catalina Herrera."

The name dropped into the room like a cymbal crash. Everything froze. Even Maurice White seemed to pause mid-verse.

Allie's body stiffened in my arms, her eyes flicking toward the sound. Whatever joy had just been dancing in her face drained away, replaced by something guarded—something wary.

I followed her gaze, already knowing who I'd find there.

And suddenly, it didn't matter that the music was still playing.

Because the past had just walked into the room.

Daddy approached with arms wide, his presence a blend of quiet authority and boundless warmth. He moved like he always had—with intention, with heart—his steps full of the same grounding love that had carried us through scraped knees, school dances, and whispered late-night tears.

His smile deepened as his eyes landed on Allie, and in that moment, his whole face lit up. His greeting carried the weight of a thousand moments—after-school pickups where he'd wait in the car with jazz humming low, the times he'd helped us untangle math problems or sneak snacks before dinner, how he sat through our endless grade school gossip without complaint. He had always made room for her, invited her into every corner of our world, even bringing her along to North Carolina for family reunions where she quickly became everyone's favorite "bonus Boricua daughter."

"Mr. Madison," Allie said with a grin that stretched wide, the kind only reserved for those who saw you before the world did.

"*Papi* Madison to you," he corrected, voice playful, wrapping her in a strong, familiar embrace that lifted her slightly off the ground. It was the kind of hug that anchored you—an embrace that said, *you're family here*.

When he pulled back, he took her in like he was seeing her for the first time. "Let me look at my Alejandra," he said, his voice softer now, almost reverent. "Always beautiful."

Then came the pause. A slow, thoughtful look settled across his face as though he saw something he hadn't noticed before—something quieter, deeper.

"I'm so happy to see you in full bloom," he added, and in that moment, his words wrapped around her like a prayer.

From behind him, Uncle Zo sauntered over, the sparkle in his eye and smooth cadence in his step unmistakable. "Hey there, Allie girl," he drawled with a crooked grin, tipping an imaginary hat. "How's life treatin' you?"

She laughed, pulling him into a tight hug. "Hi, Uncle Zo. Still slick as ever, I see."

"And you still got that spice," he winked. "Don't let these fellas around here forget it."

Daddy shook his head with a smirk. "Don't encourage her, Zo."

But we all knew he loved her exactly as she was.

"I hear you've been jet-setting across the world," Uncle Zo said with a sly grin, his voice dipped in curiosity and charm. "Tell your brother Elias I'm still waiting on some of that famous *pernil* he swears can win awards."

He licked his lips and rubbed his stomach in an exaggerated circle, earning an eye roll and a chuckle from Daddy, who muttered, "Here he go again."

"Stop harassing Allie," Daddy said, trying to sound stern, though the grin tugging at the corners of his mouth gave him away.

"I'm just saying," Zo added with a wink, "a man can dream of crispy pork and a passport stamp, can't he?"

The music thumped low, a rhythm that kept the room pulsing with life. As the night sky draped itself over the brownstone like a velvet curtain, the celebration roared on with no sign of slowing. After an enthusiastic, slightly off-key round of *Happy Birthday*—the *Stevie Wonder* version, naturally—came generous slices of red velvet cake, scoops of melting vanilla bean ice cream, and another hour of raucous storytelling, cross-generational teasing, and the kind of family gossip that could only be passed around the table between bites of cornbread and sips of spiked sweet tea.

We shared memories like heirlooms, one-liners that would be retold for years, and belly laughs that made your ribs ache in the best way.

Even as the guests slowly began to drift out, waving their goodbyes with to-go plates tucked under their arms, the energy lingered. Voices echoed off the old wood paneling and into the bones of the house, layering warmth into the walls. You could feel it—the love, the legacy, the weight of generations showing up and showing out.

Nights like this stitched us together.

Thread by thread. Song by song. Plate by plate.

And as the last laugh faded and the final door closed, the brownstone seemed to sigh, content to hold our joy a little longer.

It was well past one in the morning by the time Allie and I finally made it back to my apartment. The city had quieted into its nighttime rhythm—less honking, more humming—a distant lullaby of engines, footsteps, and the occasional burst of laughter echoing from some late-night corner of Brooklyn. The warmth of the evening still clung to our skin, a faint trace of music and cologne trailing behind us like memory.

When we left, Dad and Uncle Zo were still holding court at the kitchen table, their low voices drifting between decades-old stories and the last sips of sweet tea—though Uncle Zo's had long been spiked with something amber and unforgiving. They didn't even glance up when we slipped out, too deep in a conversation that involved someone's cousin, a fishing trip gone wrong, and a bet they both swore they had won.

Inside, the familiar scent of rosewood and vanilla greeted us. Allie immediately dropped into her usual spot on the floor, nestling into a fortress of oversized pillows like she had claimed the space long ago. She stretched her legs out with a dramatic sigh, her head leaning back as she stared at the ceiling.

"It was really good seeing your dad," she said after a beat, her voice soft, laced with the warmth of wine and nostalgia. "He and Uncle Zo? Straight up sitcom material. I swear, they've got better chemistry than half the couples on TV."

I laughed as I flopped onto the couch, already tugging the throw blanket over my legs. A yawn crept out before I could stop it, my whole body sagging into the cushions like a balloon finally losing air. "A little too much fun," I mumbled, rubbing my temples. "I cannot believe they were still going when we left. Do they ever get tired?"

Allie raised an eyebrow, her lips quirking into a lazy smile. "I think that generation was built different. They run on sweet tea, ego, and unspoken trauma."

I burst out laughing. "You forgot bourbon and gospel shade."

"Oh, true," she nodded sagely. "Can't forget the shade."

The apartment fell into a comfortable hush. Outside, the city lights blinked like stars trying to compete with the real thing. I glanced over at Allie—barefoot, makeup smudged, curls wild from dancing—and felt the familiar swell of gratitude.

For this life. For this sisterhood.

For nights that end like this.

Allie grinned, propping her elbow on a nearby pillow. "Hey Sky. Your dad was going on about meeting with some urban developer who's working with homeowners to make their houses more sustainable. Sounded like they're planning something big—solar energy, rainwater systems, even a community garden project."

She toyed with the hem of her sleeve, thoughtful. "It actually sounded pretty dope. He mentioned it like it was casual, but you know your dad—he doesn't talk much unless it matters."

That caught my attention. I sat up straighter, the fatigue momentarily falling away. "Really? He didn't say much to me about it, just mentioned he had a meeting with a firm later this week. Didn't realize it was something that far along."

Allie nodded, her expression brightening. "Yeah, and it sounded like a perfect fit for the summer program. You know—get the kids learning about sustainable architecture and environmental design. Could be a powerful hands-on addition."

I exhaled, rubbing the back of my neck as I leaned back. "You're right. That could be incredible. Real-world application, real impact."

Then her tone shifted slightly—equal parts playful and pointed. "Speaking of the summer program," she added, arching an eyebrow, "Langston and I have been carrying the baton for the last few months, but we still need to get the full team together. Like, *yesterday*."

I groaned, dragging a throw pillow over my face. "Don't

come for me. I know, I know."

Allie crossed her arms, not letting up. "Sky, we've got kids waiting. Funders watching. Parents already emailing."

I peeked out from beneath the pillow, giving her a sheepish look. "My team told me we were adding something to the calendar soon."

"Mmhmm," she said, unconvinced, her tone dripping with sarcasm. "You and that mysterious 'team' of yours better be setting alarms, because I am not about to be the only adult in the room when the school board starts asking questions."

I couldn't help but laugh. "I'm on it. Promise. I'll check in first thing tomorrow and make sure we get it scheduled."

She softened a little, but not completely. "I know you've had a lot on your plate lately, but don't forget—you're the glue in this thing."

I nodded, her words landing gently but firmly.

Allie always knew when to nudge, when to remind me of my power—especially when I was most tempted to set it down.

She didn't look convinced, but she let it slide—for now.

"Enough about the summer project," I said quickly, my voice a shade too breezy. I was desperate to pivot, to steer the conversation away from anything that might detour toward *him*. "I'm wiped. I don't know how you're still standing after yesterday. Shouldn't the jet lag have tackled you by now?"

Allie raised an eyebrow, smirking with that all-knowing glint in her eyes. "Mmhmm. I see you, Sky." She stood slowly, stretching her arms overhead like a cat who'd just claimed the softest spot in the sun. "I'll take the hint and change the subject," she teased, grabbing her bag from the chair. "But don't think for one second you're off the hook. You know I'll circle back."

I rolled my eyes, though the smile tugging at my lips gave me away. "Text me when you get home."

"Always." She stepped toward the door, then paused, her expression softening. She wrapped me in one of her signature hugs—tight, grounding, with just enough warmth to make the world feel safe again.

"Hasta luego, chica," she whispered against my shoulder, her lavender perfume clinging to the air as she slipped out into the hallway.

The door clicked shut behind her, and the silence that followed felt louder than it should have. I dropped back against the cushions, tilting my head to stare at the ceiling, tracing invisible shapes in the crown molding like I used to do as a kid when I couldn't sleep.

The family's Brooklyn brownstone, rich with memory, so full of music and laughter hours ago, now felt heavier—quieter. Or maybe that weight was just me.

I inhaled deeply, the scent of lavender still lingering, mingling with the faint aroma of the red wine we never finished. My body ached for rest, but my mind kept cycling: my dad's cryptic meeting, the unfinished details of the summer program, and the conversation I kept dodging like a dance I didn't know the steps to.

Titus.

I pushed myself up, slow and reluctant, each movement a reminder of how tired I really was. As I made my way to bed, I couldn't help but wonder how long I could keep pretending those thoughts weren't still knocking at the door.

It was finally game day, and Madison Square Garden buzzed with that once-in-a-lifetime kind of energy—the kind that vibrated in your chest and made the back of your neck tingle. The scent of buttered popcorn, sizzling hot dogs, and overpriced stadium beer hung thick in the air, mingling with the echo of rubber soles squeaking on polished hardwood and the bass thump of the pregame hype track reverberating through the stands.

The whole arena was a sea of blue and orange. Fans young and old were wrapped in Knicks jerseys, faces painted, foam fingers waving high like beacons of unshakable loyalty. Tip-off hadn't even happened yet, but the roar of anticipation was already building.

Daddy looked like a little boy on Christmas morning—eyes wide, mouth slightly open in awe as he took it all in. He soaked up every second, nodding along to the beat of the hype music, his energy electric. With Uncle Zo at his side, the two of them were in their element: old-school Knicks fans reliving glory days and trash talk like it was 1973. They leaned into each other, trading jabs, recalling iconic plays like sacred scripture passed down through generations, and laughing like they hadn't missed a beat.

Allie and I slid into our seats just as the jumbotron flashed to life. She was already locked in—her game face on. Dressed in her vintage Sprewell jersey, faded to perfection from years of wear, distressed jeans, and an orange bandana tied Rosie-the-Riveter-style around her braids, she looked like a Knicks historian and a hype girl rolled into one. Her eyes tracked the players during warmups like a coach ready to call plays.

Daddy, ever understated but still effortlessly cool, wore a navy dri-fit crewneck with the Knicks logo subtly embroidered on the chest. It was a gift from Allie, handed over that morning with a teasing grin and a "You can't come to the Garden looking like somebody's deacon." He'd laughed, tried to protest, but the moment he pulled it on and saw himself in the mirror, he didn't take it off. It wasn't flashy, but it was fresh—just like him.

"Y'all know this is the best seat I've had in twenty years," he muttered, eyes glued to the court.

"And you deserve it," I said, nudging his arm gently.

Allie leaned over with a smirk. "He's already got that 'we better win tonight' face."

Uncle Zo held up his beer like a toast. "We came to witness a win, baby. Ain't no other outcome."

The lights dimmed. The music surged. The Garden came alive.

And for the first time in a long time, I didn't think about work or relationships or what was waiting in my inbox. I just sat back, surrounded by love, loyalty, and decades of tradition—soaking in every second of game night at the world's most famous arena.

From the moment the ball went up for the tip-off, we were all in—yelling, screaming, living and dying with every whistle. The Garden pulsed with electricity, a living, breathing force. High-fives flew after a perfectly timed block, the crowd erupting as the Knicks stole possession. It wasn't just a game—it was communion. Strangers became teammates, seats became sidelines, and the adrenaline was a shared heartbeat thumping through thousands of bodies.

By halftime, the energy simmered into a buzz, and the court transformed into a stage, lights dimming just enough to soften the noise without dulling the thrill. Uncle Zo and Daddy leaned back in their seats, finally letting their shoulders drop as they nursed their drinks like old friends at a barbershop. The basketball talk slowed, and the grown-folks conversation started.

"We had a good meeting with the urban developer yesterday," Daddy said, almost offhand, taking a slow sip of his drink like the words didn't mean as much as they did.

Uncle Zo nodded, tilting his head, brow furrowed in thought. "Yeah, I was surprised to meet two brothas. Young, sharp."

"That was definitely a welcome surprise," Daddy added, his tone still casual, but the weight of it hung between us like an exclamation mark in a quiet room.

Allie and I perked up immediately. My curiosity flickered like a flame catching wind.

"Oh, really?" I asked, my voice coated in intrigue.

Daddy's smirk curled slowly, like he had been waiting for me to bite. "Yes, really. We had a great conversation—about my work as a Black architect, their work as urban developers and real estate investors. Smart guys. Focused on sustainable housing, community-first design. They want to fight displacement, not cause it. I was impressed. Inspired, even."

Allie glanced at me, then back at Daddy, a knowing look creeping into her expression—the kind that said she was five steps ahead of whatever I was just beginning to realize.

"You get their info?" she asked, her tone light but pointed.

Daddy just smiled.

My pulse quickened.

Allie leaned over and whispered, "So... are we all just going to pretend this doesn't sound exactly like someone we know?"

And that's when it hit me.

Titus.

Of course.

"I was even more surprised," Daddy continued, chuckling as he swirled the last of his soda, "when Mr. Scott and Mr. Hughes told us they were Celtics fans."

Uncle Zo groaned dramatically, nearly spilling his drink. "Poor souls," he said with a slow shake of his head. "Lost, misguided souls."

Daddy laughed. "Before the meeting was over, we were on a first-name basis. And get this—Mr. Hughes? His first name is Langston."

Allie's eyes lit up, her head whipping toward me. "No way!" she exclaimed, practically bouncing in her seat.

"Crazy, right?" Daddy said, nodding with amusement. "Langston has a whole tribe of kids—named after Black authors, no less. His wife's name?"

"Zora," I murmured before he could finish.

The name slipped out before I could stop it, like a secret I hadn't meant to say aloud. My voice was quiet, but Allie noticed. She always did. She didn't say a word—just arched one eyebrow in that Allie way that said *mmm hmm, we're circling back to this.*

Daddy turned toward me, his smirk stretching wider, now fully dipped in mischief. "And Mr. Scott's name," he added, drawing out the pause like he was delivering a punchline, "is Titus."

My stomach didn't just flip—it freefell.

The air around me thickened, the noise of the crowd growing muffled as the name settled over me like a weighted blanket. I blinked slowly, trying to keep my face neutral, but I knew I wasn't fooling anyone—not with Allie sitting two inches away, not with Daddy watching me like a man who knew exactly what he'd just done.

"Small world, huh?" he said, sipping the last of his drink.

"Yeah," I breathed, eyes fixed on the court even though I couldn't see a single thing. "Real small."

Daddy leaned back in his seat, clearly enjoying himself, his smirk spreading slow and wide. "Told him I'd only heard that name twice before—once in Bible study," he paused for effect, "and once from my daughter's recent romance."

I groaned aloud, slumping in my seat as the heat rushed to my cheeks. I could feel the blush rising from my neck all the way to the tips of my ears. The sheer impossibility of it all had my head spinning. Out of all the boroughs in New York, of all the office towers and closed-door meetings, how was it that *my* father had—of all people—sat down with *my* Titus?

The second-half countdown started above the court, the buzzer buzzing with fresh urgency. The players returned, sneakers squeaking, the crowd roaring back to life around us. The arena surged with energy, but I was stuck somewhere between disbelief and a mild out-of-body experience.

"Skylar, what's wrong with you?" Uncle Zo asked, watching me with a puzzled frown as he took a swig from his beer.

Before I could even open my mouth, Allie elbowed me gently, her grin sly and unbothered. "That Titus is a catch," she said, her voice sing-song, her amusement absolutely uncontainable.

I glared at her, but she just wiggled her eyebrows and returned her attention to the game. I let out a slow breath, dragging my palms down the front of my jeans in a futile attempt to ground myself.

My pulse thudded in my ears louder than the roar of the crowd. I glanced over at my dad—cool as ever, watching the court like nothing had happened, like he hadn't just shattered the very fragile bubble I'd built around Titus.

The ball was back in play, but I wasn't. Not really. Because all I could think about was the uncanny inevitability of it all. The universe, it seemed, had a real sense of humor.

Somehow, Titus had found his way into *my* world, and now—without warning—he'd stepped into *Daddy's* too.

And that felt dangerously close to permanent.

44

Titus

Langston and I had more than just a passing interest in tonight's basketball game. For us, it wasn't just about team loyalty or box scores—it was about something deeper, something rooted. Something still echoing after an afternoon spent on the sun-dappled stoop of Mr. Dexter and Mr. Alonzo's brownstone in Bed-Stuy.

Their home didn't just sit on a historic block—it *was* history.

Inside, the air was thick with memory. The walls wore their family's story proudly—sepia-toned portraits, faded diplomas, and framed newspaper clippings that marked not just milestones but *survival.* You could feel the generations that had lived and laughed and fought to stay here. The scent of aged wood mingled with cinnamon and cloves—Mr. Alonzo had brewed a spiced tea that tasted like it had been steeped in stories.

The living room hummed with dignity. No fancy staging, no curated aesthetic—just lived-in elegance and reverence for the past. It was clear: this wasn't just a house. It was

382

legacy in brick and mortar.

We talked for hours—about real estate, about equity, about the invisible cost of "revitalization." Mr. Dexter spoke with the slow cadence of a man who had watched an entire community rise, fall, and now hold its breath again. He told us how their family had clung to this brownstone through redlining, through the crack epidemic, through recessions and rezoning. And now, through gentrification's latest wave—polished, polite, but no less devastating.

They weren't planning to sell. Not ever. "Our kids' kids will walk these floors," Mr. Alonzo had said, his voice low, unwavering. "Not because it's easy, but because someone has to hold the line."

Langston and I left that day changed. And as we watched the Knicks warm up on the court tonight, we weren't just cheering for a team—we were thinking about everything that home represented. Ownership. Resistance. Legacy. And the responsibility we carried to protect it.

Mr. Alonzo's voice softened as he spoke of his son—a man who had long since traded New York's relentless rhythm for the quiet of Pennsylvania. Six children, a big yard, and a life that rarely intersected with the city that raised him. "He says he's done with the noise," Mr. Alonzo muttered, not bitter, just resigned. "But I think he forgot how to listen to the music."

Mr. Dexter, in stark contrast, lit up with quiet pride when he spoke of his daughter. She was the kind of woman who wore Brooklyn like both armor and gospel—unyielding in her loyalty, bold in her love for home. "Told me straight up," he said with a chuckle, "'Daddy, if you ever sell this house, I'll never forgive you.'" His smile lingered, a mix of amusement and deep respect. "And she meant every word. Said it with her whole chest."

He leaned back, his gaze drifting toward the window like he could already see both skylines. "I'm building a place down in North Carolina now—peaceful, slower pace, something for retirement. But I'll be splitting my time. Brooklyn's in our bones. That's why this brownstone matters. It's not just property. It's the heartbeat of our family."

Before he even revealed more, I already knew—felt it in my gut—that his daughter was someone I'd admire. Hell, I had the eerie sense I might already *know* her.

Our conversation slid easily from family to the very thing Langston and I came to talk about: retrofitting the brownstone with sustainable upgrades. We laid out ideas—solar panels discreetly mounted on the roofline, energy-efficient insulation that wouldn't disturb the integrity of the home's historical bones. Mr. Dexter listened closely, occasionally jotting notes in a worn leather-bound notebook that looked older than I was.

But inevitably, as conversations with Black men in New York tend to do, talk shifted to basketball.

"The Knicks game this weekend," Mr. Dexter said, eyes lighting up. "My girls are takin' me for my birthday. My daughter and her 'bonus sister,' as she calls her. Been tight since grade school. They bleed blue and orange."

He laughed, shaking his head. "I swear, that bonus girl—if the Knicks ever win a chip, she'll need a parade of her own. Shows up to every game dressed like she's part of the starting five."

Langston looked at me, eyes wide.

A chill of recognition crawled up my spine.

Bonus sister. Knicks obsession. A legacy brownstone. Fierce, Brooklyn-born daughter.

Langston's voice was low, amused. "You don't think..."

But I already knew.

Skylar.

And Allie.

As we wandered deeper into the living room, the truth unraveled slowly—first in glances, then in undeniable clarity. It was written across the framed photographs lining the mantle like breadcrumbs left for the observant.

One frame held a snapshot of a young girl, maybe eight or nine, her mischievous pigtails flying as she leaned into the camera with a wide, gap-toothed grin. Even in stillness, she radiated boldness. I recognized that smile before my mind caught up with my heart.

Another photo—this one more recent—showed the same girl, now a striking young woman with a sleek silk press, wearing a cap and gown, her arm wrapped tightly around Mr. Dexter as he beamed beside her at her college graduation. Pride poured off the frame.

Skylar.

My chest tightened. Mr. Dexter wasn't just a client. He was her father. And Mr. Alonzo—her uncle.

A hundred pieces clicked into place all at once.

I thought back to our conversations—Skylar's reverent tone when she mentioned her father, her stories filled with equal parts respect and exasperation. She spoke of him like he was larger than life, someone impossible to replicate. Now, standing in his home, surrounded by the evidence of a life built on legacy, laughter, and hard-earned wisdom, I understood why.

There was a warmth in Mr. Dexter's presence, a commanding yet comforting energy that made people lean in, listen. And the way he effortlessly pivoted between dry humor and deep thought? That was *all* Skylar. Her wit. Her sharp eyes. The fire in her spine when she believed in something. It all had a blueprint, and he was standing right in front of me.

She hadn't just inherited his features—she had inherited his fire.

And I suddenly understood something else too.

Skylar wasn't just magnetic. She was rooted. She came from legacy.

And I had just shaken hands with the man who built the soil she bloomed from.

The afternoon stretched longer than expected, hours slipping by as our conversation shifted from Mr. Dexter's career as a Black architect to a deeper meditation on urban renewal, generational wealth, and the fragile balance between progress and preservation. What started as a professional meeting quickly unraveled into something more intimate—something rooted.

At some point, the titles faded. Mr. Dexter became Dexter. Mr. Alonzo simply Alonzo. We traded insights like old friends instead of strangers brought together by property lines and zoning permits.

They chuckled when Langston introduced himself—people always did. There was something both poetic and weighty about a six-foot-three developer named after Langston Hughes. But it was when I said *my* name that the room changed.

The silver-haired, brown-skinned man with clean waves that looked fresh from the barbershop and a salt-and-pepper goatee that rivaled any GQ model tilted his head and gave me a long, knowing look. A smirk tugged at the corner of his mouth like he was solving a riddle only he knew the answer to.

"Well, isn't that something," he said, leaning back in his chair. "Titus. I've heard that name twice in my life—once in Sunday school... and the other from my daughter's short-lived romance."

Langston nearly choked on his tea.

I couldn't speak. I didn't have to.

The moment hung in the air like the trailing note of a jazz solo—soft, unfinished, full of meaning.

And now here we were, hours later, back in my house, two Knicks haters half-watching the team we usually loved to hate. The irony wasn't just amusing—it was cosmic.

I tried to act unaffected, but the truth was, I hadn't stopped thinking about her. Skylar Madison. Even when I told myself I should let go, that I had every reason to close the chapter, she lingered—like a familiar melody you can't help but hum long after the music ends.

Only now, after today, that melody had a harmony—her father's laugh, the pride in his voice when he spoke about her, the unmistakable fire in his eyes when he said her name.

Instead of frustration or regret, I felt something else.

A low flicker of curiosity. A grin I didn't bother hiding.

Maybe the universe wasn't nudging me to forget Skylar.

Maybe it was daring me to remember her... differently.

And maybe, just maybe, I was finally ready to listen.

The Knicks had pulled off a wild win, and somewhere between the final buzzer and my third fist-pump, I'd forgotten I was supposed to hate them.

Now, the sports announcers were droning on about the upset victory, their voices blending into the soft hum of the city outside. Through the tall windows of my brownstone, the streetlights cast amber streaks across the exposed brick walls, shadows dancing lazily with every passing car. The buzz of victory still hung in the air—but it didn't quite reach me anymore.

Langston sat across from me in the deep leather armchair, his arms folded across his chest, that annoyingly perceptive smirk tugging at his mouth.

"Please don't tell my father I was rooting for the Knicks tonight," I muttered, scrubbing a hand down my face. "He's already disappointed enough that I'm a Celtics fan."

Langston chuckled, slow and deliberate, like he'd been waiting all night for me to admit that. "Oh, he'd love that. You know Mr. Dexter is probably still at the Garden right now—celebrating with Mr. Zo, Allie, and Skylar."

Skylar.

Her name landed in the room like a dropped glass—quiet, but impossible to ignore.

I stretched my legs out, resting my feet on the coffee table, but the ease I'd felt just an hour ago was slipping away. During the game, I'd let myself forget for a little while— forget the way she had looked at me that last night, the way her voice had trembled with restraint, the lie she let fall from her lips like it was easier than the truth.

Langston's words cracked the seal on a box I'd been trying to keep closed.

"Can we not?" I asked quietly, though there wasn't any real bite to it.

Langston didn't push. He just tilted his head, still watching me with the same calm patience he always had when he knew I was lying to myself.

Outside, a siren wailed in the distance. Inside, the silence between us said everything.

"You gonna text her?" Langston asked, always cutting straight to the point, never one to let things stew for too long.

I sighed, flipping my phone over in my hand like it might suddenly give me the answer. "I don't know, L. Feels like too much, too soon." My thumb hovered near the screen, hesitant, like making contact would unravel something I wasn't sure I could put back together.

Langston didn't respond right away. He pushed up from the armchair with that slow, unbothered stride of his and headed into the kitchen like he paid the mortgage. The fridge gave a soft suctioned pop as he opened it, then came the familiar hiss of a ginger beer cap twisting free. The sound was sharp in the otherwise quiet apartment, a fizzy little exclamation point.

Leaning against the counter, Langston watched me, his silhouette outlined by the subtle glow of the under-cabinet lights. The cool gleam of stainless steel behind him clashed with the soft, amber light spilling in from the living room— two worlds at odds, much like the one I found myself stuck between.

"Ty," he said, voice low and knowing, "you know this ain't just coincidence. The timing, the connection—hell, Skylar's dad? That's divine comedy if I've ever seen it."

I didn't respond, just exhaled through my nose and opened my phone. Skylar's name stared back at me—unread, untouched. Still pinned at the top like it always had been.

Langston took a swig, then pointed the bottle at me with a grin. "Besides, we've got that final team meeting in a few weeks for the Garden Project. Do yourself a favor and clear the air before we all end up in the same room, playing nice for the sake of the kids."

My thumb hovered, again. No text. No call. Just inertia.

"Text, call—smoke signal," Langston said with a shrug. "Just do something. Or I swear, I'm telling Pops you damn near cried when the Knicks hit that buzzer beater."

I looked up sharply, scowling. "You wouldn't."

He smirked over the rim of his bottle, all teeth and mischief. "Oh, I absolutely would. And I'd do it while wearing my Celtics hoodie."

I narrowed my eyes, but the corner of my mouth betrayed me. I was already losing this standoff. He knew it. And honestly, so did I.

45

Skylar

My heart brimmed with warmth after a day well spent—with Dad, Uncle Zo, and Allie. The Knicks had pulled off a solid win, and I topped the night off with a slice of strawberry shortcake from the little bakery near the promenade—the one that had sweetened my childhood summers. It was the perfect mix of nostalgia and indulgence, sugar and memory.

Back home, I let the steam from a long, hot shower melt the city from my skin. The water beat against my shoulders like a soft drum, loosening muscles I hadn't realized were tense. By the time I stepped into my bedroom, towel-dried and content, the weight of the day had given way to a rare quiet.

I nudged aside one of the many decorative pillows cluttering my king-sized bed and sank into its plush center. From my window, the view stretched across the harbor, the water a sheet of black glass beneath the soft shimmer of city lights. A few brave stars had punched through Brooklyn's urban haze, winking like they knew things I didn't.

I was just starting to drift—thoughts fluttering between

the evening and dreams—when the sharp buzz of my phone cut through the stillness. The ringtone pierced the calm, jolting me upright.

My heart stuttered.

I threw back the covers and padded barefoot across the apartment, retracing my steps, trying to remember where I'd left it. It wasn't on the nightstand. Not on the kitchen counter. Finally, I found it nestled deep in the pocket of the jacket I'd worn earlier, the fabric still faintly scented with Allie's lavender perfume and the fried food aromas of the arena.

The screen glowed in the dim light.

The name alone sent a current through me—familiar, complicated.

I hesitated for the briefest moment, breath catching.

Then, without letting myself overthink, I swiped to answer.

"Hello?" I greeted, aiming for light and breezy, though my body had already stiffened with instinct.

"Skylar Madison." The voice on the other end was sharp, composed—too familiar. There was no warmth in it, just a cool knowing, like they'd been waiting for me to answer.

I shifted against the doorframe, phone tucked to my ear. "Didn't expect a call this late," I said, keeping my voice even.

"Didn't expect to be waiting this long for you to return mine," came the response. Smooth. Controlled. A sentence dressed in polite accusation.

I bristled but forced a chuckle. "It's been a week. Not a year."

"A week too long."

A pause.

Then: "Since you're finally free, let's do brunch tomorrow.

It's been forever."

"Tomorrow?" I asked, already weighing the mental gymnastics of declining.

"Yes, Skylar. Tomorrow. Pick the place. Let me know when you're coming to get me."

Still the same tone. The same choreography of command masked as invitation.

My lips pressed into a thin line. I could see the script already—tight smiles, carefully measured words, the dance we always did in public spaces.

After we hung up, I grabbed my phone and fired off a quick text to Eden.

Text to Eden:

Brunch tomorrow. She's back at it.

We need a post-brunch brunch. With cocktails. Heavy ones.

Only then, as I tossed my phone onto the nightstand and rubbed my temples, did I finally say it out loud, to no one in particular.

"Stitch."

By the next morning, the café was alive with the soft murmur of conversation, the hiss of steamed milk, and the occasional clink of a teaspoon against ceramic. Sunlight poured in through floor-to-ceiling windows, painting the room in a warm, forgiving gold that made even tension seem Instagram-worthy.

Across from me sat my mother—flawless, of course, in an ivory blouse that probably cost more than my rent, and gold hoops that swung like punctuation marks every time she turned her head. She held the menu with the same air of superiority she used to hold my report cards—expectant and ready to critique.

To anyone watching, we looked like a mother-daughter dream: elegant, composed, bonded over brunch. They couldn't hear the landmines buried beneath the small talk.

"So," she said, her voice soft as buttercream but twice as rich with intention, "when were you planning to tell me your father was in town?"

I didn't flinch. Not externally, anyway. Internally, I was already scanning for emotional exits. My therapist's voice echoed in my mind: *Breathe. Count. Ground yourself.*

One... two... three...

"It wasn't my information to share," I said, smoothing the napkin in my lap with a calm I had to download from heaven.

She blinked slowly. That was her tell. Not the twitchy kind. The sniper kind.

"Well," she sniffed, folding her menu like a closing argument, "I suppose that makes sense. After all, I was only married to him for a decade. Why should I be kept in the loop now?"

Here we go. Act One, Scene One: *The Misunderstood Ex.*

"It wasn't a party," I said, already regretting the clarification.

"A *celebration*, then," she corrected. "A family moment that I'm just hearing about through the brunch grapevine."

I wanted to tell her that not every gathering required her RSVP or approval, but I sipped my juice instead. Four... five...

"I didn't plan it," I said instead, softly.

"Ah," she nodded. "So you just showed up. No questions asked. How nice to be so... uninvolved."

She smiled—wide, tight, teeth like pearls but twice as cold. She always did that—twisted the narrative into a shape where she was both the outsider and the injured party.

The server came. Thank God.

She ordered eggs with clinical precision, then turned to me like nothing had just happened. "And what are you having, sweetheart?"

"French toast," I muttered, eyes still on the remnants of restraint on my plate.

"Oh, wonderful! I'll just try a bite of yours."

I paused mid-sip. "You always say that. And then you *commandeer* the plate like it's a diplomatic mission."

She laughed, delighted, as if being accused of food theft was charming. "Skylar, darling, don't be so dramatic."

"Not dramatic," I said, coolly. "Just observant."

She grinned. "That's your father's side showing."

She always said that when I refused to bend. As if holding a boundary meant I had inherited something defective.

Then, without missing a beat: "Speaking of which... what's this I hear about you and Sterling?"

I stiffened. Again.

"I *know* Allie didn't tell you," I said, suspicious.

"Oh, she didn't have to. Ms. Brenda saw you two at that cute little coffee spot on Atlantic. Said it looked like a *very* cozy catch-up."

She sipped her tea like she was sipping tea.

"Love life?" I snorted. "That's... a stretch."

"Well, I always liked Sterling," she offered breezily. "Sharp dresser. Good job. Charming."

Of course she did. Sterling had always known how to charm women of her ilk—polished, socially strategic, wooed by the sheen of status and good tailoring. My father, on the other hand, had seen right through him. He could spot ego wrapped in ambition from a mile away. That alone was reason enough for me to tread lightly.

Mom's approval was like a bad Yelp review—once she gave it, you started questioning all your choices.

Mental note: Whatever this is with Sterling—end it.

"And for the record," I added, tone flat but eyes steady, "my daddy is off limits."

"Oh please," she rolled her eyes. "You need someone who can keep up."

"With what? Your expectations?"

A beat of silence.

Then she smiled again, this time thinner. "I just want you to be happy. Is that so wrong?"

I held her gaze. "It is when your version of happy comes with strings."

"Oh, Sky. Always with the accusations."

She returned to her eggs like I'd just said something whimsical instead of emotionally barbed.

Then, as if on cue, she leveled me with a look over the rim of her cup. "And another thing, Skylar," she added, voice coated in faux concern. "I really wish you'd stop airing all our business with that therapist of yours. What could you possibly have to say about me that requires weekly sessions? Honestly, what exactly are you sharing in there? It's exhausting—living under a microscope like that.""

I didn't answer. I just reached for my water and counted again. One... two... three...

As she launched into an update about her latest endeavor— a spiritual writing class she was "maybe" taking online—I let my mind drift. Not too far, though. You can't daydream around Stitch. She notices. She notices everything.

Sure enough, when her fork hit the empty plate, her eyes drifted to mine like a homing beacon.

I sighed and nudged my plate toward her. "Don't say I never gave you anything."

She lit up. "You're a gem."

"No. I'm your daughter," I muttered. "Which is almost the same thing. Just with more therapy bills."

She laughed, mouth full of my cinnamon joy. "You always were the funny one."

And there it was again. The audience laughed. The curtain dropped. And the bruises stayed hidden under pearls and pressed linen.

Even brunch had battle scars.

After brunch, she insisted on stopping by the market. Not a request—never a request. "You can't live off overpriced granola and air, Skylar," she'd said, already sliding into the passenger seat and pulling out her shopping list like she was briefing a mission.

At the store, she moved like a general with a cart. Olive oil? She picked up a $40 bottle and dropped it in the cart without blinking. "This is the only one worth cooking with," she declared. Then she turned and added, without even looking at me, "You're paying, right?"

Apples? Not firm enough. Greek yogurt? "This brand tastes like regret."

She filled the cart with a mix of ingredients she deemed "basic survival tools" and what she called "a few essentials for when you have company... not that you ever do."

By the time we reached my apartment, I was already exhausted. She breezed in like she owned the place, dropped her bags, and went straight to the fridge.

"Skylar," she said, scandalized, "this refrigerator is one sad breakup away from being completely empty. Honestly, what do you eat?"

"Food, Mom. Just not all at once."

She tsked and started organizing the shelves, muttering about nutrient deficiencies like she had an honorary nutritionist degree.

Then came the closet.

"I'll just make a little space in here for when I stay over," she announced, already shifting hangers and moving my shoes like I was the guest.

"Stay over?" I echoed, trying to keep my voice neutral.

She smiled sweetly, like it was the most obvious thing in the world. "Well, I just need a little space from Parker right now. You know how he gets when he's in one of his moods—hovering, needy, always with the passive-aggressive sighs. I figured it might be nice to have a place to clear my head."

I counted again. One... two... three... then gently slid the closet door shut.

It took twenty more minutes, two false goodbyes, and one exaggerated yawn on my part to finally get her—and her bags full of overpriced groceries—back in the car. I had picked her up earlier that morning, which now meant the return trip was part of the package deal.

As I pulled away from her building, she waved like royalty being sent off on tour.

I exhaled, letting the silence settle around me like balm.

Brunch, groceries, closet diplomacy—survived.

Barely.

Sometimes, surviving breakfast with her felt more exhausting than running a marathon in heels.

"The last piece of *my* French toast," I hissed into the phone, pacing the living room, "disappeared into her mouth like it was hers all along. No shame. No hesitation. Like I ordered it *for* her."

Allie snorted. "Not the beloved French toast! Girl, I know that had whipped cream on it too."

"Whipped cream, cinnamon, the works," I said, flopping onto the couch like I had just returned from battle. "And she chewed it slow, like she was savoring a win I didn't realize we were even competing for."

"Typical Stitch," Allie muttered.

"Oh, but wait. That was just the appetizer to the emotional chaos," I continued. "She blotted her lipstick with her napkin, then goes, 'I need a little space. From Parker.' Like she was talking about switching gym memberships."

There was a beat of silence before Allie let out a long, "Oh *no*."

"Oh *yes*," I groaned. "She followed it up with, 'I'm going to stay with you for a little while.' Just like that. As if she's a casual weekend plan I forgot to pencil in."

Allie gasped, equal parts horror and delight. "Wait. Did she *ask*?"

"Nope," I said. "Just declared it. Right there between bites of *my* brunch. Like she was ordering dessert."

Allie sighed dramatically. "She really is a master of the soft ambush. All calm tone, Chanel lip gloss, and nuclear impact."

"She weaponized a lemon wedge and a linen napkin," I said. "I was defenseless."

"Did you at least push back?"

"I *tried*," I said, rubbing my temples. "But she gave me

that look. The one that says, 'You can try to resist, but you won't win.' Next thing I knew, I was mentally calculating how many clean towels I had."

"Whew," Allie said. "Sky, your mom is like a Park Avenue chess master with a flair for emotional checkmate."

"Exactly," I muttered. "She's not moving in. She's invading."

Allie chuckled. "So when does Stitchlandia arrive?"

"She didn't say. Which means... soon. Possibly with matching luggage and a dramatic monologue."

"Well," Allie said, her voice full of mischief, "let me know if I need to run interference. I'll show up with coffee and chaos."

"I'll take both," I said, exhaling into the phone. "Heavy on the coffee."

"I should've known something was brewing," I said into the phone, pacing the living room. "The signs had been stacking up for months like unopened mail."

I could hear Allie's soft hmm on the other end, the kind she made when she already knew where the story was going but let me get there myself.

"It started when she decided to crash my Thanksgiving plans. My dad had mentioned he was hosting in North Carolina this year—casual, low-key, just us. Given that she *is* still married to Parker, I figured this was the perfect opportunity to take a solo trip. *Solo* being the operative word. She called me out of the blue."

Tears. Sniffles. The usual dramatics. She rambled on about not having anywhere to go, how she couldn't possibly endure another dry, beige Thanksgiving with Parker's family be-cause they didn't "season their food *or* their conversation."

"She was invited," Allie said, casually crunching through her snack like she wasn't low-key judging me.

"Dad said she could come," I corrected, my voice tight. "After she pulled the waterworks and guilted him into it."

"But she was *still* invited," Allie replied with that annoying calm she slipped into whenever she decided to play therapist instead of friend.

"She wasn't invited by *me*. That's the point."

Allie let out a long, slow breath—her official signal that she was shifting into neutral, which in Allie-speak meant *brace yourself for a truth bomb*. "Semantics, Skylar. She was invited. Whether or not you agreed to be her chauffeur is a whole other debate. And that's not today's argument."

I pressed my lips together, biting back the retort hanging on my tongue. Our friendship had always been built on truth-telling, and sometimes—okay, *a lot* of the time—truth stung like lemon juice in a paper cut.

"She only came because I'm a sucker," I muttered.

"No," Allie said, voice softer now. "You let her come because deep down, you're still holding out hope that she'll show up for you. That one of these days, she'll actually choose *you* instead of whatever husband, hobby, or healing phase she's floating through."

The silence stretched for a beat too long.

"Well," she pivoted, brightening her tone with practiced ease. "What *did* happen with the latest and greatest husband?"

I rolled my eyes. "Greatest?"

Allie laughed. "Sky, no one will ever compare to Mr. Dexter Madison. Papi Madison had that old-school Brooklyn swagger."

Despite myself, I smiled. "That man knew how to dress."

"And how to treat a woman."

We sat with that memory for a moment, letting it bloom in the space between us. My father, with his salt-and-pepper waves, his perfectly knotted ties, and that way he made every woman feel like the most important person in the room— even when he was quietly judging their shoe choice.

He wasn't just *better* than Parker. He was *unmatched.*

And maybe that was the problem.

Eva had moved on. Married again. And again. And again. But somehow, she had never really left the shadow of the man she let go of.

And neither had I.

"He spoiled her."

"And *you*," Allie added without missing a beat.

I sighed, letting the weight of that truth press against the ache in my chest. My father had always had a softness for Stitch, a flaw of his that I'd never fully forgiven. Still, I let the memory of him—his steady hand, his easy laugh—soften me for a moment. It was fleeting.

"Back to the heart of the matter," Allie said, shifting gears with the finesse of someone who'd been navigating my family drama for over two decades. "What's going on with *Ms. Eva?*"

The weight returned instantly, like someone had dropped a sandbag right on my sternum.

"I don't know, Allie. That's the million-dollar question. If I had the answer, maybe I could also solve climate change and bring back Blockbuster."

Allie burst out laughing on the other end. I didn't.

"She didn't say the word *divorce*," I clarified, "but she said she needed 'space from Parker.' Her *exact* words."

"And then she casually asks to move in with you?" Allie said, her voice climbing in disbelief.

"Yup. Over French toast. *Mine*, to be exact."

Allie stifled a cackle. "Wait, was this before or after the pitch for the church trip?"

"Oh, it all happened in the *same* breath."

"She said the church is planning a mission trip to South America." I paused. "But by the end of breakfast, it had magically transformed into the Bahamas."

Allie gasped, then wheezed. "*Wait...* what?"

"Yup. And then she hit me with the sponsor pitch—told me the deposit was due and everything."

"She brought *receipts*?"

"Only emotionally manipulative ones. No literal receipts. Just guilt and that lemon wedge she swirls in her tea like she's conjuring a spell."

Allie snorted. "Hello, *Alejandra*," I said, dropping into my most exasperated tone. "Did you catch the part where my mother wants to *move in*? Like, live *with me*? In my apartment. *My* space."

"Sí, sí, tranquila, cariño, yes, yes, calm down" she cooed, completely unfazed. "I'm just trying to lighten the mood. I mean, a girls' trip to the Bahamas does sound nice..."

"Allie! *Focus*. Help me."

"Okay, okay." Allie took a breath, her tone shifting into big sister strategist mode. "Listen, you *know* your mom. That woman is the Beyoncé of manipulation. She doesn't *ask* to stay—she *suggests* it, lightly, like it's a weather forecast. And then just waits for you to build the whole damn storm around her."

"Exactly!" I threw my free hand in the air. "She didn't

ask. She just said it like it was already on the calendar, right between my next therapy session and trash day."

"And you..." Allie's voice slowed, laced with playful accusation. "Didn't say no?"

"I was too shocked. And also? I was hungry. Then she hijacked my French toast and I lost the will to fight."

Allie let out a belly laugh. "Not the cinnamon-sugar surrender!"

"She *devoured* it, Allie. And had the nerve to moan like it was her idea to order french toast."

I could practically hear Allie wiping tears from her eyes. "Hold up. Quinn's calling. This sounds like it needs a four-woman council of wisdom. Don't go anywhere."

Before I could object, the line clicked, and seconds later Quinn's bright, singsong voice cut through the line like sunshine through clouds.

"S-K-Y-L-A-R! What's up, queen?"

"Hey, Q," I said, sinking deeper into the cushions like they might swallow me whole.

Quinn's tone softened just enough. "You sound like mama drama has you on the ropes."

"You don't know the half," I muttered, eyes closed, already bracing for her signature brand of loving-but-blunt truth.

"Whew," Quinn said. "Give us the rundown. And please tell me this woman didn't eat your entire breakfast."

Allie chimed in, giddy. "She did. Every last bite."

"Y'all." I exhaled dramatically. "We might need a safe house."

Before I could even get the words out, Allie cut in. "Hold up—let me add Eden. I swear we all have ESP. This needs to be a full-on emergency group session."

Seconds later, Eden's smooth, measured voice joined the chaos. "Hey ladies. What's the emergency? I was mid-serum routine."

Quinn didn't skip a beat. "Skylar's mama just pulled a classic Eva sneak attack: *'I'm moving in with you'*—said it over French toast like she was requesting hot sauce."

"Oh, Lord Jesus," Eden whispered. "*Ms. Eva?*"

"Yup," I said flatly.

"It must be a full moon," Eden said, dead serious. "Mama drama is in the air like pollen. Mine just called me at 6:45 this morning, no good morning, no warning—just, *'Ahn when yah gwan gimme one nex granpickney, eh? Yuh tink ah gettin any youngah?'*"

The room *erupted* in laughter.

"Oh nooo," Allie cackled. "Not the *granpickney* guilt trip before sunrise!"

"Yup," Eden sighed. "Told her we were already late for school drop-off, and she hit me with, *'Yuh fi breed again before mi bruk mi hip!'* Like... what?!"

I wheezed. "See? This is what I'm saying. They just *insert themselves* like we're their second chance at everything."

Allie cackled while I pressed the heel of my hand into my forehead. "You're all missing the real crisis. Let me run it back."

I launched into my recap:

The lemon-twisting guilt trip.

The fake tears about spending Thanksgiving with Parker's bland family.

The miraculous transformation of a "church mission to South America" into a *resort* in the Bahamas.

The unplanned grocery run.

The passive-aggressive comments about my fridge contents.

And the grand finale: a totally unsolicited closet cleanout as she declared, "Just making space for a few things."

"*A few things?!*" Quinn echoed. "She planning to stage a whole second act in your apartment?"

"She said she's staying 'just for a bit,' like she was asking to borrow my earrings," I snapped. "Next thing I know, she'll be hosting a Bible study in my living room and labeling Tupperware."

There was a stunned silence.

"Okay, but let's circle back to the South America trip," Eden said finally, barely holding in her laughter. "Because I still have questions."

I groaned. "Eden, *seriously?* That is not the headline here."

"We need context!" she defended.

"Fine." I exhaled dramatically. "It started as a church mission trip to South America—feeding the poor, helping build schools, whatever. But somehow by the end of brunch, it became a women's ministry retreat in the *Bahamas*, and she had the nerve to say *'I'm trusting God to provide my deposit... starting with you.'*"

"I can't," Allie wheezed.

"Who needs reality TV?" Quinn added. "We've got Ms. Eva and her Deluxe French Toast Diplomacy."

I took a deep breath and dove back into the memory.

We were sitting at our usual breakfast spot in Brooklyn. She was in a new wig—dark brown, silky straight, hanging down past her shoulders. I suspected it was her latest online purchase, the kind she pretended was "on sale" but cost more than my monthly utilities.

"Sister Helen," she began with dramatic flair, "walked into the deacon's meeting looking like a knockoff Lil' Kim. Platinum wig. Green contacts. Bangs! Bangs, Skylar!"

"She's in her sixties, right?"

"Sixty-six and still chasing trends. It was shameful. I told her not to bring that mess to church again. Someone had to tell her."

"Should that someone be you?"

She gave me a side-eye and flicked the ends of her wig. "Please. This is human hair, darling."

"Okay, Foxy Brown."

"Foxy Brown wore an afro."

"Not Pam Grier. The rapper."

"There's only one Foxy Brown. Don't start, Skylar."

Then, mid-monologue, she paused to swipe another piece of my French toast.

"And by the way," she added, "I've been thinking about taking a little break. Parker's been working my nerves."

"Define break."

"I need space. I'm going to stay with you for a bit."

My fork froze midair. "Is that a question?"

"Just for a little while. Nothing permanent."

I stared, stunned, as she poured syrup over the last piece of toast on my plate. My toast. Then she launched into her next topic—how the church was planning a mission trip to South America. Or the Bahamas. Whichever came with a beach and brunch.

"You know what she said next?" I told the girls, pacing in front of my couch like I was building a case in court. "That the deposit was five hundred dollars—and she thought I could '*bless her with it.*'"

"Wow," Eden deadpanned. "That's bold. Even for her."

"Classic Stitch," Allie muttered, her tone dry enough to crack pavement.

"That's not even the best part," I continued, flopping onto the couch with an exaggerated sigh. "Right after I politely declined her fraudulent vacation-in-the-name-of-Jesus pitch, she had the nerve to tell me to stop biting my lip."

"What?" Quinn blinked.

"Said it's a 'bad habit' from when I was a child. And—*this is the kicker*—that she *hates it*."

"I'm sorry," Quinn interrupted, full-on incredulous now. "She's moving into your apartment, wants you to bankroll her Bahamian 'mission trip,' and she's out here critiquing your *coping mechanisms*?"

"You can't make this up," I said, shaking my head.

"She's like a spiritual scammer with a Pinterest board," Eden added under her breath.

"Next she'll be asking you to Venmo her for 'spiritual covering,'" Allie quipped, and we all burst out laughing—because if we didn't, we'd cry.

"I'm crying," Eden said between wheezes. "This sounds exactly like something my mom would pull."

"Oh, speaking of—guess what Ursula hit me with the other night?" Eden continued, already slipping into her mother's unmistakable Jamaican cadence. "'Eden, mi pickney, mi been workin' like mule all mi life. Mi deserve a likkle break, nuh? Jus' help mi pay di deposit. Five hundred dollar is small change. You an', your brother Clifton can mash head and sort it out.'"

We *lost* it.

"All our mothers are out here running scams," I said, wiping tears from the corners of my eyes.

"Mine didn't even bother faking a mission trip," Eden added. "She called it a *spiritual sabbatical.* I can't."

"Okay, but real talk," Allie said, reigning us back in. "What are you actually going to do about your mom?"

"I don't know," I admitted, sinking deeper into the couch. "I feel like if I say no, I'm a heartless daughter. But if I say yes, I'm signing over my peace of mind."

"Sky, has she brought it up again?" Eden asked, her tone gentle now.

"No," I said. "Not since the French toast summit."

"Then don't move," Eden advised. "Let *her* bring it back up—with a real plan. Don't you dare initiate."

"She's going to show up with her luggage like, 'Skylar, darling, where's the guest towel?'" Quinn chimed in.

"Not even a towel," Allie countered. "She'll just toss her roller bag in the hallway, light a candle, and start rearranging your feng shui."

"Classic Stitch," Eden muttered, shaking her head.

I sighed so hard my shoulders dropped. "What am I going to do?"

"Schedule therapy," Eden said dryly, and we all broke into laughter again.

Then Quinn, always the one with the follow-up questions, tilted her head. "So... how long has she even been married to Parker?"

"Not even a full year," I said, dragging out each word.

"She just got married—and now she needs a break?" Quinn blinked. "That's not a relationship, that's a layover."

"She thought marriage would fix everything," I muttered,

pushing my thumb against the rim of my mug. "But her relationships always have a shelf life. There's always an expiration date she doesn't see coming—until it's spoiled."

"Sounds like someone else I know," Quinn said, too casually.

My eyes narrowed. "Excuse me?"

She shrugged, all innocence. "I'm just saying..."

"Here we go," I muttered, leaning back against the couch cushions, bracing myself.

"Sky," Allie said gently, her voice like a soft nudge, "have you ever considered that maybe... just maybe... you act a little like your mom when it comes to men?"

The words landed like a stone in my stomach.

"That's ridiculous," I said, even though the edges of me had started to crack.

"You bail early," Quinn said, undeterred. "You've got dealbreakers for your dealbreakers."

"You mean I have boundaries," I countered, sharper than I intended.

"No," Eden cut in, her voice cool and precise. "You have escape hatches. And you're always halfway through them before you even admit you want to stay."

The silence that followed wasn't awkward—it was truthful. Heavy. Familiar.

I swallowed hard. The truth always did sound worse when someone else said it out loud.

I sucked my teeth, Eden's words hitting harder than I expected. "Escape hatches?" The phrase echoed in my head like an insult wrapped in a parable.

The four of us were mid-convo on a late-night FaceTime. I was curled up in bed, wrapped in my weighted blanket, a half-glass of wine balanced on my nightstand and my satin bonnet slightly crooked from tossing and turning. Eden was posted up in her dimly lit home office, her signature glasses perched low on her nose like she was reading me for filth and footnotes. Quinn was flopped across her sectional, the glow of a muted *Insecure* rerun flickering in the background while she alternated between sipping tea and side-eyeing me.

"Seriously, E?" I said, brows arching as I sat up a little straighter. "You of all people? Miss I've-got-a-scroll-of-deal-breakers? Don't you have, like, a laminated card of non-negotiables in your wallet?"

Quinn chuckled and lifted her mug in agreement.

"You're always the first one to remind us that if a man doesn't believe in therapy, tithing, and hot water facials, he's not worthy of your time," I added, letting the heat in my voice sharpen just enough to mask the sting I felt.

Eden blinked slowly, unimpressed. "And I *own* that. But I don't run the second it gets hard. That's the difference."

My mouth parted to respond, but no words came. Just the sound of *Insecure*'s muted credits rolling behind Quinn and my pride slowly backing itself into a corner.

Eden exhaled, her breath shaky as she leaned back in her chair. The usual steel in her voice was gone, replaced with something fragile—raw and unguarded.

"I'm starting to realize..." she began, her tone quieter now, almost reverent, "fairy tales are just that. Fairy tales."

The words hung in the air, delicate and devastating.

"If you can't be real—like *really* real... messy, scared, honest—then all you're doing is building a relationship that feels like performance art. You memorize your lines, hit your marks, smile on cue. But there's no *you* in it. Just... costumes.

Cue cards. Smoke and mirrors."

She paused, eyes distant. "And Sky... I'm struggling."

The admission knocked the air out of the room.

"This man—Jayson—the one I waited for, the one I prayed for, hand-picked like some custom order from God's boutique... he doesn't even see me." Her voice trembled. "Because I didn't *show* him me. Not fully. I gave him the polished version. The conference-ready, charity-gala, edge-laid and lips-glossed version. I showed him the sizzle reel, not the behind-the-scenes."

Her words tapered off, choked slightly by emotion. For a moment, none of us spoke. The silence was thick—weighted with unspoken truths, shared fears, and the kind of sisterhood that holds space without needing to fill it.

Then she cleared her throat, the sound sharp and jarring after so much softness. She sat up straighter, trying to laugh, but it didn't quite land.

"Anyway... enough about my little TED Talk of sadness."

But her eyes betrayed her. She wasn't done—not even close.

"I've been doing a lot of thinking," Eden said, her voice lower now, more certain. Her eyes drifted past the screen toward a framed photo behind her—one of her and Ursula at her college graduation. Her smile in the picture was radiant, but the grip Ursula had on her shoulder looked more like possession than pride.

"A lot of this," she continued, "started with Ursula."

Quinn and I both sat up a little straighter.

"From day one, she drilled it into me—find a man who *fits*. Not one who *feels*. He should have a degree, a 750 credit score, a family crest, a Black Amex, and summer plans in Martha's

Vineyard. Bonus points if his parents own property in Sag Harbor."

Quinn snorted. "Or a family trust."

Eden didn't even crack a smile. "Exactly. She sold me a dream wrapped in designer fabric and respectability politics and said *that's* what stability looks like. That's what success *feels* like. So, I chased it. And guess what? I caught it."

She paused, eyes hard. "And now I'm miserable. Quietly. Elegantly. *Miserable.*"

The words hit like glass shattering.

"I'm sinking in a life that looks perfect on paper, but it feels like a damn prison. A picket fence built from performance and pressure."

Her voice steadied with that last sentence—low and sharp, like a confession and a reckoning all at once.

Then she sat back, arms folded. "We have mommy issues," she added dryly. "Deluxe edition."

Quinn nodded slowly, her voice low. "She's right, Sky. You're out here investing in these pretty little placeholder relationships—men you *curate* instead of connect with— because somewhere deep down, you don't trust your own judgment."

The silence that followed wasn't awkward.

It was truth-filled. Heavy. Real.

And maybe exactly what I needed to hear.

I frowned, my brow knitting as I leaned further into the screen. "Trust myself to do *what* exactly?"

"To choose something *real*," Allie said, her voice floating in from the corner of the group chat like velvet laced with smoke. She hadn't said much in the last few minutes, but when she did, it landed. "You keep walking away from men who don't check every box on your perfect little list—but maybe that list is just a shield. Maybe the truth is... real love scares the hell out of you."

"Here we go," I muttered, grabbing my wineglass and taking a slow sip. "What are y'all charging for this pop-up therapy session? Because I definitely didn't sign up for a co-pay."

That cracked the tension. Eden let out a chuckle. Quinn snorted. Even Allie smirked.

But just as I was settling into that momentary relief, Quinn cut through it with surgical precision. "You're terrified of staying."

My shoulders tensed. "That's not true."

"Sterling," she said flatly.

I narrowed my eyes. "What about him?"

"You're clinging to him because he's easy," she replied, cool and cutting. "He's familiar. He's mediocre."

I blinked. "Wow. Okay. Harsh much?"

"You said it, not me," Eden jumped in. "You're not building with him. You're hiding behind him."

"I'm not hiding," I insisted, my voice tight. "I'm figuring things out."

"No, Sky," Allie said gently, "you're *stalling*."

Their words circled me like a slow storm—no raised voices, just a steady pressure I couldn't push away.

"Because you're scared," Allie added.

I sat back, the silence stretching just long enough to make me uncomfortable. "Scared of *what*?"

Quinn jumped in again, her tone shifting from teasing to sincere. "But seriously, Sky—what are you scared of?"

The question hung in the air like heavy smoke. I didn't

respond right away. Couldn't. I wasn't even sure I knew the answer.

Eden didn't hesitate. "That Sterling isn't the one... and that maybe—just *maybe*—Titus is."

The line went quiet, the weight of her words hitting like a slow exhale I hadn't realized I was holding.

And there it was.

The truth I'd been too afraid to name.

The silence between us widened, thick with everything said and unsaid—until Eden cut through it like she always did.

"Ms. Eva and Ms. Claudette are *absolutely* running game with this so-called 'mission trip.' More like a deluxe girls' trip with one scripture and a beachside prayer circle thrown in for tax exemption."

"There is *no way* I'm funding this divine vacation," she declared, her voice sharp with mock indignation.

"Eden, please," Allie jumped in. "You and Sky already have the checks written and the envelopes addressed."

"No need to call me out in front of company," I said, lifting my glass. "You know Stitch stays ready with the Zelle info saved as 'your favorite mother.'"

"And Ursula already sent me a Cash App request!" Eden groaned. Then, slipping seamlessly into her mother's Jamaican cadence, she delivered the kicker:

"'*Eden, mi love, yuh can just drop di money inna mi Cash App, y'hear? Mek sure yuh send it quick-quick—before mi start bawl or sell mi soul to go pon dis trip!*'"

She rolled her eyes so hard I thought they might stay that way.

We *lost it*. The phone line erupted in pure laughter, the kind that made your ribs hurt and your mascara run.

These were my girls. My anchor, my rhythm, my check-in and check-you crew. The only people who could pull my receipts, read me for filth, and still wrap me in laughter and love. They were grace with a side-eye, prayer with a punchline.

"Okay, ladies," Quinn said through her giggles, "my man has been waiting patiently for me to get off this phone. *Patient*—as in, he made me a cocktail and queued up my show over an hour ago."

We all groaned in envy.

"Tatum strikes again," Allie muttered. "The gold standard of husbands."

"I know he's sitting on that couch right now with that 'Take your time, baby, I'm here' look," I said, half-laughing, half-sighing.

"Disgustingly cute," Eden agreed.

"Truly nauseating," I added. "God, I want that kind of love."

"Don't hate!" Quinn chuckled eager to entertain Tatum.

"A pint of grapenut ice cream has been calling my name," Eden sighed. "Jayson's out of town, the kids are asleep, and it's just me, my spoon, and some quality self-pity tonight."

"I need to call Luz back before she ends up on my doorstep," Allie said, glancing at her screen. "She rang twice while we were on the phone. If I don't hit her back soon, she'll have Elias knocking like he's NYPD with a warrant."

I laughed, startled by how quickly time had passed. "Damn. We've really been on the phone that long?"

"Girl—*hours*," Eden confirmed, her tone both amused and exhausted.

I softened, letting the vulnerability show in my voice.

"Thanks for listening to me ramble about Stitch."

"Our pleasure," Eden replied, her voice wrapped in love. Then came the weight: "Just remember, Sky—fairy tales aren't real. But if you have the privilege of a man *seeing you*—really seeing you—and still choosing to love you? Don't fumble that."

"Whoa," Quinn murmured. "Eden, what's *in* that ice cream? Did it come with a word from the Lord?"

"She's giving you the full Iyanla Vanzant experience!" Allie added, laughing.

Quinn chuckled, then leaned in gently. "Figure out what's really scaring you, Sky. Then ask yourself—*is he worth the risk?* And if the answer is yes, stop running. Let yourself be loved. I can't wait for the day you rush me off the phone because your husband is somewhere in the background trying to pull you back into his arms."

"Love y'all," Quinn said, her voice soft, sure, and full. "Now let me go keep my man from reheating his own dinner."

"Good night, chicas," Eden added, and just like that—two clicks and they were gone.

Leaving just me and Allie.

The silence lingered for a moment, but it wasn't empty.

It was safe. It was sacred.

The kind of silence reserved for soul-deep friendships, where nothing needed to be said for everything to be understood. It wrapped around us like a soft blanket, soothing the sharp edges of our conversation.

I shifted on the couch, my eyes landing on the blank television screen. My own reflection stared back—tired, pensive, a little undone. Not the version of myself I curated for the world. This was the raw one. The real one.

"You *really* had to tell them I call him 'Two Kids Titus?'" I said, voice low and dry.

Allie didn't miss a beat. "It's one of my *better* nicknames for your situationships. Don't make me bring up 'Broke Tyrese' or 'Vanilla Ice, Esq.'"

I groaned, already bracing for the flashbacks. "You are *diabolical.*"

"Sky. Stop procrastinating," she said, her tone shifting to that gentle insistence only a best friend can pull off. "Call him."

My breath caught. "And say what, Allie?"

"Start with 'I'm sorry.' Then say, 'I'm scared.' And then... tell him the truth. That he's worth the risk."

I didn't respond right away. My thumb hovered over the edge of my phone, suddenly heavier than it should've been. The thought of dialing Titus made my pulse quicken. Not because of the kids, though that was my convenient excuse. The truth was uglier—quieter.

Titus represented everything I claimed I wanted: stability, depth, presence. Love without ego. And something inside me was terrified that I didn't know how to receive that.

Before I could untangle it, Allie cut in. "Don't argue. I've got to call Luz before she sends Elias to file a missing person report. Church with la familia mañana. Love you, chica."

Click.

And just like that, I was alone again. Alone—but not empty.

Her words hung in the air like incense—unspoken prayers and hard truths lingering between my ribs. I sat in the stillness, letting them echo.

Eventually, I picked up my phone and scrolled to his name.

I didn't press call.

Not yet.

But for the first time, I didn't scroll past him either.

And for me—that was progress. That was a crack in the armor. That was hope.

46

Titus

The soft glow of the setting sun spilled through the tall windows of my Brooklyn brownstone, casting honeyed streaks across the polished hardwood floors. The scent of roasted garlic and fresh basil still lingered in the air, clinging to the corners of the room like the echo of a conversation you didn't want to end. A lazy jazz playlist murmured in the background—Coltrane, low and soulful—spinning comfort through the open space.

Outside, spring stirred to life. Laughter floated up from brownstone stoops. Somewhere down the block, a bike bell chimed, and the soft rustle of cherry blossoms brushing against the glass reminded me that the world was still blooming, even if I wasn't sure I was.

I sat in my office—my sanctuary. Bookshelves lined the walls, filled with titles on architecture, history, and the occasional well-worn novel I refused to part with. The scent of old pages mixed with cedarwood from the diffuser on my desk. Next to my laptop sat a worn Morehouse mug and a Polaroid. The photo of Skylar and me from that impulsive afternoon at the High Line leaned against a stack of blueprints. She was laughing in it—head thrown back, curls wild, joy unfiltered. I hadn't meant to stare at it again, but her smile in that moment had the strange power to disarm me every time.

The phone buzzed. I reached for it automatically, the name flashing across the screen just as I pressed answer.

"Hi, Titus. I'm sorry—I thought I'd take a chance and call instead of texting. I hope that's okay?"

Her voice wrapped around me like warm cognac—smooth, slow, and laced with something tender and unspoken. A little breathless. A little unsure. But unmistakably her. There was vulnerability threaded through every syllable, like she was leaning against the words for balance.

I exhaled, slow and quiet, grounding myself in the moment. My eyes drifted back to the photo, and something in my chest stirred—familiar, aching, alive.

"Skylar Madison," I said, her name like a smile in my mouth. I couldn't help the warmth that slipped into my voice, even if part of me wanted to play it cool. "Can't lie and say I'm not surprised to hear from you. But I am pleasantly surprised. How are you?"

There was a pause—just long enough to feel the weight of it. I heard the small hitch in her breath, the hesitation that wasn't there the last time we spoke. It wasn't nerves. It was something else. Something heavier.

"I'm... I'm well," she said softly. "Titus, I wanted to—"

"T! Where you hiding the glasses in this place?"

The voice cut through the moment like a knife through silk—casual, confident, and far too familiar. Smooth, like a late-night radio host with a voice meant to wrap around women at 2 a.m.

I closed my eyes for a beat, jaw tightening on instinct. That voice floated through the brownstone like a saxophone riff—sultry, attention-seeking, and completely out of place in the middle of this conversation.

"Ty-tus," the voice called again, elongating each syllable with theatrical flair. The sound of cabinet doors opening and closing punctuated her search. "You've got way too many places to hide stuff in here, babe."

My hand gripped the phone tighter. I turned toward the hallway, voice low but steady.

"Skylar..." I began, my voice low, regret already curling at the edges of each word. "Would you mind if we picked this back up later? I've got something I need to tend to."

There was a beat of silence on her end—a quiet inhale, like she was steadying herself.

"Yeah... yes, of course. I understand," she said, her voice barely above a whisper, trying too hard to sound unaffected. "Let me know when you're free to talk or... maybe grab a bite?"

"I will. Definitely." I tried to match her calm, but my tone betrayed me—too earnest, too hopeful. "And hey—how'd your dad and Uncle Zo like the Knicks game?"

A breath of laughter escaped her, soft and sweet. The kind of laugh that wrapped around you before you even knew you needed it.

"They had the time of their lives," she said, and I could hear her smile again. "Like two big kids at Coney Island." Then, quieter, with a trace of something deeper: "Should I tell Allie we've got a Knicks fan in the making?"

I chuckled, rubbing the back of my neck. "Langston and

I were yelling at the screen like it was Game 7. I can only imagine the energy in the Garden."

But the warmth between us was already thinning.

Because the sound of heels—sharp and insistent—echoed down the hallway, growing louder.

"Tyyy, are you ignoring me now?" the voice called out, more flame than flirtation.

Skylar heard it. I knew she did. I didn't have to say a word— her silence told me everything.

"I'm sorry, Skylar," I said quickly. "I really have to go."

There was another pause. This one colder.

"It's okay," she replied, and though the words were gentle, her voice had shifted—cooler, distant, like she was already pulling back.

"Thanks for the call," I added, desperate to reclaim some of the moment. "It was... a good surprise. I'm glad you reached out."

A quiet beat passed before she said, simply, "Me too. Bye, Titus."

"Goodbye, Skylar."

I held the phone for a few seconds longer, long after the call ended, staring at her name as it faded from the screen.

The line went dead, and in the silence that followed, Sade's voice rose from the speaker behind me—her words hauntingly perfect. *"If you were mine, if you were mine... I wouldn't want to go to heaven."*

I closed my eyes and let the lyric hang there, suspended in the weight of everything unspoken, the weight of Skylar's voice still warm in my ear, even though she was already gone again. Like she always seemed to be.

"Ty," a voice cut in sharply.

I turned toward the doorway. Cece stood there, framed by the arch like a scene from a movie—tall and striking, her thick curls cascading around her face in effortless coils. Her curvy frame filled out her casual lounge set, and her tortoiseshell glasses framed eyes that were narrowing at me with suspicion.

Her hands were planted firmly on her hips. "Why are you sneaking off in here? Who were you on the phone with?"

I gave her a slow grin, the kind that used to charm my way out of trouble—but even I could feel the guilt tucked behind it.

"Why are you cockblocking, Cece?"

She raised a brow, one hand flying to her hip like punctuation. "Oh, so now *I'm* the problem?"

I just chuckled and walked toward her, but Skylar's voice still echoed in my ears.

That midnight whisper wasn't something you could forget. And I wasn't sure I wanted to.

Cece finally unearthed the wine glasses—God knows where I had shoved them—and helped herself to a generous pour like a queen reclaiming her throne after battle. Without missing a beat, she made herself right at home, collapsing onto my couch with the kind of authority only an older sister possesses. Her fuzzy slippers hit the floor, her legs stretched out across the cushions like she was auditioning for a Tempur-Pedic commercial.

She raised her glass in a regal toast, eyes half-lidded with dramatic flair. "I need my husband to give me a proper foot rub after all the walking you put me through today."

Her half-smile was pure Cece—exhausted but satisfied, like someone who'd carried a full load and somehow still made it look graceful.

We'd spent the whole day threading through New York's forgotten seams—corners the average tourist never touched, pockets of the city even locals didn't talk about. Between my work in urban redevelopment, months of quiet research before I moved back, and the legacy breadcrumbs dropped by Skylar and Allie—who spoke of Brooklyn like it was sacred ground—I had curated a solid list of places that meant something. Places that whispered history if you listened closely enough.

Today, Cece and I weren't just sightseeing—we were time traveling. Touching walls older than our lineage. Reading plaques that carried names we might've been named after. Unearthing stories buried beneath concrete and scaffolding.

And somewhere in all that wandering, we found pieces of ourselves too.

She took another slow sip and sighed. "Next time, warn a woman when she needs to wear compression socks."

"Stepping into the Hispanic Society Museum and Library felt like entering a time capsule," I said, the memory still fresh in my mind. "A portal to a different world."

Cece nodded, swirling her wine. "That collection of Spanish and Latin American art was insane. Who would've thought something like that was tucked away in Washington Heights?"

"I didn't." I smiled. "Allie never misses with her recommendations."

"El Barrio was just as dope," Cece added, her eyes lighting up. "That space had a whole heartbeat of its own."

I leaned forward slightly, still tasting the energy of East Harlem. "It felt like the pulse of the neighborhood—alive, layered, unapologetically rich with culture."

Cece raised her glass in agreement. "And that installation Allie curated? The mix of iconic and emerging Latino artists—stunning. It painted more than a picture. It told a whole story."

We sat for a moment in quiet appreciation, the kind only shared between people who'd truly *seen* something.

"What'd you think of the burial ground?" I asked, recalling the somber stillness of the African Burial Ground Monument in Lower Manhattan.

Cece exhaled slowly, her voice softer now. "Fifteen thousand... free and enslaved Africans buried right there in Manhattan." Her eyes clouded slightly. "I've been studying our history for years, Titus. Teaching it. Living it. But moments like that still hit me in the chest."

I leaned back, a grin pulling at the corner of my mouth. "I'm just amazed I could introduce *you* to a piece of Black history you didn't already have on speed dial."

Cece gave me the side-eye, wine glass lifted halfway like a weapon. "Let's not rewrite the script now, baby brother. *I* was the one who suggested we go there."

I tilted my head, feigning confusion. "Did you?"

Cece narrowed her eyes. "Don't start with me, Ty."

We both laughed, the sibling banter wrapping around us like a familiar blanket. The older we got, the sharper our jokes and the deeper our bond.

"Weeksville was my favorite," I said. "There was something about that space."

Cece straightened up, her historian instincts fully activated. "Most folks have no idea that free Black communities existed in Brooklyn during the 1800s. They think the South holds all the roots of slavery, but the North—New York—was just as twisted up in it."

"Wall Street. Built by enslaved people," I added, shaking my head. "Who knew?"

"They helped build the early bones of this city. Roads. Homes. Even that wall—the one that gave Wall Street its name." Cece's voice carried the weight of generations, her passion always right at the surface.

"I don't know how you store all that information in that big head of yours," I teased, needing to break the emotional tension.

Cece peered over her turquoise frames, smirking as she tipped her glass toward me. "From one big head to another."

We both laughed again, and the room felt warm with memory and meaning. She reclined, glancing out at the skyline wrapped in darkness, where the stars blinked faintly above the glowing city below.

"I loved everything we saw today," she said. "But that walk across the Brooklyn Bridge? Top tier."

"You mean the walk I *dragged* you on?"

She groaned. "Dragged is dramatic. Heavily encouraged, maybe."

I chuckled, the image of her complaining the whole first half of the walk flashing through my mind. But as I looked out the window myself, my thoughts drifted. The bridge held more than city views for me now—it held memories.

I could still hear Skylar's voice that day she called it *her* bridge. The reverence in her tone. The way she spoke of late-night escapes from her mother's wrath—feet pounding wooden planks, tears drying in the night air. How that bridge held her stories, her rage, her healing.

I imagined a younger Skylar, fierce and full of fire, walking across those steel cables under starlight, letting the city winds carry away her anger. That image stayed with me, and over time, the bridge became my place too. On quiet nights, it felt like it listened. Like it *held* you up when your thoughts tried to pull you down.

"Tiiiitus," Cece sang, cutting into my thoughts. "Come back to Earth."

I blinked, caught in a moment that had crept up on me. "Sorry. Just... the bridge is special."

"Special?" Cece raised a perfectly shaped brow, her tone suspicious but amused. "Why's the bridge so special? Don't tell me you're out here getting sentimental about architecture."

I hesitated, eyes drifting in the distance. "Someone special showed it to me," I said finally. "Helped me really *see* it."

She paused mid-sip, her gaze sharpening over the rim of her glass. "Are we talking about Skylar Madison?"

I didn't answer right away—but I didn't have to. My silence curled around her question like a confession.

Cece let out a long, knowing sigh and held her glass high like a ceremonial offering. "Welp. I'm gonna need a refill if we're going down *this* road."

I chuckled, reaching for her glass. "Snacks too, Your Highness?"

"You already know," she called out, stretching like a cat across my couch. "And bring the good chips. Not those sad, off-brand ones you keep in the pantry 'for guests.'"

As I walked toward the kitchen, the bridge still glowed in my mind's eye—an anchor to something I couldn't quite let go of. Something I maybe didn't want to.

I returned with a tray—her favorite kettle chips, a small bowl of grapes, and two fresh glasses of wine. Cece's eyes lit up the moment she spotted the chips.

"Have I told you lately that I love you?" she sang, lifting her glass like it was communion.

"That's the last pour you're getting," I said, settling beside her. "You get extra annoying after glass number three."

Cece crunched another chip and gave me *the look*. "So... earlier. Who were you talking to in your office? You were so locked in, I could've told you Snoop dropped another gospel album and you'd have waved me off."

I cracked a smile. "Didn't he already do that?"

"Exactly," she said, grinning. "And you still would've missed it, you were so caught up."

I tried to play it cool. "Nobody important."

She gave me *the look*. The one that used to make me confess to sneaking out as a teenager. "Titus, don't insult me. That goofy smile? That shift in your voice when you said 'the bridge is special'? Come on. You don't get poetic for just *anybody*."

I sighed, rubbing the back of my neck. "Skylar called. Out of nowhere."

Cece arched a brow, waiting.

"She wanted to talk. Maybe grab a bite. I had to cut it short though—somebody was yelling my name like the house was on fire."

She smirked. "I should say you're welcome... but honestly, I'm not sorry."

I gave her a half-smile, shaking my head.

"Look," she said, leaning in now, her tone shifting, "I get it. Skylar is... Skylar. But you've done the work, Ti. You built something good for yourself after everything that went down. So if she wants back in? Let *her* do the heavy lifting this time. Let her meet you where you are—not where you left off."

Her words landed hard but clean—like truth wrapped in love.

I nodded slowly, watching as the city lights blinked softly through the window, the bridge in the distance etched against the sky like a memory too stubborn to fade.

"Maybe," I said. "Or maybe some bridges aren't meant to be rebuilt."

Cece leaned her head on my shoulder. "Or maybe... they're meant to bring you home."

47

Allie

The warmth of the day still lingered in the air, hugging my skin like the arms of someone you didn't want to let go of just yet. I sat on the back deck, legs loosely crossed, shoulders dipped in that satisfying kind of exhaustion—the kind that settles in after a day wrapped in family, steeped in faith, and laced with fragile healing.

Skylar was beside me, quiet now. Her silence wasn't heavy—it was reflective, reverent. Her glass of agua fresca sat sweating on the table between us, the slow drip of condensation keeping time with the soft clinks of ice. Somewhere down the block, a dog barked once, then again. Wind danced through the chimes, scattering their tones like whispered prayers across the evening. It was the kind of night that didn't ask for conversation. It just let you breathe.

The backyard had slipped fully into its spring rhythm. The garden was alive with color—geraniums, marigolds, and creeping phlox spilling from their pots like they couldn't help themselves. Fresh mulch still released its earthy scent, and tucked between rosemary bushes and sprigs of lavender were sculptures—small, curious things I'd collected over the years. Each piece carried a memory: a jazz saxophonist in bronze, a hand-painted tile from Mexico City, a clay angel from a Harlem street fair. They peeked out from the ivy like old friends with secrets.

It looked like Eden tonight. Not the polished, biblical kind—this was lived-in, imperfect, sacred. A little wild. A little weary. My sanctuary. Maybe even Ari's, too.

We'd just returned from Jersey—my family, my roots. This morning, we stood in the front pew, watching my niece Ariana walk into the baptismal waters she'd spent years avoiding. My baby girl. My sister's firstborn. She had been adrift for so long, trying to make peace with a world that had taken her father too soon. And today, she didn't just walk into the water. She surrendered. She chose faith again.

And me? I was still trying to catch my breath from the miracle of it.

"You know," I said, turning slightly toward Skylar as the sun dipped lower behind us, "she really didn't want to make it a big deal this morning."

Skylar let out a low chuckle, her brow arching with that familiar, knowing amusement. "Ari? Dramatic? Never."

I grinned, the memory bubbling up with fresh laughter. "She was *so* over us before breakfast."

I could still picture her in her bedroom, arms flailing like a soap opera star on a deadline, while Luz and I held up dress after dress like we were prepping her for a red carpet instead of a baptism.

"Tía Chula, why are y'*all* doing the most?" she groaned, her hands waving in protest as she tried to squeeze past us with a dramatic huff. But her eyes—they betrayed her. That sparkle, that softness she tried to hide—it told the real story.

"Because, baby, *I am* the most," I declared, striking a run-way pose with one of her rejected dresses draped dramatically across my shoulder. "And this is your day. It's supposed to feel sacred *and* fabulous."

"*Mi amor*," Luz cooed, stepping in with the gentleness only a mother could offer. She kissed Ari's cheek and ran her fingers through her curls. "*Esto es un big deal.*"

"A *very* big deal," Skylar added, stepping in like Vanna White, unveiling a pale yellow sundress with a flourish like it was a Picasso.

"Ugh, *no bueno*," I muttered, throwing my hand in the air like I couldn't believe what I was witnessing.

Ari rolled her eyes with such force I half-expected her pupils to disappear. "*Y'all me están volviendo loca*, for real."

And then, true to form, she summoned all the fire of a sixteen-year-old queen in her castle, waving her hands like she was swatting flies. "*¡Fuera!* Out! *Byeeee!* Close the door!"

We barely made it down the hallway before collapsing into laughter, Luz still shouting tips through the door like a coach who refused to be benched. "*Put on lotion! Don't forget your earrings! Y ponte perfume!*"

But even through all the chaos—the flailing arms, the eyerolls, the *tía* dramatics—our girl showed up.

She was more than ready.

The sanctuary was bathed in morning light, golden and warm, filtering through stained-glass windows like God's own spotlight. The soft hush of a piano filled the air—delicate, reverent, the kind of music that wrapped itself around your spirit and made you sit up straighter without realizing. Families were already beginning to settle in, some whispering prayers, others dabbing at tear ducts with wrinkled tissues. The hum of conversation slowly gave way to something quieter, holier.

And then I saw her.

Ari took her place near the altar, and my breath caught before I even realized I'd been holding it. She looked like something out of a dream—graceful and grounded all at once, her posture regal but not rehearsed. The same little girl who used to twirl around the living room in sparkly tights and patent leather shoes now stood in front of the congregation, chin tilted slightly upward, her eyes lifted toward heaven.

I couldn't stop watching her.

I couldn't stop remembering.

She was ten when Luz called me. I'll never forget that sound—the way her voice cracked open mid-sentence, how it dissolved into sobs that didn't sound like her at all. Grief makes even the most familiar voices unrecognizable.

I dropped everything. Left my coffee half-sipped on the counter. I still remember the clang of my keys in my hand, the sharp rhythm of my heels on the apartment stairs. By the time I reached their floor, I found Ari curled in the hallway like a broken wing—knees to her chest, her face buried in Elias' oversized sweater.

Her father—my favorite brother-in-law, the man who hummed as he cooked Sunday dinners, who wrote ridiculous Bible-verse songs with too many rhymes just to make Ari laugh, who kissed Luz like he was still trying to win her over—was gone. Just like that. A senseless accident. A red light someone didn't see. A call in the middle of the day. And in an instant, everything shattered.

Ari unraveled.

She clung to Luz like a lifeline, afraid to let her out of sight. She refused to sleep unless her mother was right there beside her. She flinched at the sound of car engines. She cried if someone was even a minute late. Nightmares, anxiety, tears that came out of nowhere. She'd go quiet, then explode, then retreat again. And the thing that used to center her—church—became unbearable.

"I'm not going," she told Luz one Sunday, voice flat and sharp like a blade. "God abandoned me when Papi died."

She didn't yell. She didn't cry. She just…stated it. Like a fact that no one could argue.

And Luz, in all her wisdom and heartache, didn't try. Mami and Papi encouraged her to give Ari space, and somehow—despite her own grief—Luz found the strength to let her daughter pull away from faith without pulling away from love.

That's when I stepped in. Quietly, at first. And then more. We started what Ari eventually called her "church escapes"—weekends with me where God was off-limits, but love wasn't. We binge-watched teen dramas and documentaries. We wandered into galleries and out of bookstores. We made bagel runs in pajamas and painted our nails on my fire escape. No sermons. No prayers. Just presence. Just tethering her—without saying it out loud—to something that still felt like light.

I never forced her to talk about God. But I tried to live Him, quietly. In the way I showed up. In the way I listened. In the way I laughed with her even on the days she felt heavy.

And now here we were.

This young woman—this beautiful, wounded, wise-beyond-her-years miracle—stood at the altar in a pale blue dress, her fingers laced in front of her, chin lifted as if daring the heavens to hold her gaze.

My heart was loud in my chest. The tears I'd promised myself I wouldn't cry welled anyway.

This wasn't just a baptism. It was a resurrection.

One of those weekends last spring, we spent the entire day out here in this very yard. The weather was perfect—the kind of day that kisses your skin just right. Warm enough for shorts, cool enough that the breeze carried a hint of spring's promise. The sun filtered through the budding trees, dappling our arms and faces as we worked side by side, dirt under our nails and joy tucked between the tasks.

We were shoulder-deep in soil, repotting stubborn roots and coaxing new blooms into their ceramic homes. Ari was on weed duty, muttering dramatic complaints every time she tugged at something that wouldn't let go. We hung the new wind chimes I'd found at a Brooklyn artist market—bronze, hand-hammered, and a little crooked in the most charming way. My "Ratchet Gospel" playlist was in full effect, a sacred and slightly unholy blend of soul, praise, and hip hop that only I could justify.

Marvin Gaye crooned about mercy, then Biggie swaggered through a verse before gliding effortlessly into Maverick City. Ari tried to act unimpressed, rolling her eyes when I started lip-syncing into a trowel, but I caught her tapping her foot, just enough to betray her enjoyment.

And then it happened—that song came on.

♪ *I'm not afraid to show You my weakness... Lord, You've seen them all, and You still call me friend...* ♪

I felt it before I saw it. A subtle shift. Like the wind stilled, the air cooled. The laughter between us faded into something softer. I looked up and saw her standing motionless at the edge of the garden, the gloves she'd been wearing dangling from one hand, her other arm hanging limply by her side. Her face was turned toward the speaker, but her eyes were far away, lost in some quiet ache she hadn't spoken aloud in years.

Tears were streaming down her cheeks—quiet, unannounced.

"Ari," I said gently, brushing the dirt from my palms as I stood. I tried to keep it light, to keep her from shutting down. "It's not that deep. I promise I've got Bad Bunny up next."

She let out a small laugh—half-snort, half-sob—and wiped her face with the back of her arm. That sound, that little laugh laced with pain, cracked something in me wide open.

Then she asked it.

"Titi... is that true?"

My breath caught. "Is what true, baby?"

Her voice dropped into a whisper, like she was afraid it might disappear if she said it too loud.

"That... He still calls me friend?"

I didn't hesitate. Not for a second. I crossed the yard, kicked off my muddy shoes halfway there, and pulled her into me like I could gather every piece of her heart that had scattered since the day she lost him.

"Ay, *mi tesoro*," I whispered, clutching her tight. "Yes. Yes, He does. He never stopped."

She held on. Fierce and fragile. My strong, tender girl who had survived so much grief and still carried so much hope beneath her bravado.

I leaned back just enough to cup her face, to wipe away the tears with the kind of gentleness she hadn't allowed herself to receive in a long time.

"He calls you *beloved*," I said, my voice thick with emotion. "Somehow, He loves you even more than I do. And that's saying something."

Her lips trembled into a smile, and for the first time in a long while, her eyes didn't look lost. They looked found.

We played that song on repeat for the rest of the afternoon.

Every time it faded out, she'd whisper, "One more time," and I'd press replay without saying a word. There was no need. The music said what we couldn't, holding the space open for us to finally step into what we'd both been avoiding—truth.

We talked. Really talked.

About the ache that never quite left her chest. About how she was scared to feel joy again, because the last time she did, her daddy died. How that moment—the sound of the phone call, the way the world tilted—etched itself into her body like scar tissue.

She spoke about Alex Jr., her little brother, and how unfair it was that he'd grow up never knowing the rumble of his father's laugh or the way he used to dance in the kitchen with Luz when he thought no one was watching.

She remembered Luz crying herself to sleep for what felt like months. Remembered how she used to count the sobs through the wall and pretend not to hear them. How it did not matter how many times Tito Elias stepped in to take her to the daddy daughter dance, he could never quite fill the shape her father left behind.

She missed the smell of his cologne—sandalwood and

citrus. Missed the weight of his arms when he scooped her up after church. Missed the way he sang bedtime stories like lullabies wrapped in scripture.

And when she finally went quiet, eyes rimmed red, shoulders trembling from the weight of it all, I told her things I hadn't told anyone.

About Bryan.

About how, for a while, I mistook being needed for being loved. How I found myself wrapped in something that looked like security but felt like slow suffocation. How I learned to smile on cue, keep the peace, play my part, until I didn't recognize my own voice anymore.

I told her how I drifted from God, too. Not out of anger—but numbness. Silence. How sometimes, when you're in survival mode, even faith feels like a luxury you can't afford.

We cried. Let it pour out of us like rain that had been held back too long.

We laughed, too—about the ridiculousness of our old church crushes, about my tragic taste in early 2000s fashion, about the time she tried to baptize her Barbies in the bathtub and flooded the hallway.

Then we sat. In silence. No rush to fix anything. Just two women—one growing, one healing—sitting in the middle of a messy, blooming garden that didn't ask them to be anything but honest.

That backyard became our confessional.

And that day—that simple, music-soaked, tear-streaked, beautifully ordinary day—was the beginning of something new. A crack in the wall. A slow return to joy. A whispered yes to grace.

It was the day we both remembered we were still loved.

Still tethered. Still held.

Even in the unraveling, something sacred was being stitched back together.

So today, watching Ari step into the baptismal waters—white robe clinging softly to her frame, curls pinned back with the kind of care that said "special occasion" but still left room for her signature edge—it wasn't just a milestone. It was resurrection.

She moved with a nervous kind of grace, the kind you earn, not inherit. And just before she descended the steps, her eyes scanned the sanctuary—just once, just briefly. When they landed on us—on Luz, on Mami and Papi, on Elias, on me— her whole face lit up like a sunrise breaking through a long, dark night. It was quick, but it was everything. A flicker of joy. Of peace. Of home.

The choir swelled as she entered the water, their harmonies wrapping around her like a lullaby only heaven could compose. It wasn't dramatic or theatrical. It was sacred. A quiet awe settled in the room as the pastor gently lowered her into the water, and when she rose again, gasping slightly, eyes shut tight against the light, it felt like time had paused to witness something holy.

And afterward—after the tears, after the applause, after the hugs that didn't let go too quickly and the whispered "thank you, God" from Luz that cracked even Papi's voice— we all piled into cars and headed to brunch, buzzing with relief and reverence.

That's when she came down the stairs.

Wearing the pale yellow sundress. The same one we all lobbied for this morning while she insisted it was "too Easter

Sunday." But now? Now it looked like it was made for her.

She paired it with turquoise sandals and a tiny matching purse, her usual sneakers swapped for something just a touch more grown. The dress swayed around her like sunlight—simple, sweet, but with that little flair that was unmistakably Ari. She didn't have to say a word. Her walk said it all: I chose this. I'm different now. But I'm still me.

And we? We just stared. A little stunned. A little proud. A lot in love with the girl we'd always known, and the young woman we were now blessed to witness.

"She looked beautiful at brunch," Skylar said softly, her voice pulling me gently back into the moment.

"She did," I whispered, the image of Ari in that pale yellow dress still vivid—etched like sunlight on the back of my eyelids.

"She's definitely your niece," Skylar added with a teasing grin. "That little pop of color? The turquoise? Come on."

I smirked. "She gets it honest."

Skylar stretched her arms overhead, then let them fall lazily into her lap as she looked out over the garden. "To think... this place helped her heal."

I followed her gaze—took in the vibrant chaos of spring blooming all around us. The garden beds overflowing like they had something to prove. The painted stones Ari and I had laid in crooked little rows. The wind chimes dancing in the breeze. The tucked-away corners where sculptures peeked out like secrets. The spot by the lavender bush where she once collapsed into my arms and cried until the soil beneath us was soaked with grief.

"This garden saved me, too," I said, voice almost lost in the rustle of leaves. "Piece by piece."

I closed my eyes and let the day unfurl again, like a reel of grace I didn't want to stop watching. The worship team's harmonies climbing toward heaven. The piano's gentle echo beneath it. Ari's voice—stronger than I remembered—as she sang with her whole chest. The look on Elias' face, pure awe, like he was watching a star form in real time. And Luz—*mi hermana*—finally exhaling, her shoulders softening like the storm inside her had passed at last.

The world had handed Ari mourning, but today—today God gave her dancing.

I leaned back in my chair, let my head tilt toward the sky, and whispered it more to the breeze than to Skylar: "You turn graves into gardens."

Not a wish. Not a cliché. A truth. A quiet promise now rooted deep in my bones.

And I knew—in the marrow of my soul, in the soil beneath my feet—that spring had come.

Not just for Ari. Not just for Luz.

But for *all* of us.

48

Allie

The evening settled over Brooklyn like a velvet blanket, warm and slow, casting a golden haze across brownstones and fire escapes as the sun melted into the skyline. The city exhaled with that Sunday-night softness—less hustle, more hush. In my backyard, the scent of rosemary still clung to the breeze, mixing with the earthy notes of fresh soil and mulch from the morning's gardening.

Our stomachs, however, had zero appreciation for ambiance. Brunch was a fading memory, and hunger had made itself known in dramatic fashion.

"I am *starving*," Skylar declared, flopping back against the deck railing with exaggerated flair. "Like, hollow-leg hungry. What's in the fridge, *chica*?"

I didn't even bother standing. I shot her a look that said it all—flat, resigned, and mildly offended by my own negligence.

"Absolutely nothing," I said. "Not even a sad little yogurt cup or a mystery takeout container from two Thursdays ago."

She burst out laughing. "So you're telling me your garden

is out here flourishing like Eden, but your kitchen is giving post-apocalyptic desert?"

"Exactly. Between the baptism, the drive back, and Elias being all distracted with Lupe..."

I trailed off, letting the sentence dangle like juicy bait.

Skylar's eyebrows lifted instantly. "*Oh*, Lupe?" she repeated, her whole face lighting up with curiosity, like she'd just smelled good gossip from across the borough.

"Girl, he's been tight-lipped. All I know is she's cute, apparently has a thing for live jazz, and somehow got him to wear real shoes on a Wednesday night. That's all I've got. We *definitely* need to gang up on him for the rest."

I held up a hand and she slapped it with a grin. "Operation Cupcaking Elias is officially a go," she said.

"*Cupcaking*," I repeated with a snort. "He's gonna hate us."

"Well, if your fridge is barren and Elias is off whispering sweet nothings to Lupe, then that means one thing—takeout," Skylar announced, stretching her arms like a woman preparing for battle. "So what's the vibe—comfort food or culinary adventure?"

We launched into the usual debate. Thai? Too spicy for tonight. Pizza? Too basic for the occasion. Ethiopian? Tempting, but we didn't feel like negotiating injera portions.

Finally, we landed on sushi. Light, flavorful, and just indulgent enough.

There was a cozy little spot a few blocks over—our go-to when we wanted something delicious without the burden of real pants or full makeup. We threw on hoodies over our brunch outfits, slipped into sneakers, and made the short walk under the soft glow of streetlights and stoop lamps.

We ordered far too much, of course. California rolls, spicy tuna, miso soup, seaweed salad, and a few bonus items just because they looked cute on the menu.

As we walked back, brown paper bags swinging in hand and the sweet-salty aroma curling around us like perfume, I felt the quiet bliss of a day well spent. Brooklyn buzzed softly around us—distant laughter, the whir of a bike, the hush of families winding down.

Ari had been baptized. The garden was in bloom. Skylar was by my side.

And somehow, the sushi tasted like celebration.

As we walked, the city shifted around us. The sun slipped lower, and Brooklyn exhaled into evening. Kids were being called in for dinner, their laughter trailing behind like echoes. Stoop lights flickered on one by one, casting golden halos around neighbors deep in post-weekend catchups. The sky had softened into a watercolor wash—lavender melting into coral, dusk humming its slow lullaby.

We were halfway down my block, sushi bags swinging at our sides, when Skylar suddenly slowed her pace. She tilted her head upward, eyes locking on the street sign like she'd just spotted something sacred—or scandalous.

"What's up, Sky?" I asked, eyebrows raised, watching her study the intersection like she was decoding a map from a dream.

She didn't answer right away. Her gaze drifted down the street, thoughtful, almost wistful.

"This is Titus' block," she said finally, her voice low. Like the words had snuck up on her, too.

I blinked. "And?"

But instead of responding, she veered. Not left toward my

place. Right. Toward his.

"Skylar," I said, slowing to a stop. "My house is that way."

She waved me off like I was a breeze interrupting a thought. "I know. I just figured… since we're so close, maybe we should stop by. Say hello."

I planted my feet on the sidewalk like a tree taking root. "Girl, are you out of your entire mind?"

She paused, back still to me. The tension hung between us, thick as the city heat.

"Just last week," I reminded her, my voice sharpened with sisterly concern, "you called him. And there was a woman in the background. That is *not* a green light. That is a caution tape and flashing hazard lights."

Skylar turned around slowly. Her face wasn't smug or plotting—just wide-eyed. Vulnerable. A little cracked.

"I just…" she started, voice catching. "I don't know. I'd stop by your place if I was close."

I crossed my arms. "Skylar *Maya* Madison," I said, dragging out her full name like Mama used to when we were acting real left-field. "You popping up unannounced at Titus' place is not giving 'friendly visit.' It's giving 'season two, midmess episode of *Insecure*,' and newsflash—you are *not* Issa Rae."

That got her. Her lips twitched, and despite herself, a guilty little laugh escaped.

She just stood there at the corner of decision, the sushi bag hanging from her hand, her hair catching the last strands of sun like a halo.

I took a tentative step toward her, unsure if I should pull her back or push her forward.

"Sky," I said, softer now. "What are you really hoping to

find?"

She didn't answer.

Instead, she turned slowly toward Titus' street, eyes narrowed like she was trying to see something far off—something beyond brownstones and block numbers. Maybe a memory. Maybe a future. Maybe both.

I stood frozen, clutching takeout and holding my breath.

And she stood there, caught between one more step and walking away.

Neither of us moved.

Not yet.

Then she was already moving again—no hesitation, no explanation—just motion. Her fresh twist-out bounced with every determined step, catching the fading sunlight like a crown. Lime green kicks smacked against the sidewalk with purpose, and her black leggings and cropped tank clung to the kind of body built not by vanity but by discipline—early gym mornings, post-workout smoothies, and the quiet promise she'd made to herself to be strong again. Inside and out.

I sighed loud enough for half the block to hear, trailing behind like a reluctant chaperone. The sushi bags swung in my hands like little flags of protest, slapping against my thighs as I tried to keep pace.

Usually *I* was the one striding down Brooklyn streets like I paid rent on every corner. But tonight? Tonight I was two steps behind Skylar Madison and her full-blown romantic delusion.

The block didn't help. Of *course* it was beautiful.

Tree-lined, calm, with brownstones that looked like they belonged in glossy real estate ads. Window boxes overflowing with color. Iron railings gleaming like they'd been polished just that morning. The kind of block that made you dream stupid dreams—raising kids, walking dogs, sipping cafecito on the front steps while your person kissed your cheek and asked if you wanted one or two sugars.

"This is reckless," I muttered, more to the air than to her.

Skylar didn't flinch. Didn't turn around. She was already halfway up the steps of Titus' brownstone, each one climbed with more confidence than I knew she actually had. I could read her body like a familiar book—her shoulders held high, her hands too still, her jaw set just a little too tight.

The house was exactly what I'd expect from Titus: classic with quiet swagger. Rich brown brick, sharp black window frames, and potted plants that weren't just surviving—they were thriving. Two matching ones flanked the front door like guards with excellent skincare routines. A tasteful brass doorbell gleamed beneath the porch light.

I stopped at the bottom of the stairs, sushi bags hanging like lead from my fingers, my mouth already forming prayers or profanity—I wasn't sure which.

Maybe she'd chicken out. Maybe the sight of his door, the reality of what she was doing, would hit her square in the chest and spark some long-overdue sense.

But no.

Skylar raised her hand and, without fanfare, pressed the doorbell.

She stepped back half a pace, tucking her curls behind her ear, trying hard to look breezy and unbothered. But I saw it—how her hand shook just slightly before she slipped it into her back pocket. The telltale signs of a woman standing at the edge of something.

And me?

I just stood there, rooted to the spot like a stunned witness to a slow-motion car crash. Already regretting letting this play out. Already imagining every scenario except the one where this actually ends well.

Then the porch light clicked on.

And the door began to open.

And we both went still.

Standing in the doorway was a woman—tall, curvy, and that particular brand of beautiful that didn't ask for attention but stole it anyway. She wore a faded Howard University tee tucked effortlessly into high-waisted distressed jeans, barefoot like she owned the damn threshold. Her honey-brown curls tumbled past her shoulders in loose, intentional waves that caught the last of the sunlight, glinting like she was mid-shoot for a "carefree but accomplished" ad campaign.

She looked at Skylar, and for half a heartbeat, something passed between them. A flicker. Recognition, maybe. Familiarity that didn't quite settle into comfort. Then the woman smiled. And not just any smile.

It was the kind of smile that knew something you didn't. A slow, deliberate curve of the lips that wasn't warm or cold—it was *territorial*.

I felt my stomach drop. "*Ay, Dios mío*," I muttered under my breath, already bracing for impact. This was about to be one of *those* moments. The kind you replay in the shower months later.

Skylar froze mid-breath.

The woman leaned lazily against the doorframe, her hip cocked just enough to look casual but not enough to seem unbothered. "Can I help you?" she asked, her tone smooth, measured, and laced with just enough challenge to make it sting.

From where I stood, I could see the shift in Skylar's shoulders. The way her spine straightened just a little too fast. The flicker of heat that bloomed in her cheeks. Her voice, when it came, was tight, a little too bright.

"I, uh... I'm looking for Titus," she said, blinking like she wasn't entirely sure how she'd ended up here.

The woman's smile sharpened at the edges. "He's not here right now."

Just like that. Flat. Final. Clean as a cut.

"Oh," Skylar said, caught between grace and ego. "Okay. Um... just tell him Skylar stopped by."

"I will," the woman replied, never asking who Skylar was. Never offering a name. Just holding that same smug smile as she gently closed the door—slow, but not hesitant.

Click.

And we stood there. Just... stood there. The street noise faded into the background, and the only thing I could hear was the quiet thud of Skylar's pride landing at her feet.

"Well," I said finally, turning toward the sidewalk, "at least your twist-out got to shine."

Skylar let out a soft, breathy laugh—more disbelief than humor—and followed me down the steps like someone waking from a dream she wasn't quite ready to leave. Her face gave nothing away, but I knew that look. I'd seen it before. The sting of regret. The ache of maybe. The hollow pit where hope had been.

We didn't say much on the walk back. Didn't need to. Brooklyn hummed around us, unchanged. But everything in Skylar's silence told me this chapter had just cracked wide open.

49

Skylar

The moment we stepped back into Allie's house, it was like the evening finally exhaled. She kicked off her shoes and let them land wherever they pleased before flopping down onto her couch with the dramatic flair of someone who had just witnessed an award-winning rom-com unfold in real life.

"I am *convinced* you were on something tonight," Allie said, wide-eyed and full of judgment wrapped in affection. "I cannot believe you went up to his door and rang the bell *unannounced*."

I sank into the other end of the couch, tossing the jacket that had been wrapped around my waist in her direction. "I can hardly believe it either," I said, still a bit breathless from the whole thing. "I nearly tumbled down the stairs after that doorway greeting."

Allie burst into laughter, completely losing herself in the memory. "You looked like a deer caught in headlights. And my 'Ay, Dios mío!' did *not* help!"

We laughed until it hurt—that kind of cathartic, belly-deep laughter that only best friends can provoke. But even beneath our humor, the emotional weight of the day hummed in the air.

"I'm not sure I can take any more today," Allie sighed, pulling a pillow into her lap. "This day was packed with *every* emotion possible."

"Yes. Every single one," I agreed, sinking deeper into the cushions.

From the sacred joy of Ariana's baptism, to the serenity of Allie's garden-turned-sanctuary, and now to the full-body *whiplash* of popping up at Titus's door like some lovestruck sitcom character—I was emotionally hungover.

Allie turned to me on the couch, smirking like the cat who knew all the tea.

"You barely picked your face up off the sidewalk after that walk of shame down his brownstone steps," she teased, nudging me with her knee. "And your face when the door opened? Absolutely *priceless*. I wish I'd had popcorn."

I groaned and collapsed into the throw pillow like I was trying to disappear. "Please don't remind me. I'm still debating whether to laugh, cry, or legally change my name and disappear into witness protection."

She cackled, clearly no help at all.

But no matter how hard I tried to laugh it off, my mind kept pressing replay—looping the moment like it was part of some cosmic blooper reel starring *me*.

It started with *her*.

She was stunning. That kind of quietly lethal beauty that made you want to fix your posture. Warm golden-brown skin that glowed like it had soaked up every last drop of sun, honey-brown curls cascading around her face like she was born in soft lighting. She wore a Howard University tee like it was custom couture, tucked into perfectly distressed jeans, barefoot like the front steps of his brownstone were hers.

She opened the door and gave me *that* smile. Not warm. Not cold. Just *knowing*. Like she already had the full script while I was still on page one.

I did my best to play it cool, but my pride? Slid down those stairs faster than my feet ever could. I could feel Allie vibrating with secondhand panic behind me, and I was *this close* to making a clean exit when I heard it—

"Sky! Skylar!"

His voice.

It cracked through the tension like a sudden breeze on a hot day.

I turned. And there he was.

Titus.

Standing in the doorway behind her like a walking contradiction—soft and strong, calm and commanding. That signature easy smile tugging at the corners of his mouth. A fitted white tee clung to him like a second skin, outlining every sculpted muscle like it had been sketched by hand. His jeans hung low in that perfect, casual-on-purpose way. And the salt-and-pepper in his neatly lined goatee? Yeah. That was unfair.

But it was his eyes that got me.

Deep brown. Steady. Familiar. They found mine instantly—and just like that, the street, the noise, the awkwardness...all of it faded.

It was just us.

Two people who had lived a thousand what-ifs.

And one woman still holding the door.

"Skylar, what are you doing here?"

His voice was soft but carried enough weight to make everything else fall quiet.

I opened my mouth to speak, but my voice must've taken a detour. I had something—some combination of sushi, coincidence, and weak logic about being in the neighborhood—but none of it made it past my lips. I just stood there, caught mid-thought, mid-breath, mid-moment.

And thank God for Allie.

Forever the MVP, she stepped in like she'd been training for this exact scenario.

"Hi, Ty," she said smoothly, her voice calm and casually warm. "We were just in the neighborhood and thought we'd stop by before heading back to my place for dinner."

Titus gave us that half-grin—*his* grin. The one that had disarmed me more times than I cared to admit. "Thanks for thinking of me," he said, voice laced with that easy charm. "Why don't you stop in for a minute?"

Allie and I exchanged a look. Not long. Just a flick of the eyes. A silent check-in. *Are we really doing this?*

"Uh, I don't know," Allie said, stalling. "We don't want to intrude. You've got company."

Titus laughed, deep and low. That sound—it didn't just ripple through the air. It traveled. Down my spine, into every inch of me that still hadn't made up its mind about him.

"Company?" he repeated. "That's just Priscilla. Cece. My big sister. She doesn't bite."

As if on cue, Cece stepped forward and swatted him playfully on the back.

"He's lying. I *do* bite. Especially when people show up unannounced with nothing but charm and sushi."

Her voice was smooth, but there was steel underneath. She

had presence—curves, confidence, and a razor-sharp wit that filled the doorway. Her smile was more smirk than welcome, but not hostile. More *let's see what you're about* than *get off my porch.*

"Nice to meet you, Ms. Skylar. Ms. Allie," she said, pronouncing our names like she already knew them. Like maybe she'd heard of us long before we ever rang the doorbell.

Titus gave her a look. "Excuse my sister. She's... invested."

"I'm *protective*," Cece corrected, folding her arms. "This one's got a soft heart, even if he tries to act like he doesn't."

He rolled his eyes and held the door open wider.

And against every ounce of logic—every warning bell and voice of reason—I stepped through.

Inside, the house was exactly what I expected from Titus: warm, lived-in, intentional. Hardwood floors, exposed brick, and walls lined with vinyl records, framed art, and Black history books that made me want to pause and linger. Cece had been curled up on the couch with a glass of wine and a journal when we arrived. Within minutes, she had traded both for chopsticks.

Turns out, our comically large sushi order was more than enough.

And just like that, we were seated around the table—eating, laughing, and talking like old friends at a reunion no one planned.

Cece was hilarious—sharp-tongued, observant, and clearly the type who could read you within five minutes. And she *adored* her brother. It showed in every side-eye, every joke, every story she told with pride stitched into every syllable.

Watching them together was its own kind of intimacy.

And sitting across from Titus, with laughter humming in the background and the memory of his eyes on mine still fresh, I couldn't help but wonder—*Had I just stepped back into something unfinished? Or was this the beginning of something entirely new?*

By the end of the evening, I was half in love with her too.

Cece, with her sharp tongue, unapologetic loyalty, and those side-eyes that could slice through steel, had somehow managed to win me over—even while dragging me with every other sentence. She was a lot. But so was I. And I respected that.

As we made our way to the door, full of sushi and shared stories, Cece turned to me with a smirk that was equal parts warning and amusement.

"Skylar," she began, folding her arms with flair, "I have to admit—when I saw you outside Titus' door I was fully prepared to hate you. Like, deeply. On sight. Especially after all the emotional cardio you've put my brother through."

I raised my brows, ready to defend myself, but before I could say a word, she continued.

"But after meeting you tonight... and watching you pick your dignity up off those brownstone stairs like a true queen?" She shrugged. "You might've earned a point."

"*Yay!*" I threw my hands in the air with exaggerated joy. "A whole point!"

Cece narrowed her eyes with a half-laugh. "Don't get carried away. You're still deep in the red, ma'am. But if Titus insists on keeping you around and I'm forced to play nice... who knows. You might charm me eventually."

"Challenge accepted," I said, giving her a mock curtsy.

She smirked, muttered something about "audacity in cute

shoes," and vanished back inside, leaving behind the faint scent of wine and wise woman energy.

Titus walked us to the door, lingering as Allie stepped ahead to give us space. His hand brushed against mine—barely there, but intentional. Not a full touch. Just a promise. Or a reminder.

He looked at me, eyes warm but unreadable. "Thanks for stopping by," he said softly. "And for the sushi. And... for the surprise. It was a good one."

I nodded, unable to do much more. Words felt too small.

We stood there for a beat longer than necessary—one foot in the doorway, one in something we hadn't quite named.

And then we turned to go.

As we walked back toward Allie's place, the Brooklyn night wrapped around us like a well-worn hoodie. Streetlights flickered above, the scent of blooming jasmine threading through the breeze. I was buzzing. Not from wine. But from something far more dangerous.

Nerves.

Hope.

Attraction.

And a healthy dose of *what-the-hell-just-happened*.

It had started with a bad idea and ended with chopsticks, Cece's reluctant approval, and the soft brush of Titus's hand against mine.

And somehow, the part that scared me the most...

Was how right it had all felt.

"I *absolutely* love Ty's sister," Allie said, her voice pulling me out of my thoughts and back into the dim, cozy light of her living room.

I rolled my eyes. "Of course you do."

"Come *on*, Sky. She's stunning, smart, and loyal as hell. A whole ride-or-die. She walked that fine line between 'I will cut you' and 'I might share my wine with you' *perfectly*. What's not to love?"

I exhaled deeply, flopping back onto the couch like the weight of the night had finally caught up to me. "She's everything. I mean—*everything*."

Back on the couch, the entire day played in my head like a film reel on a loop. The sacredness of Ari's baptism. The stillness of the garden. That doorbell. That *door*.

"I'm still shocked you actually rang his bell," Allie said, wide-eyed, her voice low like she still couldn't believe it. "You—Skylar 'Guarded Heart' Madison—showed up on a man's doorstep with nothing but takeout and boldness."

"Same," I admitted, staring at the ceiling. "I surprised myself."

Without missing a beat, she burst into song, off-key and proud: *"Who's that girl?"*

I couldn't help it. I joined in, laughing. *"La la la la, la la la la la la."*

We cracked up like two teenagers in our dorm room again, the joy filling the room, softening all the sharp edges the day had left behind.

When the laughter faded, I leaned back, letting the moment stretch, a little smile tugging at my lips. "I guess I finally took the advice of a wise woman I know. I stopped procrastinating... and decided to go after someone who may not be perfect—but might be perfect *for* me."

Allie's teasing grin faded into something gentler. She nodded, her eyes soft, full of that rare kind of friendship that knows when to joke and when to hold space.

And in that quiet, laughter-laced lull—between the candles flickering low and the city humming outside the window—I let myself believe...

Maybe, just maybe, I wasn't crazy for showing up on his doorstep after all.

Maybe... I was finally just in the right place at the right time.

It was a little past eleven when I finally stepped through the door of my apartment, nudging it closed behind me with the last ounce of strength I had. The soft *click* echoed into stillness, and just like that, I exhaled.

The air inside held the faint scent of lavender and something warm and sweet—vanilla, maybe, or the memory of a candle that had burned low hours ago and left its goodbye lingering in the air. I dropped my purse by the door, kicked off my shoes, and leaned against the wall for a long beat, letting the quiet wrap itself around me like a favorite sweater. My home. My calm.

The weekend had been full—overflowing, really. Family. Friends. Faith. Food. The kind of weekend that fills you to the brim and leaves you deliciously tired, like laughter and love had wrung you out in the best way.

I smiled to myself as I walked toward the bathroom, shedding layers of clothes along the way like a breadcrumb trail of exhaustion. My earrings hit the counter with a soft *clink*, and my necklace followed, sliding off like it, too, was ready to rest.

Ari's baptism replayed in my mind like an old film reel— her sweet, serious face as the water touched her forehead, the way her eyes closed like she could feel something sacred settling in her spirit. Allie's joy, beaming across the sanctuary. Her parents' laughter. It was like I had been dipped in something holy and familiar, like God had whispered *you're exactly where you're supposed to be.*

And then there was Titus.

My steps slowed.

The memory of standing on his doorstep, heart thudding like it wanted out of my chest, rushed back. The curve of his sister's smirk. The brush of his hand against mine. That steady look in his eyes, equal parts invitation and unfinished sentence.

I had done it. The thing that scared me most.

I had shown up. Vulnerable. Unscripted. Hopeful.

And I still didn't know where it would lead—but damn if I wasn't proud of myself for stepping forward instead of running.

I turned the shower on, twisting the knob until steam curled up instantly from the glass. I let the water run hot— borderline scalding—before stepping in and letting it cascade over me. The stream drummed against my skin, washing away the day, the noise, the lingering nerves.

For a few minutes, there was only water. And silence. And heat.

Until—*BZZZ.*

My ringtone sliced through the hush, sharp and sudden, echoing off the tile and cutting through the steam like a siren. I cursed under my breath, fumbling for the knob and rushing out, slipping on the mat as I grabbed a towel and wrapped it haphazardly around me like a warrior in retreat.

I sprinted down the hallway, still dripping, heart racing.

"Hello?" I answered breathlessly, towel clinging for dear life.

And then I waited—wet, wide-eyed, and suddenly wondering who was on the other end of this call.

"Skylar, I wasn't sure I had the right number."

That sly, unmistakable voice floated through the receiver—equal parts syrup and steel. My mother. Sharp as a tack, sweet as molasses, and somehow both exhausting and mesmerizing in the same breath.

I tilted my head toward the ceiling, eyes already rolling. "Hi, Mom. Is everything okay?"

"You tell me, Sky. *Is* everything okay?" Her tone oozed judgment like it was hand-poured, decades in the making. "I've been calling and leaving messages for *days*. No response."

I counted to three. Inhale. Exhale. *Don't escalate. Don't give her a reason.*

"Skylar *Maya* Madison," she continued, weaponizing my full name like a dagger in a velvet glove, "are you ignoring me?"

In my mind, I screamed: *You damn skippy I am. Because you are exhausting and it's a Sunday night and I am standing here dripping in a towel like an emotionally burnt rotisserie chicken.*

But my mouth, praise God, knew better. "No, Mom. I've just been... busy. Ari was baptized today. Work's been nonstop. There's just... a lot going on."

I ladled it on like gravy, hoping she'd take the bait and give me a moment of grace.

"Mmm." She wasn't buying a single drop. "Is this your new number?" she asked, completely ignoring everything I'd just said.

I blinked. "Is *this* your new number?" I asked, squinting at the random digits on my screen. "Is this your *burner* phone?"

"*Burner* what? Girl, don't be silly. Never mind that," she breezed, as if I hadn't just caught her possibly phone-hopping like a low-level spy. "Why wasn't I invited to Ari's baptism? First your father's birthday, now *this*."

I sighed—long and loud. The kind of sigh that could fog glass.

"It was just close family, Mom. Intimate. Ari wanted it small."

I skipped the part about Dad's birthday on purpose. No need to reignite the 30-year-old feud she somehow still finds new chapters for. She and my father had been divorced since the Clinton administration, yet she still managed to insert herself into his family affairs like a pushy extra in a family drama she wasn't cast in.

"Well," she said with a sudden, dramatic pivot. "Mother's Day is in a few weeks. My church is having a banquet. I want that dress we saw when we were shopping in the city. The one with the flowy sleeves. Do you remember the store?"

I shifted my grip on the towel that was now hanging on by hope and friction. "Mmhmm."

"Check your calendar and let me know if you're free that Saturday. Tickets are $150 each," she added breezily. "Oh—and did you get my note about the mission trip to Belize? The deposit's due soon."

"Mom," I said, my voice barely containing the crack of midnight fatigue, "it's almost midnight. Can we please talk about this tomorrow?"

A pause. Just long enough for me to think she might actually say yes.

Then: "Skylar, I *raised* you to be more organized than this."

And that's when I realized the towel wasn't the only thing

hanging by a thread.

Just then, *salvation* arrived—my phone buzzed with an incoming call. I glanced at the screen and nearly cried.

Sterling.

"Sorry, Mom, that's my other line. Gotta go."

"Mmmhmm," she said, dragging the sound out like a judge delivering a sentence. "Is that *the* Sterling Jennings? The one you had a crush on since elementary school?"

My stomach dropped. *Lord, have mercy.* She'd clearly been gossiping again. Probably to her church friends over coffee and pound cake, giving them updates on my love life like it was a prayer request.

"Mom. *Goodnight.* Love you," I said firmly, clicking over before she could wedge in another invasive question.

I pressed the receiver to my ear. "Sterling?" I asked, more cautious than I meant to sound.

"Of course it's me. Why did you answer like that?" he chuckled, his voice smooth and self-satisfied as ever.

"You, my friend, just saved me from a late-night mono-logue from my mother about dresses, church banquets, and my eternal failures as a daughter."

He laughed—a deep, easy sound that always managed to disarm me just a little. "Not Mrs. Madison! I'm honored to play the role of your knight in shining armor."

"You have *no* idea," I said, finally sinking into my bed, towel ditched, robe on, exhaustion wrapping around me like a weighted blanket.

There was a pause, then his tone softened. "Truth is, I just wanted to hear your voice. Feels like you've been making me the last thing on your list lately."

I sighed, guilt fluttering in my chest. "Sterling, it's not

personal. This weekend was full—Ari's baptism, work, just... life. I've been in ten places at once."

"Well," he said, a smile evident in his voice, "even if I'm last on the list, I still have a request."

I braced. "What now?"

"I have an investor dinner tomorrow night," he said smoothly. "And I want you to come."

I paused. "You mean you want me to *be seen* with you. You want to *take* me—compliment the aesthetic, close the deal." I smirked. "You're giving very much Beyoncé and Jay-Z energy, minus the mutual admiration."

He laughed, totally unfazed. "Maybe."

Typical Sterling—always toeing the line between charm and manipulation, between invitation and agenda.

"Where and when?" I asked, already feeling the weight of tomorrow pressing against my eyelids.

"Chelsea. 7 p.m. I'll send the address. Wear something that makes *you* feel powerful and sexy."

I sighed. "Fine. But you owe me. No surprise pitches. No 'meet my business partner's wife, she's an interior designer, maybe you two should collab.' Just dinner."

"Deal," he said. "And Sky?"

"Yeah?"

"I'm glad you answered."

I didn't say anything back. I wasn't sure if I was, too.

After hanging up, I tossed my phone onto the nightstand like it had betrayed me and flopped back onto the pillows, ready to collapse into sleep.

But just as my eyes fluttered shut, the group chat lit up like Times Square.

Eden: Another late night at work. I call bullsh*t. Not sure

how much more I can take.

Allie: Oh chica, I'm up if you wanna talk.

Quinn: Do we need to go full Jazmine Sullivan on Jayson? Because I've got keys and rage.

I smiled, exhausted but grateful. There was something about the way we showed up for each other—even in emojis and petty threats—that grounded me.

Me: Always ready to bust the windows out his car. Just say the word.

Eden: In no mood to talk. Just needed to say it out loud. Love y'all.

Quinn: Love you too. Goodnight, sis. Rest.

I stared at the screen for a second, thumb hovering. The chat quieted down, but I noticed Allie was still active. My eyes burned, but my mind was too loud. The night was still humming with what-ifs and heartbeats I hadn't sorted yet.

Before I could overthink it, I hit "Call."

She picked up on the second ring.

"Sky, you *better* have a good reason for calling after 1:00 a.m.," she said, her voice sharp—but her tone was warm, amused. "I already took my bonnet off. You know what that means."

I laughed, letting my head sink deeper into the pillow. "Trust me, I wouldn't risk bonnet wrath unless it was serious."

"Spill," she said. "Is it Titus? Sterling? Or your mama again?"

I hesitated. "Yes."

She groaned dramatically. "Not all three, Skylar. Please don't tell me you need bail money."

And just like that, I remembered why I called. Why I always

466

called her.

Because even in the middle of the night, when the weight of the day clung to me like steam, Allie could make me laugh and tell the truth in one breath.

"Why are *you* so awake?" I asked, narrowing my eyes like I could see her through the phone.

"Why are *you* calling *me*?" she shot back, laughing. "What happened now?"

"First Stitch—aka my mother—and then Sterling."

Allie laughed so hard I thought she might've rolled straight out of bed. "This day just keeps on giving."

"She called me from some random number, like a whole burner phone, talking about, 'I wasn't sure I had the right number.'" I groaned. "Like she wasn't just yelling at me two days ago."

"*Gangsta*," Allie said between giggles. "She's out here like she's in a Netflix crime doc. Okay but—what did *Sterling* want?"

"Investor meeting. Wants me to be his plus-one."

"Ohhh," she said, instantly catching the tone. "You gonna wear *the* little black dress? You know the one—perfect neckline, makes him forget his talking points. Show up and 'complement the deal'?"

I burst out laughing. "Allie, I love you so much. I literally said those exact words to him."

"And let me guess," she said, already bracing, "he didn't get the *Beyoncé and Jay-Z* reference?"

"Not even close."

"Cornball," she muttered. "Classic fine man with no culture. Alright, I'm going to sleep before you drag me into another crisis. Don't make me miss my 6 a.m. gym class."

"Night, chica. Love you."

"Love you back. Try to rest that overthinking brain."

She hung up, and I stared at the dark screen for a moment before letting it fall to the nightstand. I lay back, eyes tracing the familiar shadows on my ceiling, the hum of the day finally starting to fade.

Even with the chaos, the curveballs, the uninvited family drama, and the unexpected dinner invitation... something about today had felt *electric*. Like I was plugged back into my own life.

I'd shown up. I'd taken a risk. I'd chosen vulnerability over silence.

And maybe—just maybe—this was what *living* felt like.

Messy. Beautiful. Alive.

50

Skylar

My 2 a.m. bedtime was catching up with me in all the wrong ways. I hadn't just stood Allie up at the gym—I had ghosted her and my ambition entirely. I dragged myself through the day like my soul was still wrapped in my comforter, clutching my throw pillow like it owed me something. By the time my final team update wrapped, I could barely keep my eyes open, eyelids fluttering like faulty Wi-Fi.

"Rushing out of the office again," Lala teased as I passed her desk, her smirk peeking out from behind a tall stack of folders. She knew my schedule better than I did—mostly because she kept it from unraveling completely.

This was the fourth dinner in a month I'd agreed to attend for Sterling. Investor meetups, partner introductions, fundraising strategy sessions. Always something. Always *someone* to impress. And always *me*, the polished ornament on his arm—articulate, strategic, charming. The one who smiled at the right people and carried the weight of the room when he needed it.

It wasn't a partnership. It was a *performance*. And I was

getting tired of being booked without benefits.

Lala glanced at me over her bright red glasses, her close-cropped curls immaculate, freckles stretching as her grin deepened.

"You tell Mr. Jennings to run his proposed dates through *me* from now on," she said dryly. "I'm not your secretary, but I'd play one for the right rate."

I gave her a tired smile and slung my bag over my shoulder, trying to shake off the tension riding shotgun with my exhaustion.

Halfway out the door, something tugged at me.

"Lala!" I called, turning back. "Did I get any messages today?"

She froze, then turned slowly like a woman who had *exactly* three seconds for foolishness. One brow arched higher than the other, judgment dressed in designer frames.

"Skylar. If someone had called or texted, I'd know. *You* know I'd know. Who are you hoping to hear from?"

I exhaled slowly, caught.

I gave a sheepish shrug. "Just... checking."

"Don't mess with me," she said with mock sternness, already walking away. "And get some damn sleep. You look like you're running on iced coffee and audacity."

"I'm planning to. Late start tomorrow?"

"Already blocked your calendar."

"You're the best."

"I know," she said, flashing a wink and handing me a small stack of documents as she disappeared down the hall.

By the time I got home, the sun was hanging low in the sky, casting amber streaks across the apartment like brushstrokes. My floor-to-ceiling windows welcomed me like warm arms, and the golden hour glow softened everything—the walls, the edges of my fatigue, even the ache between my temples.

I kicked off my heels like they had personally offended me, dropped my jacket on the back of the couch, and unfastened the silk blouse clinging to me like the day's residue. The couch called to me, whispering promises of peace, a nap, or maybe just a moment to *not* be everything for everyone.

And then my phone buzzed.

Titus.

I froze, still holding the fabric in my hands, breath hitching like I'd been caught in a memory.

"Hey, Sky," he said, his voice low and velvet-smooth—the kind that somehow slipped past my defenses and settled in places I'd long forgotten were still tender. "Is this a good time? I saw your text earlier, but I've been in back-to-back meetings. Didn't want to hit you with something generic."

"Yeah," I breathed, already feeling some of the day's tension loosen. "Now's good."

We talked for over an hour. Effortless. Like slipping into a favorite hoodie. Titus had a way of anchoring me—steady, familiar, with just the right dose of humor to make me laugh even when I was running on fumes.

"Thank you for being so gracious yesterday," I said eventually, once we'd circled through updates, jokes, and the latest Cece-isms.

"You mean for letting you in after you showed up on my doorstep like a gangster with a fitted cap and vengeance?" he teased.

"*Gangster?*" I laughed. "Cece is the gangster. I was just… lost."

"She won't admit it," he chuckled, "but you made an impression."

"A good one, I hope."

"Definitely. Having Allie in your corner didn't hurt either."

"She saves the day. Every time," I said, smiling into the phone.

There was a small pause, then his voice dipped softer. "In all seriousness... I admired your vulnerability. That took courage. It was overdue."

I took a breath, feeling that familiar tightness in my chest. "I know it's just a start. But I do want to start, Titus. I've missed this. Missed you."

He was quiet for a beat. Then: "What is *this*, Sky? Just so I know the rules of the road."

The shift in tone hit like a subtle shift in the wind—gentle, but it carried weight.

"The rules?" I repeated, already bracing.

"Yeah. I'm not expecting declarations or timelines," he said evenly. "But let's not pretend. You ghosted me, and I've got enough sense to know I wasn't the only one in your orbit."

I exhaled. "That's fair. I'll be honest. I have... an engagement tonight."

"Engagement?" he echoed, slower now. "Like a *date*?"

"I wouldn't call it that," I said, the words sticking to my tongue. "Sterling invited me to an investor dinner. He asked me to join him for a pitch."

"So, you're there to seal the deal with your beauty?" he said, trying for lightness. "Very Jay and Bey of you."

I didn't respond. Because the truth was—it didn't feel glamorous. It felt strategic. Performative. Heavy.

"So… are you and Sterling still a thing?" he asked, the ease in his voice thinning just enough to sting.

"No," I said honestly. "Honestly, I feel more like a showcase than a partner. We're falling into old patterns. But this time, I *see* them."

"Thanks for being real," he said. "I don't like it, but I get it. Just… know I'm not sitting on the bench, Sky. We both have a right to figure things out. But I'm not waiting in the shadows, either."

"That's fair," I whispered, though the thought of Titus with someone else made my stomach turn in a way I wasn't proud of.

There was another pause. He let the silence breathe before saying, "Skylar… the time apart taught me something. I want a woman who sees my worth. My past, my kids—they're not baggage. They're blessings. If someone can't honor that, they don't deserve me."

I swallowed hard. The conviction in his voice—his self-worth—was both beautiful and humbling.

"You're right," I said, voice catching. "I let fairy tales cloud my vision. I thought I needed perfect on paper when what I really needed was *real*. I *see* you now, Titus. No more noise. No more running."

The quiet that followed wasn't awkward. It was intimate.

And for the first time in a long time, I wasn't afraid of where the silence might lead.

"Good," he said gently. "I didn't call to scold. Just wanted to say… what you did took courage. And Cece—well, she thinks you might actually be worth the trouble."

I laughed. "Barely survived her."

"But you did," Titus replied, his baritone smooth, calm,

and utterly unbothered. "Now go play nice at the investor dinner. Hit me up when you want to get together."

The line went dead, but his voice lingered in my ear like a jazz riff—bold, intentional, unforgettable.

I sat there for a beat, phone still in hand, the hum of the city drifting in through my Brooklyn Heights window. Evening light spilled across the room, stretching long and gold across the hardwood, brushing the couch in honey and shadow. I should've been getting dressed—fluffing curls, sliding into heels, rehearsing my smile—but instead, I let myself sink into the cushions.

The room felt thick with everything he didn't say... and all that he did.

It wasn't just his tone. It was the quiet confidence behind it. The way he carried his worth like a tailored suit—measured, refined, effortless. Titus didn't posture. Didn't compete. He didn't need to.

No digs at Sterling. No guilt trips. Just presence. Steady, clear, *his*.

And in that clarity, he gave me space—room to wrestle, reflect, even run if I had to. But he also drew a line, gently but unmistakably: *I know who I am. I know what I bring. And if you're not ready, I won't beg you to be.*

That kind of energy? It was disarming. Sexy. Powerful in the kind of way that didn't need an audience.

The fact that he could watch me walk into an evening with a man he didn't respect and still not flinch? That told me everything. It wasn't indifference—it was mastery. Of his emotions. His boundaries. His expectations.

He wasn't trying to be chosen. He *already was*—by himself, by his kids, by the life he'd built. And still... he was willing to show up. For me.

A low sigh slipped out as I sat up, the weight of obligation pulling at my spine like a coat I didn't want to wear. The dress I'd laid out earlier suddenly felt less like allure and more like armor.

I was headed out to perform—again. But my heart was already offstage, lingering in the quiet of that call, replaying every note of a man who knew his worth and dared me to know mine too.

And somewhere deep in the back of my mind, a quiet truth stirred:

Maybe I wasn't dreaming of the next scene.

Maybe I was finally ready to write it—with him still in it. On purpose.

I lingered in front of the mirror longer than usual that evening.

The woman staring back at me was polished—yes. Impeccable makeup, sleek dress, every curl in place. But beneath the surface, there was something else. A weariness that no concealer could hide. The kind of tired that settles into your bones when you're living a life that looks good on paper but feels miles away from your truth.

I traced a fresh coat of lipstick across my lips, then paused, studying my own eyes.

Who are you getting ready for, Skylar?

Sterling?

Or the version of yourself you keep trying to convince is satisfied?

The question cut sharper than I expected.

Memories unspooled behind my eyes like old film reels— me on Sterling's arm, nodding in boardrooms, laughing on cue at rooftop parties, always camera-ready, always composed. Perfect posture. Perfect plus-one. Smiling through discomfort, ignoring the low hum of discontent for the sake of optics. Of strategy. Of *his* upward climb.

And now, there was Titus.

Unapologetic. Present. Steady. A man who didn't ask me to perform, only to *show up*. Fully. Honestly.

I had fumbled him once—mistaking comfort for complication, confusing the quiet strength of something real with the predictable performance I'd mastered. But tonight, the choice sat in front of me like an unspoken question:

Would I make the same mistake again?

Would I keep choosing curated appearances over vulnerable truth?

Dinner with Sterling went off flawlessly. Investors were charmed. His pitch landed with precision. The champagne flowed. The applause was polite, and his smile was wide—gleaming with the kind of satisfaction that had nothing to do with me, yet still somehow relied on my presence.

By the time we reached the car, he was practically glowing—lit up with ego and celebration, more inflated by the deal than the Dom Pérignon.

He opened the door for me with a flourish, like a man convinced he was winning.

And for a brief second, as I slid into the leather seat, I wondered—

Did he even *see* me?

Or just the image I'd perfected for his stage?

"Let me," he said, radiating charm.

"Thanks," I mumbled, sliding in with a sigh.

Instead of closing the door, he leaned in, close. His cologne and confidence overwhelmed me.

"Sterling..." I began, voice weary.

He mistook it for playfulness and leaned in for a kiss. I turned my head.

His lips caught my cheek.

Still undeterred, he moved to my neck.

I tensed. "Sterling, no. I'm tired. I have work to prep."

He pulled back sharply. Slammed the door. When he got into the driver's seat, the energy shifted.

"You're giving mixed signals," he snapped. "Laughing at my jokes, touching my arm. Then this?"

I looked out the window. "Do we really have to do this now?"

"Why not? You're clearly somewhere else."

He wasn't wrong.

"You're right," I replied. "And it's not fair to you."

"So I'm a placeholder now?"

"I didn't say that."

He scoffed. "I thought you were different."

We reached my building. I didn't move to get out.

He sighed. "You know, Skylar, not every woman gets the kind of attention I give you. Walk in with me, and people look."

It landed like an insult.

"You treat me like a prop, Sterling. Not a partner," I said, my voice like glass—clear, but sharp enough to cut. "I was furniture tonight. Ornamental. You didn't ask my thoughts, didn't even toast to me."

He scoffed, lips curling into that familiar smirk that used to pass for charm. "You're overthinking things again, Ciara—"

My head whipped toward him. "What did you just call me?"

He froze, the mask slipping for half a second. "It was a slip. Long night."

"Yeah," I said, pulse quickening. "Long couple of years, Sterling. You haven't changed."

He leaned back like I was the one being unreasonable. "Skylar, come on. Most women would kill to have a man like me. You really want to throw this away over one slip?"

But I wasn't in the car anymore.

I was nineteen again, in the basement of that brownstone near Columbia, clutching a red Solo cup and a heart that didn't yet know how to spot a red flag. He had me in that bodycon dress I borrowed from Allie—tight, shimmering, too grown for me—and made me feel like I belonged on his arm. At least until we walked in the room.

He switched up so fast. Suddenly I was invisible, a girl he barely introduced. When his frat brother asked if I was his girlfriend, he laughed and said, "Nah, she's just chillin'."

Just chillin'. Like I hadn't spent the whole day getting ready. Like I hadn't skipped my study group to be there for him.

And then it happened again at that rooftop party in SoHo. He called me *Tasha*. I remember blinking, thinking maybe I misheard. But when I pulled away, he had the nerve to say, "What's the big deal? I talk to a lot of people."

What was worse than the disrespect was the way he made me feel like *I* was the problem. Like I was too emotional, too clingy, too much. I was young and trying to act unbothered, but I was always waiting for him to see me—not the girl who looked good next to him in pictures, not the trophy—but *me*.

Now, years later, that same arrogance sat across from me, aged but unchanged. Polished, maybe. But still hollow.

"You wanted a showpiece," I said now, more to myself than to him. "Someone who made you look good. But you never really *chose* me."

He rolled his eyes, exasperated. "Jesus, Skylar. That was college. You really still stuck there?"

"No," I said, folding my arms. "I just finally understand it. And I won't play the fool again."

"You act like you've got options," he told me. "Like men like me are everywhere."

Back then, I believed him.

Not tonight.

I opened the door. The night air slapped me into clarity.

"You're right. This isn't new. And I do have options. I have myself. That's enough."

"So you're done?"

"No. I just remembered who I am. And I don't need you to validate that."

I shut the door.

I didn't look back.

I lingered in the shower longer than usual, the steam curling around me like a fog I couldn't shake. It clung to my skin, wrapped around my chest, made the air thick with something that felt a lot like grief.

I stood motionless beneath the water, letting it pound against me—hard and hot—like it could scrub the night off my body... and maybe, if I stayed in long enough, wash away the last twenty years too.

My tears mingled with the water, silent and steady. I wasn't even sure when I'd started crying. Maybe somewhere between Sterling's sneer and the moment he called me *Ciara* like it was a joke. Or maybe the tears had been waiting—

lingering just beneath the surface for years—and tonight was just the night they finally decided to show up and spill.

I wasn't just angry. I was *furious*.

Furious with *him*, sure—but more so with *myself*.

For the woman I kept shapeshifting into whenever Sterling walked back into my atmosphere. The one who shrank. Who smiled on cue. Who rationalized red flags like a trained diplomat. The one who confused shared history with shared future, as if familiarity could substitute for fulfillment.

I had walked myself right back into the same emotional alley I swore I'd never set foot in again. Same shadows. Same heartbreak. Just a new pair of heels.

And what made it worse—what twisted the knife—was that while I sat in Sterling's dim light, a man like Titus was out there, quietly waiting. Giving me space. Honoring my process. Showing up, without demand or fanfare. A man whose strength wasn't in how loud he could be—but in how deeply he could listen.

He didn't try to control the room. He simply *anchored* it.

Titus didn't ask me to choose him. He just made it impossible to forget his presence. It lived in the way he said my name. In the way he made space for my silence without rushing to fill it. In the way he offered steadiness—not perfection, but consistency. Substance.

And yet, I paused for Sterling.

A man who never truly saw me—just the reflection of himself in the polish of my patience. A man who used my presence as a prop. A mirror. A stage. A means to his own applause.

God, what was I thinking?

Could I really lose something *real* with Titus because I was too afraid to make room for *his* reality—his children, his responsibilities, his grown-man life?

I had told myself it was about standards. About sticking to the vision. But the truth?

Maybe I'd been hiding behind ideals. Chasing the aesthetic of love rather than the experience of it. Maybe I'd mistaken mess for misalignment—when really, real love *is* messy. It has stretch marks. Complications. It doesn't always match the mood board. But it's rooted. It's *earned.*

And if I was being brutally honest—*bone-deep* honest—Sterling's only real selling point was that no one called him "Dad."

Everything else?

Smoke and mirrors.

Lies dressed as charm.

Omissions wrapped in confidence.

Emotional malpractice in a tailored suit.

He never made my heart flutter. He made it clench.

Because my body knew the difference.

Sterling gave me knots.

Titus gave me butterflies.

And for the first time in a long time... I was ready to stop betraying myself just to keep the peace.

As if summoned by the ache in my chest, my phone lit up with Allie's name. She always had impeccable timing, like the best kind of divine meddling.

"Allie," I answered, my voice raw, nearly breaking.

She heard it immediately. "Sky, are you okay?"

"Not really," I whispered.

"Hold that thought, Quinn's on the other line. Let me patch her in."

A few clicks later, Quinn's warm voice wrapped around me like a soft blanket. "Hello, beautiful."

"Hey, Q," I murmured, still feeling like a balloon losing air.

"What's going on, Sky?" Allie cut in, direct but gentle.

"It's been a long night," I exhaled. "Sterling and I exchanged words."

"Words?" Allie's voice sharpened.

"I thought you were just playing arm candy tonight," Quinn added, confused.

"That's the problem," I said, letting the weight of the truth sit in my gut. "I wasn't a woman. I was décor. Something shiny for his colleagues to admire."

"Oh hell no," Allie said, her tone flipping like a switchblade. "What did he do?"

"He called me by another woman's name. *Ciara*, if you're curious."

A moment of stunned silence, then Quinn sighed. "I want to say I'm surprised, but..."

"But we're not," Allie finished for her. "He's a dusty rerun. Same bad script, same tired lines."

"And get this," I added, heat rising in my voice, "he told me most women would kill to have a man like him."

"He really thinks he's God's gift, huh?" Quinn muttered.

"At least he's consistent. Still a narcissist in loafers." Allie's disdain was palpable. "Sky, we've watched you run this lap before. I've been courtside since middle school."

She wasn't wrong. They both had front-row seats for the first heartbreak, the first betrayal, the first time Sterling called me "Tasha" and then said I was being too sensitive. Allie had helped me throw his clothes out of my dorm room window. Quinn had brought ice cream and red wine when I swore off men for six months. They had carried me through the wreckage more times than I cared to admit.

"My eyes are wide open," I said now, and for once, I meant it. "Really, they are. I saw the whole pattern tonight—and I saw myself in it. And I didn't like what I saw."

There was a pause on the line. A pause that held relief. Respect. Recognition.

"You're finally choosing *you*, Sky," Quinn said softly. "Not the fantasy. Not the familiar pain. Just... you."

"Yeah," I nodded, even though they couldn't see it. "And I think...I think I'm ready to be loved in real life. Not in the edited version I keep making excuses for."

"And Titus?" Allie asked carefully.

"He's not a fantasy either," I said. "He's real. Flawed. A whole man with a whole life and two kids. But he sees me. He listens. He gives me peace... and that scares me more than it should."

"Well," Quinn said, "maybe peace feels foreign because you've been fighting for scraps."

"Sky," Allie added, "you deserve the whole table. Not a seat at someone else's game."

I took a breath, deep and cleansing, as the last of the shower steam cleared from the mirror.

For the first time in a long time, I could see myself clearly.

51

Titus

The bassline of the playoffs pulsed from the television like a heartbeat, mixing with laughter, friendly trash talk, and the rhythmic clinking of glasses. The glow from the streetlights streamed through the tall windows of my Brooklyn brownstone, bouncing off polished wood floors and casting soft shadows on the exposed brick walls. Outside, spring had arrived in full bloom—the cherry blossoms fluttering just outside like confetti in the golden dusk.

Inside, it smelled like a reunion. The rich, earthy notes of sandalwood, amber, and mahogany from our colognes mingled with the mouthwatering aroma of fried chicken, flaky beef patties, and Elias' signature *pernil*—a dish so good it could bring a grown man to tears.

The buzzer blared, and the living room exploded. Cheers, groans, and high-fives ricocheted through the air. Langston, ever the coach, was pacing like he had money on the line, clapping his hands and barking imaginary orders. Elias? He was damn near on his knees, gripping the edge of the couch like it was the last lifeboat on the Titanic.

Playoff basketball had turned my home into a coliseum of emotions, and I was soaking it all in.

Watching my brothers—because that's who they were, in every way that mattered—brought back memories of the House. Late nights, hoop dreams, endless debates about life and legacy. Back then, the world outside was something we could ignore. Tonight, it felt like that again. No suits, no stress, just freedom, brotherhood, and wings.

Langston had been with me since freshman year at Morehouse—my consigliere, my children's godfather, my moral compass when mine needed recalibrating. He was there when my college girlfriend told me I was going to be a father, held me down when I was juggling two jobs and an MBA, and flew in after the divorce to make sure I remembered who the hell I was. He bet on me when I left corporate America, and together, we built an Urban Development firm brick by brick.

Elias, though newer to the circle, felt like an old soul who'd been with us forever. After a couple games at the Garden, deep convos about Skylar, and Sunday dinners at his parents' spot—where Mami Herrera's *arroz con gandules* put five-star chefs to shame—it was clear the man was cut from solid cloth.

"Take the shot, man! Shoot the damn shot!" Elias yelled at the screen, waving a chicken drumstick like a rally flag.

I smirked. "Aren't you supposed to be the chill Knicks fan? Or is Allie the only one with real loyalty in that household?"

Elias groaned, throwing a throw pillow across the room as his team turned the ball over. "Don't play me, bro."

Langston leapt to his feet, pumping his fists as his Celtics capitalized on the mistake. "Yeahhh boyyyy!" he howled in

Elias' direction, chest puffed like he'd hit the game-winner himself.

We all cracked up.

"There's still time," Elias snapped back, pointing to the scoreboard like a man clinging to hope. Four-point-two seconds. Down by one. Timeout. Game on the line.

The room fell quiet. We leaned in, eyes glued to the screen.

The ball inbounded. One dribble. A floater. It kissed the rim once, twice, then dropped.

Game.

Elias jumped like he'd just won the lottery. Langston screamed "TRAVEL!" at the TV like it owed him money. More laughter followed as the room erupted.

As the crowd trickled out over the next hour or two, we were left with the three of us—brothers by blood, sweat, and circumstance—cleaning up the aftermath of a night well-lived. Empty bottles, half-eaten wings, and the echoes of joy still floating in the air.

"So," Elias said with a grin, wiping down the counter. "Looks like your love life's about as rocky as the Knicks' playoff chances, huh?"

Langston groaned, rolling his eyes. "Please don't encourage him."

I laughed. "Might be shooting my shot again though," I said, tossing a stack of plates in the trash.

"Shooting your shot?" Langston raised a brow. "You're practically writing love letters and dreaming in Skylar."

"Don't be a hater," I warned, jabbing a finger in his direction. "You've got Zora and the kids. Let a brother dream."

"Not hating," he said, tone shifting from playful to protective. "But I *am* my brother's keeper. She ghosted you, Ty. For months. Then came back with emotional baggage and an ex on her arm. Forgive me if I'm team 'slow your roll.'"

Elias leaned against the counter, arms folded. "Skylar's good people."

Langston wasn't convinced. "I didn't say she wasn't. I said I don't think *she* knows what she wants. And I don't want you caught up in someone else's confusion."

"C'mon, man," Elias pushed back. "Skylar's not out here playing games. She's cautious. And frankly, she has every right to be."

"There's cautious," Langston said, grabbing a drink and taking a seat, "and then there's cold. She nearly fumbled a real one chasing a memory. I'm not giving her brownie points just yet."

Elias stiffened. "Well, last I checked, she doesn't need our approval. Maybe she's not perfect, but she might be exactly what Titus needs. And if they're serious about building something, we owe it to both of them to show up with some damn support."

I stepped between them, holding up my hands. "Alright, alright. Can we not turn this into First Take? There's no 'Team Skylar' or 'Team Ex.' I just need y'all to be Team Titus."

Langston tilted his head. "Same team, different playbook. I'm just trying to make sure you're not making decisions with your *soft* heart. You've always been a romantic, and this... this might not be that fairy tale."

"I love Skylar," Elias said simply. "And yeah, I might be biased. But I believe she's growing. You don't see what I see when they're together. Maybe... maybe he's finally getting the kind of love you have with Zora."

Langston's features softened at the mention of his wife. He nodded slowly, letting the edge fall away.

"Alright," he said. "But I still think her turning you into a fake Knicks fan is unacceptable."

That made Elias laugh.

"Give it time," Elias said, raising his bottle. "Skylar and Allie might have you in orange and blue before the season ends."

As I listened to them, I thought back—how Skylar lit up the charity gala in that lavender pants suit, how we vibed instantly over basketball, business, and Black excellence. I remembered the sting of telling her I had two kids and the silent rejection that followed. Her distance. Her ghosting. The late-night calls with Langston as I tried to make sense of the silence. I remembered how that pain turned into clarity— clarity about my worth, about the kind of love I deserved, and the kind of woman who could love my kids like they were her own.

Then I thought about these last few months—how we found our rhythm again. Laughing over takeout, dreaming together about the community we want to build, sharing stories about our families, trading vulnerability for vision.

It felt different now. Solid. Possible.

Langston caught me staring into space, a small smile tugging at my lips.

"That look right there." He pointed. "That's how I know it's real."

"Celtics in six," he added quickly, just to keep me grounded.

We all cracked up again, the tension dissolving like sugar

in sweet tea.

Somewhere in the background, the TV played the game highlights. But the real victory was this—brotherhood, accountability, and the quiet hope that maybe, just maybe, love was still worth the risk.

The last of the dishes had been put away. The laughter faded into the walls, and the echo of sneakers against hardwood lingered like a memory. The night had slipped into stillness, and with Langston and Elias gone, I finally sat—alone—with my thoughts.

I leaned back into the couch, eyes drifting toward the window. The streetlights still spilled their golden hue across the floor, but the noise of the game, the banter, the tension—it had all quieted into something tender.

Skylar's name floated through the quiet like a whispered promise.

She had challenged me, cracked open parts of me I thought were already healed. She forced me to hold my own heart up to the light—and my children's too—and ask who deserved to hold it.

There were no guarantees. No perfect stories.

But there was something in the way she laughed now. In the way she reached for my hand during quiet moments. In the way her eyes softened when I talked about Duece and Kayla, like she saw them—not as baggage—but as blessings.

Maybe that was enough.

Maybe love wasn't about getting it all right. Maybe it was about trying again, this time with eyes wide open.

I grabbed my phone, hesitated, then typed:

"You up?"

Three dots appeared, then disappeared. Then appeared

again.

Skylar:

"For you? Always."

I smiled, and in that moment, it wasn't about the past or even the promise of the future. It was about now.

And now... was a good place to begin.

52

Epilogue

The DJ had just dropped *"Remind Me"* by Mary J. Blige, and the dance floor throbbed with nostalgia—like a shared heartbeat syncing across two decades of memories. That opening beat hit like muscle memory, stirring something deep in my chest. A hum I hadn't realized I missed. A melody I forgot I loved.

We were back in Brooklyn. But not *this* Brooklyn—the one with million-dollar brownstones, yoga studios where laundromats used to be, and bodegas rebranded as "artisanal markets."

No. *Tonight*, we were in *our* Brooklyn.

The Brooklyn of mixtapes and MetroCards.

Of hallway makeouts and corner store crushes.

Of hoop earrings big enough to double as bangles.

Of Saturday block parties with folding chairs and bass lines.

Of Sunday stoops and aunties in house dresses giving side-eye and advice.

The ballroom at the Dumbo Loft had been transformed. String lights spilled across the ceiling like constellations. A warm haze floated through the room, casting a golden filter over every memory we hadn't shared yet. It smelled faintly of cologne—Tom Ford now, not the Curve or Cool Water of our teenage days—but the energy? The energy was pure 2000. Throwback magic.

High School Class of '00. Twenty-five years later and somehow, everyone looked the same—just glossier. Tighter at the waist, looser in the hairline. A little more polished, a little more paid, but still flashing that same Brooklyn edge in their smiles. The kind of edge you couldn't unlearn, even if you tried.

I stood near the entrance with Allie, Eden, and Quinn— my sisters in spirit, in secrets, in survival. We were draped in sequins and confidence, grown-woman glam and well-earned sass. We swapped knowing glances, raised brows at exes we hadn't seen since Y2K, and whispered inside jokes like sacred scripture.

Each of us had lived whole lives since those cap-and-gown days. We'd buried dreams, birthed new ones, fallen in and out of love, lost ourselves and found our way back again. But tonight? Under these lights, with this beat, in this room—we were those girls again.

Just sharper.

Smarter.

Still fly.

Still standing.

Still *us*.

Eden wore red like a weapon—fitted, strapless, unapologetic. Her jet-black Halle Berry cut framed her cheekbones like art. Champagne flute in hand, she scanned the room like she was collecting data for a story she hadn't written yet. "Tell me why this DJ playing the entire '90s Black love starter pack like it's still prom night?"

We cackled. But our laughter softened when Jayson strolled past us again, his phone glued to his ear like a lifeline he refused to cut. Another whispered work call. Another apology diamond glinting on Eden's collarbone. The man came dressed like a husband, but acted like a client. She didn't flinch—Eden knew how to stand alone in stilettos—but something in her exhale said it still hurt.

Quinn, in soft mauve satin, stood next to me, her thick curls tinged with hints of gray that suited her like wisdom worn well. She claimed Taylor, her teenage tornado, was the reason for the gray. Maybe. But we knew better. She'd weathered heartbreak, motherhood, and the ache of losing her mother— each time coming back softer in spirit but stronger in spine. Tatum, her college sweetheart turned soulmate, was coaxing her toward the dance floor with a smile that could melt marble. When she finally let him lead her out, his hands on her waist, his lips mouthing the lyrics to make her laugh, I felt the ache of joy.

Somewhere between "Sweet Thing" and "Back in the Day," Allie leaned into me. She looked incredible. Short white lace dress, turquoise heels, legs sculpted by her morning Peloton hustle, and blonde highlights fading into honey brown waves. The way the room looked at her—like she *was* the spotlight— made my heart swell. But it wasn't just the dress or the hair. Something about Allie had shifted. She was softer, lighter, like she'd laid something heavy down. I couldn't name it yet. But I saw it. And I knew whatever it was, it mattered.

Her eyes narrowed, and I followed her gaze.

Sterling.

Of course.

Clean-shaven. Suit tailored within an inch of its life. Swagger on ten. Still moving like the room owed him applause.

"Ugh. Sterling Jennings. Walking Red Flag since 1999," Allie muttered, loud enough for only us.

I smirked and lifted my glass. "You knew he'd show. A man like that doesn't miss a chance to peacock."

"Man, I wish Titus was here to stick it to him," Eden said, eyes glittering with shade. "You remember the last time they were in the same room? Sterling looked like somebody revoked his VIP status."

"Always the dog trying to mark his territory..." Allie added.

"Well, good thing I'm not his to mark," I said, the steel in my voice surprising even me. There was something beautiful about finally knowing your worth and walking like it.

"Where is Ty anyway?" Eden asked, twisting her lips into a suspicious smile.

"He surprised Deuce and Kayla with a trip to Portugal. Said Allie's travel stories got them hyped. He booked it before they announced the date for the reunion."

We danced, we clowned, we sang into our drinks. Every time I looked around, I caught a piece of our old selves— huddled at lockers, slow dancing in the gym, skipping class to chill in Fort Greene Park. Time had aged us, but it hadn't dimmed us.

"Twenty-five freaking years later and we're still here," I said, raising my glass. "To surviving, thriving, and—"

I didn't finish. Because I felt it first—his hand, warm and familiar, sliding around my waist like it belonged there.

Allie's eyes flashed wide before she broke into a grin. "Girl..."

"Ladies," came that velvet baritone, the one that always made the air shift around me, "do I need to be worried about this recap?"

I turned to find him, my heart doing somersaults. "Ty? What—how—"

He pulled me close with both arms, chuckling as he kissed my temple. "Deuce and Kayla said showing up tonight would lock in my #1 draft pick status with you and your girls."

Tatum clapped him on the back. "Well played, brother. That's how you stay in the game."

Allie nodded, smirking. "We won't fumble the bag. You're prime time all day."

Titus grinned. "Can you believe they took my man in the fifth round?"

"That was straight bull," Tatum said, pulling Quinn in tighter.

"Don't get him started," Quinn warned, laughing.

I leaned into Titus, heart full. "You good?"

"I see a lot of your past in here," he said, eyes scanning the room. "But none of it scares me."

"Not even Sterling?"

"Especially not Sterling." His thumb grazed my shoulder, slow and certain. "And if there *was* a choice—"

"There *wasn't*," I cut in, smirking.

The DJ dropped "Lady" by D'Angelo and the floor turned velvet.

Titus pulled me toward the center, the crowd melting around us.

"You know," he whispered as we moved, "we could've been high school sweethearts... if you weren't so damn Brooklyn."

"And you weren't so DC," I laughed.

"But I'll take grown-up us over teenage confusion any day."

Same.

His hand rested at my lower back, our steps slow and synced, even as the tempo picked up. The room blurred—exes, rivals, rumors, regrets—and all I saw was him. This man. This love. This life I almost left behind, but thank God I didn't.

I turned back to my girls—Quinn slow dancing with Tatum, their rhythm a quiet testament to second chances; Eden holding steady, even as the fault lines in her marriage threatened to give way beneath her; and Allie, radiant as ever, glowing with a kind of healing she hadn't put into words yet. I raised my glass again, grateful for the beauty, the brokenness, and the bond between us.

"To healing. To real love. To outgrowing what we thought we needed."

And to everything still unwritten.

About the Author

Bryant Lee is a storyteller shaped by legacy, guided by roots, and committed to honoring the depth and richness of Black and Brown lives. With a pen dipped in memory and melody, Bryant Lee writes to celebrate the nuances, sounds, vibrancy, and struggles of culture, identity, and love. Every word is a tribute—to the trailblazers who spoke truth in hush tones and bold lines, to communities that birth brilliance in the face of adversity, and to the art of storytelling passed down like heirlooms. Through fiction, reflection, and soul-stirring prose, Bryant Lee paints with language, preserving the beauty of heritage while illuminating the path forward.